THE OXFORD BOOK OF

FRENCH

SHORT STORIES

Edited by
Elizabeth Fallaize

OXFORD
UNIVERSITY PRESS

OXFORD
UNIVERSITY PRESS

Great Clarendon Street, Oxford OX2 6DP

Oxford University Press is a department of the University of Oxford.
It furthers the University's objective of excellence in research, scholarship,
and education by publishing worldwide in

Oxford New York

Auckland Cape Town Dar es Salaam Hong Kong Karachi
Kuala Lumpur Madrid Melbourne Mexico City Nairobi
New Delhi Shanghai Taipei Toronto

With offices in

Argentina Austria Brazil Chile Czech Republic France Greece
Guatemala Hungary Italy Japan Poland Portugal Singapore
South Korea Switzerland Thailand Turkey Ukraine Vietnam

Oxford is a registered trade mark of Oxford University Press
in the UK and in certain other countries

Published in the United States
by Oxford University Press Inc., New York

First published 2002
Reissued 2010

British Library Cataloguing in Publication Data

Data available

Library of Congress Cataloging in Publication Data

Data available

Typeset by Footnote Graphics
Printed in Great Britain
on acid free paper by
Clays Ltd, St Ives plc

ISBN 978–0–19–958317–1

Acknowledgements

I am grateful for the help of many friends, colleagues, and members of my family in discussing the gradual development of a project which has been deeply satisfying to work on. At an initial stage, the advice of Terence Cave was, as always, just what was needed, and he responded generously to later calls for help. I shall miss him deeply as a colleague. David Coward was my first choice for the nineteenth-century stories for which we commissioned translations: we were delighted that he agreed to take them on, and he produced a series of magnificent translations with his customary brio, efficiency, and good cheer. Marie Elven provided support on my own translations, reading everything for me with great care and attention to detail and making a series of excellent suggestions for which I am very grateful. On the editorial side, George Miller has worked with me from the beginning: his personal enthusiasm for the project, his determination to make everything as easy for me as possible, and his own knowledge of the field have all made him a tremendous editor. My thanks are also due to Rebecca O'Connor for her sterling work on chasing up so many publishers and extracting permissions. Alan Grafen has lived with the stories, reading many of them along the way: this book is for him, with my love and thanks.

Contents

Contents

Contents

Contents

Introduction

I read my first French short story at school in 1966. The story was Guy de Maupassant's 'The Necklace' and I revelled in its savagery, my pleasure untouched by the least suspicion that I would still be thinking about the French short story more than thirty years later. Like my younger self, most readers of this collection are likely to have come across or heard the names of some of the great French short story writers: Maupassant of course, Mérimée perhaps, especially for his 'Carmen', the story which was the inspiration for Bizet's opera, or possibly Stendhal, Balzac, Zola, or Flaubert. All these names are from the nineteenth century, rightly acclaimed as a golden age of the French short story. Not only do those stories retain their appeal for a twenty-first-century reader by virtue of their imaginative power, their wit, and their virtuoso handling of the form, but some have in addition made a re-entry into contemporary culture through their reworking as films: thus, for example, the great film director Jean Renoir adapted Maupassant's 'A Day in the Country' in 1936 to produce a lyrical and much admired film, whilst Balzac's 'Le Colonel Chabert' has had two film versions made of it to date. However, the French short story by no means begins or ends with these famous names of the nineteenth century, and one of the aims of this collection is to introduce readers to a range of different voices and stories, written in a variety of places where French is spoken.

[The Short Story in French Literature]

When does the French short story begin? Strong candidates for this honour include 1456, when an anonymous collection of short pieces of fiction published under the title *Les Cent Nouvelles Nouvelles (A Hundred New Short Stories)* appeared, presenting itself as importing the Italian tradition of *The Decameron* into France. But both the oral character of these stories and their brief form strongly recall the French medieval 'fabliau' and 'lai'—the first a short, often earthy and comic narrative; the second a lyric form of the troubadours. The tradition of short fiction in France is thus a long one. In the seventeenth century the short form tended to great complexity and length, making it difficult to recognize as a short story for the modern reader. Towards the end of the eighteenth century the work of Florian and Sade brings it back to a more unified form, closer to the genre's origins: indeed, I chose the Marquis de Sade story 'The Husband Who Said Mass' to open this collection not only because it gets us off to a lively start, but also because its boisterous tone and humour are reminiscent of the medieval tale.

The eighteenth century is also rich in short fiction which belongs in this era to the separate tradition of the *conte*: Voltaire and Diderot, for example, practised the philosophical *conte*, and in the seventeenth and eighteenth centuries the genre also included the fairy tale, widely popularized by Charles Perrault, and stories based on animals, such as the *Contes* of La Fontaine. Up until the end of the eighteenth century, the French short story was thus proceeding along two different tracks—the *conte* as just described, whose name foregrounds storytelling, and the *nouvelle*, a term which originally implied that the story was about a recent event. It is remarkable that neither French term includes the word 'short', an indication perhaps of differing perspectives on what matters about the 'short' story on different sides of the Channel. In so far as the two traditions are separate, this collection follows the development of the *nouvelle* rather than the *conte*; however, the distinction disappears in the nineteenth century, when the traditions merged in the explosion of the success of the genre. All the great writers of the age turned at one time or another to short fiction: Hugo, Balzac, Gautier, Zola, Sand, Daudet, Flaubert, and many more. However, it was Prosper Mérimée and Guy de Maupassant who became the two most famous practitioners of the genre. Mérimée, the pioneer and virtuoso of elegant ambiguity, published only eighteen stories: he considered his 'The Venus of Ille' (1837), in which a statue is invested with mysterious supernatural powers, to be his masterpiece. In contrast Maupassant, the undisputed master of the form, wrote 300 stories on a great variety of subjects; his affinities with the naturalist movement led him to observe milieux which famously include the life of the Normandy peasantry, the world of the prostitute and that of the petite bourgeoisie. In each case Maupassant ruthlessly exposes the foibles and weaknesses of human beings, to the relish of his reader. To mark his special position with regard to the French short story, he is the only author in this collection represented by two stories.

The status of the short story in the nineteenth century is closely associated with the development of the press. By 1900, almost the whole of the adult French nation was literate, and the number of books published rose from about 2,000 per year at the end of the eighteenth century to 15,000 by the end of the nineteenth. A similar explosion took place in the newspaper press from the 1830s onwards as new printing techniques brought down production costs; hundreds of short-lived literary journals appeared, many carrying short fiction or serialized novels. In the twentieth century popular demand for reading of this kind slackened considerably; the number of newspapers and journals published fell and the short story lost an important publication outlet. The first half of the twentieth century is often described as a somewhat thin era for the short story; nevertheless, collections by Colette, by Marcel Arland, and Marcel Aymé—the last mentioned a gifted and often underrated short story writer—and by Jean-Paul Sartre remind us that the genre was alive and well.

The second half of the century witnessed some exciting developments. Camus's *Exile and the Kingdom* (1957), the last work he published before the accident in which he met his death, marks a haunting high point and provides one of the best examples of the short story cycle—a collection of stories designed as a whole in which the reading of each is affected by the reading of the others. The title of Camus's collection is not the title of any of the individual stories, and the two terms of the title, 'exile' and 'kingdom', are implicit rather than explicit themes of most of the stories. In 'The Guest', included here, the young French teacher at the centre of the story struggles with a dilemma which leaves him feeling exiled in the Algeria which he loves—yet he also catches a frustrating glimpse of a possibility of human solidarity which might be thought of as a kingdom. The story—and the collection—work through suggestion and symbol, depending for their effect on making a striking impact on the reader's imagination.

The decision by those bastions of the French literary establishment, the Académie Française and the Académie Goncourt, to attribute prizes to the short story as well as to the novel marked a significant gain in status for the short story in the closing decades of the twentieth century. New prizewinning writers dedicated to the form, such as Christiane Baroche and Annie Saumont, have contributed to the renewal of interest in the genre; literary reviews dedicated to the short story have appeared; and the range of distinct genres appearing under the umbrella of the short story has widened to include, for example, the erotic short story, the detective fiction short story, the science fiction short story, etc. There is a self-awareness about the genre which makes it part of a postmodern sensibility. One of the most striking examples of this is Frédéric Fajardie's story 'The Underwear of the Woman Up Above', published in 1985, a playful piece of writing which works on a number of levels. It makes a number of nods to the traditional detective story (the reader can compare it to the Maigret story also in this collection), most obviously by placing the lone policeman at the centre of the story, but, far from being a guardian of political and moral order, he turns out to be an anarchist with a mildly masochistic fetish surrounding women's underwear. Popular culture is brought into play not only through the whole tradition of the detective story (known as the 'polar') which has such a strong hold in France, but through the English and American pop culture of the 1960s which the superintendent uses to lure his neighbour; a reference to the links between film and the short story is effected via the inspector's admiration for the cult 1934 Jean Vigo film *L'Atalante*, and the actress Juliette Dita Parlo who figured in it.

However, the most striking development of the later twentieth century can perhaps be found in the way in which the short story form has opened up to writing by women and by non-metropolitan writers. The sudden surge in names of women writers parallels their increasing place in novel writing in the second half of the twentieth century but, interestingly, women have won more official recognition in the form of prizes for the short story than they have for the novel. Belgian, Swiss, African, and French Canadian writers have increasingly been drawn into the mainstream of the French short story and have found publishing outlets in Paris and deservedly won critical attention. The difficulty for different kinds of writers coming into the short story genre is amusingly parodied by Annie Saumont in 'The Finest Story in the World'. The title is a reference to Rudyard Kipling: the central female character has learned from Kipling's story that woman is a barrier to the short story not a potential creator. All she manages to write is a series of lists of tasks to be achieved and which constantly intrude on her time and space for writing. Yet, as the character remarks, 'Women do write,' and Saumont herself is an immensely successful short story writer with over twenty published collections and a number of literary prizes. She specializes in putting humble characters into her work, with humdrum lives and popular vocabularies, but they face emotional crises and everyday dilemmas which Saumont delivers to us with wry humour.

Assia Djebar, the Algerian writer, also foregrounds women's exploration of their identity in *Women of Algiers in their Apartment* (1980), but here in relation to the family, to the male, and to the fact of exile in France. Monique Proulx, a young French Canadian writer with the shortest story collected here, demonstrates how six paragraphs can suffice to set up a contemporary drama at a metro station in central

Montreal, to deflate it and deliver a barbed approach to heroism and media exploitation at the end of the twentieth century. The sharply chiselled tales of the horrors of everyday life which make up her collection *Montreal Dawns* (1996) recall, in tone at least, the cruel tales of Villiers de l'Isle-Adam published a century earlier in a metropolitan France which did not think of Quebec as part of mainstream French culture. René Depestre, the Haitian writer in exile, offers a fable of racial and sexual identity in his 'The Negro with the White Shadow', published in 1973. Birago Diop, born in Senegal, has published several volumes of the folk tales and legends of French West Africa, in which the tale 'An Errand' collected here features. The animals of tropical Africa have a strong presence in Diop's tales, and 'An Errand' is no exception. Finally, the brief story by Hervé Guibert, a metropolitan writer who gained iconic status in France when he wrote about AIDS, from which he died a few days after his thirty-sixth birthda, in 1991, presents us with an apparently insignificant incident—a child refuses to undress for a medical check-up. The minuscule weight of the episode, however, is used as a springboard to evoke a strong sense of the potency of the naked human body, and the transfer of power which offering the body to the medical gaze entails. The final line of the story strikes home in time-honoured fashion. The short story may have changed in the twentieth century, drawing different voices to it which contribute to its range and attract new readers, but it has the same constraints and the same possibilities to work with which its predecessors down the centuries have always manipulated to great effect.

[*Formal Matters*]

Writers of the short story tend to be intensely conscious of questions of form, and the French are no exception. I have already referred to the perhaps surprising fact that the French terms for the genre do not include any reference to shortness. Even a cursory glance at this volume attests to the fact that the stories of the collection are by no means all 'short': they vary enormously in length, from Flaubert's 'A Simple Heart' at one end of the spectrum, running to about 15,000 words and covering decades in its main character's life, to Monique Proulx's 'Public Transit', which comes in at well under 1,000. The early twentieth-century writer André Gide turned this question round by thinking about the reader: like Baudelaire and American short story writer Edgar Allan Poe before him, Gide thought that the short story should be able to be read in a single sitting. Instead of being read like the novel in a series of irregular bursts, interspersed by ordinary life, the short story thus has the power to take hold of the reader's imagination and bring an entire fictional construct to fruition without interruption. But how long is a single sitting? Poe thought an hour about right. Baudelaire, whose enthusiasm for Poe led him to translate Poe's stories and essays into French, effecting a rapid transfer of ideas about the short story from America to France in the mid to late nineteenth century, opined that a sitting might stretch to two hours if the story were read aloud. Radio listeners today are used to hearing short stories read aloud in much shorter sessions of thirty or even fifteen minutes.

The key appears to be not the length itself but the intensity of effect on the reader. Most short story writers strive for the utmost economy of means, scaling down plot developments and stripping out all unnecessary detail. The intensity of the form derives from this challenge to the writer to set up a situation and resolve it, to bring characters to life and let them go, in the minimum of pages. The reading pause which naturally occurs at the end of the story, however long or short the story may be, is a rich and fertile space, often the goal towards which the whole story is geared. The novel frequently reaches its climax before the end, with the last few pages functioning as a gradual disengagement. The short story, on the other hand, characteristically creates a surprise effect at the very last moment, causing the reader to stop short, to reconsider what has gone before or simply to laugh aloud. A paradoxical situation results: the reader feels from the beginning that the author is in charge and knows exactly where he or she is headed; on the other hand, a great deal is of necessity left to the reader's imagination and the mechanism which forces us out of the story at the end and onto a terrain of reflection creates a strong interaction between reader and writer. One French critic has remarked that reading a short story always makes him feel intelligent, and this result seems like too good an opportunity to miss.

[*The Drive to an Ending*]

Many theorists of the short story have made strong narrative drive and an unexpected ending crucial features of the genre. Both of these elements can indeed be found in abundance in the stories which follow. However, they are certainly not absolutely necessary features. In Christiane Baroche's 'Do You Remember the Rue d'Orchampt?' the pace of the story is slow, and the focus is above all on atmosphere, as the narrator winds along a reflective path which follows the dictates of memory. Eventually, the path leads to a moment of self-knowledge which does assume the status of a minor epiphany, but the twist of the closing lines remains enigmatic and place, as suggested by the title, is as important to the story as plot. Another recent example is Hervé Guibert's 'The Check-up', which recounts only a brief scene in which a child visits the doctor's surgery: the impact of the story comes from the intensity of the interaction between the two participants, an intensity deftly and economically underlined in the final sentence. This type of story, which has been termed the *nouvelle-instant* because of its focus on a particular moment of individual significance rather than on a more complex narrative of more general import, is more widespread in the twentieth century than in earlier periods. Alphonse Daudet's 'The Last Class', written in the late nineteenth century, describes a period of time hardly longer than that of Guibert's story, since it covers only a single class attended by a schoolboy in Alsace, but the class turns out to mark a culturally significant moment of history, and the story raises issues of language and culture which go well beyond individual experience and indeed beyond its own time. Equally Joris-Karl Huysmans' 'Knapsack at the Ready', published in the 1880s, does not have a strong narrative drive but it paints a broad canvas of the chaos of the Prussian War.

Nevertheless, many of the stories do make splendidly effective use of plot, as we can see in the case of Mérimée's 'The Venus of Ille', published in the 1830s and generally acknowledged to be one of the finest of French short stories. It sets up a thrilling mystery story which anticipates the format of the detective story in its use of an outsider figure confronted with a dramatic and mysterious set of events surrounding an antique statue. Here the mystery is never fully elucidated, making the story part of a strong nineteenth-century tradition of fantasy in the short story. Mérimée was clear that what he was looking for in building a short story was a truly fascinating and bizarre episode: 'I've taken the most extravagant and most atrocious subject that I could find,' he wrote to a correspondent about one of his stories with evident glee. In a less atrocious vein, Gautier's 'The Coffee Pot', subtitled 'conte fantastique', in which the majority of the characters step out of paintings, provides another example of this tradition, creating an enjoyable mystery and exploiting an essentially whimsical idea to both humorous and poignant effect.

The equally strong tradition of the realist or naturalist short story often depends on a strong narrative with a final twist. Maupassant's 'The

Necklace', a satirical account of the pretensions of the wife of a minor civil servant, and an archetypal point of reference in the French short story, brings its full ironic weight to bear in the whip of revelation of its final sentence. Zola's 'Story of a Madman' is also precisely socially situated and creates an ironic narrative reversal reaching its climax in a closing sentence of only three words. Sharing the same tradition of social satire focused on relations within the married couple, Marcel Aymé's 'The Walking Stick' (1934) takes us on an apparently innocent Sunday afternoon family walk which proceeds through a tightly structured series of power battles to the triumph of the wife's closing words. A supreme example of a narrative which ruthlessly prepares its ending from its beginning, stripping away the love objects of a humble servant until only a moth-eaten parrot is left, will be recognizable to readers of Flaubert (or Julian Barnes) as Flaubert's 'A Simple Heart'. Unlike the other stories of social satire just mentioned, however, the narrative's humour does not prevent the reader from empathizing with the luckless Félicité. An altogether different use is made of a final twist to a strong narrative in Sartre's 'The Wall'. A group of prisoners sentenced to death who must pass their last night together seems to provide a situation with only one exit, but a grotesque joke takes an unexpected twist and the final surprise of the story invites the reader to engage in philosophical reflection about the meaning of death and life.

The predilection for the sting in the tail works against the short story as a natural vehicle for happily concluded romance. Stendhal's entrancingly entitled 'Vanina Vanini', set in Italy, starts out as the romantic tale of a beautiful young aristocratic lady who falls for a handsome revolutionary; he in turn loves her 'as a man loves for the first time when he is nineteen and Italian'. The numerous cross-dressings which occur in the story heighten the tension and raise the gender identity stakes. However, political and romantic intrigue soon begin interfering with each other's progress and the marriage which ends the story is indeed a sting rather than the traditional seal on the romance plot. In a more recent example, Michel Tournier's 'The Lily of the Valley Lay-by' offers a promisingly romantic construct as a young long-distance lorry driver develops a passion for a country girl encountered on the motorway which looks set to equal his passion for his gleaming vehicle. As he manoeuvres his huge articulated lorry down country lanes in pursuit of his love it seems that he must be rewarded for negotiating the usual barriers with such determination and intrepidity. Alas, disaster is once again looming. Baudelaire compared the short story form to a stiff uphill climb, from the vantage-point of which one might contemplate the view spread at one's feet. Happy couples seem unlikely to be thickly populating the panorama.

[*Tellers of Tales*]

Whether satirical or fantastic, realist or imaginative, humorous or philosophical, the short story frequently accords a significant role to the teller of the tale, thus emphasizing the short story's connections with oral storytelling and allowing for the introduction of a lively and informal spoken style. There is scope for a complex web of tellers: there may be a third person narrator who passes the baton to a first person speaker; a first person narrator may tell their own story or a story they have heard from a third party; occasionally they hand over to the third party who continues the story and who may or may not hand it back at the end. This last scenario occurs in Villiers de L'Isle-Adam's 'Gloomy Tale, Gloomier Teller' in which the emphasis of the story falls on a teller who recounts his tale at a supper party attended by the first person narrator and other playwrights. After setting the scene the narrator ostensibly hands over to the teller, though this does not in fact prevent the narrator from commenting on the teller's demeanour throughout and the audience of playwrights reacts to the account as if listening to a potential play. At the end of the teller's account the narrator takes back the story to tell us how he in turn recounted the tale he had heard to a friend who comments: 'That's almost a short story! (. . .) Why don't you write it!' The version we are reading is thus presented as the third account: as listeners we have been preceded not only by the other guests at the supper party, including the narrator, but the narrator's friend. The tale—which might also have been a play—has become a short story by virtue of being retold and, in moving between versions, the tale slips intriguingly in status between the real and a variety of fictional forms. The narrator also assumes considerable importance in Balzac's 'The Message', where the narrator becomes the double or substitute of the young man at the centre of the narrative. The two men meet by chance on a journey and discover themselves to be caught up in parallel love affairs; a dramatic turn of fate then intervenes which leads the narrator to visit the other man's mistress and become the carrier of a terrible message, before returning to his own mistress and carrying the message to us as readers.

In these cases, the narrative situation is complex, and the person of the narrator and/or storyteller foregrounded, but despite the complications the narrative is presented as trustworthy. In two of the twentieth-century stories in this collection, the reader is clearly invited to unpick the delusions of the first person narrator. Renée Vivien issues this invitation with humour and irony in her story 'The Lady with the She-Wolf' in which a preening male narrator reveals the depths of his own foolishness through his account of his meeting with the lady with the wolf. His asides to the gentlemen in his audience, in which he draws on a supposedly common culture of assumptions about women, are particularly entertaining. Much darker is Simone de Beauvoir's 'Monologue', in which a woman who has driven her daughter to suicide finds herself alone on New Year's Eve. She fills her solitude with the construction of a monologue in which she stars as a victimized and dutiful wife and mother—her monologue is so plainly self-deluded as to be on the edge of madness. The oral tradition of storytelling, so clearly elaborated in these examples, also has a strong and differently inflected presence in Birago Diop's prizewinning collection *Tales of Amadou Koumba*. Here Diop presents himself as the translator and recorder of the tales of Koumba, the 'griot' or teller whose task it is to keep the tradition of local storytelling alive in his village in Senegal, where Diop first heard the tales as a child at nighttime from his grandmother. The three tellers—Diop, his grandmother, and the 'griot'—thus link together storytelling, family, and cultural tradition.

[*Translations and the Construction of an Anthology*]

The reading of any one of the stories in this volume is the result of a series of choices—the reader's choice to select a particular story to read next, the editor's choices about which stories to include, translators' choices about how to mediate between the original French text and English-speaking readers at the turn of the century. Translators no longer aim, if they ever did, for an unrealizable goal of exact equivalence but instead try to find ways of introducing unfamiliar concepts and meanings to readers eager to extend their own understanding of other cultures. The Algerian-born French writer Hélène Cixous has described reading as a process of crawling like an ant over a text, inspecting it up close, and then crawling away from it back to the self, bringing back crumbs and incorporating them into our own understanding of ourselves. What is true of reading is even more true of translation—the translator has to listen to the text and try to bring what he or she understands back to his or her own culture, expressed in terms which preserve a degree of the text's strangeness, which avoid flattening it into something that could have been written in English in the first place, and yet which can stand up as a fluent and creative text. Twelve of the stories included here have been newly translated for this volume; six of them have been translated for the first time into English. The translations thus range in age from 1949 (Lloyd Alexander's translation of Sartre) to 2001, a range which presents its own interest. When we read a 1949 translation into English of a 1939 text, we are dealing with a number of cultural moments: the moment of original composition, the moment of English translation (much closer after all to the original than we are), and our reading today. No translation is for all time, as the example of the translations of the Bible shows. As readers, we are aware that in reading a translation we are dealing with a version of a text, and we are all experienced in handling versions, from the film version of a Jane Austen novel to remakes of old films. As for the selection of the pieces to construct an anthology, all sorts of versions of what constitutes the French short story would be perfectly possible. In a virtual version it would be possible to start much earlier than the end of the eighteenth century, and still not be limited to only the best-known canonical pieces. I have tried to ensure that this version is wide-ranging and engaging but, to be entirely scrupulous, I can only offer one guarantee: every story in this collection rates in my estimation as a good read. I hope you will agree.

The Husband Who Said Mass

A Provençal Tale

Translated by David Coward

Between the town of Menerbe in the country of Avignon and Apt in Provence, there stands a small, isolated Carmelite monastery, called Saint-Hilaire, perched on the flank of a hill where even grazing goats venture with difficulty. This modest place acts more or less as a dumping-ground for all the Carmelite communities in the area, for to it each consigns those Brothers who have brought dishonour to their calling. It may easily be deduced that the company in such a house is far from wholesome. Drunkards, womanizers, sodomites, and gamblers, such broadly speaking are the noble elements of which it is composed: so many recluses foregathered in scandalous retreat to offer up to God as best they can hearts which the rest of the world does not want. One or two châteaux close by and the town of Menerbe, no more than a league from Saint-Hilaire, form the entire social purview of these goodly monks who, their cassocks and calling notwithstanding, do not find all doors open to them in the surrounding district.

For some considerable time now, Father Gabriel, one of the saints of this holy place, had coveted a certain woman of Menerbe whose husband—one of life's natural cuckolds—was called Monsieur Rodin. Madame Rodin was a black-haired little thing of 28, with a pert eye, a round bottom, and everything required of a dish to set before a monk. As for Monsieur Rodin, he was a decent sort who went calmly about his business. He had sold cloth for a living and served as Provost[1] and was therefore what is called an honest burgher. Not altogether certain of the virtue of his better half, he was enough of a philosopher to realize that the best way of keeping the horns that sprout on a husband's forehead to reasonable proportions is to appear unaware that any have sprouted at all. He had studied for the ministry, spoke Latin as well as Cicero, and regularly played draughts with Father Gabriel who, sly and attentive wooer that he was, knew that it is always important to decoy the husband if you want to hook the wife. Among the sons of Elijah, Father Gabriel

---

[1] A municipal appointment equivalent to the office of local magistrate. [*Author's note*]

was a stallion. The mere sight of him was enough to give anyone every confidence that the business of propagating the whole human race could safely be left to him, for if ever there was a begetter of children, it was he. With a solid pair of shoulders, a back a yard wide, swarthy, tanned features and the brow of Jove, he stood six feet tall and was, people said, as well endowed as the province's finest mules (always a distinctive feature of Carmelite friars). What woman would not be irresistibly attracted to such a lusty brute? And he did indeed most marvellously appeal to Madame Rodin who was anything but accustomed to encountering appurtenances quite so sublime in the lord and master her parents had picked out as a husband for her. Outwardly, as we have said, Monsieur Rodin appeared to notice nothing. But this does not mean he was not jealous. He never said anything but he was always there, and he was often there at times when he might have been wished elsewhere. But the apple was ripe for plucking. The naïve Madame Rodin had brazenly told her lover that all she was waiting for was an opportunity to respond to desires which seemed to her much too ardent to be resisted any longer, while on his side Father Gabriel had given Madame Rodin to understand that he was quite ready to accommodate her. In a brief instant snatched when Rodin had been obliged to go out, Gabriel had even shown his delicious mistress credentials calculated to make up the mind of any woman who might still be inclined to hesitate. All that was needed now was an opportunity.

One day Rodin called on his friend from Saint-Hilaire to invite him to lunch, with a notion of suggesting they might go hunting together. The two of them having emptied a few bottles of Lanerte wine, it struck Gabriel that circumstances had conspired to favour his desires.

'By God, Provost!' said the friar to his friend, 'I am very glad you're here. You couldn't have come at a better moment for my purposes. There's something I must attend to, most urgent, and you could be a great help to me.'

'What is it, Father?'

'Do you know a man in town called Renoult?'

'Renoult the hat-maker?'

'That's him.'

'What about him?'

'Well, the rogue owes me a hundred écus and I have just heard that his business is about to go to the wall: even as I speak he might be clean away and across the county boundary. I must get away and see him, but I can't.'

'What's stopping you?'

'My mass, for God's sake, I have to say mass. If I had my hundred écus in my pocket, mass could go to blazes!'

'Isn't there any way you could be excused?'

'Excused! Out of the question! There are three of us here and if we don't spout out three masses between us every day, the Superior who never manages to say any at all would report us to Rome. But there is a way you could help. Do you want to know what it is so you can think about it? It's entirely up to you, of course.'

'I'd be glad to help. What do you have in mind?'

'There's just myself here and the sexton. The first two masses have been said and all the friars have gone out and about. No one would know. The congregation won't be very big, just a handful of peasants and that nice woman, very devout, who lives in the château of —— just half a league from here, an angelic creature who believes that by strict observance she can make up for all the wild oats her husband keeps sowing. I believe you once told me you studied for the priesthood?'

'That's right.'

'So you must have learned how to say mass?'

'I can say mass like an archbishop!'

'Then, my dear old friend,' Gabriel went on, throwing his arms around Rodin's neck, 'for God's sake, slip my habit on, wait until it strikes eleven—it is ten now—and when it does would you say my mass for me? Please? The Brother who is the sexton is a good sort. He won't give us away. If anyone says they did not think it was me, we'll say it was a new Brother just arrived, and the rest needn't be told anything. I'll get to Renoult's house, the rogue, as quick as I can, kill him or have my money, and I'll be back here inside two hours. Wait for me. Put the sole on the grill and the eggs in the pan and draw the wine. When I return we shall sit down and eat, and then we'll go and hunt. O yes, we'll go hunting and I have a feeling that this time we might just bag something. I'm told that a pair of antlers was spotted near here only just the other day. By God! I'd love us to pot it, even if it meant saddling ourselves with twenty lawsuits from the lord of the manor!'

'The plan is excellent,' said Rodin, 'and I'd do absolutely anything I could to help out. But wouldn't it be sinful?'

'Sin doesn't come into it. Perhaps it might if mass were said and said badly. But if someone who is not qualified celebrates it, then whatever is said would be the same as if nothing was said at all. Take it from me: I am a trained casuist and in this matter there is nothing which might be described as a venial sin.'

'Would I have to say the words?'

'And why ever not? The words mean something only when they are said by us: the power is in us, not in them. Look here, I'd only have to say those words over your wife's belly for the tabernacle of your conjugal devotions to be immediately transformed into the body of Christ. No, only we have the power of transubstantiation. You could say the words twenty thousand times and you would never persuade the Holy Spirit to descend on anybody. And even with us it doesn't always work. It's entirely a matter of faith. With an ounce of faith a man can move mountains, you know, Jesus Christ Himself said so. But a man who has no faith cannot move anything. Take me, for instance. Sometimes when I'm giving mass, my mind is more on the girls and the women in the congregation than on that damned bit of wafer I wave about in my hand. How do you think I could manage to get anything to descend then? I'd be better off believing in the Koran than filling my head with that sort of thing. Which means that your mass will be to all intents and purposes just as valid as the ones I give. So don't give it another thought. Go to it! Brace yourself!'

'By God!' said Rodin. 'But haven't I an appetite on me! And lunch isn't for another two hours yet!'

'But what's to prevent you having a bite to eat? Here, we've plenty.'

'But what about the mass I'm supposed to say?'

'God in heaven! What difference does it make? Do you think God is more defiled if He fetches up in a full stomach than in an empty belly, or if there's food under Him or on top of Him? I'm damned if I can see it makes the slightest difference! Listen, if I had to go to Rome and make a clean breast of things every time I broke my fast before saying mass, I'd spend all my time on the road. Anyway, you aren't a priest and the rules don't apply to you. All you'll be doing is making it look like mass, not actually saying it. So you can do whatever you want before or after. You could even pleasure your wife if she was there. Just do what I do, that's all. You won't be celebrating mass or consummating the sacrifice.'

'In that case,' said Rodin, 'I'll do it. Don't give it another thought.'

'Good,' said Gabriel, making off and leaving his friend well recommended to the sacristan. 'You can depend on me. I'll be back inside two hours and then I'm your man.'

Overjoyed, the friar hurried on his way.

With an expeditiousness which is only too easily imagined, he rushed round to the house of the Provost's wife. Surprised to see him there when she believed he was with her husband, she asked what the reason was for this unexpected visit.

'Let's be quick, my sweet,' said the breathless friar. 'Hurry! We have only a few moments to ourselves. First a glass of wine and then to work!'

'But my husband?'

'He's saying mass.'

'Saying what?'

'Yes, by God, saying mass, my pretty,' replied the Carmelite as he tumbled Madame Rodin on to her bed. 'It's true, light of my soul. I've turned your husband into a priest and while the booby is celebrating a mystery divine, let's be quick and consummate a passion profane.'

The friar was strong and there were few arguments that could be put up against him once he had come to grips with a woman. Anyway, the case he made out being so conclusive, he quite won over Madame Rodin. Since he did not find the business of convincing a pert little thing of 28 summers and a combustible Provençal disposition in any way irksome, he put his case more than once.

'Oooh, you angel man,' said she at last, now perfectly convinced. 'But look at the time! We must part. If our revels are supposed to last as long as it takes to say mass, then he must have got to the *ite missa est* long ago.'

'Not at all, my sweet,' said the Carmelite, who still had one argument left to put to Madame Rodin. 'Come, dear heart, there's plenty of time. Just once more, my dear, my sweet, once more. Beginners like him don't rush it as we do. Believe me, just one more time. I'll wager that husband of yours still hasn't got to the part where God the Wafer has to be held aloft.'

But part they had to, though they did not separate without promising to see each other again and agreeing several new strategies for doing so. Then Gabriel went off to rejoin Rodin who had said mass as well as any archbishop.

'The only part I got slightly wrong,' he said, 'was the *quod aures*. I started eating instead of drinking. But the sexton put me right. Now what about your hundred écus, Father?'

'In the bag, my son. The rogue tried to put up a fight. But I got hold of a pitchfork and, by God, I gave it to him. On the head and all over.'

The meal came to an end and the two friends went hunting. When he got home, Rodin told his wife all about the good turn he had done Gabriel.

'I said mass,' the great booby announced gleefully. 'Said it like a proper priest, by God, while our friend went off and took Renoult's measure with a pitchfork. He browbeat him, light of my life, what do you say to that! Raised great bumps on his head! Ah! Dear heart, it's so funny!

Anyone who ends up with bumps on his head makes me laugh! Now what about you, my dear, what were you doing while I was saying mass?'

'O my sweet!' said the Provost's wife. 'Heaven must surely have inspired us both today! Don't you see, we were both filled with the celestial spirit and never knew it! While you were saying mass, I was reciting the beautiful prayer which the Virgin offered up to the angel Gabriel when he appeared unto her and announced that she would be with child by the Holy Ghost. O my dear! We shall surely both remain on the road to salvation as long as each of us, in our separate ways, goes on performing such good works.'

Vanina Vanini,

Or

Particulars concerning the latest Cell of the *Carbonari*
to be eradicated in the Papal States

Translated by David Coward

It was a spring evening in the year 182*. All Rome seethed with excitement. The famous banker, the Duke de B***, was giving a ball at his new residence in the Place de Venise. All the splendour produced by the arts of Italy and the luxury of Paris and London had been brought together to embellish his palazzo. The throng was immense. The fair-haired, demure beauties of noble England had fought for the honour of being present at the ball: they arrived in large numbers. The handsomest ladies of Rome vied with them in beauty. A young woman whose flashing eyes and jet-black hair proclaimed her a daughter of Rome made her entrance on her father's arm: all eyes were on her. Her every movement radiated uncommon pride.

As they went in, foreigners were seen to be forcibly struck by the magnificence of the ball. 'None of the festivities of any of the kings of Europe', they said, 'come near to matching this.'

Kings do not have palaces designed by Roman architects and they are also obliged to invite the great ladies of their courts. The Duke de B*** never invited any save pretty women and that evening he had been fortunate with his invitations. The men were dazzled. Among so many striking women an argument arose as to which was the most beautiful. The verdict remained unsettled for some time but eventually Princess Vanina Vanini, she of the black hair and blazing eyes, was proclaimed Queen of the Ball. At once the foreign gentlemen and the youth of Rome forsook all other rooms and crowded into the salon where she was.

Her father, Prince Asdrubale Vanini, had insisted that she should dance first with two or three of Germany's royal sovereigns. She then accepted invitations from several handsome, very aristocratic Englishmen but their starched manners bored her. She seemed to find more enjoyment in teasing young Livio Savelli, who was visibly besotted with her. He was the most brilliant young man in Rome and moreover he too was a prince. But if you had offered him a novel to read, he would have tossed it away after twenty pages saying that it made his head ache. That was, in Vanina's eyes, not an advantage.

Around midnight, a rumour spread through the ball and produced a considerable effect. A young *carbonaro* who was being held captive in the fortress of Sant'Angelo had escaped that very evening by means of a disguise and, with a startling piece of romantic bravado, had reached the outer guardroom where he had fallen on its occupants with a dagger. But he himself had been wounded, the myrmidons of the law had chased him through the streets and there was every chance that he would be retaken.

While this story was doing the rounds, Don Livio Savelli, dazzled by the loveliness and sensational success of Vanina with whom he had just danced, and almost maddened by love, asked her as he led her back to her place:

'Tell me, I beg you, what sort of man could ever please you?'

'This young *carbonaro* who has just escaped,' replied Vanina. 'At least he has done more than simply go to the bother of getting himself born.'

Prince Asdrubale came up to his daughter. He was a rich man who for twenty years had not discussed his finances with his steward, who lent him back his own money at a very high rate of interest. If you met him in the street, you would take him for an elderly actor. You would not notice that his hands were primed with five or six enormous rings each set with very large diamonds. Both his sons had become Jesuits and subsequently died mad. He had forgotten them long ago but was exasperated by the fact that his only daughter, Vanina, had no wish to marry. She was already nineteen years of age and had refused proposals from the most illustrious suitors. What was her reason for doing so? The same given by Sylla for abdicating: *contempt for the people of Rome*.

The day after the ball, Vanina observed her father, normally the most lax and casual of men who all his life had never bothered with keys, in the process of cautiously locking the door to a small staircase which led to an apartment situated on the third floor of the palazzo. This apartment had windows which overlooked a terrace planted with orange trees. Vanina went into Rome and paid a number of social calls. When she returned, the main gate to the palazzo was blocked by the preparations for a firework display so her carriage used a rear entrance. Vanina happened to look up and to her surprise saw that one of the windows of the apartment which her father had so carefully locked up was open. She dismissed her companion, made her way up to the eaves of the house, and after a thorough search succeeded in finding a small, barred window which overlooked the terrace with the orange trees. The open window which she had noticed was now only feet from her. Obviously the room was occupied: but by whom? The next day, Vanina managed to get hold of the key to a small door which admitted her to the orange-tree terrace.

Furtively, she crept towards the window which was still open, her approach hidden by a Venetian blind. Inside the room was a bed and there was someone in it. Her first instinct was to go away, but then she saw a woman's dress on the back of a chair. Looking more closely at the figure in the bed, she made out someone with fair hair who seemed very young. She had no doubt in her own mind that it was a woman. There were blood stains on the dress draped over the chair. There was also blood on a pair of women's shoes which stood on a table. The figure stirred and Vanina saw that she was wounded. A wide blood-stained dressing covered her bosom. It was tied in place with ribbons and was clearly not the work of a doctor.

Vanina observed that every day around four o'clock, her father locked himself in his rooms and then went up to see this woman. He would come down again soon afterwards, climb into his carriage, and drive off to call on Countess Vitteleschi.

The moment he left, Vanina climbed up to the terrace from which she could see the unknown occupant. Her sympathies were fervently roused by the plight of the unfortunate young woman. She wondered what had happened to her. The blood-stained dress thrown over the chair had slits in it which seemed to have been made by a dagger. Vanina was able to count them. One day, she had a clearer view of the woman: her blue eyes were staring out at the sky and she seemed to be praying. Soon, the eyes filled with tears. With difficulty, the Princess bit back an urge to speak to her. The next day, Vanina was bolder and hid on the terrace before her father arrived. She saw Don Asdrubale come in through the door. He was carrying a small basket containing provisions. The Prince seemed worried and said very little. He spoke in a whisper so that, although the window was open, Vanina could not make out what he said. He left again almost immediately.

'Poor creature! She must have made terrible enemies,' she said to herself, 'to make my father, usually so easy-going by nature, reluctant to confide in anyone and willing to climb a hundred and twenty steps every day.'

One evening, as Vanina was poking her head round the woman's window, she suddenly found herself staring into a pair of eyes and the secret was let out of its bag. Vanina fell to her knees and cried out:

'I am your friend! I will do anything to help you!'

The unknown woman beckoned to her to come in.

'I owe you a profound apology,' exclaimed Vanina. 'You must be thoroughly offended by my stupid curiosity. I swear to keep your secret and, if you ask, I shall never come here again.'

'Whose heart would not rejoice to see you?' said the woman. 'Do you live here?'

'Of course,' said Vanina. 'I see you do not know who I am. I am Vanina, daughter of Don Asdrubale.'

The woman looked at her in amazement, blushed profusely, and added:

'May I hope that you will come to see me every day? But I would prefer if the Prince knew nothing of your visits.'

Vanina's heart raced. The woman's manner seemed to her to breathe refinement and distinction. No doubt the poor creature had offended some powerful man. Perhaps she had killed her lover in a fit of jealousy! Vanina could not believe that her predicament was due to some ordinary cause. The woman told her she had received a wound in the shoulder which had gone deep into her chest and caused her considerable pain. She could often taste blood in her mouth.

'And you have not been attended by a doctor!' exclaimed Vanina.

'You know that in Rome,' said the woman, 'doctors must provide a detailed report of any wounds they treat to the police. The Prince himself was kind enough to bind up my wounds with the dressing that you see.'

The woman avoided dwelling on her injuries with infinite good grace and tact. Vanina's affection for her was unbounded. Yet one thing surprised Vanina extremely: in the middle of what seemed a very earnest conversation, the young woman clearly had great difficulty in suppressing a sudden urge to laugh.

'I should very much like', said Vanina, 'to know your name.'

'My name is Clémentine.'

'Very well, dearest Clémentine, I shall come to see you tomorrow, at five.'

The next day, Vanina found her new friend feeling very ill.

'I want to send for a doctor for you,' said Vanina as she embraced her.

'I'd rather die,' said the woman. 'I have no wish to compromise those who have helped me.'

'The doctor who attends Monsignor Savelli-Catanzara, the governor of Rome, is the son of one of our servants,' Vanina continued eagerly. 'He is absolutely devoted to us and, given his position, fears no one. My father underestimates his loyalty. I shall go and send for him.'

'I refuse to see a doctor,' said the woman with a brusqueness which took Vanina aback. 'Keep coming to see me. If it please God to call me to him, I shall die happy in your arms.'

The next day, the woman's condition had deteriorated further.

'If you love me,' said Vanina as she left her, 'you will see a doctor.'

'If one comes, my happiness will vanish.'

'I am going to send for him,' said Vanina firmly.

Without speaking, the woman detained her and took her hand which she covered with kisses. There was a long silence. There were tears in the woman's eyes. Finally, she released Vanina's hand and, looking as tragic as though she were about to be led away to the scaffold, said:

'I have an admission to make. The day before yesterday, I lied when I told you my name was Clémentine. I am in fact a wretched *carbonaro* . . .'

Startled, Vanina pushed her chair back and stood up.

'I feel', said the *carbonaro*, 'that my admission will snatch from me the only good thing which binds me to life. But in deceiving you I dishonour myself. My name is Pietro Missirilli and I am nineteen. My father is a poor doctor at Sant'Angelo-in-Vado and I am a *carbonaro*. There was a surprise attack on our organization. I was brought in chains from the Romagna to Rome and was thrown into a cell where a lamp was kept burning night and day: there I remained for thirteen months. A charitable soul conceived a plan of escape for me. I was dressed in women's clothes. As I was leaving the prison and walking past the guards at the last gate, one of them cursed the *carbonari*. I punched him. I assure you that it was no empty gesture of bravado, merely an unthinking reflex. For my imprudence, I was chased in the dark through the streets of Rome. Wounded by several bayonet thrusts and growing weak, I climbed the steps of a house whose door stood open. I could hear the soldiers coming after me. I found my way into a garden and collapsed several paces from a lady who was strolling there.'

'It was Countess Vitteleschi, my father's friend!' said Vanina.

'How do you know this? Did she tell you?' exclaimed Missirilli. 'But no matter. That lady, whose name must never be spoken, saved my life. At the moment when the soldiers swept into her house to arrest me, your father was driving me away from it in his carriage. I feel very ill. For several days now the bayonet wound in my shoulder has been making it difficult for me to breathe. My days are numbered and I shall die in despair because I shall see you no more!'

Vanina had listened with impatience. Then she rushed out of the room. Missirilli had seen no pity in those lustrous eyes, merely the reflection of a haughty character which had just been offended.

Night had just fallen when a doctor appeared. He was alone. Missirilli was in the depths of despair, for he feared he would never see Vanina again. He plied the doctor with questions, but the man bled him and did not reply. The same silence was observed in the days which followed. Pietro's eyes remained fixed on the terrace window through which Vanina usually came. He felt very unhappy. Once, about midnight, he thought he saw someone in the shadow which lay across the terrace. Was it Vanina?

Vanina came each night and pressed her cheek against the young *carbonaro*'s window pane.

'If I speak to him,' she told herself, 'I am lost! No! I must never see him again!'

Now that this was decided, she remembered, against her better judgement, the feelings of friendship she had conceived for the young man when she had been foolish enough to believe he was a woman. They had been so close, so easy together and yet now she would have to blot him from her mind! In calmer mood, Vanina felt afraid of the change which had come about in her ideas. Ever since Missirilli had identified himself, everything that she normally thought had, so to speak, furred over and become very distant.

Before a week had gone by, Vanina, pale and trembling, appeared in the young *carbonaro*'s room with the doctor. She came to tell him that he must try to persuade the Prince to allow a servant to take over his ministrations. She stayed for moments only. But a few days later, she returned with the doctor, as part of her human duty. One evening, although Missirilli was much better and Vanina could no longer use fears for his life as her excuse, she was bold enough to come alone. When he saw her, Missirilli was overjoyed but told himself he must hide his feelings; above all, he knew that he should not depart from the dignity which so becomes a man. Vanina, who had come to his room with her cheeks flushed red, fearing he might speak of love, was quite disconcerted by the noble, devoted but hardly tender declarations of friendship with which he received her. She left. He made no attempt to detain her.

A few days later, when she returned, she met with the same behaviour, the same assurance of respectful devotion and undying gratitude. Far from having to think how she might apply a brake to the young *carbonaro*'s incandescent passion, Vanina wondered if she was the only one to be in love. She who until that moment had been so proud, was now all too bitterly aware of the extent of her infatuation. She feigned cheerfulness, even cool indifference, came less often but could not bring herself to stop seeing her young patient altogether.

Missirilli, consumed by love but aware both of his undistinguished birth and the urgings of his personal honour, had vowed he would not stoop to speaking of love unless Vanina went a whole week without coming to visit him. The young Princess's pride fought him every inch of the way.

'So be it!' she told herself in the end. 'If I see him, it shall be for me, to please myself. I shall never admit to his face what feelings he has aroused in me.'

She paid Missirilli long visits. He spoke to her as he would have done had there been a score of people present. One evening, after a day spent hating him and vowing to be even colder and more unbending to him than usual, she said she loved him. Soon, she was in no position to refuse him anything.

If Vanina's folly was extreme, it must also be said that she was blissfully happy. Missirilli stopped thinking of the dignity which so becomes a man. He loved her as a man loves for the first time when he is nineteen and Italian. He conscientiously observed the proper protocol of true love even to the point of admitting to his proud Princess the stratagem he had used to make her love him. He was amazed by how excessively happy he was. Four months passed quickly.

One day the doctor declared that his patient was free to go.

'What shall I do?' thought Missirilli. 'Shall I stay hiding in the house of one of the most beautiful women in Rome? If I do, the vile tyrants who kept me locked up for thirteen months and never let me once see the light of day will think they have won! Italy, you are lost if your sons desert you for such flimsy reasons!'

Vanina never doubted that Pietro's greatest happiness was to remain by her side for ever. Certainly he appeared blissfully happy. Yet something General Bonaparte once said reverberated unpleasantly in the young man's soul and dictated the way he behaved with women. In 1796, as Bonaparte was leaving Brescia, the city fathers who escorted him to the city gate told him that its inhabitants loved liberty more than all other Italians.

'Quite,' he replied, 'they like nothing better than talking about it to their mistresses.'

Missirilli said to Vanina, in a somewhat strained voice:

'As soon as it's dark, I must leave.'

'Take good care to be back before daybreak. I shall be waiting for you.'

'At daybreak I shall be several miles from Rome.'

'I see,' said Vanina. 'And where will you be going?'

'To the Romagna, to avenge myself.'

'Since I am so rich,' Vanina went on calmly, 'I trust you will at least allow me to provide you with weapons and money.'

Missirilli looked at her without blinking for several moments and then, clasping her to him:

'Soul of my life,' he cried, 'when I am with you I forget all else, even my duty. But heed your noble heart and you will understand me.'

Vanina wept copiously and it was agreed that he would not leave that day, nor the next, but the day after.

'Pietro,' she said on the morrow, 'you have often told me that a man in the public eye—a Roman prince let's say—with vast wealth to command, would be well placed to render the greatest service to the cause of liberty if ever the attention of Austria were to be deflected from us by some great war elsewhere.'

'That is so,' said Pietro in surprise.

'Well then! You are brave and all you lack is a high position. I offer you my hand and an income of two hundred thousand livres. As to persuading my father to give his consent, you may leave that to me.'

Pietro fell at her knees. Vanina was radiant with joy.

'I love you passionately,' said he. 'But I am an unworthy servant of my country. The more wretched Italy is, the more loyal I must be. To obtain the consent of Don Asdrubale, I would be forced for years to play a shabby role. Vanina, I refuse your proposal.'

Missirilli hastened to commit himself by these words, for he felt his resolve melting away.

'My tragedy,' he exclaimed, 'is that I love you more than life and that for me to leave Rome is the most agonizing of tortures. Oh! why has not Italy been freed from the yoke of the barbarians? How happy I should be if I could sail away with you and live in America!'

An icy hand clutched at Vanina's heart. Hearing him refuse her offer had shaken her pride. But soon she threw herself into Missirilli's arms.

'I never saw you more adorable than you are at this moment!' she cried. 'You are my little country doctor and I am yours for ever. You have the greatness of our ancient Romans!'

All thoughts of the future, every dismal consideration urged by common sense vanished: it was a moment of perfect love. When they became rational again:

'I shall reach the Romagna almost as soon as you,' said Vanina. 'I shall arrange to take the waters at Poretta. I will stay at the fortress we have at San Nicolo, near Forli . . .'

'There I shall spend the whole of my life with you!' cried Missirilli.

'Henceforth my fate shall be to flinch from nothing,' Vanina went on with a sigh. 'I shall be ruined on your account, but no matter . . . Could you love a woman who has lost her honour?'

'Are you not my woman, my wife,' said Missirilli, 'a wife who shall be worshipped for all eternity? I will love you, I shall protect you.'

Vanina had social obligations which she could not neglect. As soon as she had left him, Missirilli began to find his behaviour barbaric.

'What is a man's *country*?' he asked himself. 'It is not a person to whom we owe a debt of gratitude for some benefit received, who might feel disappointed and curse us if we fail to discharge it. A man's *country* and his *freedom* are like his coat, a thing useful to him which in truth he must buy if his father has not bequeathed it to him. So I love my country and freedom because they are things which are useful to me. If I care nothing for them, or if they serve no more purpose than an overcoat in August, what is gained by buying them, and at so high a price? Vanina is so beautiful! She is a person of quite extraordinary spirit! Other men will try to please her; she will forget me. What woman ever had just one lover? All these Roman princes, whom I despise as citizens, have so many advantages over me! How can they not be irresistible? Oh! If I leave now, she will forget me and I shall lose her for ever!'

Vanina came to see him in the middle of the night. He told her about the uncertainty into which he had been plunged and, because he loved her, about the debate he had conducted on the great subject of 'my country'. Vanina was delighted.

'If he had to make a simple choice, one way or the other, between his country and me,' she told herself, 'I would win.'

The clock of the nearby church struck three. The time had come for the last farewell. Pietro tore himself from her loving arms and was already going down the narrow staircase when Vanina, choking back her tears, said with a smile:

'If you'd been nursed by some poor country woman, would you leave without some acknowledgement? Wouldn't you try to pay her? The future is uncertain, you will be travelling through enemy country: give me three days as my recompense, as though I were that poor woman, to repay me for my trouble.'

Missirilli stayed.

Eventually, he left Rome. Using a passport bought from a foreign embassy, he returned to his family. He was greeted with joy, for he had been given up for dead. His friends wanted to give him a rousing welcome by shooting a couple of *carabiniere* (as officers of the law are called in the Papal States).

'We must avoid the unnecessary killing of any Italian who can use a gun,' said Missirilli. 'Our country, unlike fortunate England, is not an island. What we lack are soldiers to resist the encroachments of the kings of Europe.'

A little while later, Missirilli, hard pressed by the *carabiniere*, killed two of them with pistols which Vanina had given him. A price was put on his head.

There was no sign of Vanina in the Romagna. Missirilli thought he had been forgotten. His vanity was hurt. He began to give much thought to the difference in rank which separated him from his mistress. In a moment of tender regret for his past happiness, it entered his head to return to Rome to see what Vanina was doing. This extravagant idea was about to get the better of what he believed was his duty when one evening the angelus rang from a mountain church in the oddest manner, as though the bell-ringer's mind was not on his task. It was the signal for a meeting of the cell of the *carbonari* to which Missirilli had been affiliated when he had arrived back in the Romagna. That night, all its members gathered in a certain hut in the woods occupied by two hermits who, drowsy with opium, were quite unaware of the use to which their little house was being put. When Missirilli arrived, feeling very dejected, he learned that the cell's leader had been arrested and that he, though a young man just turned twenty, was about to be elected leader of a cell which included men aged fifty and more who had been party to conspiracies ever since Murat's expedition in 1815. When he received this unexpected honour, Pietro felt his heart beat faster. The moment he was alone, he made up his mind that he would think no more of the girl from Rome who had forgotten him but devote his every thought to the task of *delivering Italy from the barbarian*.[1]

Two days later, Missirilli discovered, in the list of arrivals and departures which was sent to him as leader of the cell, that Princess Vanina had

---

[1] *Liberar l'Italia de' barbari*: a phrase first used by Petrarch in 1330 and subsequently repeated by Jules II, Machiavelli, and Count Alfieri.

just reached her fortress at San Nicolo. Reading her name aroused more anxiety than pleasure in his heart. He tried in vain to convince himself that his country came first by denying an urge to ride like the wind to the fortress at San Nicolo that same evening. But the thought of Vanina, whom he was neglecting, prevented him from carrying out his duties efficiently and he saw her the next day: she loved him as she had loved him in Rome. Her father, anxious to find a husband for her, had delayed his departure. She had brought two thousand sequins for him. This unexpected windfall proved extremely useful in raising Missirilli's standing as the group's new leader. Daggers were ordered from Corfu; a hold was acquired over the private secretary of the Legate who was entrusted with the task of hunting down the *carbonari*; a list was obtained of the names of priests who spied for the government.

It was at this time that arrangements were completed for one of the least absurd conspiracies ever mounted in strife-torn Italy. I shall not enter into superfluous detail. I will limit myself to observing that had the enterprise proved successful, Missirilli could have claimed, with every justification, a large share of the glory. Through his work, several thousand insurgents would have risen up when the signal was given and would have waited, fully armed, for their most senior chiefs to arrive. The decisive moment was drawing near when, as invariably happens, the plot was halted by the arrest of its leaders.

Vanina had been in the Romagna for only a short time when she thought it likely that love of country would make her inamorato forget every other kind of love. Her pride was offended. She tried to reason with herself, but to no avail. A black cloud of melancholy descended on her: she was surprised to find herself cursing liberty. One day, when she had come to Forli to see Missirilli, she was unable to control her feelings, which until then her pride had kept well in check.

'Be honest,' she told him, 'you love me like a husband. That is not what I deserve.'

Soon her tears were flowing, but they were tears of shame for allowing herself to descend to the level of common fault-finding. Missirilli reacted to them like a man who had more important things on his mind. Suddenly it struck Vanina that she should leave him and return to Rome. She felt a cruel pleasure in punishing herself for the weakness which had prompted her to say what she had. After a brief silence, she saw clearly what was to be done. She would be, in her own eyes, unworthy of Missirilli if she did not leave him. She thought with pleasure how surprised, how heart-broken he would be when he looked for her and could not find her. But then the realization that she had failed to win the love of a man for whom she had committed so many follies filled her with warmer feelings. She broke her silence and did her utmost to extract a tender, loving word from him. He said a few affectionate things but his thoughts were elsewhere and it was in an altogether more passionate voice that he spoke of his political plans, exclaiming tragically:

'*Ah! If this present business fails, if the government gets wind of it again, I shall give up the game!*'

Vanina froze. For the past hour, she had believed she was seeing her lover for the last time. What he had just said planted a fateful idea in her mind. She told herself:

'The *carbonari* have got several thousand sequins out of me. No one can doubt my enthusiasm for their plottings.'

Vanina cut short her musings and said to Pietro:

'Would you like to spend twenty-four hours with me at the fortress at San Nicolo? The meeting tonight does not call for you to be there. Then tomorrow morning, at San Nicolo, we shall go for a long walk—it will calm your mind and help you regain the composure you will need to see you through this testing time.'

Pietro agreed.

Vanina left him to make the arrangements for the journey. As usual, she locked the door of the room in which she had hidden him.

She hurried off to find one of her maids who had left her service to get married and had opened a small shop at Forli. When she arrived, she took a prayer-book she had got from her room and, in the margin, scribbled down the exact location where the meeting of the *carbonari* was due to be held that very night. She concluded her denunciation with these words: 'This cell has nineteen members. Their names and addresses are as follows.' When she had written out the list, which was complete with the exception of one name, that of Missirilli, which she omitted, she said to the woman, whom she trusted completely:

'Take this book to the Cardinal-Legate. He is to read what is written in it and then return it to you. Here are ten sequins. If he ever mentions your name, you will surely die. But you will save my life if you persuade the Legate to read the page I have just written.'

Everything went smoothly. The Legate lived in a state of such terror that he did not behave like the aristocrat that he was. He agreed to see the common woman who asked to speak to him and allowed her to appear with her face masked, but only on condition that her hands were tied. In this state she was ushered into the presence of the great man, whom she found safely ensconced behind an immense table covered in green baize.

The Legate read the page in the prayer-book, holding it at arm's length, fearing that it might be the carrier of some subtle poison. He gave it back to the woman and did not order her to be followed. In less than forty minutes after leaving her lover, Vanina, who waited until her former maid was safely returned, rejoined Missirilli believing that henceforth he was hers alone. She told him that there was great activity in the town: patrols of *carabiniere* had been seen in streets where they never normally went.

'If you want my opinion,' she said, 'we should leave for San Nicolo without wasting another moment.'

Missirilli agreed. They set out on foot for the young Princess's carriage which, together with the lady who attended her, a discreet, handsomely paid confidante, stood waiting for them half a league outside the town.

On reaching the fortress of San Nicolo, Vanina, greatly troubled by the unwonted step she had taken, became even more attentive and affectionate. But even as she told him how much she loved him, she had the feeling that she was acting a part in a play. The evening before, as she betrayed him, she had felt no remorse. But now, as she folded her lover in her arms, she thought:

'There is a word that someone might say to him, and once that word is spoken, at that instant and for ever after, he will hate me.'

In the middle of the night, one of Vanina's servants burst into her room. The man was a *carbonaro*, although she had never suspected it: clearly, there were things which Missirilli kept from her, even small things like this. She trembled. The man had come to warn Missirilli that during the night the houses of nineteen *carbonari* at Forli had been surrounded and they had been arrested as they returned from the meeting. Despite being ambushed, nine had escaped. The *carabiniere* had marched the ten captives to the citadel's prison. As they were going in, one had leapt into the well, which was very deep, and had been killed.

Vanina turned deathly pale. Fortunately, Pietro did not notice. Had he done so, he would have seen the guilt in her eyes.

'At present,' the servant went on, 'the garrison at Forli is lined up in every street. Each soldier is close enough to the next man to be able to speak to him. Nobody can cross from one pavement to the other except at points where an officer has been posted.'

When the man had gone, Pietro thought for a brief instant and then said:

'There's nothing to be done for the moment.'

Vanina thought she would die. She trembled every time her lover looked at her.

'What on earth has got into you?' he asked.

Then his thoughts reverted to other matters and he turned his eyes away. At about noon, she ventured to say:

'So that's another cell that's been discovered. I imagine you'll have to lie low for some time.'

'*Oh, very low!*' answered Missirilli with a smile which made her blood run cold.

She went out to pay an unavoidable call on the priest of the village of San Nicolo who was, perhaps, a Jesuit spy. When she got back for dinner at seven, she found no one in the little room where her lover had been hiding. Beside herself, she ran all over the house looking for him. He was not there. She returned in despair to his room and it was only then that she saw the note. It said:

I am going to the Legate to give myself up. I have lost hope in our cause: heaven is against us. Who betrayed us? Probably the swine who threw himself down the well. Since my life is of no use to hapless Italy, I do not want my comrades, when they realize that I alone was not arrested, to think that I was the man who sold them out. Farewell. If you love me, avenge me! Kill, exterminate the scoundrel who betrayed us, even if the traitor should prove to be my father.

Vanina collapsed on to a chair, barely conscious and overcome by the most terrible gloom. She could not speak. Her eyes were dry and inflamed. Finally she fell to her knees:

'Oh God on high,' she cried, 'hear the vow I now make. Yes, I shall punish the traitor. But first, Pietro must be freed!'

Within the hour, she was on her way to Rome. For some time, her father had been urging her to return. He had arranged her marriage with Prince Livio Savelli. The moment she got back, he broached the subject nervously. To his amazement, she consented at once. That same evening, in the house of Countess Vitteleschi, her father, in more or less official terms, presented Don Livio to her. She conversed with him at length. He was the most elegant young man and owned the finest horses. But although he was generally credited with great wit, his character was considered so frivolous that the government believed him to be quite harmless. Vanina thought that if she first turned his head, she could convert him into a useful pawn. Since he was the nephew of Monsignor

Savelli-Catanzara, governor of Rome and Minister of Police, she assumed that government spies would not dare watch his movements.

For several days, Vanina showered the amiable Don Livio with attentions. Then she told him he would never be her husband. His mind, she said, was too frivolous.

'If you were not such a boy,' she said, 'your uncle's agents would have no secrets from you. For instance, what is being done about the *carbonari* who were arrested the other day at Forli?'

Two days later, Don Livio called to inform her that all the *carbonari* arrested at Forli had escaped. She fixed her large black eyes on him, treated him to a bitter smile of the deepest contempt, and would not speak to him for the rest of the evening. Two days later, Don Livio returned and blushingly admitted that he had, at first, been misled:

'But,' he said, 'I have managed to get hold of a key to my uncle's study. Among his papers I found one which said that a *congregation,* or committee, of the foremost cardinals and prelates is to meet in the greatest secrecy to decide whether it would be better to try the *carbonari* in Ravenna or Rome. The nine captured at Forli and their leader, a man named Missirilli who was stupid enough to give himself up, are currently being held in the fortress at San Leo.[2]

When she heard the word 'stupid', Vanina nipped him as hard as she could.

'I would very much like', she said, 'to see those official papers for myself and break into your uncle's study with you. I expect you read them wrongly.'

When he heard this, Don Livio quailed. What Vanina was asking was virtually impossible. But her determined spirit gave wings to his love. A few days later, Vanina, disguised as a man, wearing a becoming suit in the livery of the Savelli household, spent half an hour reading through the most secret papers of the Minister of Police. She felt a thrill of joy when she came across the daily reports on the prisoner Pietro Missirilli. Her hands shook as she held the paper and she felt a little faint. As they left the palazzo of Rome's governor, she allowed Don Livio to kiss her.

'You have made a commendable start,' she told him, 'on the tests I have decided to set you.'

When he heard this, the young Prince would have burned down the Vatican to please Vanina.

---

[2] Near Rimini in the Romagna. It was in this fortress that the famous Cagliostro died. Local people claim that he was suffocated.

That evening, there was a ball given by the French ambassador. She danced a great deal and almost exclusively with him. Don Livio was drunk with happiness. But he had to be prevented from thinking.

'Really! My father sometimes behaves in the most infuriating way,' she said to him one day. 'This morning, he dismissed two of his servants. They came to me in tears. One wanted me to find him a position in the household of your uncle, the governor of Rome. The other, who used to be an artilleryman under the French, would like me to get him something at the fortress of Sant'Angelo.'

'They can both enter my service,' the young Prince said eagerly.

'Is that what I asked you?' Vanina answered haughtily. 'Do I have to repeat the exact request which those two poor men made to me? They must have what they asked for, not some second best.'

It proved an impossible task. Monsignor Cantazara was anything but careless and never allowed anyone he did not know personally to enter his household.

Living a life apparently filled with every imaginable pleasure, Vanina, gnawed by remorse, was very unhappy. She found the slow pace of events worse than torture. Her father's steward had produced money for her. Should she leave home, travel to the Romagna, and try to find a way of helping her lover to escape? Although the plan was quite irrational, she was about to carry it out when chance smiled on her.

'The ten *carbonari* belonging to Missirilli's cell are about to be transferred to Rome, but they are to be executed in the Romagna after sentence is passed. My uncle received notification to that effect from the Pope this very evening. Only you and I in all Rome know about this. Are you satisfied?'

'You are growing up,' replied Vanina. 'You may give me a portrait of yourself as a present.'

The day before Missirilli was due to arrive in Rome, Vanina found an excuse for visiting Città-Castellana. It is in this town's gaol that *carbonari* spend the night when they are being transferred from the Romagna to Rome. She saw Missirilli the next morning as he was being led out of the prison. He was in chains and rode by himself in an open cart. She thought he looked pale but did not appear down-hearted. An old woman threw him a bunch of violets. Missirilli smiled as he thanked her.

Now that Vanina had seen her lover again, her ideas quickened once more and she was filled with renewed courage. Some considerable time previously, she had succeeded in obtaining a handsome preferment for the abbé Cari, now almoner at the fortress of Sant'Angelo where her lover was about to be locked up. She had taken this good priest as her confessor. It is no small matter in Rome to act as confessor to a princess who happens to be the governor's niece.

The trial of the Forli *carbonari* did not last long. As revenge for their presence in Rome, an affront they could not prevent, the extreme conservative party arranged for the committee appointed to judge the rebels to be packed with the most ambitious clerics. The committee was chaired by the Minister of Police.

The law against the *carbonari* is unambiguous. The men from Forli had nothing to hope for. Even so, they fought for their lives using every possible line of defence. Their judges not only condemned them all to death but several recommended they be put to the most appalling torture, have a hand cut off and so forth. The Minister of Police, whose fortune was already made (for when a man relinquishes that office a cardinal's hat awaits him), had no need of amputated hands. When he conveyed the verdict to the Pope, he succeeded in having the sentence of all the prisoners commuted to a few years in prison. Pietro Missirilli was the only exception. The Minister considered this young man to be a dangerous fanatic and, besides, he had also been given a death sentence for the murder of the two *carabiniere,* as we have already mentioned. Vanina read the verdict and the commuted sentence only moments after the Minister had returned from seeing the Pope.

The next day, Monsignor Catanzara returned to his palazzo around midnight. His valet was nowhere to be found. The Minister, very puzzled, rang several times and eventually an aged, extremely stupid servant appeared. The Minister, losing patience, decided he would undress himself. He locked his door. As it was very warm, he took off his coat and tossed it in a heap on a chair. The coat, thrown too vigorously, sailed over the back of the chair and struck the muslin curtain at the window where it revealed the outline of a man. The Minister sprang to his bedside and reached for a pistol. As he was making his way back to the window, a young man, wearing his livery, advanced towards him, also holding a pistol. When he saw this, the Minister raised his pistol and squinted down the barrel. He was about to fire when the young man laughed and said:

'Oh Monsignor! Don't you recognize Vanina Vanini?'

'What is the meaning of this tasteless jest?' replied the Minister furiously.

'Let us think calmly,' the young woman said. 'To begin with, your pistol is not loaded.'

The startled Minister checked and saw that it was so. Then he reached for a dagger from a pocket of his waistcoat.[3]

With a firm but charming gesture, Vanina said:

'Shall we take a seat, Monsignor?'

She sat down calmly on a sofa.

'May I take it you are alone?'

'Quite alone, you have my word on it,' replied Vanina.

But the Minister insisted on seeing for himself. He walked round the room and looked everywhere. Then he sat down on a chair three paces from Vanina.

'What would I gain', she said calmly and sweetly, 'by making an attempt on the life of a moderate man who would only be replaced by some weak-minded hothead quite capable of ruining himself and taking others down with him?'

'So what is it you want?' said the Minister tetchily. 'I do not care for this little drama and have no wish to prolong it.'

'What I am about to say', Vanina went on imperiously, suddenly forgetting her gracious manner, 'concerns you more than it does me. The life of the *carbonaro* Missirilli is to be spared. If he is executed, you will survive him by no more than one week. I have no personal interest in this matter. I have committed what you choose to call an act of folly first, for my own amusement, and second, as a favour for a friend of mine, a lady. What I wanted', she went on, reverting to the drawing-room manner, 'was to lend a helping hand to an extremely able man who will soon be my uncle and will in all likelihood carry the fortunes of his family to the highest pinnacle.'

The Minister stopped looking angry. Vanina's beauty was doubtless a factor which contributed to this rapid change. Few in Rome were unaware of Monsignor Catanzara's liking for pretty women and, disguised as a footman of the Savelli household, in smooth silk stockings, red waistcoat, that short sky-blue coat with silver facings, and with a pistol in her hand, Vanina was irresistible.

'So you are to be my niece,' said the Minister, barely repressing a

---

[3] A Roman prelate would doubtless be unable to lead a body of troops with dash and flair, as happened several times with a general who was Minister of Police in Paris at the time of Mallet affair. But he would never let himself be so easily cornered in his own house. He would be much too afraid of being the butt of his colleagues' jokes. A Roman who knows that he is hated never walks abroad without being well armed. It has not been thought necessary to point out several other differences in the way people behave and speak in Paris and in Rome. Far from wishing to minimize these differences, we have chosen to write them boldly. The Romans who are sketched here do not have the honour of being French.

laugh. 'You realize that you are doing a very foolish thing—and I doubt very much that it will be the last.'

'I hope that a man as wise as you', answered Vanina, 'will keep my guilty secret, especially from Don Livio. And to encourage you to do so, dearest uncle, if you grant me the life of the man who so interests my friend, I shall give you a kiss.'

By continuing to maintain the conversation on this level of semi-serious banter, which Roman ladies adopt to further their gravest interests, Vanina succeeded in giving the conversation, which she had begun with a pistol in one hand, the tone of a social call paid by the young Princess Savelli on her uncle, the governor of Rome.

Soon Monsignor Catanzara, imperiously dispelling any impression that he could be forced to act through fear, began acquainting his niece with all the difficulties he would face if he tried to save Missirilli's life. As he spoke, the Minister walked around his study with Vanina. He reached for a carafe of lemonade which stood on the mantelpiece and filled a crystal glass. As he was about to raise it to his lips, Vanina took it from him and, after toying with it for some time, dropped it, accidentally it seemed, into the garden. A moment later, the Minister chose a chocolate drop from a box. Vanina snatched it out of his hand and said with a laugh:

'You should take more care. Everything is poisoned here. For there are people who want you dead. But I have arranged for the life of my future uncle to be spared so that I do not have to enter the Savelli family absolutely empty-handed.'

Monsignor Catanzara, startled out of his wits, thanked his niece and held out high hopes of Missirilli's continuing existence.

'Then our business is concluded!' exclaimed Vanina. 'And to seal it, here is your reward,' she said and she kissed him.

The Minister accepted his reward.

'But let me make one thing clear, Vanina, my dear,' he added. 'I hate bloodshed. Besides, I am still young though I probably seem very old to you and I live in times when blood that is spilt today may leave stains which will appear tomorrow.'

Two o'clock was striking when Monsignor Catanzara escorted Vanina to a side-gate of his garden.

Two days later, as the Minister, feeling none too sure of how to frame the request he was about to make, was being shown into the presence of the Pope, His Holiness said:

'Before we begin, I have a favour to ask of you. One of the *carbonari* from Forli has been sentenced to death. The thought of it is preventing me from sleeping. The man's life must be spared.'

The Minister, seeing that the Pontiff's mind was made up, raised many objections but in the end drafted a decree, or *motu proprio*, which the Pope signed, although it was contrary to custom.

Vanina had thought that she might obtain a pardon for her lover but feared that someone would try to poison him. The previous evening, the abbé Cari had brought Missirilli several packets of ship's biscuit with instructions that he was not to touch any food provided by the State.

Vanina subsequently learned that the Forli *carbonari* were to be transferred to the fortress at San Leo and wanted to see Missirilli as he passed through Città-Castellana. She reached the town twenty-four hours before the prisoners. There she found the abbé Cari who had arrived several days previously. He had persuaded the gaoler to allow Missirilli to attend mass, at midnight, in the prison chapel. But he obtained even more: provided Missirilli allowed his arms and legs to be chained, the gaoler would withdraw to the chapel door, so that he could still see the prisoner for whom he was responsible, but not hear what he said.

The day which would decide Vanina's fate finally dawned. Early in the morning, she took up her station in the prison chapel. Who can say what troubled thoughts ran through her mind during the long hours of waiting? Did Missirilli love her enough to forgive her? She had betrayed his cell but had saved his life. When reason gained the upper hand in her tortured mind, Vanina hoped that he would agree to leave Italy with her: if she had sinned, love had driven her to it. Four o'clock was striking when, in the distance, she heard the clatter of the horses of the*carabiniere* in the cobbled streets. The sound of every hoof seemed to reverberate in her heart. Soon, she made out the rumble of the carts which transported the prisoners. They halted in the small square outside the prison gate. She saw two *carabiniere* lift Missirilli, who had been placed in a cart by himself and was bound by so many chains that he could not walk unaided.

'At least he is alive!' she told herself, with tears in her eyes. 'They have not poisoned him yet!'

She spent a cruel evening. The altar lamp, set very high and smoking because the gaoler saved money by buying cheap oil, was the only light that pierced the chapel gloom. Vanina's eyes strayed to the tombs of a number of medieval lords who had died in the prison close by. Their effigies looked wild and fierce.

All sounds had grown still long ago. Vanina was absorbed in her black thoughts.

A little after midnight had struck, she thought she heard a faint noise, like the sound of a bat's wings. She stood up, tried to walk, and stumbled half-conscious over the altar rail. At that very moment, two ghostly figures appeared at her side, though she had not heard them approach. It was the gaoler and Missirilli so closely bound in chains that he was, so to speak, swaddled by them. The gaoler opened the window of a lantern which he placed on the altar rail, close to where Vanina lay, so that he would be able to see his prisoner. Then he walked to the back of the church and stood by the door. As soon as he had gone, Vanina flung her arms around Missirilli's neck. She held him close but could feel only his cold, sharp chains. Who put these chains on him? she thought. She took no pleasure in holding him. This disappointment was followed by another which was more distressing by far: Missirilli reacted so icily that she thought for a moment that he knew the secret of her treachery.

'Oh my dear,' he said after a moment's silence, 'I am heartily sorry you love me as you do. I can find no merit in me to explain it. It would be best, believe me, if we reverted to more Christian sentiments and forgot the illusions which once led us astray. I cannot be yours. The awful fate which has dogged my every undertaking is perhaps a consequence of the state of mortal sin in which I live constantly. But even if I invoke the ordinary standards of human judgement, why was I not arrested with my friends that fatal night at Forli? Why, when the danger was greatest, was I not at my post? Why did my absence give credence to the most hurtful suspicions? Because I had another love which was greater than my desire to see Italy free!'

Vanina was bewildered by the shock produced in her by the alteration in Missirilli. Although he did not seem to have lost weight, he looked at least thirty. Vanina attributed the change to the treatment he had suffered in prison. She burst into tears.

'But,' said she, 'the gaolers swore that they would treat you with kindness.'

The truth was that, when faced by the prospect of imminent death, the religious principles which were consistent with his love of Italian freedom had resurfaced in the heart of the young *carbonaro*. Gradually, Vanina realized that the change she noticed in the man she loved was of the spiritual variety and had nothing to do with his physical treatment. Consequently, her unhappiness, which she thought had reached its zenith, soared to new heights.

Missirilli had stopped speaking. Vanina seemed about to choke on her sobs. Then, in a voice not entirely bereft of feeling, he said:

'If I were ever to love anything or anyone on this earth, it would be you, Vanina. But, by the grace of God, I now have only one aim in life. I shall die, either in prison or in attempting to give Italy her liberty!'

There was another silence. It was clear that Vanina could not speak. Missirilli went on:

'Duty is a cruel master, my dear. But if there were not pain to overcome, where would be the heroism? Give me your word that you will never try to see me again.'

Insofar as his chains allowed, he made a small movement with his hand and held out his fingers to Vanina.

'If you will allow a man who once was dear to you to offer a word of advice: be sensible, marry the worthy man whom your father has chosen for you. Never reveal any dangerous secrets to him, but on the other hand never try to see me again. Let us from this day on be strangers to each other. You gave a large sum of money to our country's cause. If ever Italy is delivered from her tyrants, it will be repaid to you out of the public purse.'

Vanina felt utterly crushed. All the time Pietro had spoken to her, the only time his eyes had lit up was when he pronounced the words 'our country's cause'.

Eventually, her pride came to her rescue. She had come provided with diamonds and a set of small files. Without giving Missirilli an answer, she offered them to him.

'I accept because it is my duty,' said he, 'for I must try to escape. But I shall never see you again, this I swear by the new gifts you bring me. Farewell, Vanina. Promise me you will never write or attempt to see me. Leave me free to give my all to Italy. Think of me as though I were dead. Farewell!'

'No,' replied Vanina in a rage. 'I want you to know what I did for love of you!'

And she recounted everything she had done from the time Missirilli had left the fortress at San Nicolo to give himself up to the Legate. When her tale was finished:

'But that is nothing,' she said, 'I did much more and I did it because I loved you.'

Then she told him how she had betrayed him.

'Oh, you monster!' cried Pietro, white with fury, and he lunged at her, attempting to bludgeon her with his chains.

And he would have succeeded too had the gaoler not come running and restrained him.

'Here, take these, I have no wish to be obliged to a monster like you!' Missirilli said to Vanina, and though hampered by his chains, he threw her files and diamonds back at her, then turned and hurried off.

Vanina was left utterly broken. She returned to Rome.

The newspapers report that she has just married Prince Livio Savelli.

The Coffee Pot

A Fantastic Tale

Translated by David Coward

This sight I saw high in heaven:
Stars (they were eleven)
And also Moon and Sun
Bowed down to me as one,
and in silence kept
Their heads bent all the time I slept
Joseph's Vision

I

Last year, I was invited, together with a couple of friends from the studio, Arrigo Cohic and Pedrino Borgnioli, to spend a few days on a country estate in the depths of Normandy.

The weather when we set out promised to be superb but made up its mind to change all of a sudden, and so much rain fell that the sunken lanes along which we walked turned into raging torrents.

We were soon up to our knees in mire. A thick layer of sticky mud clung to the soles of our boots and, being very heavy, so slowed our progress that we did not reach our destination until an hour after the sun had set.

We were exhausted. Accordingly, as soon as we had finished dinner, our host, observing the efforts we made to stifle our yawns and keep our eyes open, had us shown to our rooms.

Mine was huge. As I went through the door, I felt a nervous shiver, for I had the impression that I was entering a different world.

And I might well have been, for I seemed to have stepped back into the Regency period to judge by the Boucher paintings of the four seasons over the doors, the furniture cluttered up with rococo ornaments of appalling taste, and the mirrors in their heavy carved frames.

Nothing had been disturbed. The dressing table, strewn with comb-cases and powder-puffs, looked as though it had been in use the day before. Two or three shot-silk dresses and a fan spangled with silver sequins littered the highly polished floor and, to my great surprise, a tortoise-shell snuffbox stood open on the mantelpiece, its contents still fresh.

I did not notice all this until the footman, setting down the candlestick on the bedside table, had wished me a good night's sleep. But then, I freely admit, I began to shake like a leaf. I undressed quickly, got into bed, and to banish my ridiculous fears, turned my face to the wall and closed my eyes.

But I found it impossible to remain in this position. The bed heaved under me like a wave and my eyelids were forced open. I had no choice but to turn and look.

The flickering flames in the hearth cast a reddish glow over the room so that it was perfectly possible to make out the people in the tapestries and the faces of the smoke-blackened portraits which hung on the walls.

These were of our host's ancestors, knights in armour, bewigged councillors, and handsome ladies with painted faces and white-powdered hair, each holding a rose.

Suddenly, the fire blazed up in the strangest way. An unearthly brightness illuminated the room and I saw quite clearly that what I had taken for a mere collection of paintings was in fact real. The eyes of the personages in their frames moved and glinted eerily. Their lips opened and closed as mouths do when people speak, but all I heard was the ticking of the clock and the sigh of the autumn wind.

I was overcome by a feeling of irresistible terror. My hair stood on end, my teeth chattered until I thought they would break, and my whole body broke out in a cold sweat.

The clock struck eleven. The reverberation of the last stroke hung long in the air and when it died away completely . . .

But no, I hardly dare say what happened next, no one would believe me and people would think me mad.

The candles acquired flames spontaneously. The bellows, wheezing like an asthmatic old man, though no human hand could be seen working it, breathed life into the fire, while a pair of tongs raked through the embers and the ash was collected by a pan.

Then a coffee pot jumped off a table where it had been standing and waddled to the fireplace where it settled on the glowing coals.

Almost immediately the armchairs began to quiver and, stirring their twisted legs in the most amazing fashion, advanced to form a half-circle around the hearth.

II

I had no idea what to make of what I was seeing. But what I was about to see was more extraordinary still.

One of the portraits, the most ancient, of a stout man with round cheeks and a grey beard who looked exactly as I had always imagined old Sir John Falstaff must have looked, poked his head out of his frame with a scowl and then, after a struggle, heaved his shoulders and vast stomach through the narrow square and jumped heavily to the floor.

When he had caught his breath, he took from the pocket of his doublet a tiny key. He blew on it to make sure the blade was clean and then inserted it into every frame in turn.

The frames expanded until they were large enough for all the persons they held to step out quite easily.

Rosy-cheeked clerics, withered, yellow-skinned dowagers, grave-faced magistrates wreathed in long black robes, fops in silk stockings and sloe-coloured breeches with the point of their swords held high—all these figures made such a bizarre sight that, despite my fears, I could not help but laugh.

These worthies then sat down. The coffee pot hopped nimbly back on to the table. They drank their coffee from blue-and-white Japanese porcelain cups which came running spontaneously from a cabinet, each arriving with its own sugar lump and dainty silver spoon.

When they had finished with the coffee, pot, cups, and spoons vanished in a trice and they then began a conversation which was the weirdest I ever heard, for none of the strange participants looked at the others when they spoke but kept their eyes glued to the clock.

I too found it impossible not to look at it nor could I prevent myself following the hands which crawled towards midnight with barely perceptible movements.

Finally, midnight struck. A voice whose timbre exactly matched that of the clock boomed out. It said:

'All change! It's time for dancing!'

The entire company rose. The chairs moved back of their own accord. Then each gentleman took the hand of a lady and the same voice said:

'And now, members of the orchestra, music please!'

I omitted to mention that the subject of the tapestry at one end of the room was a group of Italian musicians and at the other a stag-hunt which included a number of huntsmen blowing horns. Both they and the musicians who, up to this point, had not moved a muscle, now inclined their heads to indicate that they were ready.

The maestro raised his baton and lively, rhythmic music struck up from opposite sides of the room. First they danced a minuet.

But the rapid notes of the score from which the musicians were playing were at variance with grave bowing and curtseying and within moments each couple began to whirl round and round like spinning tops. The ladies' silk dresses, brushing against each other in this dancing maelstrom, made a distinctive sound, rather like the flapping wings of pigeons in flight. The air rising from the floor made their skirts swell prodigiously, with the result that they looked like so many handbells set in motion.

The bows of the fiddlers flew so quickly across the strings that sparks of electricity were given off, the fingers of the flautists rose and fell as though made of quicksilver, the huntsmen's cheeks were as big as balloons, and together they all made a deluge of such busy notes and trills, of such convoluted scales which rose and fell, that not even the devils of hell could have kept up with that tempo for two minutes.

It was a pitiful sight to watch the efforts made by the dancers to keep up with the rhythm. They hopped and skipped, flung their legs out, executed jetés, performed entrechats three feet off the ground until the perspiration which ran from their foreheads into their eyes washed away their face-powder and beauty patches. But it was no use, the orchestra was always three or four notes ahead of them.

The clock struck one. They stopped. Then I saw something which had escaped my attention: a woman who had not danced.

She was sitting in a wing-chair in one corner of the hearth and seemed supremely indifferent to what was going on around her.

Never, not even in my dreams, had I set eyes on so perfect a creature. Dazzling white skin, ash-blond hair, long eyelashes, and blue eyes so limpid and so transparent that through them I could see her soul as clearly as a pebble on the bed of a stream.

Instantly I knew that if ever I were to fall in love, it would be with her. I leaped out of my bed in which until that point I had remained paralysed, and walked towards her, impelled by some inner force which I could not explain. Then I found myself kneeling before her, with her hand in mine, chatting away as though I had known her for twenty years.

Yet, through some very mysterious phenomenon, I noticed as I talked that my head nodded in time to the music which had not stopped playing. And although I could not have been happier than to be talking to such a beautiful creature, my feet were itching to dance with her.

However, I did not dare suggest it. But she seemed to understand what I wanted, for she raised the hand I was not holding and, pointing to the clock-face, said:

'When the pointer reaches there, we shall see, dearest Théodore.'

I cannot explain why but I was not in the least surprised to hear myself called by my name and we went on chatting together. Eventually, the time she had indicated struck and the voice of the silver-toned bell reverberated through the room once more:

'Angela, you may dance with the gentleman if that is your wish. But you know what the consequence will be.'

'I don't care,' said Angela sulkily.

She put her creamy, ivory arm around my neck.

'*Prestissimo!*' cried the voice.

And we began to waltz. Angela's bosom was touching my chest, her velvet cheek brushed against mine, and her sweet breath hovered over my mouth.

I had never felt such emotion in all my life. My nerves quivered like steel springs, blood coursed through my veins like a torrent of lava, and I heard my heart beat as loudly as though I had a watch attached to each ear.

Yet there was nothing distressing in my situation. I bubbled with unutterable happiness and wished I could have gone on like this for ever. Oddly enough, although the orchestra was now playing three times as fast, we did not have to make any conscious effort to keep up.

The onlookers, amazed by our nimbleness, shouted 'Bravo!' and clapped their hands for all they were worth, though this produced no sound.

Angela, who up to this point had waltzed with astounding energy and surefootedness, suddenly seemed to tire. She leaned on my shoulder as though her legs were about to give way. Her tiny feet which only the moment before had skimmed the floor, now grew sluggish and earthbound, as though lead weights had been attached to them.

'Angela, you're tired,' I said. 'Shall we rest a moment?'

'Very well,' she replied, wiping her brow with her handkerchief. 'But while we've been waltzing, the others have all sat down. There's only one chair left and there are two of us.'

'Does it matter, my angel? You shall sit on my knee.'

III

Without raising the least objection, Angela sat down, curling her arms around my neck like a white scarf, burying her head in my chest for warmth, for she had become as cold as marble.

I cannot say how long we remained in that position for all my senses were engaged by my contemplation of this mysterious, magical creature.

I had ceased to have any notion of time and place. The world no longer existed for me and all the ties which bound me to it were snapped. My soul, freed from its earthly prison, hovered in the fathomless realms of infinity. I understood what no man can understand, for Angela's thoughts were transmitted to me without need of speech. For her soul shone out of her like an alabaster lamp and the light radiating from her heart illumined every dark recess of mine.

A lark began to sing and the curtains were suffused by a pale glow.

The instant Angela became aware of it, she stood up quickly with a gesture of farewell, took a few steps, gave a cry, and collapsed in a heap.

Gripped by fear, I rushed to help her to her feet . . . My blood runs cold at the mere thought of it: all I found was the coffee pot smashed to smithereens.

When I saw it, I was convinced that I had been the victim of some diabolical illusion. I was seized by such dread that I fainted clean away.

IV

When I came to my senses, I was lying down, comfortably tucked up. Arrigo Cohic and Pedrino Borgnioli were standing by my bedside.

The moment I opened my eyes, Arrigo exclaimed:

'And about time too! I've been rubbing your temples with eau de cologne for nearly an hour. What the devil did you get up to last night? When I noticed you hadn't come down this morning, I came up to see where you were and found you stretched out on the floor, got up like an old-time French gentleman clutching a piece of broken porcelain crockery as though it was a pretty girl.'

'Good lord! These are the clothes my grandfather wore to his wedding,' said our host.

And he raised one of the coat-tails which was pink silk patterned with green leaves.

'These are the paste and filigree buttons he was always telling us about. I expect Théodore found it somewhere or other and put it on for a laugh.'

'By the bye, what came over you?' asked Borgnioli. 'Fainting should be left to pretty girls with shoulders like alabaster. Gives you an excuse for loosening her laces, removing her collars, her scarf . . . creates no end of opportunities for flirting.'

'I just felt faint. I do sometimes,' I replied sharply.

I got up and took off the ridiculous costume I was wearing.

Then we had lunch.

My three friends ate large quantities and drank even more. But I hardly touched a thing, for the memory of what had happened was strangely distracting.

When lunch was over it was pouring with rain and there was no question of our going out. We each amused ourselves as best we could. Borgnioli tapped out military marches on the window panes, Arrigo and our host played draughts, and I took a square of thick paper from my sketchbook and began to draw.

The faint, barely visible outline traced by my pencil, to whose meandering I gave no conscious thought, ended up looking like an amazingly accurate picture of the coffee pot which had played a central role in the previous night's drama.

'Extraordinary! That face looks exactly like my sister Angela,' said our host who, having finished his game, was watching me work over my shoulder.

He was right. What a moment before had looked to me like a coffee pot was actually the profile of sweet, melancholy Angela.

'By all the saints in heaven! Is she living or dead?' I exclaimed in a voice which shook as though my very life depended on his answer.

'She died two years ago of pneumonia. Came down with it after a ball.'

'Alas!' I replied sorrowfully.

And holding back a tear which was about to fall, I replaced the sheet in my sketchbook.

I had just realized that from that day forth there would be no happiness for me in this life!

The Message

Translated by David Coward

For the Marquis Damaso Pareto

I have always wanted to tell a tale so simple, so true that on hearing it a young man and the girl he loves would shiver with fear and seek refuge in each other's arms, like children who cling together when they chance upon a snake at the edge of a wood.

At the risk of deflating any interest my narrative might have, or of seeming pretentious, I state thus the aim of my tale at the outset. I played a part in this fairly unexceptional little drama; if it fails to interest you, the fault will be as much mine as the authentic truth. Many true things are supremely dull. Which is why the better half of talent consists of selecting from what is true that which can be made poetic.

In 1819, I was travelling from Paris to Moulins. I was obliged by the meagre state of my purse to take a seat on the roof of the coach. As you know, the English consider the seats located in this aerial part of the vehicle to be the best. For the first few leagues we travelled, I found many excellent reasons to justify the opinion of our neighbours.

A young man, who seemed to me a little better off than I was, clambered by choice on to the bench beside me. He greeted my opinion of the matter with inoffensive smiles. Soon a certain conformity of age, outlook, a mutual love of the open air and of the expansive views which unfolded before us as the lumbering coach proceeded, together with an indefinable magnetic attraction impossible to explain, all combined to produce between us a kind of fleeting intimacy to which travellers surrender all the more readily because such passing closeness is guaranteed to end promptly and commits neither party to any future obligation.

We had not travelled thirty leagues before we were speaking of women and love. Watching our words with all the circumspection required in such situations, it was only natural that we soon got round to our mistresses. We were both young and were still at the stage of *the older woman*, that is a woman who is between thirty-five and forty years of age.

Now, had there been a poet to eavesdrop on us from Montargis to I forget which staging post, he would have garnered such a haul of burning phrases, captivating portraits, and tender confidences! Our youthful fears, unspoken exclamations, and still bashful looks were charged with an eloquence whose innocent charm I have never recaptured. No doubt anyone who wishes to understand youth must remain young. In other words, we understood each other perfectly on all the basics of passion.

So to start with, we had begun by agreeing in fact and in principle that there was nothing more absurd than a birth certificate; that many women of forty were younger than some at twenty; and that, in short, women were only as old as they seemed. This theory set no time limit on love and meant that we could set sail in all honesty upon a boundless sea.

Eventually, having made our mistresses young, attractive, faithful, aristocratic, with exquisite taste and the finest wit; after granting them pretty feet and silky, even delicately perfumed skin, we each owned up and admitted, he that Madame So-and-so was thirty-eight and I, for my part, that I worshipped a lady who would not see forty again.

Whereupon, now that our qualms were dispelled, we both became more expansive in our disclosures on discovering that we were brothers in love. It turned into a contest to establish which of us had the better claim to fine feeling. One of us had once ridden two hundred leagues to spend an hour with his mistress. The other had run the risk of being mistaken for a wolf and shot in the grounds of a grand house so that he could keep a midnight tryst. Ah, such folly! If there is enjoyment to be got from recalling past dangers, is there not also delight to be had by remembering pleasures which have fled? To do so is to live them again. Perils, joys large and small, we held nothing back, not even the lighter moments. My friend's countess had smoked a cigar to please him. Mine insisted on preparing my chocolate with her own fair hands and could never let a day go by without seeing me or writing a note. His had stayed in his rooms for three days, though by doing so she jeopardized her reputation. Mine had done better—or worse, if you prefer.

Our countesses were adored by husbands who were slaves to the charms which all loving women possess. And unsuspecting beyond the call of duty in these matters, they provided us with that whiff of danger which we needed to enhance our pleasure. Oh how quickly our tender words and gentle mockery were borne away on the wings of the wind!

When we reached Pouilly, I looked closely at my new friend. I had no hesitation whatsoever in believing that he was capable of inspiring passionate love.

Picture a young man of average height, but well proportioned, with an engaging, expressive face. He had black hair and blue eyes. His lips were a delicate pink and his teeth white and even. An attractive pallor heightened his fine features and faint dark-brown rings circled his eyes as though he were recovering from an illness. Add to this that his hands were white, well shaped, and as carefully manicured as any pretty woman's, that he seemed cultured and was certainly a man of wit, and you will have no difficulty in agreeing with me that my companion would have done honour to any countess. In sum, many a young girl would have had him for a husband, for he was a viscount and had a private income of twelve or fifteen thousand a year, not counting his expectations.

A league after leaving Pouilly, the coach ran into a ditch. My unfortunate comrade, thinking to save his neck, decided to jump to safety on the edge of a freshly ploughed field, instead of holding on to the seat and following the momentum of the coach, as I did. Perhaps he caught his foot or slipped, I couldn't say how the accident happened, but he was crushed by the coach, which fell on him. We carried him to a farm-labourer's cottage.

Through the groans induced by the agonizing pain that racked him, he was able to ask me to carry out the kind of task which the last wishes of a dying man turn into a sacred duty. Even as his end approached, the poor boy, with all the frankness of which we are often the victim at his age, was tortured by the thought of the pain his mistress would suffer if she were to learn of his death suddenly, through a newspaper. He entreated me to go and tell her myself. Then he told me to look for a key hanging on a ribbon which he wore across his chest. I found it: it had been half-pressed into his flesh. The dying man made not the slightest complaint as I retrieved it, which I did as gently as I possibly could, from the laceration it had caused. He was giving me the last of the instructions I would need to go to his house at La Charité-sur-Loire and get the love letters she had written to him and was begging me to return them to her, when his voice failed in mid-sentence. But his final gesture made me understand that the fatal key was the pledge I should need in my mission to his mother.

Grieved to be unable to pronounce a word of thanks, for he was in no doubt of my zeal, he looked pleadingly at me for a moment, said goodbye with a movement of his eyelids, then his head went slack and he died. His death was the only fatality caused by the accident to the coach.

'All the same, it was 'alfway 'is own fault,' the driver told me.

At La Charité, I carried out the unwritten wishes of my poor travelling companion. His mother was not at home, which was no little relief to me. Even so, I had to contend with the grief of an old serving-woman who reeled when I told her that her young master was dead. She collapsed half-dead into a chair when she saw the key which was still stained with blood. But since my mind was preoccupied with sorrow of a higher order, that of a woman from whom fate had snatched her last love, I left the old woman to her lamentations and left, taking with me the precious correspondence which had been carefully sealed by the friend I had known for one day.

The château where the Countess lived was eight leagues from Moulins and there were several more leagues of the estate to cross before I got there. This made it rather difficult for me to deliver my message. Through a combination of circumstances which I need not explain, I had only enough money to take me as far as Moulins. However, with the enthusiasm of youth, I resolved to complete the rest of the journey on foot and to make all possible speed and arrive before the report of bad news, which always travels very fast.

I enquired which was the shortest route and set off through the Bourbonnais carrying, so to speak, a dead man on my back. As I neared the Château de Montpersan, I grew increasingly alarmed by the singular pilgrimage I had undertaken. My imagination bred a succession of romantic fancies. I pictured every possible circumstance in which I might meet the Countess de Montpersan, or, as they say poetically in novels, the *Juliette* who had been so loved by my young friend, the traveller. I devised witty answers to the questions which I assumed would be put to me. Behind every tree, at every bend in the road, I ran through the scene with Sosie and her lantern in which he gives an account of the battle. I am ashamed in my heart to say it, but at first I thought only of my appearance, my wit, the cleverness I intended to show. But when I got within striking distance of the place, a sinister thought blasted my whole being like a bolt of lightning which sunders and shreds a curtain of grey cloud. What appalling news to bring a woman who was even now thinking about her young lover and anticipating with every hour that passed a bliss for which there was no name, after all the infinite pains she had taken to find a legitimate pretext for bringing him to her.

In short I felt the cold charity implicit in my role as Death's messenger. Accordingly I hurried on, muddying my boots as I trudged along the miry lanes of the Bourbonnais. Soon I reached a long avenue of chestnut trees at the end of which the great pile of the Château de Montpersan loomed up against the sky like sepia clouds edged with light and moulded into fantastic shapes.

When I got to the great door of the château, I found it standing open. This unforeseen circumstance disrupted my plans and assumptions. Nevertheless, I stepped boldly inside and was immediately besieged by two hounds which barked as only country dogs can. On hearing the noise, a fat maid came running and when I told her that I wished to speak to the Countess, she gestured vaguely at the massed trees of the English-style estate which coiled around the château and said:

'The Mistress is over there . . .'

'I am obliged to you,' I said ironically. Her 'over there' might well lead me a merry dance round the grounds for a couple of hours.

Meanwhile, a pretty little girl with curls, wearing a pink sash, a white dress, and a pleated cape, had appeared from nowhere. She either heard or made out both the question and the answer. Taking one look at me, she ran off shouting in a small, high-pitched voice:

'Mama! There's a gentlemen who wants to talk to you!'

I set off in pursuit, following the twists and turns of the paths and walks, never losing sight of that skipping, bobbing white cape which, like a will o' the wisp, showed me which way the little girl was going.

I must hold nothing back. On first arriving, when I got to the bush at the end of the avenue, I had pulled my shirt collar up, brushed my battered hat and trousers with my coat lapels, my coat with my cuffs and my cuffs with each other, then I buttoned my coat to show the back of the lapels which are always less worn than the rest. I had also pulled my trouser bottoms on to my boots which I had artistically wiped clean in the grass. Thanks to my improvised titivations, I hoped not to be taken for an exciseman sent by the local tax office. But today, when my thoughts take me back to that time of my youth, I sometimes laugh at my former self.

Suddenly, as I was putting the final touches to the dash I intended to cut, I saw, in a loop of a winding green path, surrounded by innumerable flowers lit by a warm stream of sunlight, Juliette and her husband. The pretty little girl was holding her mother's hand and it was easy to see that the Countess had quickened her step after hearing her daughter's cryptic words.

Surprised to see a stranger who offered his hand in such an awkward manner, she stopped, looked at me with a cool, polite expression and a delightful purse of her lips in which I believed I saw all her dashed hopes. I tried in vain to remember the fine phrases which I had prepared with such labour. At that moment, as we both stood there hesitating, her husband came up and joined us. Innumerable thoughts passed through my mind. Respecting the courtesies, I said a few meaningless words, asking if they were the Count and Countess of Montpersan, in person. My questions were vacuous but they allowed me to judge at a glance and analyse, with a perspicacity rare at the age I then was, a husband and wife whose private world was soon to be rudely shattered.

The husband appeared to be a typical representative of the country gentleman who is at the present time the finest flower of France's provinces. He was wearing stout shoes with thick soles. I mention these first because they struck me even more forcibly than his faded black coat, worn trousers, the slack jabot, and the curling collar of his shirt. There was a whiff of the justice of the peace about him, but also a stronger reek of district councillor, the self-important local mayor who lets nothing stand in his way or the sour candidate who puts his name forward periodically but has been rejected since 1816, an inconceivable mixture of good country sense and stupidity, a man who had none of the manners and all the arrogance of the rich, who deferred much to his wife but considered himself her master, ready to take to the barricades over trifles but indifferent to matters of moment, with a face, moreover, that was sunken-cheeked, lined, and weather-burned, and surrounded by wisps of long, grey, lank hair: such was the man.

But the Countess! Oh what a vivid, unexpected contrast she made next to her husband! She was small, with a trim, supple waist and an enchanting figure, dainty and so delicate that you would be afraid to touch her lest she break. She wore a white muslin dress, a pretty hat with pink ribbons, a rose-coloured sash, a little cape which her shoulders and beautifully swelling contours filled so temptingly that the sight of them quickened the pulse and put the spur to desire. Her eyes were quick, black, and expressive, her movements gentle, and her feet small and well made. An ageing Don Juan would not have believed she was above thirty years of age, such was the bloom of youth which still clung to her brow and every delicate detail of her head. As to her character, she seemed to me to have something about her of both the Countess de Lignolles and the Marquise de B***, two types of women who remain fresh in the memory of any young man who has read the novel by Louvet de Couvray.

I suddenly felt as though I knew everything there was to know about this couple and decided upon a diplomatic course of action worthy of an experienced ambassador. It was perhaps the only time in my life when I showed any finesse and really understood the skill of those who move in court circles and fashionable society.

Since those carefree days, I have fought too many battles to worry about analysing every trifling passage of life and nowadays merely go through the motions, observing the requirements of etiquette and good manners which can shrivel up the most genuine emotions.

'May I have a word with you in private, Count?' said I mysteriously, stepping back a few paces.

He followed me. Juliette left us together and turned away like a woman who was confident of learning her husband's secrets whenever she chose to ask. Briefly I acquainted the Count with the death of my travelling companion. The effect my words produced on him proved to me that he felt a genuine affection for his young colleague, and this knowledge emboldened me to reply as follows in the exchange which took place between us.

'My wife will be distraught,' he exclaimed, 'and I shall have to be very careful in choosing the right way of breaking the news of this most regrettable accident to her.'

'Sir, by speaking first to you,' said I, 'I have discharged a duty. It was never my intention to deliver a message from a stranger to your wife without first informing you. But he entrusted me with what might be called an obligation of honour, a secret which I am not at liberty to disclose as I wish. If I may judge by the high estimate he gave me of your character, I believed you would not object to my carrying out his last wishes. The Countess is of course free to break the silence which binds me.'

Hearing his praises sung, the Count nodded his head sagely. He replied with a somewhat involved compliment and in the end gave me a free hand. We retraced our steps.

At that moment a bell announced that dinner was served. I was invited to stay. Finding us so grave and silent, Juliette observed us furtively.

Strangely puzzled to hear her husband devise an unconvincing pretext for leaving us alone, she paused and threw me one of those looks which only women can give. Her eyes brimmed with the proper curiosity of a hostess receiving a stranger who has suddenly appeared in her house out of nowhere. They were full of questions prompted by my clothes, my youth, and my face, which formed an assemblage of odd contrasts! But they also oozed with the disdain of an adored mistress to whom all men, save one, are nothing. In them were apprehensiveness, fear, and the irritation of having to cope with an unexpected guest when no doubt she had been planning to spend her moments alone in happy contemplation of her love.

I understood all that her silent eloquence signified and replied with a wistful smile, a smile full of pity and compassion. And I paused a moment, observing the full splendour of her beauty, on that serene day, as she stood in the middle of a narrow walk lined with flowers. As I gazed on this exquisite picture, I could not contain a sigh.

'I fear, Madame, that I have reached the end of an arduous journey which I undertook . . . for your sake.'

'Oh sir!' she exclaimed.

'I am here,' I went on, 'in the name of a man who called you Juliette.' She turned pale. 'You will not see him today.'

'Is he ill?' she whispered.

'Yes,' I answered. 'But please, you must remain calm. He asked me to give into your keeping certain private affairs which concern you. You must believe that no messenger could ever be more discreet or more devoted than I.'

'What has happened?'

'What if he has stopped loving you?'

'That cannot be,' she exclaimed, and she allowed herself a faint smile which was nothing if not candid.

Suddenly, she gave a shudder, shot me a wild, urgent look, blushed and said: 'Is he alive?'

God! What a question! I was too young to know how to deal with the emotion with which it was charged. I did not reply but stood staring at the unhappy women in a daze.

'Sir, you will give me an answer!' she exclaimed.

'Yes, Madame.'

'Is it true? Oh, tell me the truth. I can bear it. Tell me! Anything, however painful, would be easier to bear than this uncertainty.'

My answer was contained in the tears brought to my eyes by the extraordinary tone of voice which accompanied her words.

She leaned against a tree and uttered a faint whimper.

'Madame,' I said, 'your husband is coming!'

'Husband? I have no husband.'

And so saying, she fled and disappeared from sight.

'Look lively,' exclaimed the Count, 'the dinner is getting cold. Come, sir!'

Upon which I followed the master of the house, who led the way to a dining room where a meal was served with all the luxury to which the

Paris fashion has accustomed us. Five places were set: those of the husband and wife, their little daughter, *mine* which should have been *his*, and the last for a canon from Saint-Denis who, after saying grace, asked:

'But where is the dear Countess?'

'Oh, she'll be along presently,' answered the Count, who hastily ladled out the potage for each of us and then served himself a very generous helping which he expedited with amazing speed.

'Nephew,' chided the canon, 'if your wife were here you would not behave so unreasonably.'

'Papa will make himself ill,' said the little girl knowingly.

A moment after this peculiar gastronomic incident and just as the Count was enthusiastically carving some cut or other of venison, a maid entered and said:

'Oh sir! We can't find the mistress anywhere!'

Hearing these words I leaped quickly to my feet fearing that something dreadful had happened, and my alarm was so clearly imprinted on my face that the old priest followed me out into the garden. The husband, for form's sake, came as far as the door.

'Don't go! Stay! There's no cause for concern,' he called after us.

But he did not come with us.

The canon, the maid, and I scoured the walks and lawns of the grounds, calling, listening, and becoming anxious to the point that I told them all about the death of the young Viscount. As we hurried on, I related the details of how the fatal accident had occurred and realized that the maid was extremely fond of her mistress, for she sensed the secret direction of my terror far better than the canon. We went to the water garden, we combed the grounds but did not find the Countess or any trace of her. And then, returning along the course of a wall, I heard low, heavily stifled moans which seemed to be coming from a barn of sorts. At a venture, I went in. There we found Juliette who, driven by the instincts of despair, had burrowed into the middle of the hay. She had buried her head in it to muffle her terrifying screams, unable to overcome the urge to hide her misery: she sobbed, she wept like a child, but more vehemently and more plaintively. Nothing existed in the whole world for her now. The maid disentangled her mistress, who did not resist but behaved with the limp indifference of a dying animal.

Over and over the maid kept repeating: 'Come along, Madame, come along . . .'

The old priest asked: 'What's wrong with her? What's the matter, niece?'

Finally, with the help of the maid, I carried Juliette to her room. I left careful instructions that she should not be left and that if anyone asked they should be told that the Countess had a headache. Then the canon and I went back down to the dining room.

It was some time since we had left the Count. I had not given him a moment's thought until I was walking through the columned hall. I was surprised that he had shown so little concern but my amazement grew when I found him sitting patiently at the table.

He had eaten virtually all the food on the table, much to the delight of his daughter, who smiled to see her father deliberately flouting the orders of the Countess.

The strange unfeelingness of the husband was explained to me in a brief altercation which suddenly erupted between he and the canon. The Count was supposed to be on a strict diet which his doctors had prescribed to cure him of some serious illness the name of which escapes me. Impelled by the rabid gluttony which will be all too familiar to anyone who is recovering from illness, animal appetite had gained the ascendant over all human feeling.

In that moment, I saw nature in all its truth, in two very different lights which thrust comedy into the heart of the most harrowing grief.

The evening passed dismally. I was tired. The canon used all his powers of reasoning to get to the root of his niece's tears. The Count digested in silence after accepting a rather hazy explanation of the Countess's indisposition which she had conveyed to him through her maid and which was, I believe, not unrelated to ailments natural to women. We all went up to bed early.

I was shown to my room by a footman. As I passed the door of the Countess's apartment, I shyly enquired how she was. Recognizing my voice, she sent for me and tried to speak. But the words would not come and she bowed her head. I withdrew.

Despite the cruel emotions which I had lately felt with all the earnestness of youth, I slept deeply, exhausted by my long forced march.

Some time towards morning, I was woken by the jangle of rings clattering over metal rods as my curtains were suddenly flung wide open. I saw the Countess sitting at the foot of my bed. Her face was brightly lit by the lamp on my bedside table.

'Is it really true?' said she. 'I do not know how I shall go on living after the horrible blow I have been struck. But I feel calm now. I want to know everything.'

Calm? I said to myself as I observed the ghastly pallor of her face which contrasted starkly with the brown of her hair and heard the croak that was now her voice, for I was stunned by the change in her to which her altered appearance bore visible testimony. She had been drained of colour, like the sere leaf which has lost the last of the tints conferred upon it by autumn. Her eyes, red and swollen and robbed now of their former beauty, were reflections only of deep and bitter grief. It was like seeing grey cloud where once the sun had danced.

In a few words I recapitulated, without going into certain details too painful for her to bear, the brief event which had plucked her lover from her. I told her about the first day of our journey together which had been filled by memories of their love.

She shed no tears but listened avidly, with her head bent towards me, like a zealous doctor scanning a patient for symptoms. Seizing a moment when she seemed to have opened her heart fully to her suffering and to be on the point of surrendering to her grief with all the burning intensity that comes with the feverish onset of despair, I spoke of the fears which had tormented the dying man and explained why he had entrusted me with my sombre mission.

She stopped weeping, her tears dried by the grim fires which smouldered in the deepest recesses of her soul. Her pallor deepened. When I held out the letters which I produced from beneath my pillow, she took them mechanically. Then she gave a violent start and said in a whisper:

'But I burned his! Every one! I have nothing left of him! Nothing!'

And she struck herself forcibly on the forehead.

'Madame . . .' I said.

She looked at me and shuddered:

'From his head,' I went on, 'I cut a lock of his hair. I have it here.'

I presented it to her, an imperishable relic of the man she loved.

Had you felt as I did when those burning tears fell on to my hands, you would know what gratitude is when it follows so promptly the gift that is given!

She clasped my hands and, in a voice which broke and with a look bright with fever in which a precarious joy shone through her dreadful suffering:

'Ah!' she said, 'you know what love is! May you always be happy and never lose the one you love . . .'

She did not finish but fled with her treasure.

The next day, this nocturnal encounter, which had merged into my dreams, seemed like something out of a novel. It took a fruitless search for the letters under my pillow to convince me that it was all too painfully real.

Nothing would be gained by relating the events of that day. I stayed on for a few hours with Juliette whom my unfortunate travelling companion had praised so highly. Her least word, her every gesture, her smallest act demonstrated a nobility of soul and a delicacy of feeling which raised her to the level of those women beyond price who are all love and self-sacrifice but of whom there are precious few on this earth.

That evening, the Count de Montpersan himself drove me back to Moulins. As we arrived, he said with an embarrassed smile:

'Sir, at the risk of trespassing further on your kindness and of appearing to act indiscreetly towards a stranger who has already obliged us, may I ask if you would be good enough, since you are going to Paris, to deliver to Monsieur de *** (I forget the name) in the rue du Sentier, a sum of money I owe him which he has asked me to convey to him with all convenient speed?'

'Gladly,' I said.

And innocent that I was, I took a rouleau of twenty-five gold louis from him, the transportation of which took care of the expense of my return to Paris and which I faithfully took to the Count de Montpersan's supposed associate.

It was only on reaching Paris and presenting myself with the money at the address which he had given me, that I understood the ingenious means Juliette had found to pay me for my trouble. Surely the way that gold was loaned to me and the discretion with which my all-too-obvious poverty was treated reveal the spirit of a loving woman in all its glory?

How gratifying to have had an opportunity of telling this story to a woman who, taking fright, held you close and said:

'Oh dearest, you won't die, will you?'

The Venus of Ille

Translated by Nicholas Jotcham

Ἵλεως ἦν δ' ἐγώ, ἔστω. ὁ ἀνδριὰς
καὶ ἤπιος, οὕτως ἀνδρεῖος ὤν.
ΛΟΥΚΙΑΝΟΥ ΦΙΛΟΨΕΥΔΗΣ

I was descending the final slope of Mount Canigou, and although the sun had already set, on the plain I could make out the houses of the little town of Ille, which was my destination.

'I don't suppose you know where Monsieur de Peyrehorade lives?' I asked the Catalan who had been acting as my guide since the previous day.

'Why, of course I do!' he exclaimed. 'I know his house as well as I know my own. If it weren't so dark I'd point it out to you. It's the finest house in Ille. He's a rich man, is Monsieur de Peyrehorade, and he's marrying his son to a girl who's wealthier still.'

'And is this marriage to take place soon?' I asked him.

'Soon! I daresay they've already hired the musicians for the wedding feast. Perhaps this evening, or tomorrow or the day after, I couldn't say. The wedding's taking place at Puygarrig, because it's Mademoiselle de Puygarrig that young Monsieur de Peyrehorade is marrying. Oh yes, it will be a grand occasion!'

I had been given an introduction to Monsieur de Peyrehorade by my friend Monsieur de P——. He was, my friend had told me, a most erudite antiquary, and infinitely obliging. He would be delighted to show me all the ruins for ten leagues around. I had been counting on him to give me a conducted tour of the country around Ille, which I knew to be rich in ancient and medieval monuments. This marriage, which I was now hearing of for the first time, looked like upsetting all my plans.

I'm going to be in everybody's way, I said to myself. But I was expected; now that my arrival had been announced by Monsieur de P——, I would have to present myself.

'I'll bet you, sir,' my guide said to me as we came onto the plain, 'I'll bet you a cigar I can guess what you're going to do at Monsieur de Peyrehorade's.'

'Why, that's not very hard to guess,' I said, offering him a cigar. 'At this time of day, after a six-league trek over Mount Canigou, supper is the main item on the agenda.'

'Yes, but what about tomorrow?—Come on, I'll lay odds you've come to Ille to see the idol. I guessed as much when I saw you drawing those pictures of the saints at Serrabona.'

'Idol! What idol?' The word had aroused my curiosity.

'Why, didn't they tell you in Perpignan how Monsieur de Peyrehorade came to unearth an idol?'

'An earthen idol? Do you mean a terracotta statue, one made out of clay?'

'No, no, a real copper one. It must be worth a packet, weighs as much as a church bell. We found her deep in the ground, at the foot of an olive tree.'

'Were you present at the discovery, then?'

'Yes, sir. A fortnight ago, Monsieur de Peyrehorade told us, me and Jean Coll, to grub out an old olive tree which had caught the frost last year, for it was a hard winter, you know. So there was Jean Coll going at it for all he was worth, takes a swing with his pick, and I heard this "dong", as if he'd struck a bell. "What's that?" I says. So we dug and dug, and gradually this black hand appears, like a dead man's hand reaching up out of the ground. So then I got frightened, I went off to monsieur, and I said to him: "Dead men, master, under the olive tree. Better call the priest!" "What dead men?" he says to me. He came, took one look at the hand, and exclaimed, "An antiquity, an antiquity!" Anyone would have thought he'd found treasure. And there he was, digging away with the pick and with his hands, working almost as hard as the two of us put together.'

'And what did you eventually find?'

'A great black woman, more than half naked, begging your pardon, sir; solid copper, and Monsieur de Peyrehorade told us it was an idol from pagan times—you know, from the time of Charlemagne!'

'I see. Some bronze Virgin plundered from a convent.'

'A Virgin? Oh, dear me, no! I'd soon have recognized it if it had been a Virgin. It's an idol, I tell you—you can tell from the look of her. She looks at you with these big white eyes of hers . . . it's as if she was staring at you. You can't look her in the eyes.'

'White eyes? No doubt they are embedded in the bronze. It sounds as if it may be a Roman statue.'

'Roman, that's it! Monsieur de Peyrehorade says it's a Roman lady. Ah! I can see you're a scholar like him!'

'Is it intact, in a good state of preservation?'

'Oh, there's nothing missing, sir! It's a lovely bit of work, even better than the painted plaster bust of Louis-Philippe in the town hall. All the same, I don't like the look of her. She looks vicious . . . and what's more, she is, too.'

'Vicious? Has she done you any harm?'

'Not me exactly. But let me tell you. We was trying for all we was worth to get her upright, Monsieur de Peyrehorade too, he was pulling on the rope as well, though he's got no more strength than a chicken, bless him! After a lot of heaving we got her upright. I was picking up a bit of tile to wedge her with when, crash! down she went flat on her back again. "Watch out!" I said. Not quick enough, though, because Jean Coll didn't have time to get his leg out of the way.'

'And was he hurt?'

'Why, his poor leg was snapped clean through like a vine-prop. Poor lad, when I saw what had happened I was livid. I was all set to smash up the idol with my pick, but Monsieur de Peyrehorade held me back. He gave Jean Coll some money, but all the same he's still in bed a fortnight after it happened, and the doctor says he'll never walk as well on that leg as on the other. It's a shame, he was our best runner and, apart from Monsieur de Peyrehorade's son, the best *pelota* player. Young master Alphonse was proper upset about it, because Coll and him, they used to play against one another. What a sight it was to see them returning the balls—thump! thump! they never touched the ground.'

Discoursing in this vein we entered Ille, and I soon found myself in the company of Monsieur de Peyrehorade. He was a little old man, still hale and hearty, powdered, red-nosed, and with a jovial, bantering manner. Before he had even had time to read Monsieur de P——'s letter, he had sat me down at a generously spread table and had introduced me to his wife and son as a distinguished archaeologist who was destined to rescue Roussillon from the oblivion to which scientific indifference had condemned it.

While tucking in with zest, for nothing whets the appetite better than the keen mountain air, I was studying my hosts. I have already said a word about Monsieur de Peyrehorade. I should add that he was vivacity personified. He was constantly talking, eating, getting up, running to his library, bringing me books, showing me etchings, pouring me wine; he was never still for two minutes. His wife, who was rather too plump, like most Catalan women over the age of 40, struck me as an out-and-out provincial, totally absorbed in running her household. Although there was enough supper for at least six people, she ran to the kitchen, ordered pigeons to be killed and maize cakes fried, and opened I don't know how many pots of preserves. In a moment the table was laden with dishes and bottles, and I should certainly have died of indigestion if I had so much as tasted everything I was offered. However, with each dish I refused there were renewed apologies. They were afraid I should not be comfortable in Ille. Resources are so limited in the provinces, and Parisians are so hard to please!

Amid his parents' comings and goings, Monsieur Alphonse de Peyrehorade sat motionless like a Roman *Terminus*. He was a tall young man of 26, whose features were fine and regular but somewhat expressionless. His athletic figure and build certainly bore out the reputation he enjoyed locally of being an indefatigable *pelota* player. That evening he was dressed elegantly, exactly in the style illustrated in the latest number of the *Journal des modes*. But he seemed to me to be inconvenienced by his clothes; he was as stiff as a peg in his velvet collar, and moved his whole body as he turned. His large, sunburned hands and short nails contrasted strangely with his attire: they were the hands of a ploughman emerging from the sleeves of a dandy. Furthermore, although he scrutinized me keenly on account of my Parisian credentials, he spoke to me only once in the course of the evening, and that was to ask me where I had bought my watch chain.

'Well now, my dear guest,' Monsieur de Peyrehorade said to me as supper drew to an end, 'I have you at my mercy. You are in my house, and I'll not let you go until you've seen all the curiosities our mountains have to offer. You must get to know our Roussillon, and you must do it justice. You can't imagine how much there is to show you. Phoenician, Celtic, Roman, Arab, and Byzantine monuments—you will see everything from the cedar tree to the hyssop. I shall take you everywhere, and I shall not spare you a single brick.'

A fit of coughing obliged him to break off. I took this opportunity to tell him that I should be sorry to inconvenience him at a time of such significance for his family. If he would be so good as to give me the benefit of his excellent advice on what excursions I should make, then, without putting him to the trouble of accompanying me, I should be able . . .

'Ah! You're referring to that boy's wedding,' he exclaimed, interrupting me. 'A mere trifle. It will be all over two days hence. You shall celebrate with us, as one of the family. The bride-to-be is in mourning for an aunt who died leaving her all her money, so there will be no reception, no ball. A pity, you'd have been able to see our Catalan girls dancing. They are pretty, and perhaps you would have felt like taking a leaf out of

Alphonse's book. One marriage, they say, leads to another. . . . On Saturday, once the young couple are married, I shall be free, and we'll begin our excursions. I must ask your pardon for inflicting a provincial wedding on you. For a Parisian, bored with parties . . . and a wedding without a ball, at that! However, you will see a bride . . . what shall I say?—you will be delighted with her. But then you are a serious-minded man, you're not interested in women any more. I've got better things to show you. Wait till you see the fine surprise I've got up my sleeve to show you tomorrow.'

'Upon my word,' I said, 'it's not easy to have a treasure in one's house without everyone getting to hear about it. I think I can guess the surprise you have in store for me. But if it's your statue we're talking about, the description my guide gave me of it has only served to arouse my curiosity and to predispose me to admire it.'

'Ah! he told you about the idol—for that's what they call my beautiful Venus Tur . . .—but I shan't say another word. Tomorrow you shall see her in daylight, and then you can tell me whether I am justified in considering her a masterpiece. To be sure, you couldn't have arrived at a better moment! There are some inscriptions which, ignorant as I am, I have interpreted to the best of my ability. But perhaps you, a scholar from Paris, will laugh at my interpretation, for the fact is, I have written a monograph. I, your humble servant, an elderly provincial antiquary, have put pen to paper. . . . I want to make the presses groan. If you would be so good as to read and amend what I have written, I might hope. . . . For example, I am very curious to know how you will construe this inscription on the pedestal: *CAVE* . . .—but I shall ask you nothing yet! Tomorrow, tomorrow! Not another word about the Venus today!'

'You are right not to keep going on about your idol, Peyrehorade,' said his wife. 'Can't you see you are preventing monsieur from eating? Why, he has seen much more beautiful statues than yours in Paris. At the Tuileries there are dozens of them, bronze ones, too.'

'Such is the ignorance, the blessed ignorance of the provinces!' Monsieur de Peyrehorade interrupted. 'Fancy comparing a marvel of antiquity with Coustou's lifeless figures!'

> With what irreverence
> My wife doth speak of the gods!

'Do you know, my wife wanted me to melt down my statue to make a bell for our church. She would have been the sponsor, you see. A masterpiece by Myron, sir!'

'Masterpiece? Masterpiece? A fine masterpiece she is, breaking a man's leg!'

'I tell you, my dear,' said Monsieur de Peyrehorade resolutely, extending towards her a right leg clad in shot silk, 'if my Venus had broken this leg of mine, I would not regret it.'

'Good heavens, Peyrehorade, how can you say such a thing! Fortunately the man is recovering. . . . Even so, I can't bring myself to look at a statue that does such wicked things. Poor Jean Coll!'

'Wounded by Venus, sir,' said Monsieur de Peyrehorade with a hearty laugh. 'Wounded by Venus, and the rascal complains.

Veneris nec praemia noris.

'Which of us has not been wounded by Venus?'

Monsieur Alphonse, whose French was better than his Latin, gave a knowing wink, and looked at me as if to say: 'And you, Parisian, do you understand?'

Supper finished. It was an hour since I had eaten anything. I was tired, and I could not manage to stifle my frequent yawns. Madame de Peyrehorade was the first to notice the fact, and observed that it was time to go to bed. At this they again began to apologize for the poor accommodation I was going to have. It would not be like Paris. There are so few comforts in the provinces. I must show indulgence towards the people of Roussillon. In vain did I protest that after a journey through the mountains I would be delighted with a heap of straw for a bed; they continued to beg me to forgive poor countryfolk if they did not treat me as well as they would have wished. At last I went up to the room that had been prepared for me, accompanied by Monsieur de Peyrehorade. The staircase, whose upper flight was of wood, ended in a corridor extending to either side, with several bedrooms opening onto it.

'To your right', my host said to me, 'are the rooms I am setting apart for the future Madame Alphonse. Your bedroom is at the end of the other corridor. Of course,' he added, doing his best to sound discreet, 'you realize that newlyweds must have privacy. You are at one end of the house, they are at the other.'

We entered a well-appointed bedroom, in which the first object that caught my eye was a bed seven feet long, six feet wide, and so high that one needed a step-ladder to hoist oneself into it. After showing me where to find the bell, checking for himself that the sugar bowl was full and that the flasks of eau de cologne had been duly placed on the washstand,

and asking me several times if I needed anything, my host wished me goodnight and left me alone.

The windows were shut. Before undressing I opened one of them so as to breathe in the fresh night air which, after that long supper, seemed delicious. Opposite lay Mount Canigou, a magnificent sight in any weather, but which that evening, by the light of a resplendent moon, seemed to me the most beautiful mountain in the world. I stood for a few minutes contemplating its marvellous outline, and was about to close my window when, lowering my eyes, I noticed the statue on a pedestal about a hundred yards from the house. It stood at one corner of a quick-set hedge separating a little garden from a large square of perfectly level ground which, I later learned, was the town *pelota* court. This ground, which was the property of Monsieur de Peyrehorade, had been made over by him to the community, in response to insistent demands by his son.

At that distance it was hard for me to make out the appearance of the statue; I could only judge its height, which seemed to me to be around six feet. At that moment two local lads were crossing the *pelota* court, quite near the hedge, whistling the pretty Roussillon tune *Montagnes régalades*. They stopped to look at the statue; one of them even addressed it in a loud voice. He spoke in Catalan, but I had been in Roussillon long enough to be able to get the gist of what he said.

'So there you are, you hussy!' (the Catalan term was stronger). 'There you are!' he said. 'So it's you that broke Jean Coll's leg! If you were mine I'd break your neck.'

'Huh! What with?' said the other. 'She's made of copper, and it's so hard that Étienne broke his file trying to cut into her. It's copper from pagan times, and harder than I don't know what.'

'If I had my cold chisel' (apparently he was a locksmith's apprentice) 'I'd soon gouge those big white eyes out for her, like prising almonds out of their shells. There's more than a hundred sous' worth of silver in them.'

They began to walk away.

'I must just say goodnight to the idol,' said the taller of the two apprentices, stopping suddenly.

He bent down, and doubtless picked up a stone. I could see him straighten an arm, then throw something, and immediately the bronze emitted a resonant note. At the same moment the apprentice put his hand to his head and uttered a cry of pain.

'She threw it back at me!' he exclaimed.

And the two young lads took to their heels. Evidently the stone had rebounded off the metal and punished the rascal for this act of sacrilege against the goddess.

I shut the window, laughing heartily.

'Another vandal punished by Venus. May all destroyers of our ancient monuments get their heads broken in the same way!' On this charitable thought, I fell asleep.

It was broad daylight when I woke. At one side of my bed stood Monsieur de Peyrehorade, in his dressing-gown; at the other, a servant sent by his wife, holding a cup of chocolate in his hand.

'Come on, Parisian, up we get! How lazy they are in the capital!' my host was saying as I dressed hastily. 'Eight o'clock and still in bed. I've been up since six. This is the third time I've come upstairs. I tiptoed to your door: nothing stirring, no sign of life. It's not good for you to sleep so much at your age. And you haven't even seen my Venus yet! Quick, drink this cup of Barcelona chocolate, it's real contraband. . . . You won't get chocolate like that in Paris. Get your strength up, for once you are standing before my Venus we won't be able to tear you away.'

In five minutes I was ready: that is to say, half-shaved, ill-buttoned, and burned by the scalding chocolate I had gulped down. I went down into the garden and found myself looking at a splendid statue.

It was indeed a Venus, and a marvellously beautiful one. The upper part of her body was naked, as was customary among the ancients when depicting great divinities. Her right hand was raised to the level of her breast, with the palm turned inwards, the thumb and first two fingers extended, and the other two slightly bent. The other hand, held near her hip, supported the drapery that covered the lower part of her body. The attitude of the statue recalled that of the *Mora Player*, which for some reason or other is known as *Germanicus*. Perhaps someone had wanted to portray the goddess playing the game of *mora*.

Be that as it may, nothing could be more perfect than the body of that Venus; nothing softer or more voluptuous than her contours; nothing more elegant or more noble than her drapery. I had been expecting some work of the Lower Empire; what I saw was a masterpiece from the finest period of statuary. What especially struck me was the exquisite truth of the forms, so perfect that one could have thought them moulded from nature, had nature ever produced such models.

The hair, brushed up from the brow, seemed at one time to have been gilded. The head, which was small, like that of almost all Greek statues, was tilted slightly forward. As for the face, it had a strange quality which defies description, and which resembled that of no other ancient statue I can recall. It had none of that calm and severe beauty of the Greek sculptors, who systematically imparted a majestic immobility to every feature. Here, on the contrary, I observed with surprise that the artist had clearly intended to render a mischievousness bordering on the vicious. All the features were contracted slightly: the eyes a little slanting, the mouth turned up at the corners, the nostrils somewhat flared. Disdain, irony, cruelty could be read in that face, which, notwithstanding, was incredibly beautiful. The fact is, the more one looked at that admirable statue, the more one became aware of the distressing truth that such wonderful beauty could go hand in hand with a total absence of feeling.

'If ever there was a model for this statue,' I said to Monsieur de Peyrehorade, 'and I doubt that Heaven ever brought forth such a woman, how I pity her lovers! She must have delighted in letting them die of despair. There is something ferocious in her expression, and yet I have never seen anything so beautiful.'

'*C'est Vénus tout entière à sa proie attachée!*' exclaimed Monsieur de Peyrehorade, satisfied at my enthusiasm.

Her expression of diabolical irony was perhaps heightened by the contrast between the very bright eyes, of inlaid silver, and the blackish-green patina with which time had overlaid the rest of the statue. Those bright eyes produced an illusion of reality, of life. I recalled what my guide had told me, that she made those who looked at her lower their eyes. It was almost true, and I could not help being momentarily angry with myself for feeling ill at ease in the presence of this bronze figure.

'Now that you have admired everything in detail, my dear fellow-student of bric-à-brac,' said my host, 'let us hold a learned colloquium. What is your view of this inscription, which you have not yet noticed?'

He was pointing at the base of the statue, on which I read these words:

CAVE AMANTEM.

'*Quid dicis, doctissime?*' he asked me, rubbing his hands. 'Let's see if we can agree on the meaning of this *cave amantem.*'

'Well,' I replied, 'there are two possible meanings. One could translate it as: "Beware of him who loves you, mistrust lovers". But I don't know whether, if that were the sense, *cave amantem* would be very good Latin. Having seen the lady's diabolical expression, I am more inclined to believe that the artist wanted to put the beholder on his guard against this terrible beauty, and I would therefore translate as follows: "Beware if *she* loves you".'

'Hmm!' said Monsieur de Peyrehorade. 'That's a splendid meaning. But, if you'll forgive me, I prefer the first translation, on which, however, I shall elaborate. You know who was the lover of Venus?'

'She had several.'

'Yes, but the first was Vulcan. Don't you think what is meant is: "Despite all your beauty, your disdainful air, you shall have an ugly, lame blacksmith for a lover"? An object-lesson, sir, for coquettes.'

I could not suppress a smile, so far-fetched did the explanation seem to me.

'Latin is a shocking language for concision,' I observed, to avoid open disagreement with my antiquarian friend; and I stepped back a few paces so as to get a better view of the statue.

'One moment, my dear colleague,' said Monsieur de Peyrehorade, seizing me by the arm to detain me, 'you have not seen everything yet! There is another inscription. Climb onto the pedestal and look on the right arm.' As he spoke he was helping me up.

I clung rather unceremoniously to the neck of the Venus, with whom I was beginning to get on familiar terms. For a moment I even looked her boldly in the face, and from close up I found her even more vicious and even more beautiful. Then I noticed that engraved on the arm were what looked to me like some characters in ancient cursive script. With much recourse to spectacles, I spelled out the following inscription, while Monsieur de Peyrehorade repeated each word as I uttered it, with sounds and gestures of approval. What I read was:

> VENERI TVRBVL . . .
> EVTYCHES MYRO
> IMPERIO FECIT.

After the word *TVRBVL* in the first line, it looked to me as if a few letters had been worn away; but *TVRBVL* was perfectly legible.

'Meaning . . .?' my host asked me, beaming, but with a glint of mischief in his smile, for he was quite sure that *TVRBVL* was going to give me a hard time.

'There's one word that I haven't worked out yet,' I said. 'The rest is easy. "Eutychus Myron made this offering to Venus at her command."'

'Excellent. But *TVRBVL*, what do you make of that? What is *TVRBVL*?'

'*TVRBVL* has me baffled. I'm racking my brains to try to find some well-known epithet for Venus that might come to my aid. Let's see, what would you say to *TVRBVLENTA*? Venus who disturbs, who disrupts. . . .'

As you can see, I am still preoccupied with her vicious expression. *TVRBVLENTA*, that's not too bad an epithet for Venus,' I added modestly, for I was not myself very satisfied with my explanation.

'Venus the turbulent! Venus the reveller! So you think that my Venus is a Venus of the taverns? Not a bit of it, sir, my Venus keeps good company. But now I shall explain *TVRBVL* . . . to you. Promise me one thing: not to reveal my discovery until my paper has been printed. The fact is, you see, I'm rather proud of my find. . . . You must leave us poor devils in the provinces a few ears of corn to glean. You Paris scholars are so well off!'

From the top of the pedestal, on which I was still perched, I promised him solemnly that I would never stoop so low as to plagiarize his discovery.

'For *TVRBVL* . . ., sir,' he said, drawing closer and lowering his voice lest anyone other than myself should hear him, 'read *TVRBVLNERAE*.'

'I am none the wiser.'

'Listen carefully. A league from here, at the foot of the mountain, there is a village called Boulternère. The name is a corruption of the Latin word *TVRBVLNERA*—nothing is commoner than these inversions. Boulternère, sir, was a Roman city. I had always suspected as much, but I never had any proof. This is the proof I was seeking. This Venus was the local deity of the city of Boulternère; and the word Boulternère, whose ancient origin I have just demonstrated, proves something more curious still, namely, that before being a Roman city, Boulternère was a Phoenician city!'

He paused for a moment to get his breath and to enjoy my surprise. I managed to suppress a strong inclination to laugh.

'In fact,' he resumed, '*TVRBVLNERA* is pure Phoenician: *TVR*, pronounced *Tour*. *Tour* and *Sour* are the same word, aren't they?— "Sour" is the Phoenician name for Tyre (there's no need to remind you of the meaning). *BVL* is "Baal"; Bâl, Bel, Bul—minor differences in pronunciation. As for *NERA*, that gave me a bit of trouble. Having failed to find a Phoenician word, I am tempted to believe that it comes from the Greek νηρός, humid, marshy. In that case this would be a hybrid word. In order to justify νηρός, I will show you at Boulternère how the streams from the mountain form stagnant pools there. On the other hand, the termination *NERA* may have been added much later in honour of Nera Pivesuvia, wife of Tetricus, who may have granted some favour to the city of Turbul. But on account of the pools I prefer the derivation from νηρός.'

He took a pinch of snuff with a self-satisfied air.

'But enough of the Phoenicians—let's get back to the inscription. I therefore translate it: "To Venus of Boulternère Myron dedicates at her command this statue, his work."'

I took good care not to criticize his etymology, but I wanted to have a chance to show some proof of my own perceptiveness, and I said: 'Not so fast, sir. Myron dedicated something, but I certainly don't see that it need have been this statue.'

'What!' he exclaimed. 'Wasn't Myron a famous Greek sculptor? The talent must have been handed down in the family; it was one of his descendants who made this statue, nothing could be more certain.'

'But I can see a small hole on the arm,' I replied. 'I think it was for attaching something, a bracelet, for example, that this Myron offered to Venus as an expiatory gift. Myron was an unhappy lover. Venus was angry with him, and he propitiated her by dedicating a gold bracelet to her. Bear in mind that *fecit* is very often used with the meaning of *consecravit*; the terms are synonymous. I could show you more than one example if I had Gruter or Orelli to hand. It's only natural that a lover should dream of Venus, and that he should imagine her to be commanding him to give a gold bracelet to her statue. Myron dedicated a bracelet to her. Then the barbarians, or perhaps some sacrilegious thief . . .'

'Ah! How easy it is to see that you have written novels!' exclaimed my host, reaching out a hand to help me down. 'No, sir, it is a work of the school of Myron. Just look at the workmanship and you will agree.'

Having made it a rule never to persist in contradicting stubborn antiquarians, I lowered my head as if conceding defeat and said: 'It is an admirable piece.'

'Good Heavens!' cried Monsieur de Peyrehorade, 'another act of vandalism! Someone has been throwing stones at my statue!'

He had just noticed a white mark a little above the breast of the Venus. I noticed a similar trace of white on the fingers of the right hand. At the time I supposed that they had been grazed by the stone in its flight, or that a fragment had broken off on impact and ricocheted onto the hand. I recounted to my host the insult I had witnessed and the prompt punishment which had been its sequel. He laughed a good deal at this, comparing the apprentice to Diomedes and expressing the wish that, like the Greek hero, he might see all his companions changed into white birds.

The bell for lunch interrupted this classical discussion, and, as on the evening before, I was obliged to eat enough for four. Then some of

Monsieur de Peyrehorade's tenant farmers called by, and while he was attending to them his son took me out to see a carriage which he had bought in Toulouse for his fiancée, and for which, needless to say, I expressed admiration. Then I went with him to the stables, where he detained me for half an hour, boasting of his horses, giving me their pedigrees, and recounting to me the prizes they had won at races in the *département*. Finally, by way of a grey mare that he was reserving for her, he brought the conversation round to his bride-to-be.

'We shall see her today,' he said. 'I don't know whether you will find her pretty. You Parisians are hard to please, but everyone here and in Perpignan finds her charming. The best thing about her is that she's got lots of money. Her aunt in Prades left everything to her. Yes, I shall be very happy!'

I was deeply shocked to see a young man seemingly more moved by his bride's dowry than by her beautiful eyes.

'You know all about jewels,' Monsieur Alphonse continued. 'What do you think of this? It's the ring I shall be giving her tomorrow.'

As he spoke he drew from the first phalange of his little finger a large ring encrusted with diamonds, in the form of two interlocked hands—an allusion I found profoundly poetic. It was an ancient piece of workmanship, but I judged that the diamonds were a later addition. Inside the ring, in gothic lettering, were engraved the words *Sempr'ab ti*, that is, 'always with you'.

'It's a pretty ring,' I said. 'But these diamonds that have been added detract from its character somewhat.'

'Oh, it's much finer like that,' he replied with a smile. 'There's twelve hundred francs' worth of diamonds there. My mother gave it to me. It's a family ring, and very old—it dates from the age of chivalry. It used to be my grandmother's, and she had it from her own grandmother. Lord knows when it was made.'

'In Paris,' I said, 'it is customary to give quite a simple ring, usually composed of two different metals, such as gold and platinum. Look, that other ring, the one you've got on that finger, would be most appropriate. This one, with its diamonds and the hands in relief, is so large that you couldn't wear a glove over it.'

'Oh, Madame Alphonse will do as she sees fit. I'm sure she'll always be very pleased to own it—it's nice to have twelve hundred francs on one's finger. That little ring', he added, looking with an air of satisfaction at the perfectly plain ring he wore on one hand, 'was given to me by a woman in Paris one Mardi Gras. Ah, what a time I had when I was in Paris two years ago! That's the place to enjoy yourself . . .' And he sighed with regret.

We were to dine that day at Puygarrig, with the bride's relatives. We got into a carriage and drove to the château, which was about a league and a half from Ille. I was introduced and welcomed as a friend of the family. I shall not speak of the dinner, nor of the conversation that followed, in which I took little part. Monsieur Alphonse, seated next to his bride, spoke one word in her ear every quarter of an hour. As for the bride, she scarcely raised her eyes, and each time that her fiancé spoke to her she blushed modestly but replied without embarrassment.

Mademoiselle de Puygarrig was 18 years old; her supple and delicate figure contrasted with her robust fiancé's angular form. She was not only beautiful, but captivating. I admired the perfect spontaneity of all her responses; and her air of kindness, not without a tinge of mischief, put me involuntarily in mind of the Venus of my host. Comparing them mentally, I wondered whether the superiority in beauty that one had surely to concede to the statue was not very largely attributable to its tigress-like expression; for energy, even in evil passions, always awakens in us a feeling of astonishment and a kind of instinctive admiration.

'What a pity', I said to myself on leaving Puygarrig, 'that such a delightful person should be rich, and that her dowry should earn her the attentions of a man so unworthy of her!'

Returning to Ille, and unsure what to say to Madame de Peyrehorade, to whom I felt it proper to address a few words now and then, I exclaimed:

'You are certainly free-thinkers down here in Roussillon! Why, madam, you are celebrating a marriage on a Friday! In Paris we would be more superstitious. No one would dare to get married on that day.'

'Goodness, don't even speak of it!' she said. 'If it had been up to me, we would certainly have chosen another day. But it's what Peyrehorade wanted, and we had to let him have his way. But it distresses me all the same. Suppose there were some misfortune? And there must be a good reason for it, for why else should everyone be afraid of Fridays?'

'Friday', exclaimed her husband, 'is the day of Venus! A splendid day for a wedding! You see, my dear colleague, I think only of my Venus. Upon my word, it was on her account that I chose a Friday. If you like, tomorrow, before the wedding, we will make her a little sacrifice; we will sacrifice two wood-pigeons, and if I knew where to get hold of some incense . . .'

'Shame on you, Peyrehorade!' interrupted his wife, utterly scandalized. 'Burning incense before an idol? That would be an abomination! Whatever would they say about us in the district?'

'At least', said Monsieur de Peyrehorade, 'you will allow me to place a wreath of roses and lilies on her head:

Manibus date lilia plenis.

You see, sir, the constitution is mere empty words: we do not enjoy freedom of worship!'

The arrangements for the following day were as follows: everyone was to be ready and dressed for the occasion at ten o'clock prompt. Having drunk our chocolate, we would go by carriage to Puygarrig. The civil ceremony was to take place at the village *mairie*, and the religious service at the chapel in the château. Next would come lunch. After lunch we would amuse ourselves as best we could until seven o'clock. At seven o'clock we would return to Ille, to Monsieur de Peyrehorade's house, where the two families were to dine together. The rest would follow as a matter of course: as there would be no dancing, the intention was to eat as much as possible.

At eight o'clock I was already seated before the Venus, pencil in hand, beginning my twentieth attempt at drawing the statue's head, yet still not managing to capture its expression. Monsieur de Peyrehorade kept hovering around me, giving me advice, repeating to me his Phoenician etymologies; then arranging bengal roses on the pedestal of the statue and, in tragi-comic tones, addressing prayers to it for the couple who were soon to live under his roof. Around nine o'clock he went indoors to see about getting dressed, and at the same moment Monsieur Alphonse appeared, wearing a tight-fitting new dress coat, white gloves, patent leather shoes, chased buttons, and a rose in his buttonhole.

'Will you do a portrait of my wife?' he said to me, leaning over my drawing. 'She is pretty too.'

At that moment a game was beginning on the *pelota* court of which I have spoken; this at once attracted Monsieur Alphonse's attention. And, weary of drawing and despairing of ever rendering that diabolical face, I too soon went over to watch the players. Among them were some Spanish muleteers who had arrived the day before. They were from Aagon and Navarre, and almost all wonderfully skilled at the game. Consequently, though spurred on by the presence and advice of Monsieur Alphonse, the men from Ille were rapidly vanquished by these new champions. The local spectators were dismayed. Monsieur Alphonse looked at his watch; it was still only half-past nine. His mother had not yet finished having her hair dressed. He hesitated no longer: he took off his dress coat, asked for a jacket, and challenged the Spaniards. I watched him, smiling and a little surprised.

'The honour of the province must be upheld,' he said.

It was then that I found him truly handsome. He was in the grip of his enthusiasm. His clothes, about which he had been so concerned a moment before, had ceased to matter to him. A few minutes earlier he would have been afraid to turn his head for fear of disarranging his cravat. Now he had no thought for his curled hair or his carefully pleated jabot. And what of his fiancée? Upon my word, if it had been necessary, I believe he would have had the marriage postponed. I watched him hastily don a pair of sandals, roll up his sleeves, and place himself confidently at the head of the defeated side, like Caesar rallying his troops at Dyrrhachium. I leaped over the hedge and placed myself comfortably in the shade of a nettle tree, so as to have a good view of the two camps.

Contrary to general expectation, Monsieur Alphonse missed the first ball; admittedly it came skimming low over the ground, driven with surprising force by an Aragonese who seemed to be the captain of the Spanish team.

He was a man of about 40, lean and sinewy, six feet tall, with an olive complexion that was almost as dark as the bronze of the Venus.

Monsieur Alphonse hurled his racquet to the ground in fury.

'That confounded ring!' he exclaimed. 'It stopped me bending my finger, and made me miss an easy ball.'

Not without difficulty, he removed the diamond ring. I stepped forward to take it, but he forestalled me, ran to the Venus, slipped the ring on to her third finger, and returned to his place at the head of the men from Ille.

He was pale, but calm and determined. From then on he didn't once miscalculate, and the Spaniards were soundly beaten. The spectators' enthusiasm was a fine sight to see: some cheered exuberantly and threw their caps in the air; others shook him by the hand, calling him a credit to the province. Had he repelled an invasion, I doubt that he would have received livelier and more sincere congratulations. The chagrin of the losers added still more to the lustre of his victory.

'We shall play you again, my good fellow,' he said to the Aragonese in a tone of condescension, 'but I shall give you points.'

I could have wished Monsieur Alphonse more modest, and I was quite upset at his rival's humiliation.

The Spanish giant keenly resented this insult. I saw him go pale under his tanned skin. He looked dejectedly at his racquet and clenched his teeth; then, in an undertone, he muttered the words: '*Me lo pagarás.*'

The sound of Monsieur de Peyrehorade's voice cut short his son's triumph; my host was greatly astonished not to find him supervising the preparation of the new carriage, and even more so to see him standing drenched in sweat and with a racquet in his hand. Monsieur Alphonse ran to the house, washed his face and hands, again put on his new coat and patent leather shoes; and five minutes later we were trotting briskly along the road to Puygarrig. Every *pelota* player in the town and a large number of spectators followed us with cries of joy. The sturdy horses that drew us could barely keep ahead of the intrepid Catalans.

We were at Puygarrig, and the procession was about to set off for the *mairie*, when, striking his brow, Monsieur Alphonse whispered to me:

'What a blunder! I've forgotten the ring! It's still on the Venus's finger, devil take her. Whatever you do, don't mention it to my mother. Perhaps she won't notice.'

'You could always send for it,' I said.

'Not a chance. My servant stayed behind in Ille, and I don't trust any of the servants here. Twelve hundred francs' worth of diamonds might be too much of a temptation for some of them. And besides, what would people think of my absent-mindedness? I should seem too ridiculous. They would say I was married to the statue. . . . Just so long as nobody steals it! Fortunately that rabble are afraid of the idol, they daren't go within an arm's length of it. Oh well, no matter, I've got another ring.'

The two ceremonies, civil and religious, were performed with suitable pomp; and Mademoiselle de Puygarrig received the ring of a Paris milliner, never suspecting that her fiancé was sacrificing a love-token on her behalf. Then we sat down to table, where we drank, ate, and even sang, all at great length. I pitied the bride for the outbursts of vulgar mirth to which she was exposed; yet she put a better face on it than I would have expected, and her embarrassment was neither gauche nor affected.

Perhaps courage comes to us in difficult situations.

It was four o'clock when a merciful Heaven saw fit to put an end to lunch. The men went to stroll in the grounds, which were magnificent, or watched the peasant-girls of Puygarrig, decked out in their holiday best, dancing on the lawn of the château. In this way we filled a few hours. Meanwhile the women were fussing around the bride, who was showing off the wedding presents to them. Then she got changed, and I noticed how she covered her beautiful hair with a bonnet and a plumed hat; for women are in a great hurry to assume at the earliest opportunity the adornments that custom forbids them to wear whilst they are still unmarried.

It was almost eight o'clock when we prepared to leave for Ille. But first there occurred a pathetic scene. Mademoiselle de Puygarrig's aunt, a very old and very devout lady, who was like a mother to her, was not to accompany us to the town. On our departure, she gave her niece a touching lecture on her conjugal obligations, which led to a torrent of tears and interminable embraces. Monsieur de Peyrehorade compared this separation to the rape of the Sabine women. We finally managed to get away, and on the road home we all did our utmost to entertain the bride and bring a smile to her lips; but to no avail.

At Ille, supper was waiting for us—and what a supper! If the vulgar mirth of that morning had shocked me, I was far more shocked by the jokes and *double entendres* that were now directed particularly at the bride and groom. The groom, who had disappeared for a moment before sitting down to table, was pale and chillingly grave in his manner. He kept taking gulps of old Collioure wine that was almost as strong as brandy. I was seated next to him, and I felt obliged to warn him:

'Take care! They say that wine . . .' I do not remember what stupid remark I made so as to enter into the spirit of the festivities.

He nudged my knee and said to me in a very low voice:

'When we leave the table, . . . may I have a word with you?'

His solemn tone surprised me. I looked more closely at him, and I noticed how extraordinarily his features had changed.

'Are you feeling ill?' I asked him.

'No.'

And he resumed his drinking.

Meanwhile, amidst cheers and applause, an 11-year-old child, who had crawled under the table, was showing the company a pretty pink and white ribbon, commonly known as a garter, which he had just removed from the bride's ankle. It was immediately cut into bits and distributed to the young men, each of whom put a piece of it in his buttonhole, in accordance with an age-old custom that still survives in a few ancient families. This caused the bride to blush to the roots of her hair. But her confusion was crowned when, having called for silence, Monsieur de Peyrehorade sang her some verses in Catalan, made up on the spur of the moment, or so he claimed. This is how they went, if I understood them correctly:

'What then is this, my friends? Is the wine I have drunk making me see double, or are there two Venuses here?'

The groom turned his head sharply with a startled look, causing everybody to laugh.

'Yes,' continued Monsieur de Peyrehorade, 'there are two Venuses under my roof. One I found in the ground like a truffle; the other, descended from the skies, has just shared out her girdle among us.'

He meant her garter.

'My son, choose, between the Roman and the Catalan Venus, the one whom you prefer. The rogue has chosen the Catalan Venus, and he has the better of the bargain. The Roman Venus is black, the Catalan Venus is white. The Roman is cold, the Catalan enflames everything that approaches her.'

This ending provoked such acclaim, such clamorous applause, and such uproarious laughter that I thought the ceiling was going to fall about our heads. Around the table there were only three serious faces, those of the bride and groom, and my own. I had a fearful headache; and besides, I don't know why, but a wedding always depresses me. This one, furthermore, disgusted me rather.

When the last couplets had been sung by the deputy mayor—and pretty ribald they were, I must say—we moved into the drawing-room to celebrate the departure of the bride, who was soon to be escorted to her chamber, for it was nearly midnight.

Monsieur Alphonse drew me into the embrasure of a window and, averting his eyes, said to me:

'You're going to laugh at me . . . but I don't know what's the matter with me. I'm bewitched! The Devil's making off with me!'

The first thought that occurred to me was that he felt threatened by some misfortune of the sort alluded to by Montaigne and by Madame de Sévigné: '*All Love's empire is full of tragic histories*', et cetera. 'I thought misfortunes of that sort only befell men of intelligence,' I said to myself.

'You've drunk too much of that Collioure wine, my dear Monsieur Alphonse,' I said to him. 'I warned you.'

'Yes, no doubt. But there's something far worse than that.'

His voice kept breaking. I thought he was completely drunk.

'You know that ring of mine?' he went on after a silence.

'Well? Has it been taken?'

'No.'

'In that case, have you got it?'

'No. I . . . I can't get it off the finger of that damned Venus.'

'So, you didn't pull hard enough!'

'Yes, I did. But the Venus . . . has bent her finger.'

He was staring at me wild-eyed, clutching the window-hasp to prevent himself from falling.

'A likely story!' I said. 'You pushed the ring on too far. Tomorrow you can get it off with some pliers. But be careful not to damage the statue.'

'No. I tell you the finger of the Venus is bent, curled in. Her fist is clenched, don't you understand? It seems she is my wife, since I've given her my ring. Now she won't give it back.'

I felt a sudden shudder, and for a moment I had gooseflesh. Then he heaved a great sigh that sent a blast of wine fumes in my direction, and all my emotions evaporated.

'The wretch is completely drunk,' I thought.

'You are an antiquarian, sir,' added the bridegroom plaintively. 'You are familiar with these statues. Perhaps there is some spring, some fiendish device I don't know about. Could you go and see?'

'Gladly,' I said. 'Come with me.'

'No, I'd rather you went alone.'

I went out of the drawing-room.

The weather had changed during supper, and rain was beginning to fall heavily. I was about to ask for an umbrella when a thought stopped me short. I would be a complete fool, I said to myself, to go out to confirm a drunken man's story. Besides, perhaps he means to play some practical joke on me, to raise a laugh among these good provincials; and the very least I can expect is to get soaked to the skin and catch my death of cold.

From the door I cast a glance at the statue, which was streaming with water, and I went up to my bedroom without returning to the drawing-room. I went to bed, but sleep was a long time coming. All the scenes of that day passed through my mind. I thought of that girl, so beautiful and chaste, abandoned to a brutal drunkard. What an odious thing a marriage of convenience is, I said to myself. A mayor dons a tricolour sash, a priest a stole, and lo and behold, the most charming girl in the world is delivered up to the Minotaur! What can two beings who are not in love find to say to one another at such a moment, which two lovers would purchase with their lives? Can a woman ever love a man when once she has seen him acting boorishly? First impressions are never obliterated, and I am certain that Alphonse will richly deserve to be hated.

During my monologue, which I have abridged a good deal, I had heard much to-ing and fro-ing in the house, the sound of doors opening and closing and of carriages leaving; then I thought I could hear on the stairs the light footsteps of several women heading for the other end of the corridor on which my bedroom was situated. No doubt it was the bride being escorted to bed by her entourage. Then I heard people returning downstairs. Madame de Peyrehorade's door closed. How distressed and ill at ease that poor girl must feel!' I said to myself. I was tossing and turning in my bed with ill-humour. A bachelor cuts a ridiculous figure in a house where a marriage is being celebrated.

Silence had reigned for some time when it was disturbed by heavy footfalls mounting the stairs. The wooden steps creaked loudly.

'What an oaf!' I exclaimed. 'I'll lay odds he's going to fall downstairs!'

Everything became quiet again. I picked up a book to turn my thoughts to other things. It was a volume of statistics on the *département*, graced with an article by Monsieur de Peyrehorade on the Druidic monuments of the Prades arrondissement. I nodded off on page three.

I slept badly and woke several times. It must have been five in the morning, and I had been awake for more than twenty minutes, when the cock crew. Day was breaking. At that moment I distinctly heard the same heavy footfalls, the same creaking of the stairs that I had heard before falling asleep. This struck me as strange. Yawning, I tried to fathom why Monsieur Alphonse should be getting up so early. I could think of no plausible explanation. I was on the point of closing my eyes again when my attention was once more aroused by strange scufflings, soon joined by the sound of bells being rung and of doors being noisily opened. Then I heard confused shouts.

'My drunken friend must have set fire to something!' I thought as I leaped from my bed.

I dressed hastily and went out into the corridor. From the other end came cries and lamentations, with one piercing voice dominating all the rest: 'My son, my son!' It was clear that some misfortune had befallen Monsieur Alphonse. I ran to the bridal chamber; it was full of people. The first sight that greeted me was the young man, half undressed and sprawled across the bed, the timber frame of which was broken. He was ashen-faced and motionless. His mother was weeping and lamenting by his side. Monsieur de Peyrehorade was bustling about, rubbing his son's temples with eau de cologne and holding smelling-salts to his nose. Alas! his son had been dead for some time. On a couch at the other end of the bedroom lay the bride, in the throes of dreadful convulsions. She was uttering inarticulate cries, and two strong maidservants were having the utmost difficulty in restraining her.

'What in Heaven's name has happened?' I exclaimed.

I approached the bed and lifted the body of the unfortunate young man; it was already stiff and cold. His clenched teeth and blackened features betokened the most dreadful anguish. It was quite apparent that his death had been violent and his last struggle a terrible one. Yet there was no trace of blood on his clothes. I lifted his shirt and saw on his chest a livid imprint that extended to his ribs and back. It was as if he had been squeezed in an iron hoop. I trod on something hard which was lying on the carpet; I bent down and saw the diamond ring.

I hauled Monsieur de Peyrehorade and his wife away to their room; then I had the bride taken there. 'You still have a daughter,' I said to them. 'You owe her your care.' Then I left them alone.

It seemed to me that Monsieur Alphonse had undoubtedly been the victim of murderers who had found a way into the bride's bedroom in the night. Those bruises on the chest, however, and their circular conformation, puzzled me greatly, for they could not have been caused by a stick or an iron bar. Suddenly I remembered having heard that, in Valencia, *bravos* use long leather bags filled with fine sand to strike down those they have been hired to kill. At once I remembered the Aragonese muleteer and his threat; however, I hardly dared think that he would have exacted so terrible a vengeance for a trivial jest.

I was going around the house searching for evidence that it had been broken into, but I found none anywhere. I went into the garden to see whether the murderers might have got in that way; but I found nothing definite. The previous day's rain had in any case made the ground so wet that it would not have retained any distinct traces. I did, however, observe some deep footprints in the ground; there were two sets, running in opposite directions but along the same path, from the corner of the hedge adjoining the *pelota* court to the front door of the house. They might have been the footprints left by Monsieur Alphonse when he went to fetch his ring from the statue's finger. On the other hand, since the hedge was less thick at this point than elsewhere, it might have been here that the murderers had penetrated it. Walking back and forth in front of the statue, I stopped for a moment to gaze at it. This time, I must confess, I could not contemplate without awe its expression of vicious irony; and, with my head still full of the horrible scenes I had just witnessed, I felt as if I were looking at an infernal deity applauding the misfortune which had overtaken this house.

I returned to my room and stayed there until midday. Then I emerged and enquired after my hosts. They were somewhat calmer. Mademoiselle de Puygarrig, or rather Monsieur Alphonse's widow, had regained consciousness. She had even talked to the public prosecutor from Perpignan, who happened to be in Ille on circuit at the time, and that judge had received her deposition. He asked me for mine. I told him all I knew, and did not conceal from him my suspicions regarding the Aragonese muleteer. He ordered the man to be arrested at once.

'Did you learn anything from Madame Alphonse?' I asked the public prosecutor when my deposition had been written and signed.

'The unfortunate lady has gone mad,' he told me with a sad smile. 'Mad! Totally mad! This is her story:

'She had been in bed, she says, for a few minutes, with the bed-curtains drawn, when her bedroom door opened and someone came in. At the time Madame Alphonse was lying at the very edge of the bed with her face turned towards the wall. She did not move, sure that it was her husband. After a moment the bed groaned as if under an enormous weight. She was very frightened, but did not dare turn her head. Five minutes, perhaps ten minutes—she cannot say how long—passed in this way. Then she made an involuntary movement, or else the person in the bed did, and she felt the contact of something as cold as ice—those were her words. She pressed herself closer to the side of the bed, trembling in every limb. A little later, the door opened a second time, and someone came in and said, "Good evening, my little wife". Soon afterwards the curtains were drawn back. She heard a stifled cry. The person who was in the bed beside her sat upright and seemed to reach out their arms. Thereupon she turned her head and saw, so she says, her husband kneeling by the bed with his head on a level with the pillow, in the arms of a sort of greenish giant that was crushing him in a tight embrace. She says—and she repeated it a score of times, poor woman—she says that she recognized—can you guess?—the bronze Venus, Monsieur de Peyrehorade's statue. Ever since it turned up, everyone has been dreaming about it. But to return to this poor crazed woman's story: at this sight she fainted, and she had probably taken leave of her senses several moments before. She is quite unable to say how long she remained in a faint. When she came to, she again saw the ghost, or the statue, as she persists in calling it, motionless, with its legs and the lower part of its body in the bed, its torso and arms extended forwards, and in its arms her husband, quite still. A cock crew. Thereupon the statue got out of bed, dropped the corpse, and went out. Madame Alphonse made a grab for the bell pull and the rest you know.'

They brought in the Spaniard. He was calm, and defended himself with great composure and presence of mind. In any case, he did not deny saying the words I had overheard; but he explained them by claiming he had meant nothing more than that, on the following day, when he was rested, he would have defeated his victorious opponent in another game of *pelota*. I remember him adding:

'When he is insulted, a man from Aragon does not wait till the next day to take his revenge. If I had thought that Monsieur Alphonse had meant to insult me, I would have run my knife into his belly there and then.'

They compared his shoes with the footprints in the garden; his shoes were much larger.

Finally the keeper of the inn at which he was staying assured us that the man had spent the whole night rubbing down and administering medicine to one of his mules that was sick.

Besides, the Aragonese was a man of good repute, well known in the region, which he visited every year on business. So he was released, with apologies.

I almost forgot to mention the statement of a servant who had been the last person to see Monsieur Alphonse alive. It was at the moment when he was about to go up to his wife, and he had called this man and asked him anxiously if he knew where I was. The servant replied that he had not seen me. Monsieur Alphonse heaved a sigh and stood in silence for more than a minute. Then he said: 'Oh well, the Devil must have made off with him too!'

I asked this man whether Monsieur Alphonse had had his diamond ring when he spoke to him. The servant hesitated before replying. Finally he said that he thought not, but that in any case he had not paid any attention to the matter. On second thoughts he added, 'If he'd been wearing the ring I'm sure I would have noticed it, since I supposed he had given it to Madame Alphonse.'

Questioning this man, I experienced something of the superstitious terror that Madame Alphonse's statement had spread throughout the household. The prosecutor looked at me, smiling, and I refrained from questioning him further.

A few hours after Monsieur Alphonse's funeral, I prepared to leave Ille. Monsieur de Peyrehorade's carriage was to take me to Perpignan. Despite his weak state, the poor old man wished to accompany me as far as his garden gate. We passed through the garden in silence; he could barely drag himself along, supporting himself on my arm. As we parted, I looked one last time at the Venus. I was confident that, although he did not share the fear and hatred it inspired among one section of his family, my host would wish to be rid of an object which would serve as a constant reminder of a dreadful misfortune. My intention was to urge him to place it in a museum. I was plucking up the courage to broach the subject when Monsieur de Peyrehorade turned his head mechanically in the direction in which he could see me staring. He saw the statue and at once burst into tears. I embraced him, and, not daring to say a single word to him, I got into the carriage.

Since my departure I have not heard that any new light has been shed on this mysterious catastrophe.

Monsieur de Peyrehorade died a few months after his son. In his will he left me his manuscripts, and perhaps I shall have them published one day. I found no trace among them of the monograph concerning the inscriptions on the Venus.

P.S. My friend Monsieur de P—— has just written from Perpignan, informing me that the statue no longer exists. After her husband's death Madame de Peyrehorade's first concern was to have it melted down and recast into a bell, and in this new shape it serves the church in Ille. But, adds Monsieur de P——, it seems that misfortune dogs those who possess this bronze. Since the bell has been ringing at Ille the vines have frozen twice.

ÉMILE ZOLA (1840–1902)

Story of a Madman

Translated by Douglas Parmée

Isidore-Jean-Louis Maurin was a worthy middle-class citizen, the owner of several blocks of flats in Belleville and residing on the first floor of one of them. He had grown up in the back rooms of this old house, tending his garden and idling away his days like many a Parisian with time on his hands. At the age of forty he was foolish enough to marry the daughter of one of his tenants, an eighteen-year-old blonde whose grey eyes with their occasional sparkle were as shining and gentle as a cat's.

Six months later she had found her way upstairs to the flat of a young doctor who lived on the floor above. This happened as naturally as anything, one evening during a thunderstorm while Maurin had gone out for a stroll along the fortifications of Paris. Their love grew into a devouring passion. They soon found that the few odd minutes they were able to steal together in secret were not enough; they dreamt of living together as man and wife. Their close proximity, the fact that they were separated from each other by nothing more than the thickness of a ceiling, sharpened their desire still more. At night, the lover could hear the husband coughing in bed.

Mind you, Maurin was a decent sort, known in the district as a model husband; he didn't pry and he was as kind and tolerant as anyone could be. But that was exactly what made him such an exasperating obstacle; with his contented nature, he hardly ever left the flat and the very simplicity of his tastes meant that his young wife was a prisoner in the house. After a few weeks, she had run out of excuses for visiting the second floor and so the lovers decided that the old fellow must be got rid of.

They were reluctant to resort to violence or crime. How could you possibly slit the throat of such a tame sheep? Besides, they were afraid of being found out and sent to the guillotine. In any case, the doctor, who was an ingenious young man, hit on a less risky but equally effective method, the bizarre nature of which fired the young woman's romantic imagination.

One night the whole house was aroused by dreadful screams coming from the owner's flat. They forced open the door and found the young woman in a terrible state, kneeling on the floor, all dishevelled and shrieking, her shoulders covered in red weals. Maurin was standing in front of her, trembling and quite bewildered. His speech was slurred like that of a drunken man and when pressed he was quite incapable of replying coherently.

'I can't understand it,' he stammered, 'I didn't go near her, she suddenly started screaming.'

When Henriette had somewhat recovered her composure, she herself stammered something, giving her husband a strange look full of a kind of frightened pity. The neighbours went away greatly intrigued and even rather horrified, muttering to themselves that 'it wasn't at all clear'.

Similar scenes recurred regularly and the whole house was soon living in a state of constant alarm. Every time the screams were heard and the neighbours forced their way into the flat, they saw the same scene: Henriette was lying on the floor in a state of collapse and trembling like someone who had just been mercilessly beaten, while Maurin was running round the room in a state of bewilderment, unable to offer any explanation.

The poor man became careworn. Every evening he would go to bed trembling with the secret fear that he would be awakened by Henriette's screams. He could not make head or tail of her strange fits: she would suddenly leap out of bed, hit herself violently round the shoulders, tear her hair and roll about on the floor without giving him the slightest idea as to the cause. He concluded that she must be mad and he made a vow to himself not to answer any questions and to keep this private drama to himself. But his easygoing way of life had vanished with his peace of mind; he lost weight and looked pale and ill; his self-satisfied smile had gone for good.

Meanwhile a rumour—the source of which no one quite knew—was spreading in the neighbourhood that almost every night the poor man was subject to an attack of fever during which he thrashed the unfortunate Henriette to within an inch of her life. His pale, stricken face and his evasive answers, as well as his sad and embarrassed demeanour, served only to confirm this rumour.

From then onwards Maurin could not do anything that was not interpreted as the action of a madman. As soon as he went out, he became the focus of everyone's eyes, monitoring his every move and leading to strange interpretations of every word he uttered: nobody more resembles a madman than someone who is perfectly sane. If his foot slipped, if he looked up at the sky, if he blew his nose, people would laugh and shrug their shoulders in pity. Street urchins followed him about as though he were some strange animal. At the end of a month, everyone in Belleville knew that Maurin was mad, stark, staring mad.

People would whisper extraordinary things about him. One woman said she had met him on one of the outer boulevards walking in the rain without a hat. It was quite true: it had just been blown off his head by a gust of wind. Another woman declared that he used to walk round his garden at midnight every night, carrying the sort of candle used in churches and chanting the funeral service. This seemed quite terrifying. The truth was that the woman had seen Maurin on one occasion using a lamp to discover the slugs which were eating his lettuces. Gradually they pieced together a whole indictment of queer actions, an overwhelming dossier of mad behaviour. Tongues were busily wagging: 'Such a nice, kind, gentle man! What a shame! But that's how it is! . . . All the same, we'll have to get him put away in the end! . . . He's killing his poor dear wife, such a wonderful well-bred woman . . .'

They went to the police and one fine morning, after a dreadful scene, played to perfection by Henriette, Maurin was bundled into a cab on some pretext or other and taken off to Charenton. When he reached there and realized what was happening, in his rage he bit a warder's thumb right off. They put him into a straitjacket and dumped him among the violent madmen.

The young doctor had arranged for the poor man to be kept shut up in a cell as long as possible. He claimed to have been following Maurin's illness and observing such strange symptoms in him that his colleagues thought they had discovered a new form of madness. Moreover, the whole of Belleville was there to provide circumstantial details. Mental specialists conferred and learned articles were written. The lovers slipped away to enjoy their honeymoon in a leafy retreat in Touraine.

It took Henriette eleven months to become tired of her young doctor. Often, in between kisses, her thoughts had turned to her poor wretch of a husband screaming in his mad-cell. She began to feel a growing affection for him now that such a dreadful fate had overtaken him and he was no longer able to go out and look at his lettuces or take his stroll along the fortifications. Women with grey cat's eyes tend to be subject to such whims. She left her lover and went post-haste to Charenton, determined to make a full confession.

She had often felt surprised that the doctors were taking so long to discover that Maurin was not mad. At best, she had relied on enjoying only a few weeks' freedom. When they took her to her husband she saw in a shadowy corner of his cell a pale, thin, filthy, animal-like figure, more ghost than a man, who stood up and looked at her with eyes full of mindless, imbecilic horror. The poor man failed to recognize her. And as she stood there in terror, he began to sway to and fro with an idiotic laugh. Suddenly he burst out sobbing and stammered: 'I can't understand it, I can't understand it . . . I didn't go near her! . . .'

Then he hurled himself flat on the floor, exactly as Henriette had done, and kept hitting himself on the shoulders as he screamed and rolled around on the ground.

'He does that trick twenty times a day,' said the warder who had accompanied the young woman.

With her teeth chattering with fear and almost fainting, she covered her eyes to avoid looking at the man she had reduced to this brute beast. Maurin was mad.

ALPHONSE DAUDET (1840–1897)

The Last Lesson

As remembered by a boy from Alsace

Translated by David Coward

That morning I was very late going to school and was really afraid of getting into trouble with Monsieur Hamel, especially as he had told us he would be testing us on our participles and I didn't know any of them. For one moment I thought I would miss class and spend the day in the fields instead.

It was such a warm, sunny day!

At the edge of the wood, you could hear the blackbirds singing and in Rippert's field, behind the sawmill, the Prussians were practising marching up and down. It was all much more enticing than the rules about participles. But I managed to resist the temptation and ran as fast as I could to school.

As I passed the town hall, I saw a crowd had gathered around the wire-fronted noticeboard. For the last two years, it was on that board that all the bad news had landed, battles lost, official requisitions, orders from the military. Without stopping I wondered:

'What's it this time?'

Then, just as I was running across the square, Wachter, the blacksmith, who was there with his apprentice reading the notices, shouted to me:

'No need to run like that, boy. You'll get to school soon enough!'

I thought he was making fun of me and when I got to Monsieur Hamel's playground I was out of breath.

Normally at the start of school there was always this tremendous racket which could be heard outside in the street, desk-lids banging open and shut, lessons being chanted out loud, all together, fingers in ears to learn better, and the teacher's thick ruler thwacking desks as he shouted:

'A little less noise!!!'

I had been counting on the usual pandemonium to get to my place without being noticed. But that day, it was as quiet as a Sunday morning. Through the open window, I could see all my classmates already in their places, and also Monsieur Hamel, who was striding up and down with his fearsome metal ruler under his arm. I had to open the door and walk into the hushed silence. You can imagine how red my face was and how scared I felt.

But I needn't have been. Monsieur Hamel looked at me without getting angry and said mildly:

'Quick as you can, go to your seat, Frantz, my lad. We were about to start without you.'

I swung one leg over the bench and sat down at my desk at once. Only then, when I was beginning to get over my fright, did I notice that our teacher was wearing his best green coat, his finely pleated jabot, and his black silk academic cap with the embroidery on it that he only got out for school inspections and prize-givings. What's more, there was something strangely solemn about the whole class. But the thing that surprised me most was seeing, at the back of the room, on the benches which were usually unoccupied, rows of people from the village who were sitting as quietly as we were, old Hauser in his three-cornered hat, our former mayor, the retired postman, and others besides. They all looked grim-faced. Hauser had brought along an old, dog-eared spelling book which he held open on his knees, with his thick spectacles laid slantwise across the pages.

While I was taking all this in, Monsieur Hamel had gone to his high desk and in the same quiet, serious voice with which he had spoken to me, said:

'Children, this is the last time I shall take this class. Orders have come from Berlin that only German is to be taught in schools in Alsace and Lorraine . . . Your new teacher will be here tomorrow. Today is your last French lesson. I want you to listen very carefully.'

I was stunned by these words. So that's what the brutes had posted on the noticeboard!

My last French lesson!

But I hadn't learned to write properly yet! I'd never learn now! I'd be stuck where I was! Oh, how bitterly I regretted all the time I'd wasted, the classes I'd skipped to look for birds' nests or go sliding on the frozen Saar! My books which only a moment before had seemed so boring, so heavy to carry, my grammar, my tales from Scripture, now felt like old friends I'd be very sad to say goodbye to. The same went for Monsieur Hamel. The idea that he was going away, that I'd never see him again blotted out all the times he'd punished me and rapped my knuckles with his ruler.

Poor Monsieur Hamel!

It was in honour of this last class that he'd got dressed up in his Sunday best and now I understood why the old village people were sitting there at the back of the class. It was as if they were regretting that they hadn't come back to the school more often. It was also a way of thanking our teacher for his forty years of faithful service, and of paying their patriotic respects to their country which would soon be no more . . .

I had got this far with my thoughts when I heard my name called. It was my turn to be tested. I would have given anything if I could have reeled off the blessed rules governing participles in a loud, clear voice, without a mistake. But I got stuck after a few words and just stood at my desk, rocking on my heels, on the verge of tears, not daring to look up. I heard Monsieur Hamel say:

'I'm not going to tell you off, Frantz my boy, you're probably feeling bad enough as it is . . . But that's what happens, isn't it? Every day you say: "Oh, I've got heaps of time. I'll learn that tomorrow." But you see how things turn out . . . This has been the downfall of Alsace, always putting education off until tomorrow. And now those people can turn round and say quite rightly: "What! Call yourselves French! And you can't even read or write your own language!" . . . It's a shame, Frantz, but there are others who are far more to blame than you. We all share the guilt.

'Children, your parents never thought your schooling was important enough. They preferred to send you out to work in the fields and the mills so they'd have a little extra money coming in. But don't think I am beyond criticism. How many times have I sent you out to water my garden instead of working at your books? And whenever I felt like going out trout-fishing, did I ever hesitate to give you the day off? . . .'

And then, after one thing and another, Monsieur Hamel started talking about the French language, saying how it was the best in the world, the clearest, the most solidly constructed, and how we should always hang on to it among ourselves and never forget it, because when people become slaves then as long as they keep their language alive it's as though they have the key to their prison[1]. . . Then he picked up the grammar book and went through the lesson. It was amazing: I understood every word. Everything seemed so simple, so easy. But I also think I had never concentrated properly before nor had he ever explained things so patiently. It was as if poor Monsieur Hamel, before he left for good,

[1] 'If a people cleaves to its language, it holds the key which will loose its chains' (F. Mistral)

wanted to pass on everything he knew and was trying to cram it all into our heads in one go.

When grammar was finished, it was time for writing. For that day, Monsieur Hamel had prepared special new sheets for us. On them he had written, in his finest copperplate: *France, Alsace, France, Alsace.* Pinned to the rails of our desks, they looked like little flags hanging all round the classroom. You should have seen how hard everybody tried. And how quiet it was! All you could hear was the scratch of pens on paper. At one point, several large beetles flew in. But no one turned a hair, not even the little ones who were concentrating on their pen-strokes as earnestly and conscientiously as if making marks with a pen was the same as writing French . . . On the roof of the school, pigeons cooed softly and as I listened to them I wondered:

'Will they make them sing in German too?'

From time to time, when I looked up from my work, I saw Monsieur Hamel sitting quite still at his high desk. He was staring at all the things around him as if he thought that he could scoop up his little schoolhouse in his mind's eye and take it away with him. Just imagine. For forty years he had sat there, in the same place, looking at the same yard and the same classroom. Only now the benches and desks gleamed, polished by use. The walnut trees in the yard had grown tall and the hop he had planted himself trailed round the windows and climbed onto the roof. How heart-breaking it must have been for the poor man to have to leave all that, to hear his sister toing and froing in the room overhead as she shut the lids of their trunks! For they were due to go the next day, to vanish from the place for ever.

Even so, he found the heart to carry on teaching us to the bitter end. After writing, we had history. Then the little ones chanted A is for Apple, B is for Book. At the back of the classroom, old Hauser put his glasses on and, holding his spelling book in both hands, said his letters with them. You could tell that he too was doing his best. His voiced cracked and wobbled and it was so funny to hear him that we all wanted to laugh and cry. I shall always remember that last morning at school . . .

Suddenly, the church clock struck noon and then the angelus. Simultaneously, the trumpets of the Prussian soldiers who were returning from their exercises blared just outside our windows . . . Monsieur Hamel, deathly pale, stood up at his desk. I never remembered him looking so tall.

'My friends,' he said, 'my friends . . . I . . . I . . .'

But the words would not come and he could not finish his sentence.

Then he turned to the blackboard, picked up a piece of chalk and, pressing as hard as he could, wrote in letters as large as the board would take:

'Vive la France!'

Then he stood there, leaning his head against the wall and, without saying a word, made a gesture with his hand:

'It's all over . . . Away you go.'

GUSTAVE FLAUBERT (1821–1880)

A Simple Heart

Translated by A.J. Krailsheimer

For half a century the good ladies of Pont-l'Évêque envied Madame Aubain her servant Félicité.

For one hundred francs a year she did the cooking and the housework, sewing, washing, and ironing, she could bridle a horse, fatten up poultry, churn butter, and remained faithful to her mistress, who was not however a very likeable person.

Madame Aubain had married a handsome but impecunious young man, who died at the beginning of 1809, leaving her with two very young children and heavy debts. So she sold her properties, except the farms at Toucques and Geffosses, which brought in five thousand francs a year at the very most, and moved out of her house at Saint-Melaine into a less expensive one, which had been in her family for generations and stood behind the market-hall.

This house, faced with slates, lay between an alley and a lane running down to the river. Inside there were changes of level which could make you stumble. A narrow entrance hall separated the kitchen from the living-room, where Madame Aubain sat all day long in a basketwork armchair by the window. Against the white-painted panelling were ranged eight mahogany chairs. On an old piano, beneath a barometer, rested a pyramid of piled-up boxes and cartons. A tapestry wing-chair stood on each side of a yellow marble mantelpiece in Louis XV style. The clock in the middle of it represented a temple of Vesta—and the whole place smelled slightly of mildew, for the floor was lower than the garden.

On the first floor there came first 'Madame's' bedroom, very large, papered in a pale floral pattern, and containing a portrait of 'Monsieur' dressed as a dandy of days gone by. This led into a smaller room, in which were two children's cots without mattresses. Then came the drawing-room, always kept shut up, and full of furniture covered in dust-sheets. Next, a corridor led to a study; books and papers filled the shelves of a bookcase whose three sides surrounded a large black wooden desk. The two corner panels were lost to view beneath pen-and-ink drawings, gouache landscapes, and Audran prints, relics of better days and vanished luxury. A skylight on the second floor provided light for Félicité's room, which looked out over the meadows.

She would get up at dawn, so as not to miss Mass, and work without a break until evening; then, with dinner over, the dishes put away and the door securely locked, she would pile ashes over the log and doze in front of the hearth, her rosary in her hand. When it came to haggling no one was more persistent. As for cleanliness, her gleaming pots and pans were the despair of the other servants. Very thrifty, she ate slowly, and with her finger gathered up all the crumbs left on the table from her loaf of bread— a twelve-pound loaf, baked specially for her, which lasted three weeks.

Year in, year out, she wore a calico print neckerchief, fastened at the back with a pin, a bonnet which covered her hair, grey stockings, a red skirt, and over her jacket an apron with a bib, such as nurses wear in hospitals.

She had a thin face and a sharp voice. At twenty-five she was taken for forty. Once past fifty she could have been any age; and with her perpetual silence, straight back, and deliberate gestures she looked like a wooden dummy, driven by clockwork.

II

Félicité had had, like anyone else, her love story.

Her father, a mason, had been killed falling off scaffolding. Then her mother died, her sisters scattered, a farmer took her in and while she was still a child employed her as cowherd in the open fields. She shivered with cold in her rags, lay flat to drink water out of the ponds, was beaten for no reason at all, and was finally thrown out for the theft of thirty sous, which she had never stolen. She went to another farm, was put in charge of the poultry, and as the owners liked her the other farmhands were jealous.

One evening in August (she was then eighteen) they took her with them to the village fair at Colleville. Straight away she was dazed, deafened by the noise of the fiddles, the lights in the trees, the medley of brightly coloured costumes, lace, gold crosses, this mass of people all hopping about in time. She was standing shyly to one side when a prosperous-looking young man, who had been smoking a pipe as he leaned with both arms on a cart-shaft, came up and invited her to dance. He bought her cider, coffee, cake, a silk scarf, and imagining that she had guessed his intentions, offered to see her home. On the edge of a field of oats he brutally tumbled her over. She was frightened and began to scream. He made off.

Another evening, on the Beaumont road, she tried to get past a large haywain which was travelling slowly in front of her, and, brushing by close to the wheels, she recognized Théodore.

He greeted her quite calmly, saying that she must forgive his behaviour, since it was all 'the fault of the drink'.

She did not know how to reply, and wanted to run away.

At once he began talking about the crops and the leading figures of the commune, for his father had left Colleville for the farm at Les Écots, so that they were now neighbours. 'Ah!' she said. He added that his people wanted him to settle down, but he was in no hurry, and was waiting for a wife who would suit him. She bowed her head. Then he asked if she was thinking of getting married. She replied with a smile that it was wrong to make fun of people. 'But I'm not, I swear!', and he put his left arm round her waist; she walked on supported by his embrace; they slowed down. There was a soft breeze, the stars were shining, the huge load of hay swayed in front of them; and the four horses kicked up the dust as they plodded on. Then, unbidden, they turned off to the right. He kissed her again. She vanished into the darkness.

The following week Théodore persuaded her to agree to several assignations.

They would meet in some corner of a farmyard, behind a wall, under some isolated tree. She was not innocent in the way that young ladies are—she had learned from the animals—but her reason and innate sense of honour kept her from losing her virtue. Her resistance sharpened Théodore's desire, so that in the hope of satisfying it (or perhaps out of sheer naïvety) he proposed marriage to her. She was unready to believe him. He swore solemnly that he meant it.

Soon he had a matter of some concern to confess: his parents, the year before, had bought a substitute to do his military service; but he was liable at any time to be called up again; the idea of serving in the Forces appalled him. Such cowardice was for Félicité proof of his affection; it made hers all the stronger. She would slip out at night to meet him, and once she arrived, Théodore would torment her with his worries and his pleas.

Finally he announced that he was going to the Prefecture himself to make enquiries, and would report the result the following Sunday night between eleven and midnight.

At the appointed time she hastened to her lover.

In his place she found one of his friends.

From him she learned that she was never to see Théodore again. In order to be exempt from conscription Théodore had married a very wealthy old woman, Madame Lehoussais of Toucques.

Her grief was uncontrollable. She flung herself on the ground, screamed, called on God, and stayed moaning all alone in the fields until sunrise. Then she returned to the farm, announced her intention of leaving, and at the end of the month was paid off; with all her meagre possessions wrapped in a kerchief she made her way to Pont-l'Évêque.

In front of the inn she asked some questions of a lady in a widow's hood, who was in fact just looking for a cook. The girl did not know much, but seemed to be so willing and modest in her demands that Madame Aubain finally said:

'Very well, I will take you!'

A quarter of an hour later Félicité was installed in her house.

At first she lived there in a state of fear and trembling brought on by 'the kind of house' it was and the memory of 'Monsieur' hanging over everything! Paul and Virginie, the former aged seven, the latter barely four, seemed to her to be made out of some precious material; she would give them rides on her back like a horse, and Madame Aubain told her to stop kissing them all the time, which hurt her deeply. However she was happy there. In such an agreeable environment her gloom had faded away.

Every Thursday the same regular visitors came to play a game of boston. Félicité prepared the cards and footwarmers in advance. They arrived punctually at eight o'clock and left before it struck eleven.

Every Monday morning the secondhand dealer who lived down the lane would spread out on the ground his bits and pieces. Then the town would resound with the buzz of voices, mingled with horses neighing, lambs bleating, pigs grunting, and carts clattering through the streets. Towards noon, when the market was at its height, a tall, old peasant, with a hooked nose and his cap on the back of his head, would appear on the doorstep: it was Robelin, who farmed Geffosses. Shortly afterwards came Liébard, who farmed at Toucques, short, red-faced, stout, wearing a grey jacket and leggings fitted with spurs.

They both offered their landlady chickens or cheese for sale. Wily as they were, Félicité invariably got the better of them, and they would go off filled with respect for her.

At irregular intervals Madame Aubain would receive a visit from the Marquis de Grémanville, an uncle of hers, ruined by debauch, who lived at Falaise on the last remnant of his land. He always arrived at lunchtime, with a dreadful poodle which soiled all the furniture with its paws. Despite his efforts to act the nobleman, going so far as to raise his hat every time he said: 'My late father', yielding to force of habit he would pour himself one drink after another, and come out with ribald remarks. Félicité would politely push him out: 'You have had enough, Monsieur de Grémanville! Some other time!' And would close the door on him.

It was a pleasure for her to open it to Monsieur Bourais, a former solicitor. His white tie and bald head, his frilled shirt-front, his ample brown frock-coat, the way he curved his arm when he took a pinch of snuff, his whole person affected her with that agitation which the spectacle of exceptional men commonly provokes.

As he managed 'Madame's' properties, he would shut himself up with her for hours in 'Monsieur's' study; he was always afraid of compromising himself, had boundless respect for the judiciary and some pretentions to knowledge of Latin.

As a way of combining instruction with pleasure, he gave the children an illustrated geography-book. The pictures represented scenes from different parts of the world, cannibals with feather headdresses, an ape abducting a young lady, bedouins in the desert, a whale being harpooned, etc.

Paul would explain these engravings to Félicité. This was indeed the only literary education she ever had.

That of the children was provided by Guyot, a poor devil employed at the Town Hall, famous for his fine handwriting, who used to sharpen his penknife on his boot.

When the weather was fine they would set out early for the farm at Geffosses.

The farmyard lies on a slope, with the house in the middle, and the sea appears in the distance as a patch of grey.

Félicité would take slices of cold meat out of her bag, and they would eat their lunch in a room connecting with the dairy. It was all that remained of a country house no longer to be seen. The tattered wallpaper stirred with every draught. Madame Aubain would bow her head, overwhelmed with memories; and the children did not dare to go on talking. 'Do go and play!' she would say; they made themselves scarce.

Paul would go into the barn, catch birds, play ducks and drakes on the pond, or bang a stick against the massive casks, which were as resonant as drums.

Virginie fed the rabbits, or rushed off to pick cornflowers, running so fast that her little embroidered knickers showed.

One autumn evening they went back through the fields.

The moon in its first quarter lit up part of the sky, and mist floated like a scarf over the winding river Toucques. Cattle lying in the middle of the grass looked peaceably at these four people going past. In the third meadow some of them stood up, then formed a circle in front of them. 'Don't be afraid!' said Félicité, and keening softly she stroked the back of the nearest animal; it turned about, the others followed suit. But when they began to cross the next field a fearsome bellowing rent the air. It was a bull, hidden in the mist. It advanced on the two women. Madame Aubain was about to run. 'No! no! not so fast!' They walked more rapidly all the same, and could hear behind them the sound of heavy breathing coming closer. Hooves thudded like hammerblows on the grass; now it was charging at a gallop! Félicité turned round, and with both hands took up clods of earth which she threw into the bull's eyes. It lowered its muzzle, tossed its horns and was shaking with rage as it bellowed horribly. Madame Aubain, at the end of the field with the two children, was frantically looking for some way to get over the high bank. Félicité kept retreating in front of the bull, continually hurling clumps of turf which blinded it, crying all the while: 'Hurry! Hurry!'

Madame Aubain went down into the ditch, pushed Virginie, then Paul, up the bank and fell several times trying to climb it herself, before she finally succeeded after strenuous efforts.

The bull had backed Félicité up against a barred gate; it was slavering close enough to spatter her face, another second and it would gore her. She just had time to slip between two of the bars, and the great beast stopped in its tracks in amazement.

This event was talked about for many years at Pont-l'Évêque. Félicité took no pride in it, and had no idea that she had done anything heroic.

She was exclusively concerned with Virginie, who had developed a nervous ailment as a result of this fright; Monsieur Poupart, the doctor, advised sea-bathing at Trouville.

In those days not many people went there. Madame Aubain made enquiries, consulted Bourais, and made preparations as though for a long journey.

Her luggage went off the day before, in Liébard's cart. Next day he brought along two horses, one of which had a woman's saddle, with a velvet back-rest; and on the crupper of the other a rolled-up cloak formed a seat of sorts, on which Madame Aubain rode, sitting behind him. Félicité took charge of Virginie, and Paul mounted Monsieur Lechaptois's donkey, which he had lent on condition that they took great care of it.

The road was so bad that the eight kilometres took them two hours. The horses sank up to their pasterns in mud, and worked free by jerking their hindquarters; or else they stumbled against the ruts; at other times they had to jump. Liébard's mare would suddenly stop at certain points. He would wait patiently for her to go on again, and talk about the people whose property lay beside the road, adding moral reflections to his account of them. Thus in the middle of Toucques, as they passed beneath windows wreathed in nasturtiums, he said with a shrug of his shoulders: 'That's where a certain Madame Lehoussais lives. Instead of taking a young man . . .'. Félicité did not hear the rest; the horses were trotting, the donkey galloping; then they all turned on to a path, a gate opened, two lads appeared, and they dismounted by the cesspool, just in front of the door.

Mère Liébard effusively expressed her delight at the sight of her mistress. She served up a meal consisting of a sirloin, tripe, black pudding, fricassee of chicken, sparkling cider, a fruit tart, and plums in brandy, accompanied by compliments to Madame, who was looking much better, Mademoiselle, who had become 'simply gorgeous', young Monsieur Paul, who had 'filled out' wonderfully, without forgetting their deceased grandparents, whom the Liébards had known, having been in the family's service for several generations. The farm, like them, looked somewhat antique. The ceiling beams were worm-eaten, the walls black with smoke, the window-panes grey with dust. An oak dresser held all kinds of utensils, pitchers, plates, pewter bowls, wolf-traps, sheep-shears; an enormous syringe amused the children. There was not one tree in the three yards without fungus growing at its foot or a clump of mistletoe in its branches. The wind had brought down a lot of them. They had started growing again from the middle; and they all bent under the weight of their apples. The thatched roofs, like brown velvet of uneven thickness, stood up to the fiercest gusts. The cart-shed, however, was falling down. Madame Aubain said that she would see to it, and gave the order to harness the animals again.

It took a further half-hour to reach Trouville. The little caravan had to dismount to pass by the Écores, a cliff overhanging the boats below, and three minutes later, at the end of the quayside, they went into the courtyard of the Golden Lamb, kept by Mère David.

Virginie after the first few days did not feel so weak, as a result of the change of air and sea-bathing. She bathed in her chemise, since she did not have a costume; and her maid dressed her afterwards in a Customs hut used by the bathers.

In the afternoons they went off with the donkey beyond the Roches-Noires, in the direction of Hennequeville. At first the path led up through undulating ground like the lawns in a park, then came out on to a plateau where pasture and ploughland alternated. By the wayside, holly bushes grew up out of bramble thickets; here and there a tall dead tree traced against the blue sky the zigzag pattern of its branches.

They almost always rested in a meadow, with Deauville on the left, Le Havre on the right, and the open sea facing them. It sparkled in the sunshine, smooth as a mirror, so calm that one could barely hear the murmur of the waves; sparrows chirped out of sight, and the immense vault of the heavens arched over everything. Madame Aubain sat doing her needlework; Virginie beside her plaited rushes; Félicité picked lavender flowers; Paul was just bored and wanted to move on.

At other times they crossed the Toucques in a boat and went looking for seashells. Low tide uncovered sea-urchins, scallops, called locally 'godefiches', jellyfish; and the children would run to catch the bubbles of foam blown away by the wind. As the waves broke sleepily on the sand, they rippled out along the shore, which stretched as far as the eye could see, but on the landward side was bounded by the dunes separating it from the Marais, a wide meadow shaped like a racecourse. When they came back that way, Trouville on the hillside in the background grew larger with every step, and with all its varied houses seemed to be blooming in cheerful disarray.

On days when it was too hot they never left their room. The dazzling brightness from outside interposed bars of light between the slats of the drawn blinds. Not a sound came from the village. Below, on the pavement, not a soul. Such widespread silence increased the general impression of tranquillity. In the distance caulkers hammered away at the hulls, and the smell of tar was borne on the sultry breeze.

The main entertainment was provided by the fishing boats coming in. As soon as they had passed the marker buoys, they began to tack. Their sails were lowered two-thirds of the way down the masts; and with the foresail bellying out like a balloon, they slid forward with waves lapping their sides to the middle of the harbour, where they suddenly dropped anchor. Then each boat took its place at the quayside. The sailors threw the squirming fish ashore, where a line of carts waited, and women in cotton bonnets reached forward to take the baskets and embrace their menfolk.

One day one of these women approached Félicité, who shortly afterwards came into the room quite overjoyed. She had found one of her sisters; and Nastasie Barette, whose married name was Leroux, appeared, clutching a baby to her breast, another child in her right hand, and on her left a little ship's boy, with hands on hips and beret cocked over one ear.

After quarter of an hour Madame Aubain sent her off.

They kept coming across them, outside the kitchen, or when they went out for walks. The husband did not make an appearance.

Félicité became very fond of them. She bought them a blanket, some shirts, a stove; they were obviously exploiting her. This weakness annoyed Madame Aubain; besides she did not like the familiar way in which the nephew addressed her son, and as Virginie had developed a cough and the best of the season was over, she returned to Pont-l'Évêque.

Monsieur Bourais advised her on the choice of a school. The one at Caen was considered to be the best. Paul was sent there, and bravely said goodbye to everyone, pleased that he was going to live somewhere where he would have other boys to keep him company.

Madame Aubain resigned herself to her son's departure, because it had to be. Virginie thought about him less and less. Félicité missed the noise he used to make. But something else came up to keep her busy and distract her; starting at Christmas she took the little girl to catechism every day.

III

After genuflecting at the door, she would walk between the double row of chairs beneath the lofty vault of the nave, open Madame Aubain's pew, sit down and look around.

The choir stalls were filled with boys on the right, girls on the left; the curé stood by the lectern; one stained-glass window in the apse depicted the Holy Spirit above the Virgin; another showed her kneeling before the infant Jesus, and behind the tabernacle a wooden carving represented Saint Michael slaying the dragon.

The priest began with a summary of Sacred History. In her mind's eye she saw Paradise, the Flood, the Tower of Babel, the cities destroyed by fire, whole peoples dying, idols overthrown; and this dazzling vision left her with lasting respect for the Almighty and fear of his wrath. Then she wept as she listened to the story of the Passion. Why had they crucified him, he who loved children, fed the multitude, healed the blind, and had been willing, in his meekness, to be born among the poor, in the muck of a stable? Sowing, harvesting, pressing, all these familiar things of which the Gospel speaks were part of her life; God had sanctified them with his passing presence; and she loved lambs more dearly from love of the Lamb of God, doves because of the Holy Spirit.

She found it hard to visualize what he looked like, for he was not just a bird, but a fire as well, and at other times a breath. Perhaps it was his light fluttering at night on the edge of the marshes, his breath driving the clouds, his voice making the bells ring tunefully; and she sat lost in worship, enjoying the coolness of the walls and the peaceful church.

As for dogma, she did not understand, did not even attempt to understand, a word of it. The curé would say his piece, the children would repeat it, she would eventually doze off; and would wake with a start at the noise of their sabots clattering down the stone paving on their way out.

This was how she learned the catechism, from hearing it repeated, for her religious education had been neglected in her youth; and as for practice, from that time on she simply copied Virginie, fasting like her, going to confession with her. At Corpus Christi they made an altar of repose together.

The First Communion worried her a great deal beforehand. She fussed about the shoes, the rosary, the prayer book, the gloves. How she trembled as she helped Virginie's mother dress her!

All through the Mass she was on tenterhooks. Monsieur Bourais blocked her view of one side of the choir; but directly opposite her the band of maidens with their white wreaths worn over their lowered veils looked like a snowfield; and she recognized the precious child even at a distance by her slender neck and devout bearing. The bell tinkled. Heads were bowed; there was silence. As the organ thundered out choir and congregation intoned the Agnus Dei; then the boys began to file up, and after them the girls stood up. In slow procession, hands folded, they went up to the brightly lit altar, knelt on the first step, received the host in turn, and in the same order returned to their stalls. When it came to Virginie's turn, Félicité leaned forward to see her; and imagining things as one can when moved by genuine affection, it seemed to her that she herself was that child; the child's face became her own, she wore the child's dress, the child's heart beat in her breast; when the moment came to open her mouth and close her eyes Félicité all but fainted.

Early next morning she went to the sacristy and asked Monsieur le curé to give her communion. She received it most devoutly, but without the ecstasy she had experienced the day before.

Madame Aubain wanted her daughter to be endowed with every accomplishment; and as Guyot was unable to teach her English or music, she decided to send her as a boarder to the Ursulines at Honfleur.

The child raised no objections. Félicité sighed, finding Madame heartless. Then she reflected that her mistress might be right. Such matters were beyond her capacities.

Finally one day an old break drew up at the door; and out stepped a nun who had come to fetch Mademoiselle. Félicité hauled the luggage up on the roof, gave the coachman instructions, and stowed in the boot six pots of jam and a dozen pears, with a bouquet of violets.

At the last moment Virginie was overcome by a fit of sobbing; she hugged her mother, who kissed her on the forehead, repeating: 'Come now! be brave! be brave!' The step was raised and the break moved off.

Then Madame Aubain collapsed; and that evening all her friends, the Lormeaus, Madame Lechaptois, *those* Mesdemoiselles Rochefeuille, Monsieur de Houppeville, and Bourais came round to console her.

At first she found it extremely painful to be without her daughter. But three times a week she had a letter from her, and on the other days wrote back. She walked in her garden, read a little, and in this way filled the empty hours.

In the morning, from force of habit, Félicité would go into Virginie's room, and look round the four walls. She missed having to comb the girl's hair, lace up her boots, tuck her up in bed—and constantly seeing her sweet face, holding her hand when they went out together. With nothing else to do she tried her hand at lace-making. Her clumsy fingers broke the threads; she could not concentrate, was losing sleep, in her own words was 'undermined'.

'To take her mind off it' she asked if she might be allowed to receive visits from her nephew Victor.

He would arrive on Sundays after Mass, rosy-cheeked, bare-chested, and smelling of the countryside he had come through. She would straight away lay a place for him. They would have their lunch facing each other; and though she herself ate as little as possible to save expense, she would fill him up with so much food that he would end by falling asleep. As soon as the bell began to ring for Vespers she roused him, brushed his trousers, tied his tie and made her way to church, leaning on his arm with maternal pride.

His parents always told him to get something out of her, a packet of brown sugar, perhaps, or some soap, brandy, sometimes even money. He would bring her his clothes to mend; and she was happy to accept the task, because it meant that he would have to come back.

In August his father took him on voyages round the coast.

It was the time of the school holidays. The children's arrival consoled her. But Paul was becoming capricious, and Virginie was now too old to be spoken to familiarly as a child; that caused a certain constraint, set up a barrier between them.

Victor went successively to Morlaix, Dunkirk, and Brighton; he brought her back a present from each voyage. The first time it was a box decorated with seashells; the second time a coffee cup; the third time a big gingerbread man. He was turning out a handsome lad, with his slim waist, a faint moustache, a good honest look and a little leather cap, worn on the back of his head, like a pilot. He entertained her by telling stories mixed up with nautical language.

One Monday, the fourteenth of July 1819 (she never forgot the date) Victor announced that he had signed on for an ocean voyage, and on the Wednesday night would be taking the packet-boat from Honfleur to join his schooner, which was due to sail shortly from Le Havre. He might be away for as much as two years.

The prospect of such a long absence grieved Félicité deeply, and wanting to bid him another farewell, on the Wednesday evening, after Madame's dinner, she put on her clogs and made short work of the four leagues between Pont-l'Évêque and Honfleur.

When she reached the Calvary, instead of bearing left, she bore right, got lost in the shipyards, retraced her steps; some people she approached urged her to hurry. She went all round the docks, which were full of shipping, stumbling over mooring ropes; then the level of the ground fell, there were beams of light criss-crossing in all directions, and she thought she was going mad when she saw some horses up in the air.

On the quayside others were whinnying, frightened by the sea. A hoist was lifting them up and lowering them into a boat, where passengers jostled among casks of cider, baskets of cheese, sacks of grain; hens were clucking, the captain swearing; and a cabin boy was leaning on the cathead, quite indifferent to everything. Félicité, who had not recognized him, cried 'Victor!' repeatedly, and he looked up; she rushed forward, but the gangway was suddenly pulled up.

The packet-boat, hauled by women singing as they went, left harbour. Its ribs creaked, heavy waves lashed its bows. The sail had swung round, there was no longer anyone to be seen; and against the sea shining silver in the moonlight it stood out as a dark patch, which steadily faded, sank away, disappeared.

As Félicité went past the Calvary she wanted to commend to God all that she held most dear; and she stood praying for a long time, her face wet with tears, her eyes lifted up to the clouds. The town slept, Customs men did their rounds; and water poured incessantly through the holes in the lockgate, sounding like a torrent. It struck two.

The convent parlour would not be open before daylight. If she were late back Madame would certainly be annoyed; and despite her desire to embrace the other child, she started home. The girls in the inn were just waking up as she came into Pont-l'Évêque.

So the poor lad would be rolling about on the ocean waves for months on end! His earlier voyages had not alarmed her. People came back from England and Brittany; but America, the Colonies, the Islands, that was away in some remote, vague region at the other end of the world.

From that moment Félicité's only thoughts were for her nephew. On sunny days she worried about his thirst; when there was a thunderstorm she was afraid that he would be struck by lightning. As she listened to the wind howling in the chimney and blowing off roof slates, she saw him battered by the same gale, on the top of some shattered mast, his whole body bent back beneath a blanket of foam; or else, as she remembered the geography picture-book, he was being eaten by savages, caught in a forest by apes, perishing on some deserted shore. And she never talked about her worries.

Madame Aubain had her own worries, concerning her daughter.

The nuns found her affectionate, but delicate. The slightest excitement tired her out. She had to give up the piano.

Her mother insisted on regular letters from the convent. One morning when the postman had not called she grew impatient; and paced up and down the room, from her chair to the window. It was quite extraordinary! Four days now without news!

Trying to console her with her own example, Félicité said to her:

'But Madame, I haven't had any for six months!'

'From whom . . .?'

The servant quietly replied:

'Why, from my nephew!'

'Oh! your nephew!' And shrugging her shoulders Madame Aubain resumed her pacing, which meant: 'I never thought of him! . . . Besides, what do I care! A worthless cabin boy, of no account! . . . Whereas my daughter . . . Just imagine!'

Félicité, though brought up the hard way, was angry with Madame, then forgot about it.

It seemed so easy to her to lose one's head on account of the little girl.

The two children were of equal importance to her; they were united by the bond in her heart, and their destiny should be the same.

She learned from the pharmacist that Victor's boat had arrived in Havana. He had read the information in a newspaper.

Because of the cigars she imagined Havana as a place where nobody did anything but smoke, and she saw Victor walking about among negroes in a cloud of tobacco smoke. 'In case of need' could one come back overland? How far was it from Pont-l'Évêque? To find out she asked Monsieur Bourais.

He got out his atlas and began to explain all about longitudes; and put on a pedantically superior smile at Félicité's bewilderment. At length he pointed with his pencil at an imperceptible black dot somewhere in the indentations of an oval patch, adding: 'There it is.' She bent over the map; the network of coloured lines tired her eyes without making her any the wiser; and when Bourais asked what was bothering her, she begged him to show her the house where Victor was living. Bourais flung up his arms, sneezed, laughed uproariously, revelling in such ingenuousness; and Félicité could not understand why—her intelligence was so limited that she might even be expecting to see her nephew's portrait!

It was a fortnight later that Liébard came as usual into the kitchen at market time, and handed her a letter sent by her brother-in-law. As neither of them could read, she had recourse to her mistress.

Madame Aubain, who was counting the stitches in her knitting, laid it aside, opened the letter, gave a start, and looking intently at her said in a low voice:

'They are writing to give you some . . . bad news. Your nephew . . .'

He was dead. There were no further details.

Félicité fell on to a chair, rested her head against the wall, and closed her eyelids, which suddenly reddened. Then with head bowed, hands dangling, fixed stare, she repeated time after time:

'Poor young lad! Poor young lad!'

Liébard sighed as he watched her. Madame Aubain was trembling slightly.

She suggested that Félicité should go and see her sister at Trouville.

Félicité made a gesture to indicate that there was no need.

There was a silence. Liébard decided that he ought to leave.

Then she said:

'Them! It means nothing to them!'

Her head drooped again; and from time to time without thinking she picked up the long knitting-needles from the work table.

Some women went by in the yard carrying some laundry, still dripping, on a kind of stretcher.

Seeing them through the window reminded her of her own washing; she had boiled it up the day before, so today she had to rinse it; and she left the room.

Her washboard and tub lay beside the Toucques. She threw a pile of shifts down on the river bank, rolled up her sleeves, picked up her beater, and pounded so hard with it that the sound could be heard in the adjoining gardens. The meadows were empty, the wind ruffled the river; on the bottom long weeds streamed out like the hair of corpses floating in the water. She held back her grief, and was very brave until the evening; but in her bedroom she gave way to it, lying prone on the mattress, face pressed into the pillow, fists clenched against her temples.

Much later she heard from Victor's captain himself the circumstances of his death. He had been taken to hospital with yellow fever, and they had bled him too much. Four doctors had held him at once. He had died immediately, and the head one had said:

'Right! one more . . .!'

His parents had always treated him with inhumanity. She preferred not to see them again; and they made no advances, either from forgetfulness or the callousness of the poor.

Virginie was growing weaker.

Frequent difficulty in breathing, coughing, continual fever, and blotches on her cheeks indicated some deep-seated ailment. Monsieur Poupart had advised a stay in Provence. Madame Aubain decided on that, and would have brought her daughter straight home, but for the climate of Pont-l'Évêque.

She came to an arrangement with a man who hired out carriages, and he took her to the convent every Tuesday. In the garden is a terrace with a view of the Seine. Virginie would walk there, on her arm, treading on fallen vine-leaves. Sometimes the sun coming through the clouds made her blink as she looked at sails in the distance and the whole horizon, from the castle at Tancarville round to the lighthouses of Le Havre. Then they would have a rest beneath the arbour. Her mother had obtained a small cask of excellent Malaga wine; and laughing at the idea of getting tipsy, Virginie would take two sips, never more.

Her strength began to return. The autumn passed by quietly. Félicité spoke reassuringly to Madame Aubain. But one evening when she had been out on some errand nearby, she came upon Monsieur Poupart's cabriolet in front of the door, and he was in the hall. Madame Aubain was fastening her hat.

'Give me my footwarmer, my purse, my gloves; do hurry up!'

Virginie had pleurisy; it might be hopeless.

'Not yet!' said the doctor; and they both got into the gig, with snowflakes swirling down. It would soon be dark. It was very cold.

Félicité rushed to the church to light a candle. Then she ran after the gig, caught up with it an hour later, nimbly jumped on behind, and was clinging to the fringed hood when she suddenly thought: 'The courtyard was never locked up! What if thieves broke in?' And she jumped down.

Next day, at first light, she went round to the doctor's house. He had returned, and gone off again on his country rounds. Then she waited at the inn, thinking that was where strangers would bring a letter. Finally, as dusk fell, she took the coach coming from Lisieux.

The convent lay at the end of a steep lane. About halfway down she heard a strange sound, the tolling of a death-knell. 'It's for someone else,' she thought; and Félicité banged the door-knocker violently.

After several minutes she heard slippers shuffling along. The door opened a crack and a nun appeared.

The good sister said sorrowfully that 'she had just passed away'. At the same moment the tolling from Saint-Léonard's grew louder.

Félicité reached the second floor.

From the doorway of the room she could see Virginie lying on her back, with hands folded, mouth open, and head thrown back beneath a black crucifix which leaned towards her, her face still paler than the curtains hanging motionless on either side. Madame Aubain was clinging to the foot of the bed, choking with sobs of anguish. The Mother Superior stood on the right. Three candlesticks on the chest of drawers added splashes of red, and the fog was turning the windows white. Nuns led Madame Aubain away.

For two whole nights Félicité never left the dead girl. She kept repeating the same prayers, sprinkling holy water over the sheets, sitting down again, gazing at her. At the end of the first vigil she noticed that the face had turned yellow, the lips blue, the nose was becoming pinched, the eyes more sunken. She kissed the eyes several times; and would not have been vastly astonished if Virginie had opened them; for such souls the supernatural is quite simple. She laid out the corpse, wrapped it in the shroud, lowered it into the coffin, put on a wreath, spread out the hair. It was fair hair, exceptionally long for her age. Félicité cut off a large lock, and slipped half of it into her bosom, determined never to let it go.

The body was brought back to Pont-l'Évêque, in accordance with the wishes of Madame Aubain, who followed the hearse in a closed carriage.

After the Mass it took another three-quarters of an hour to reach the cemetery. Paul walked in front, sobbing. Monsieur Bourais came behind him, then the leading townsfolk, the women in long black veils, and Félicité. She was thinking of her nephew, to whom she had been unable to pay these last respects, and this added to her sorrow, as if he were being buried with the other child.

Madame Aubain's despair knew no bounds.

First she rebelled against God, whom she looked on as unjust for taking away her daughter—she had never done anything wrong, her conscience was so clear! But no! She should have taken her to the South of France. Other doctors would have saved her! She blamed herself, wanted to join her daughter, cried out in distress in the middle of her dreams. One dream in particular obsessed her. Her husband, dressed as a sailor, was returning from a long voyage, and told her with tears that he had been ordered to take Virginie away. Then they would put their heads together to discover some safe hiding-place.

Once she came in from the garden quite distraught. A moment before (she showed the exact spot) father and daughter had appeared to her side by side; they were not doing anything; they just looked at her.

For several months she stayed in her room in a state of apathy. Félicité gently chided her; she must look after herself for her son's sake, and for her husband's, in memory of 'her'.

'Her!' replied Madame Aubain, as if waking from sleep. 'Oh! yes! yes! . . . You are not forgetting her!' Referring to the cemetery, where she had been strictly forbidden to go.

Félicité went there every day.

Punctually at four o'clock she skirted the houses, went up the hill, opened the gate and came to Virginie's grave. It consisted of a small pink marble column, with a tombstone at the bottom, surrounded by chains enclosing a little garden plot. The beds were completely covered over with flowers. She would water their leaves, put down fresh sand, go down on her knees to dig the ground more thoroughly. When Madame Aubain was finally able to go there, she felt relieved, somehow comforted, by this.

Then years went by, all alike and without incident, apart from the great festivals as they came round: Easter, Assumption, All Saints.

Domestic events marked a date, subsequently used as a point of reference. Thus in 1825 two glaziers whitewashed the hall; in 1827 part of the roof fell into the courtyard and narrowly missed killing a man. In the summer of 1828 it was Madame's turn to present the blessed bread; at about that time Bourais went mysteriously absent; and old acquaintances gradually departed: Guyot, Liébard, Madame Lechaptois, Robelin, Uncle Grémanville, who had been paralysed for years.

One night the driver of the mail-coach brought Pont-l'Évêque the news of the July Revolution. A new sub-prefect was appointed a few days later: Baron de Larsonnière, a former consul in America, whose household included, apart from his wife, his sister-in-law with three young ladies, already quite grown-up. They could be seen on their lawn, dressed in loose smocks; they owned a negro and a parrot. Madame Aubain received a formal call from them, and did not fail to return it. At the first glimpse of them in the distance Félicité would run to warn her. But only one thing could arouse her feelings; her son's letters.

He could not follow any career, because he spent all his time in taverns. She paid his debts, he contracted new ones; and as Madame Aubain sat knitting at the window she would sigh loudly enough for Félicité to hear as she turned her spinning-wheel in the kitchen.

They would stroll together beside the espalier, and always talked about Virginie, discussing whether she would have liked this or that, or what she would probably have said on such and such an occasion.

All her modest belongings filled a cupboard in the children's bedroom. Madame Aubain inspected them as seldom as possible. One summer's day she resigned herself to do so; and moths flew out of the wardrobe.

Her dresses hung in a row under a shelf containing three dolls, some hoops, a set of doll's furniture, and the wash-basin she had used. They also took out petticoats, stockings, handkerchiefs, and spread them out on the two beds before folding them up again. The sun shone brightly on these shabby things, showing up the stains, and creases caused by movements of her body. The air was warm, the sky blue, a blackbird trilled, every living thing seemed to be full of sweetness and light. They found a little hat, made of furry brown plush; but it was all moth-eaten. Félicité asked if she might have it. Their eyes met, filled with tears; finally the mistress opened her arms, the servant fell into them; and they embraced, appeasing their grief in a kiss which made them equal.

It was the first time in their lives, for Madame Aubain was not naturally forthcoming. Félicité was as grateful to her as if she had received a gift, and from then on loved her with dog-like devotion and religious adoration.

Her natural kindness began to develop.

When she heard the drums of a regiment marching down the street, she would stand at the door with a jug of cider, offering the soldiers a drink. She looked after cholera victims. She took the Poles under her wing; and one of them even announced that he would like to marry her. But they fell out; for one morning, coming back from the Angelus service, she found him in her kitchen; he had found his own way in, and dressed himself a salad which he was calmly eating.

After the Poles, it was Père Colmiche, an old man reputed to have committed atrocities in 1793. He lived by the river in a tumbledown old pigsty. The village boys used to watch him through cracks in the wall, and throw stones which fell on the pallet where he lay, constantly racked by bronchial coughing; he had very long hair, inflamed eyelids and a tumour on the arm bigger than his head. She got him clean linen, tried to clean up his hovel, dreamed about moving him into the bakehouse, without giving Madame Aubain any trouble. When the cancer burst, she dressed it every day, sometimes brought him cake, put him out in the sunshine on a bale of hay; and the poor old fellow, dribbling and shaking, would thank her in his feeble voice, was afraid of losing her, and stretched out his hands as soon as he saw her going. He died; she had a Mass said for the repose of his soul.

On that particular day she had a great stroke of fortune; at dinnertime, Madame de Larsonnière's negro arrived, holding the parrot in its cage, with its perch, chain, and padlock. A note from the Baroness informed Madame Aubain that her husband had been promoted to a Prefecture and they were leaving that evening; and she begged her to accept the bird as a memento and token of her respects.

The parrot had filled Félicité's thoughts for some time past, for it came from America; that word reminded her of Victor, and prompted her to question the negro about it. She had even once said: 'Madame would be so happy to have it!'

The negro had repeated the remark to his mistress, who, being unable to take the bird with her, disposed of it in that way.

IV

He was called Loulou. His body was green, his wingtips pink, the front of his head blue, his breast gold.

But he had the tiresome habit of chewing his perch, pulling out his feathers, scattering his droppings, upsetting the water in his birdbath; Madame Aubain found him a nuisance, and gave him to Félicité for good.

She began training him; soon he could repeat: 'Nice boy! Your servant, Sir! Hail Mary!' He was placed beside the door, and a number of people were surprised that he did not answer to the name of Jacquot, since all parrots are called Jacquot. They described him as 'silly as a goose, thick as a plank'; Félicité was deeply wounded every time by such remarks. How odd that Loulou should perversely fall speechless as soon as anyone looked at him!

All the same he was eager for company; for on Sundays, while *those* Mesdemoiselles Rochefeuille, Monsieur de Houppeville and some new friends: Onfroy, the apothecary, Monsieur Varin and Captain Mathieu, were playing their game of cards, he would bang the window-panes with his wings and make such a dreadful fuss that one could not hear oneself speak.

There was no doubt that he found Bourais's face very funny. As soon as he saw him Loulou began to laugh and laugh with might and main. His peals of laughter rebounded round the courtyard, the echo repeated them, the neighbours looked out of their windows, laughing too; and to avoid being seen by the parrot, Monsieur Bourais would slink along the wall, hat pulled down to hide his face, go down to the river and then come in by the garden gate; and the looks he gave the bird were anything but affectionate.

The butcher's boy had once given Loulou a smack for taking the liberty of sticking his head into his basket; and ever since Loulou was always trying to nip him through his shirt. Fabu threatened to wring his neck, although he was not really cruel, despite his tattooed arms and heavy whiskers. On the contrary! he had rather a liking for the parrot, and in jovial mood went so far as to teach him some swear-words. Félicité, horrified at such behaviour, put him in the kitchen. His chain was removed, and he had the run of the house.

When he went down the stairs, he would press the curve of his beak against the steps, and raise first his right foot, then the left; and she was afraid that such gymnastics would make him dizzy. He fell ill, could not talk or eat any more. This was due to a callus under his tongue, such as chickens sometimes have. She cured him by peeling off this bit of skin with her nails. One day Monsieur Paul was foolish enough to blow cigar smoke up his nose; another time when Madame Loumeau was teasing him with the tip of her sunshade he snapped up the ferrule; finally he got lost.

She had put him down on the grass to take the air, gone off for a moment, and when she came back, there was no parrot! First she hunted for him in the bushes, down by the river, and on the rooftops, paying no heed to her mistress who was shouting at her: 'Do take care! you must be crazy!' Then she searched all the gardens of Pont-l'Évêque, and kept stopping passers-by—'You haven't by any chance seen my parrot, have you?' If they did not know the parrot, she described him. Suddenly she thought she could make out something green, fluttering behind the windmills at the bottom of the hill. But on top of the hill, there was nothing! A pedlar told her that he had come across him a short while ago at Saint-Melaine, in Mère Simon's shop. She hurried there. They did not know what she was talking about. At last she came home, exhausted, her slippers torn to shreds, with death in her heart; she sat down in the middle of the seat by Madame, and was recounting all her efforts, when she felt a light touch on her shoulder: Loulou! What on earth had he been doing? Perhaps he had been on a tour of the neighbourhood!

She had difficulty getting over this experience, or rather she never got over it.

Following a chill, she had an attack of quinsy; shortly afterwards, ear trouble. Three years later she had gone deaf, and used to talk very loudly, even in church. Although her sins could have been published in every corner of the diocese without bringing her into disrepute or upsetting anyone, Monsieur le curé judged it more suitable in future to hear her confessions in the sacristy.

On top of all her other troubles, buzzings in her ears made her imagine things. Her mistress would often tell her: 'Goodness! how stupid you are!' and she would reply: 'Yes, Madame', as she looked round for something.

The narrow range of her ideas shrank even further, and the pealing of the bells, the lowing of the cattle ceased to exist for her. Every living thing moved in ghostly silence. A single sound now reached her ears: the voice of the parrot.

As if to entertain her he would reproduce the regular clicking of the spit turning, the fishmonger's shrill cry, the sawing of the carpenter who lived opposite; and when the doorbell rang, he would imitate Madame Aubain: 'Félicité! the door! the door!'

They would hold conversations, he repeating *ad nauseam* the three phrases of his repertory, and she answering with words which were equally disconnected but came from the heart. In her isolation Loulou was almost like a son, a lover to her. He would climb up her fingers, nibble her lips, cling to her bodice; and as she bent forward, wagging her head as nurses do, the wide wings of her bonnet and those of the bird quivered in unison.

When the clouds banked up and thunder rumbled, he would squawk, perhaps remembering the downpours of his native forests. The water streaming down sent him into a frenzy; he would frantically flutter about, go up to the ceiling, knock everything over, and fly out of the window to splash about in the garden; but he would soon come in again, and hopping up and down on one of the firedogs to dry his feathers, displayed his beak and his tail alternately.

One morning in the terrible winter of 1837, she had put him down in front of the hearth because of the cold, when she found him dead, hanging head down in the middle of the cage, his claws clutching the bars. He had probably died of a stroke. She thought he might have been poisoned with parsley; and despite the lack of any evidence, her suspicions settled on Fabu.

She cried so much that her mistress said to her: 'All right! Have him stuffed!'

She went to ask the pharmacist for advice, as he had always treated the parrot kindly.

He wrote to Le Havre. A certain Fellacher took on the job. But as parcels sent by the mail-coach were sometimes lost, she decided to take this one herself as far as Honfleur.

Leafless apple trees lined either side of the road. The ditches were frozen over. Dogs barked round the farms; and with her hands tucked under her cape, her little black sabots and her bag she walked briskly along the middle of the roadway.

She crossed the forest, passed by Le Haut-Chêne, reached Saint-Gatien.

Behind her, in a cloud of dust, gathering speed downhill, a mail-coach driven at full gallop hurtled on like a whirlwind. At the sight of this woman who did not move out of the way, the driver stood up above the hood, and the postillion shouted too, while the four horses, which he could not rein in, galloped all the faster; the two leading ones just missed her; with a jerk on the reins he drove them on to the verge, but raising his arm in fury, he lashed out with his great whip, catching her such a mighty blow from waist to head that she fell over backwards.

Her first action on recovering her senses was to open the basket.

Fortunately Loulou was unharmed. She felt her right cheek burning; when she touched it her hands came away red. It was bleeding.

She sat down on a pile of stones, dabbed her face with her kerchief, then ate a crust of bread, which she had put in her basket as a precaution, and consoled herself for her injury by looking at the bird.

When she came to the top of the hill at Ecquemauville she could see the lights of Honfleur twinkling in the darkness like a mass of stars; blurred in the distance, the sea stretched out in all directions. Then a sudden weakness made her stop; and her wretched childhood, her first unhappy love affair, her nephew's departure, Virginie's death, all came back to her at once like a rising tide, and welling up in her throat made her choke.

Then she asked to speak to the captain of the boat; and without telling him what her parcel contained, asked him to take great care of it.

Fellacher kept the parrot for a long time. He was always promising it for the following week; after six months he reported that a box had gone off; that was the last she heard. Loulou would probably never come back. 'They must have stolen him!' she thought.

At last he arrived—looking splendid, standing on a tree branch, which was screwed on to a mahogany pedestal, one foot in the air, head cocked sideways, and biting a nut which the taxidermist, whose tastes ran to the grandiose, had gilded.

She shut him up in her room.

This place, to which few people were ever admitted, looked like a chapel and a bazaar combined, with its collection of religious objects and assorted oddments.

A large wardrobe obstructed the opening of the door. Facing the window overlooking the garden, another small round one gave on to the courtyard; a table, beside the humble bed, bore a water jug, two combs and a block of blue soap in a chipped dish. On the walls were displayed: rosaries, medals, several pictures of the Virgin, a holy-water stoup fashioned out of a coconut shell; on the chest of drawers, draped like an altar with a cloth, the seashell box that Victor had given her; then a watering-can and a ball, some exercise-books, the geography picture-book, a pair of bootees; and hanging from the nail that held the mirror the little plush hat! Félicité carried this sort of respect so far that she even kept one of Monsieur's frock-coats. All the old odds and ends for which Madame Aubain had no further use were picked up by Félicité for her room. That is how there came to be artificial flowers along the edge of the chest of drawers, and a portrait of the Comte d'Artois in the window recess.

Loulou was installed on a small shelf fixed on to a chimney-breast which projected into the room. Every morning as she awoke she saw him by the first light of day, and would then recall the days gone by and the smallest details of unimportant events, without sorrow, quite serenely.

Never communicating with anyone, she lived with senses dulled as if sleepwalking. The Corpus Christi processions would bring her back to life. She would call on the neighbours to collect candlesticks and mats to embellish the altar of repose being set up in the street.

In church she always gazed at the Holy Spirit, and noticed that he looked something like the parrot. The likeness seemed still more evident in a popular print of Our Lord's baptism. With his purple wings and emerald green body he was the very image of Loulou.

She bought the print and hung it up in place of the Comte d'Artois, with the result that she could take them in together with a single glance. They became associated in her mind, so that the parrot became sanctified from this connexion with the Holy Spirit, which in turn became more lifelike and readily intelligible in her eyes. The Father could never have chosen to express himself through a dove, for those creatures cannot speak, but rather one of Loulou's ancestors. And Félicité would look at the print as she said her prayers, but with a sidelong glance from time to time at the bird.

She wanted to join the Children of Mary. Madame Aubain talked her out of it.

An important event was suddenly in the offing: Paul's marriage.

He had been first a lawyer's clerk, then in trade, in the Customs, in the Revenue, and had begun an application to the Waterways and Forests Department; now, at thirty, by some heaven-sent inspiration, he had suddenly discovered the right path: Registration Office for Deeds! There he demonstrated such remarkable talents that an auditor had offered him his daughter's hand, and promised to take him under his wing.

Paul, who now took life seriously, brought her to visit his mother.

She sneered at the way things were done at Pont-l'Évêque, acted high and mighty, upset Félicité. Madame Aubain felt a sense of relief when she left.

The following week came news of Monsieur Bourais's death, in Lower Brittany, in an inn. Rumours of suicide were confirmed; doubts were raised as to his honesty. Madame Aubain examined her accounts, and it was not long before she became aware of the catalogue of his infamies:

embezzlement of arrears, disguised sales of timber, forged receipts, etc. In addition he had fathered a natural child, and had had 'relations with a person from Dozulé'.

Such base conduct grieved Madame Aubain deeply. In March 1853 she suddenly felt pains in her chest; her tongue seemed to have an opaque coating, leeches did nothing to relieve the difficulty in breathing; and on the ninth evening she expired, being just seventy-two years old.

People thought she was younger, because of her brown hair, worn in coils round her pale, pockmarked face. Few friends missed her, for her haughty ways put people off.

Félicité wept for her, but not just as a servant for an employer. The idea that Madame should die before her she found disturbing, against the natural order of things, unacceptable and monstrous.

Ten days later—the time it took to hurry there from Besançon—the heirs arrived. The daughter-in-law ransacked the drawers, picked out some pieces of furniture, sold the rest, and then they went back to the Registration Office.

Madame's easy chair, her pedestal table, her footwarmer, the eight upright chairs had all gone. Yellow squares in the middle of the walls marked where the prints had been. They had taken the two children's cots, with their mattresses, and every trace of Virginie's things had vanished from the cupboard! Félicité went back upstairs, sick with grief.

Next day there was a notice on the door; the apothecary shouted in her ear that the house was for sale.

She reeled, and was obliged to sit down.

What grieved her most was the thought of having to leave her room— so convenient for poor Loulou. Gazing at him in anguish, she implored the help of the Holy Spirit, and fell into the idolatrous habit of saying her prayers on her knees in front of the parrot. Sometimes the sun coming through the skylight would catch his glass eye, so that a great beam of light flashed out from it, and this entranced her.

She had been left an annuity of 380 francs by her mistress. The garden provided her with vegetables. As for clothes, she had enough to wear for the rest of her days, and saved the cost of lighting by going to bed as soon as it was dusk.

She hardly ever went out, to avoid the secondhand shop, where some of the furniture from the house was on display. Since her dizzy spells, she was lame in one leg; and as she grew weaker, Mère Simon, whose grocery shop had come to grief, came in every morning to chop wood and pump water for her.

Her sight began to go. The shutters were never open any more. Many years went by. The house remained unlet and unsold.

For fear of being evicted Félicité never asked for repairs. The roof laths became rotten; for the whole of one winter her bolster was soaked. After Easter she began spitting blood.

At that Mère Simon called in the doctor. Félicité wanted to know what was wrong with her. But she was too deaf to hear the answer, and caught just one word: 'Pneumonia.' That was a word she knew, and she softly replied: 'Oh! like Madame', finding it perfectly natural to follow her mistress.

The time for the altars of repose was drawing near.

The first was always at the bottom of the hill, the second in front of the post office, the third about halfway up the street. There were rival claims for that one; the ladies of the parish finally chose Madame Aubain's courtyard.

The fever got worse, and she found it harder and harder to breathe. Félicité was distressed that she was not doing anything for the altar. At the very least she could have put something on it! Then she thought of the parrot. It was not suitable; the neighbours objected. But the curé granted permission; that made her so happy that she begged him to accept Loulou, the only valuable thing she owned, when she died.

From the Tuesday to the Saturday, the eve of Corpus Christi, she coughed more frequently. By evening her face was drawn with illness, her lips stuck to her gums, she began to vomit; and first thing next morning she had a priest called.

Three women stood round her during the administration of Extreme Unction. Then she announced that she needed to speak to Fabu.

He arrived in his Sunday best, ill at ease in this funereal atmosphere.

'Forgive me,' she said, making an effort to stretch out her arm, 'I thought it was you who killed him!'

What could such nonsense mean? Suspecting him of murder, a man like him! And he waxed indignant, was about to make a fuss. 'Her mind's begun to wander, anyone can see that!'

Félicité spoke from time to time to shadows. The good women left. Old Mère Simon had her lunch.

A little later she took Loulou, and bringing him close to Félicité said:

'Now then! Say goodbye to him!'

Although he was not a corpse, he was all worm-eaten, one of his wings was broken, the stuffing was coming out of his stomach. But now quite blind, she kissed his head and held him against her cheek. Mère Simon took him back, to put him on the altar of repose.

V

From the meadows rose the scent of summer; flies buzzed; the sun glinted on the river, warmed the slates. Mère Simon had come back into the room and was quietly dozing.

The sound of bells ringing woke her up; they were coming out of Vespers. Félicité's delirium calmed down. As she thought about the procession, she could see it as if she had been following it.

All the schoolchildren, the choristers, and the fire brigade walked on the pavements, while down the middle of the street advanced first the uniformed verger, armed with his halberd, then the beadle with a great cross, the schoolmaster superintending the boys, the nun fussing over her little girls; three of the prettiest, with curly hair like angels, were throwing rose petals up in the air; the deacon, with arms outstretched, conducted the band; and two thurifers turned round at every step towards the Blessed Sacrament, borne by Monsieur le curé in his splendid chasuble, beneath a canopy of crimson velvet carried by four churchwardens. A throng of people pressed on behind, between the white cloths hung out over the walls of the houses; and they came to the foot of the hill.

A cold sweat bathed Félicité's temples. Mère Simon wiped it off with a cloth, telling herself that one day she would have to go through it too.

The noise from the crowd swelled, was very loud for a moment, faded away.

A volley of shots rattled the windows. It was the postillions saluting the monstrance. Félicité rolled her eyes, and said, as loudly as she could, 'Is he all right?'—worrying about the parrot.

Her death agony began. Laboured breathing, coming faster and faster, made her sides heave. Bubbles of froth formed at the corners of her mouth, and she was trembling all over.

Soon the booming of the ophicleides could be heard, the clear voices of the children, the deeper tones of the men. They all fell silent now and then, and the tramping of feet, deadened by flowers strewn on the ground, sounded like a herd of cattle moving over grass.

The clergy appeared in the courtyard. Mère Simon climbed on a chair to reach the little round window, so that she could look down on to the altar of repose.

Garlands of greenery hung on the altar, which was decorated with a frill of English lace. In the middle was a small frame containing relics, two orange trees stood at the corners, and all the way along were silver candlesticks and china vases, from which projected sunflowers, lilies, peonies, foxgloves, bunches of hydrangea. This pile of bright colours sloped down diagonally from the first floor to the carpet spread over the paving stones; and some rare objects caught the eye. A silver-gilt sugar bowl had a wreath of violets, pendants of Alençon gemstones sparkled on a bed of moss, two Chinese screens displayed landscapes. All that could be seen of Loulou, hidden beneath some roses, was the blue front of his head, like a plaque of lapis-lazuli.

The churchwardens, the choristers, the children, formed up round the three sides of the courtyard. The priest slowly mounted the steps and set on the lace the great golden sun, which shone radiantly. All knelt. There was a great silence. Then the censers, swung with might and main, slid up and down their chains.

A cloud of blue incense smoke rose up to Félicité's room. She opened wide her nostrils as she breathed it in deeply, in an act at once sensual and mystical. She closed her eyes. Her lips smiled. Her heartbeats grew steadily slower, fainter every time, softer, like a fountain running dry, like an echo fading; and as she breathed her last, she thought she saw, as the heavens opened, a gigantic parrot hovering over her head.

The Necklace

Translated by David Coward

She was one of those pretty, delightful girls who, apparently by some error of Fate, get themselves born the daughters of very minor civil servants. She had no dowry, no expectations, no means of meeting some rich, important man who would understand, love, and marry her. So she went along with a proposal made by a junior clerk in the Ministry of Education.

She dressed simply, being unable to afford anything better, but she was every whit as unhappy as any daughter of good family who has come down in the world. Women have neither rank nor class, and their beauty, grace, and charm do service for birthright and connections. Natural guile, instinctive elegance, and adaptability are what determines their place in the hierarchy, and a girl of no birth to speak of may easily be the equal of any society lady.

She was unhappy all the time, for she felt that she was intended for a life of refinement and luxury. She was made unhappy by the run-down apartment they lived in, the peeling walls, the battered chairs, and the ugly curtains. Now all this, which any other woman of her station might never even have noticed, was torture to her and made her very angry. The spectacle of the young Breton peasant girl who did the household chores stirred sad regrets and impossible fancies. She dreamed of silent antechambers hung with oriental tapestries, lit by tall, bronze candelabras, and of two tall footmen in liveried breeches asleep in the huge armchairs, dozing in the heavy heat of a stove. She dreamed of great drawing-rooms dressed with old silk, filled with fine furniture which showed off trinkets beyond price, and of pretty little parlours, filled with perfumes and just made for intimate talk at five in the afternoon with one's closest friends who would be the most famous and sought-after men of the day whose attentions were much coveted and desired by all women.

When she sat down to dinner at the round table spread with a three-day-old cloth, facing her husband who always lifted the lid of the soup-tureen and declared delightedly: 'Ah! Stew! Splendid! There's nothing I like better than a nice stew . . .', she dreamed of elegant dinners, gleaming silverware, and tapestries which peopled the walls with mythical characters and strange birds in enchanted forests; she dreamed of exquisite dishes served on fabulous china plates, of pretty compliments whispered into willing ears and received with Sphinx-like smiles over the pink flesh of a trout or the wings of a hazel hen.

She had no fine dresses, no jewellery, nothing. And that was all she cared about; she felt that God had made her for such things. She would have given anything to be popular, envied, attractive, and in demand.

She had a friend who was rich, a friend from her convent days, on whom she never called now, for she was always so unhappy afterwards. Sometimes, for days on end, she would weep tears of sorrow, regret, despair, and anguish.

One evening her husband came home looking highly pleased with himself. In his hand he brandished a large envelope.

'Look,' he said, 'I've got something for you.'

She tore the paper flap eagerly and extracted a printed card bearing these words:

The Minister of Education and Madame Georges Ramponneau request the pleasure of the company of Monsieur and Madame Loisel at the Ministry Buildings on the evening of 18 January.

Instead of being delighted as her husband had hoped, she tossed the invitation peevishly onto the table and muttered: 'What earthly use is that to me?'

'But, darling, I thought you'd be happy. You never go anywhere and it's an opportunity, a splendid opportunity! I had the dickens of a job getting hold of an invite. Everybody's after them; they're very much in demand and not many are handed out to us clerks. You'll be able to see all the big nobs there.'

She looked at him irritably and said shortly: 'And what am I supposed to wear if I do go?'

He had not thought of that. He blustered: 'What about the dress you wear for the theatre? It looks all right to me . . .' The words died in his throat. He was totally disconcerted and dismayed by the sight of his wife, who had begun to cry. Two large tears rolled slowly out of the corners of her eyes and down towards the sides of her mouth.

'What's up?' he stammered. 'What's the matter?'

Making a supreme effort, she controlled her sorrows and, wiping her damp cheeks, replied quite calmly: 'Nothing. It's just that I haven't got anything to wear and consequently I shan't be going to any reception. Give the invite to one of your colleagues with a wife who is better off for clothes than I am.'

He was devastated. He went on: 'Oh come on, Mathilde. Look, what could it cost to get something suitable that would do for other occasions, something fairly simple?'

She thought for a few moments, working out her sums but also wondering how much she could decently ask for without drawing an immediate refusal and pained protests from her husband who was careful with his money. Finally, after some hesitation, she said: 'I can't say precisely, but I daresay I could get by on four hundred francs.'

He turned slightly pale, for he had been setting aside just that amount to buy a gun and finance hunting trips the following summer in the flat landscape around Nanterre with a few friends who went shooting larks there on Sundays. But he said: 'Very well. I'll give you your four hundred francs. But do try and get a decent dress.'

The day of the reception drew near and Madame Loisel appeared sad, worried, anxious. Yet all her clothes were ready. One evening her husband said: 'What's up? You haven't half been acting funny these last few days.'

She replied: 'It vexes me that I haven't got a single piece of jewellery, not one stone, that I can put on. I'll look like a church mouse. I'd almost as soon not go to the reception.'

'Wear a posy,' he said. 'It's all the rage this year. You could get two or three magnificent roses for ten francs.'

She was not convinced. 'No. . . . There's nothing so humiliating as to look poor when you're with women who are rich.'

But her husband exclaimed: 'You aren't half silly! Look, go and see your friend, Madame Forestier, and ask her to lend you some jewellery. You know her well enough for that.'

She gave a delighted cry: 'You're right! I never thought of that!'

The next day she called on her friend and told her all about her problem. Madame Forestier went over to a mirror-fronted wardrobe, took out a large casket, brought it over, unlocked it, and said to Madame Loisel: 'Choose whatever you like.'

At first she saw bracelets, then a rope of pearls and a Venetian cross made of gold and diamonds admirably fashioned. She tried on the necklaces in the mirror, and could hardly bear to take them off and give them back. She kept asking: 'Have you got anything else?'

'Yes, of course. Just look. I can't say what sort of thing you'll like best.'

All of a sudden, in a black satinwood case, she found a magnificent diamond necklace, and her heart began to beat with immoderate desire. Her hands shook as she picked it up. She fastened it around her throat over her high-necked dress and sat looking at herself in rapture. Then, diffidently, apprehensively, she asked: 'Can you lend me this? Nothing else. Just this.'

'But of course.'

She threw her arms around her friend, kissed her extravagantly, and then ran home, taking her treasure with her.

The day of the reception arrived. Madame Loisel was a success. She was the prettiest woman there, elegant, graceful, radiant, and wonderfully happy. All the men looked at her, enquired who she was, and asked to be introduced. All the cabinet secretaries and under-secretaries wanted to waltz with her. She was even noticed by the Minister himself.

She danced ecstatically, wildly, intoxicated with pleasure, giving no thought to anything else, swept along on her victorious beauty and glorious success, and floating on a cloud of happiness composed of the homage, admiration, and desire she evoked and a kind of complete and utter triumph which is so sweet to a woman's heart.

She left at about four in the morning. Since midnight her husband had been dozing in a small, empty side-room with three other men whose wives were having an enjoyable time.

He helped her on with her coat which he had fetched when it was time to go, a modest, everyday coat, a commonplace coat violently at odds with the elegance of her dress. It brought her down to earth, and she would have preferred to slip away quietly and avoid being noticed by the other women who were being arrayed in rich furs. But Loisel grabbed her by the arm: 'Wait a sec. You'll catch cold outside. I'll go and get a cab.'

But she refused to listen and ran quickly down the stairs. When they were outside in the street, there was no cab in sight. They began looking for one, hailing all the cabbies they saw driving by in the distance.

They walked down to the Seine in desperation, shivering with cold. There, on the embankment, they at last found one of those aged nocturnal hackney cabs which only emerge in Paris after dusk, as if ashamed to parade their poverty in the full light of day. It bore them back to their front door in the rue des Martyrs, and they walked sadly up to their apartment. For her it was all over, while he was thinking that he would have to be at the Ministry at ten.

Standing in front of the mirror, she took off the coat she had been wearing over her shoulders, to get a last look at herself in all her glory. Suddenly she gave a cry. The necklace was no longer round her throat!

Her husband, who was already half undressed, asked: 'What's up?'

She turned to him in a panic: 'I . . . I . . . Madame Forestier's necklace . . . I haven't got it!'

He straightened up as if thunderstruck: 'What? . . . But . . . You can't have lost it!'

They looked in the pleats of her dress, in the folds of her coat, and in her pockets. They looked everywhere. They did not find it.

Are you sure you still had it when you left the ballroom?' he asked.

'Yes, I remember fingering it in the entrance hall.'

'But if you'd lost it in the street, we'd have heard it fall. So it must be in the cab.'

'That's right. That's probably it. Did you get his number?'

'No. Did you happen to notice it?'

'No.'

They looked at each other in dismay. Finally Loisel got dressed again. 'I'm going to go back the way we came,' he said, 'to see if I can find it.' He went out. She remained as she was, still wearing her evening gown, not having the strength to go to bed, sitting disconsolately on a chair by the empty grate, her mind a blank.

Her husband returned at about seven o'clock. He had found nothing.

He went to the police station, called at newspaper offices where he advertised a reward, toured the cab companies, and tried anywhere where the faintest of hopes led him. She waited for him all day long in the same distracted condition, thinking of the appalling catastrophe which had befallen them.

Loisel came back that evening, hollow-cheeked and very pale. He had not come up with anything.

'Look,' he said, 'you'll have to write to your friend and say you broke the catch on her necklace and you are getting it repaired. That'll give us time to work out what we'll have to do.'

She wrote to his dictation.

A week later they had lost all hope.

Loisel, who had aged five years, said: 'We'll have to start thinking about replacing the necklace.'

The next day they took the case in which it had come and called on the jeweller whose name was inside. He looked through his order book.

'It wasn't me that sold the actual necklace. I only supplied the case.'

After this, they trailed round jewellers' shops, looking for a necklace just like the other one, trying to remember it, and both ill with worry and anxiety.

In a shop in the Palais Royal they found a diamond collar which they thought was identical to the one they were looking for. It cost forty thousand francs. The jeweller was prepared to let them have it for thirty-six.

They asked him not to sell it for three days. And they got him to agree to take it back for thirty-four thousand if the one that had been lost turned up before the end of February.

Loisel had eighteen thousand francs which his father had left him. He would have to borrow the rest.

He borrowed the money, a thousand francs here, five hundred there, sometimes a hundred and as little as sixty. He signed notes, agreed to pay exorbitant rates of interest, resorted to usurers and the whole tribe of moneylenders. He mortgaged the rest of his life, signed papers without knowing if he would ever be able to honour his commitments, and then, sick with worry about the future, the grim poverty which stood ready to pounce, and the prospect of all the physical privation and mental torture ahead, he went round to the jeweller's to get the new necklace with the thirty-six thousand francs which he put on the counter.

When Madame Loisel took it round, Madame Forestier said in a huff: 'You ought really to have brought it back sooner. I might have needed it.'

She did not open the case, as her friend had feared she might. If she had noticed the substitution, what would she have thought? What would she have said? Would she not have concluded she was a thief?

Then began for Madame Loisel the grindingly horrible life of the very poor. But quickly and heroically, she resigned herself to what she could not alter: their appalling debt would have to be repaid. She was determined to pay. They dismissed the maid. They moved out of their apartment and rented an attic room.

She became used to heavy domestic work and all kinds of ghastly kitchen chores. She washed dishes, wearing down her pink nails on the greasy pots and saucepans. She washed the dirty sheets, shirts, and floor-cloths by hand and hung them up to dry on a line; each morning she took the rubbish down to the street and carried the water up, pausing for breath on each landing. And, dressed like any working-class woman, she shopped at the fruiterer's, the grocer's, and the butcher's, with a basket over her arm, haggling, frequently abused and always counting every penny.

Each month they had to settle some accounts, renew others, and bargain for time.

Her husband worked in the evenings doing accounts for a shopkeeper and quite frequently sat up into the early hours doing copying work at five sous a page.

They lived like this for ten years.

By the time ten years had gone by, they had repaid everything, with not a penny outstanding, in spite of the extortionate conditions and including the accumulated interest.

Madame Loisel looked old now. She had turned into the battling, hard, uncouth housewife who rules working-class homes. Her hair was untidy, her skirts were askew, and her hands were red. She spoke in a gruff voice and scrubbed floors on her hands and knees. But sometimes, when her husband had gone to the office, she would sit by the window and think of that evening long ago when she had been so beautiful and so admired.

What might not have happened had she not lost the necklace? Who could tell? Who could possibly tell? Life is so strange, so fickle! How little is needed to make or break us!

One Sunday, needing a break from her heavy working week, she went out for a stroll on the Champs-Elysées. Suddenly she caught sight of a woman pushing a child in a pram. It was Madame Forestier, still young, still beautiful, and still attractive.

Madame Loisel felt apprehensive. Should she speak to her? Yes, why not? Now that she had paid in full, she would tell her everything. Why not? She went up to her.

'Hello, Jeanne.'

The friend did not recognize her and was taken aback at being addressed so familiarly by a common woman in the street. She stammered: 'But . . . I'm sorry . . . I don't know . . . There's some mistake.'

'No mistake. I'm Mathilde Loisel.'

Her friend gave a cry: 'But my poor Mathilde, how you've changed!'

'Yes, I've been through some hard times since I saw you, very hard times. And it was all on your account.'

'On my account? Whatever do you mean?'

'Do you remember that diamond necklace you lent me to go to the reception at the Ministry?'

'Yes. What about it?'

'Well I lost it.'

'Lost it? But you returned it to me.'

'No, I returned another one just like it. And we've been paying for it these past ten years. You know, it wasn't easy for us. We had nothing. . . . But it's over and done with now, and I'm glad.'

Madame Forestier stopped. 'You mean you bought a diamond necklace to replace mine?'

'Yes. And you never noticed the difference, did you? They were exactly alike.' And she smiled a proud, innocent smile.

Madame Forestier looked very upset and, taking both her hands in hers, said:

'Oh, my poor Mathilde! But it was only an imitation necklace. It couldn't have been worth much more than five hundred francs! . . .'

GUY DE MAUPASSANT (1850–1893)

At Sea

Translated by David Coward

The following report recently appeared in several newspapers:

Boulogne-sur-Mer, 22 January: From a correspondent. News of a horrific tragedy has shocked local fishermen here already severely demoralized by similar disasters over the last two years. A fishing-vessel, commanded by its owner, Captain Javel, attempting to make port, was driven too far west on to the breakwater of the harbour wall where it broke up. In spite of the efforts of the lifeboat and the use of rocket-launched life-lines, four crewmen and the cabin boy were lost. The bad weather shows no signs of letting up. Further losses are feared.

Who is this Captain Javel? The brother of the Javel with one arm?

If the poor mariner who was washed overboard and now perhaps lies dead in the wrecked timbers of his shattered boat is indeed the man I'm thinking of, then eighteen years ago he was also involved in another tragedy, which was as awesome and simple as disasters at sea always are.

The elder Javel was then skipper of a trawler.

Now the trawler is the very best kind of fishing-boat there is. Built to withstand any weather, broad-beamed, bobbing like a cork on the surging waves, always at sea, continually buffeted by the grim, salt winds of the English Channel, she works the sea tirelessly, bent under taut sail, dragging a great net slung over the side which drags the bottom of the sea, scouring and scooping up any creatures lurking under rocks: flatfish which cling to the sand, great lumbering crabs with hooked claws, and lobsters with pointed whiskers.

When the wind is fresh and the sea choppy, the boat begins to fish. The net is slung on a long wooden iron-clad boom which is lowered by means of two hawsers paid out by windlasses fore and aft. As it drifts with wind and current, the boat drags the trawl-net with it, plundering and devastating the sea bed.

On board, Javel had with him his younger brother, four crew, and a cabin boy. He had sailed out of Boulogne in fine, clear weather to lay his drag-net.

Soon, however, the wind got up and a sudden squall forced the trawler to run before it. She got as far as the English coast. But the raging sea tore at the cliffs and flung itself at the land, making it impossible to enter harbour. So the small boat headed back out to sea and made for the coast of France. But the storm continued unabated, making the breakwaters impassable and shrouding the approaches to all ports with spray, thunder, and danger.

The trawler put about again, running on the backs of the waves, pitching and tossing, shuddering, huge seas breaking over her decks, battered by walls of water, but in good heart for all that, for she was used to heavy weather which sometimes kept her out for five or six days toing and froing between the two neighbouring countries and unable to land in either.

Eventually, the gale decreased. Since they were in open water, though there was a heavy swell running, the skipper ordered the drag-net to be broken out.

The cumbersome tackle was lowered over the side, and two men in the bow and two in the stern began feeding the ropes holding it through the windlasses. Suddenly it touched bottom. At the same instant, a huge sea made the boat heel over and the younger Javel, who was in the bow directing operations, was thrown off balance and trapped his arm between the rope, which had momentarily gone slack under the impact, and the wooden barrel of the windlass over which it was being paid out. He made desperate efforts to free it, using his other hand to lift the hawser. But the net was already trawling and the taut rope was immovable.

Rigid with pain, he gave a shout. The other hands all came running. His brother left the helm. They heaved on the rope in an attempt to free the arm which was being crushed. They could not budge it. 'We got to cut it,' said one sailor, and from his pocket took a large knife. With a couple of strokes, it could save young Javel's arm.

But cutting the rope would mean losing the net, and the net was worth money, a lot of money—1,500 francs. And it belonged to Javel senior, who was a man who aimed to keep what was his.

In an agony of indecision, he shouted: 'No! Don't cut it. Wait, I'll bring her head round' And he ran to the wheelhouse and put the helm hard over.

The boat barely responded, inhibited by the drag of the net, which absorbed its momentum, and borne along by the force of drift and wind.

Young Javel was now on his knees, teeth clenched, eyes bulging. He did not speak. His brother returned, still afraid one of the sailors would use his knife, and said: 'Hang on! Don't cut it! We'll let go the anchor!'

The anchor was dropped, and all its chain with it. Then they began turning the boat on the capstan to reduce the tension on the ropes holding the drag-net. Eventually they slackened and released the arm which now hung lifelessly in the blood-stained cloth of its sleeve.

Young Javel looked numb. They removed his jersey and were horrified by what they saw—a pulp of mangled flesh spurting blood as fast as though it were being evacuated by a pump. The man took one look at his arm and said: 'It's buggered.'

The haemorrhage spread a pool of blood on the deck. One of the crew yelled: 'He's goin' to be drained dry. We got to tie that artery up tight.'

They found a length of twine, thick, brown, tarred twine, and, looping it around the arm above the break, pulled it as tight as they could. The spurting slowed and finally stopped altogether.

Young Javel stood up, his arm dangling uselessly at his side. He took hold of it with his other hand, lifted it, turned it this way and that and shook it. It was completely shattered. Every bone in it was broken. Only the muscles still joined it to his body. He stared at it grim-faced and thoughtful. He sat down on a furled sail. His shipmates said he should keep the wound wet to prevent gangrene setting in.

They left a bucket within reach and every few minutes he dipped into it with a tumbler and bathed the ghastly mess by trickling fresh water over it.

'You'd be more comfy below,' said his brother. He went. But an hour later he came back up on deck. He did not like being on his own and besides he preferred fresh air. He sat down on the sail again and bathed his arm some more.

The fishing was good. Broad-backed, white-bellied fish littered the deck around him, twitching in the spasms of death. He stared at them, bathing his mangled arm all the while.

As they were about to put back to Boulogne, the wind suddenly picked up again. The tiny vessel resumed its headlong flight, pitching and reeling wildly, jolting and jarring the injured man.

Darkness fell. The heavy weather continued until first light. As the sun rose, they made out the coast of England again, but as the sea was moderating, they headed back to France, beating to windward.

Towards evening, young Javel called to his comrades and showed them spots of black, ugly signs perhaps that the arm which no longer belonged to him was beginning to go bad.

The sailors all had a look and said what they thought:

'Could be gangrene,' suggested one.

'It ought to have sea-water on it,' declared another.

So they brought a bucket of sea-water and poured it over the wound. The injured man's face turned grey. He gritted his teeth and winced but did not cry out.

When the pain had subsided, he turned to his brother and said: 'Give us your knife.' His brother gave him the knife.

'Lift my arm up. Hold it straight and keep it like that.'

His brother did what he asked.

Then he began to cut. He worked carefully, deliberately, slicing through the remaining tendons with the razor-sharp blade. And soon all that was left was a stump. He heaved a deep sigh and said: 'Had to be done. I'd a been a goner for sure.'

He seemed relieved and breathed deeply. Then he resumed pouring water on what was left of his arm.

That night the weather remained foul and they were unable to make land.

When it got light, young Javel picked up his severed arm and stared at it for some time. Gangrene had set in. His mates came and had a look too. They passed it round, prodded it, turned it over, and held it to their noses.

His brother said: 'Time you chucked the thing over the side.'

But young Javel shouted angrily: 'I'll do no such thing! I don't want to! I can do what I like with it! It's my arm!'

He took it back and put it carefully between his feet.

'That'll not stop it going off,' said his brother. Then the crippled Javel had an idea. When they were out for long periods at sea, they packed their catch in barrels of salt to prevent it going bad.

He asked: 'How'd it be if I bunged it in the pickling-water?'

'Now there's a notion,' said the others.

They emptied one of the barrels which contained the last few days' haul and placed the arm at the bottom. They tipped salt over it and then put the fish back one by one.

One of the sailors joked: 'As long as we don't sell it with the rest of the catch!'

Everyone laughed, except the Javel brothers.

The wind was still strong. Thy headed into it and tacked about within sight of Boulogne until ten next morning. All this time, the injured man continued to bathe his arm.

From time to time he got up and walked the length of the boat and back.

At the wheel, his brother watched him, shaking his head.

They finally sailed into port.

The doctor examined the wound and said it was on the mend. He dressed it properly and ordered complete rest. But Javel refused to take to his bed until he had reclaimed his arm, and he hurried back to the quayside to find the barrel which he had marked with a cross.

His mates emptied it for him and he picked up the arm, perfectly preserved in the brine. It was wrinkled but otherwise in good condition. He wrapped it in a towel he had brought for the purpose and went home.

His wife and children carefully inspected this fragment of their father, feeling the fingers, poking out grains of salt from under the nails. Then they sent for a carpenter who measured it up for a miniature coffin.

The next day, the whole of the crew of the trawler walked to the cemetery behind the severed arm. The two brothers, side by side, led the procession. The parish sexton carried the corpse tucked under one arm.

Young Javel never went back to sea. He got some job or other in the docks and when later on he talked about his accident, he would always add in a confidential whisper: 'If my brother had been willing to cut the line, I'd still have my arm to this day. No doubt about it. But he wasn't the sort who could ever let go of anything that belonged to him.'

Gloomy Tale, Gloomier Teller

For Monsieur Coquelin cadet
Ut declamatio fiat.

Translated by Robert Baldick

I was invited that evening, in a very formal fashion, to a supper-party
given by some playwrights to celebrate a colleague's success. It was at
B——'s, the restaurant patronized by the writing fraternity.

To begin with, the meal was naturally sombre.

However, after a few glasses of vintage Léoville had been tossed off,
the conversation grew livelier. All the more so in that it turned on the
constant duels which formed the subject of a great many Parisian conversations about that time. Each guest, with appropriate nonchalance,
recalled brandishing a sword and tried to insinuate, casually, vague ideas
of intimidation under a show of scientific theories and of knowing winks
on the subject of fencing and shooting. The most ingenuous of them all,
who was rather drunk, seemed to be absorbed in imitating a second's
cross-stroke, over his plate, with his knife and fork.

All of a sudden, one of the guests, Monsieur D—— (a man well up in
all the tricks of the theatrical trade, a master at constructing plots, and
altogether the playwright who has afforded more proof than all the rest
of knowing how 'to bring off a success'), exclaimed:

'Ah! What would you say, gentlemen, if you had been in my place the
other day?'

'That's true!' replied the guests. 'You were that Monsieur de Saint-
Sever's second, weren't you?'

'How about telling us—but honestly—what happened?'

'If you like,' replied D——, 'although I still feel sad at heart when I
think of it.'

After a few silent puffs at his cigarette, D—— took up his story (which
I now leave him to tell) as follows:

'A fortnight ago, one Monday, at seven o'clock in the morning, I was
awoken by a ring at the bell: I thought it was Peragallo. A card was
brought in to me, and on it I read: Raoul de Saint-Sever. It was the name
of my best friend at school. We had not seen each other for ten years.

'He came in.

'It was him all right!

' "It's been a long time since we last met," I said to him. "I'm delighted to see you again! We can chat about old times over breakfast. I suppose you have just arrived from Brittany?"

' "I got here yesterday," he said.

'I pulled on a dressing-gown, poured out some Madeira, and once I had sat down, I went on:

' "Raoul, you look worried and thoughtful. Is that normal?"

' "No, I'm suffering from an outburst of emotion."

' "Of emotion? Have you lost some money on the Stock Exchange?"

'He shook his head.

' "Have you ever heard of duels to the death?" he asked me very simply.

'The question surprised me, I must admit: it was so unexpected.

' "What an absurd question!" I replied, to keep the dialogue going.

'And I looked at him.

'Remembering his literary tastes, I imagined that he had come to ask my opinion about the denouement of a play he had written in the silence of the countryside.

' "Have I ever heard of duels to the death? But it's my profession as a playwright to think up, arrange, and settle affairs of that sort. Indeed, duels are my speciality, and everyone agrees that I excel at them. Don't you ever read the Monday papers?"

' "Well," he said, "as it happens, it is a question of something like that."

'I examined him. Raoul seemed pensive, absent-minded. His eyes and voice were quiet and ordinary. There was a great deal of Surville about him at that moment . . . indeed Surville in his best parts. I told myself that he was in the grip of inspiration and that he might have some talent—undeveloped talent, but something all the same.

' "Quick!" I said. "The situation! Tell me the situation! Perhaps if we go into it thoroughly. . . ."

' "The situation?" Raoul replied, opening his eyes wide. "But it's very simple. Yesterday morning, on arriving at my hotel, I found an invitation waiting for me, to a ball that very evening, at Madame de Fréville's house in the Rue Saint-Honoré. I had to go. There, in the course of the evening—you can imagine what must have happened—I found myself obliged to throw my glove in a gentleman's face, in front of everybody."

'I realized that he was acting the first scene of his play for my benefit.

' "Oh!" I said. "But how do you lead up to that? Yes, it's a beginning. There's youth and fire in it. But the rest? the motive? the arrangement of the scene? the idea of the play? the whole concept, in fact? In its broad outlines. . . . Go on! Go on!"

' "It was a question of an insult to my mother, my dear fellow," replied Raoul, who did not appear to be listening. "My Mother. Is that an adequate motive?" '

(Here D—— broke off to look at the guests, who had been unable to refrain from smiling at these last words.)

'You smile, gentlemen?' he said. 'So did I. The idea of "fighting for my mother" above all struck me as nauseatingly artificial and old-fashioned. It was appalling. I imagined the thing on the stage. The audience would have held its sides with laughing. I was dismayed by Raoul's lack of theatrical experience, and I was on the point of dissuading him from what I took to be the stillborn plot of the crudest of plays, when he added:

' "Prosper, a friend of mine from Brittany, is downstairs: Prosper Vidal. He came with me from Rennes, and he is waiting for me in the carriage outside. In Paris, you are the only person I know. Tell me, will you act as my second? My adversary's seconds will be calling on me in an hour. If you agree, get dressed quickly. We have a five-hour journey before us in the train from here to Erquelines."

'Then, and only then, did I realize that he was talking to me about something from life, from real life! I was flabbergasted. It was only after a while that I took his hand. I was terribly upset. I'm no fonder of cold steel than anybody else; but I do believe that I should have been less disturbed if I had been the person involved.'

'That's true! People do feel like that!' exclaimed the guests, who wanted to profit by the remark.

' "You ought to have told me that straight away!" I replied. "I shan't indulge in any flowery phrases. Those are only fit for the public. Rely on me. Go downstairs, and I'll join you in a moment." '

(Here D—— paused, visibly stirred by the memory of the incident which he had just described to us.)

'Once I was alone,' he went on, 'I worked out my plan, while I dressed quickly. There was no question here of adding anything: the situation (admittedly commonplace for the theatre) struck me as perfectly adequate for life. And its sentimental side, if I may say so without offence, disappeared in my eyes when I thought that what was at stake was my poor Raoul's life. I went downstairs without wasting a minute.

'The other second, Monsieur Prosper Vidal, was a young doctor, very restrained in his words and gestures; with a distinguished, rather stern profile, like Maurice Coste in his old parts. He seemed to me to be ideal for the occasion. You can picture him, can't you?'

All the guests, who had become very attentive, gave the knowing nod called for by this clever question.

'When the introductions had been completed, we drove to Raoul's hotel on the Boulevard Bonne-Nouvelle (near the Gymnase). I went upstairs. In his room we found two gentlemen in tightly buttoned coats, who looked just right, although slightly old-fashioned too. (Between ourselves, I find that people are all rather behind the times, in real life!) We exchanged greetings. Ten minutes later agreement had been reached on the arrangements. Pistols, twenty-five paces, at the word of command. Belgium. The next day. Six o'clock in the morning. In short, the usual routine.'

'You might have thought of something new,' broke in, with an attempt at a smile, the guest who was practising lunges with his knife and fork.

'My dear fellow,' retorted D—— with biting sarcasm, 'you're a clever one, you are! You make out you know what's what! You see everything through a pair of opera glasses. But if you had been there, you would have aimed at simplicity like me. There was no question here of proposing the paper-knife of *The Clémenceau Case* as a weapon. You must understand that life isn't all a play! Speaking for myself, I often get enthusiastic over real things, natural things, things that happen! Everything isn't dead in me, dammit! And I assure you that it was no laughing matter when, half an hour later, we took the train for Erquelines, with our weapons in a suitcase. Upon my word, my heart was beating faster than it ever beat on a first night.'

Here D—— broke off, and drank a glass of water at a single draught: he was white-faced.

'Go on!' said the guests.

'I shall spare you the journey, the frontier, the customs, the hotel, and the night,' murmured D—— in a hoarse voice.

'I had never felt a more sincere friendship for Monsieur de Saint-Sever. I did not sleep a single second, in spite of the nervous strain from which I was suffering. At last dawn broke. It was half-past four. The weather was fine. The time had come. I got up and splashed cold water over my face. I did not take long getting dressed.

'I went into Raoul's room. He had spent the night writing. We have all produced scenes like that. I had only to remember in order to be natural. He was asleep in an arm-chair by the table; the candles were still burning. At the noise I made going in, he awoke and looked at the clock. I was expecting him to do that: I know that effect. I saw at that moment how true to life it is.

'Thank you, old fellow,' he said. 'Is Prosper ready? We have half an hour's walk before us. I think it is time to call him.'

'A few minutes later, all three of us were on our way downstairs, and when five o'clock struck, we were on the main road to Erquelines. Prosper was carrying the pistols. I had the wind up, and I'm not ashamed to admit it.

'They were talking together about family affairs as if nothing were happening. Raoul was magnificent, all in black, solemn and determined, very calm, and extremely impressive, he was so natural. . . . There was an authority about his bearing. . . . Like Bocage, if you ever saw him at Rouen, in his eighteen-thirties repertory. Oh, he had some flashes of genius there! Perhaps even finer than in Paris.'

'Oh, come now!' protested a voice.

'That's going a bit far!' broke in two or three guests.

'In any case, Raoul impressed me as I've never been impressed before,' D—— continued. 'You can take my word for that. We reached the duelling-ground at the same time as our opponents. I felt something like a foreboding.

'The adversary was a cold man, who looked like an officer from a good family; he had a face like Landrol, but less of a swagger. Attempts at reconciliation proved vain, so the pistols were loaded. I counted the paces, and I had to hold in my spirit (as the Arabs say) to conceal my asides. The best plan was to keep to the classical tradition.

'I played the scene in a thoroughly restrained style. I did not stumble once. At last the distance was marked out. I came back to Raoul. I embraced him and shook hands with him. I had tears in my eyes, not conventional tears, but real ones.

' "Come now, my dear D——," he said to me. "Calm yourself. What's the matter?"

'At these words I looked at him.

'Monsieur de Saint-Sever was simply magnificent. Anybody would have thought he was on the stage! I admired him. Until then I had believed that that sort of sang-froid was to be found only on the boards.

'The two adversaries took up position facing each other, with one foot on the mark. There was a sort of pause. My heart was beating wildly. Prosper handed Raoul the pistol at full cock, ready to fire; then, turning my head away with a feeling of dreadful anguish, I returned down-stage, by the ditch.

'And the birds were singing! I could see flowers at the foot of the trees! Real trees! Cambon never produced such a beautiful morning. What a terrible contrast!

' "One! ... Two! ... Three!" shouted Prosper at equal intervals, clapping his hands.

'I was in such an agitated state that I thought I could hear the stage-manager's three knocks. Two shots rang out at the same time. . . . Oh, God! God!'

D—— broke off, and buried his head in his hands.

'Oh, come now! We know you have a soft heart. . . . Finish the story!' cried the guests from all sides, deeply moved in their turn.

'Very well!' said D——, 'Raoul had fallen on the grass, on one knee, after spinning round. The bullet had struck him full in the heart, or at any rate here!' (And D—— struck his chest.) 'I rushed over to him.

' "My poor mother!" he murmured.'

(D—— looked at the guests: they, as men of tact, realized that this time it would be in bad taste to repeat their superior smiles. 'My poor mother' was therefore allowed to pass; the exclamation, being really appropriate here, became acceptable.)

'That was all,' D—— went on. 'Blood filled his mouth.

'I looked across at his adversary: he for his part had one shoulder shattered.

'He was being attended to.

'I took my poor friend in my arms. Prosper supported his head.

'In the space of one minute—just imagine!—I recalled our happy childhood years, the playtimes, the merry laughter, the days out, and the holidays . . . when we used to play at *fighting*. . . .'

(All the guests nodded their heads, to show that they appreciated the allusion.)

D——, who was getting visibly worked up, passed his hand across his forehead. He went on in an extraordinary tone of voice, his eyes staring into space:

'It was like . . . like a dream. . . . I was looking at him. He could not see me any longer: he was dying. And so simple! So dignified! Not a single complaint. Altogether very restrained. I was overcome with emotion, I must say. And two big tears came into my eyes. Two real tears, they were. Yes, gentlemen, two tears. . . . I wish Frédérick Lemaître could have seen them. *He* would have understood them. I stammered out a farewell to my poor friend Raoul and we laid him out on the ground.

'He lay there, rigid, without any posturing or posing, as true-to-life as ever. Blood on his coat. His cuffs all red. His forehead already very white. His eyes closed. I had no other thought but this: I found him *sublime*. Yes, gentlemen, sublime. That's the only word for it. . . . Why, it's as though I can still see him. I was beside myself with admiration! I lost my head! I forgot what had happened! I became confused! . . . I started clapping! I . . . I wanted to call him back. . . .'

Here D——, who had been carried away to the extent of shouting, suddenly stopped short; then, in an extremely calm voice and with a sad smile went on:

'Alas, yes! . . . I would have liked to call him back . . . to life.'

(A murmur of approval greeted this felicitous phrase.)

'Prosper dragged me away.'

(Here D—— stood up, with staring eyes; he seemed genuinely distressed.) Then, slumping back on his chair, he added in an undertone:

'Well, we are all mortal!'

(Then he drank a glass of rum, banged it back down on the table, and the next moment pushed it away like a cup of woe.)

Finishing like this, in a broken voice, D—— had ended up by captivating his audience so thoroughly, as much by the impressive nature of his story as by the vivacity of his delivery, that when he fell silent there was a burst of applause. I felt I should join my humble congratulations to those of his friends.

Everybody was deeply moved. Deeply moved.

'*A succès d'estime!*' I thought.

'That fellow D—— really is talented!' each guest murmured in his neighbour's ear.

All came and shook hands warmly with him. I left.

A few days later, I met one of my friends, a writer, and I told him Monsieur D——'s story *just as I had heard it*.

'Well,' I said when I had finished, 'what do you think of it?'

'Yes', he replied after a pause. 'It's almost a short story. You ought to write it.'

I looked him in the eyes.

'Yes', I said, '*Now* I can write it: it is complete.'

JORIS-KARL HUYSMANS (1848–1907)

Knapsack at the Ready

Translated by David Coward

The moment I finished my last year at school, my parents in their wisdom decided I should appear before the Board, in reality, a table covered in green baize over which loomed the upper halves of a number of elderly men anxious to learn if I had absorbed enough dead languages to be awarded my leaving certificate.

I had. I passed.

At a dinner to which the whole of my family tribe was invited, my success was celebrated, concern was expressed about my future and eventually it was resolved that I should study law.

I got through my first exams somehow and spent the enrolment fees for my second year on a blonde who said she was fond of me, when it suited her.

I was an assiduous habitué of the Latin Quarter where I learned a great many things, among others to take an interest in students who spouted their political ideas into their beer every evening, and also to dip into the works of George Sand and Heine, Edgar Quinet and Henri Murger.

I had reached the puberty of foolishness.

This lasted a year. I gradually grew up. The final electoral battles of the Empire left me cold. I was the son neither of a senator nor of a political leper. All that was asked of me was that I step out, regardless of who was in power, on the road to mediocrity and poverty which had long been the family tradition.

I did not care much for law. I thought the Civil Code had been badly drafted on purpose to provide a certain class of men with endless opportunities to quibble and cavil over the most insignificant words: even now, I fail to see how a clearly written sentence can be made to yield such widely divergent meanings.

I had just taken myself in hand with a view to finding a line of work which I would not find unspeakably loathsome when our late Emperor found one for me. He called me up and I became a soldier as a result of his political ineptitude.

The war with Prussia broke out. To be frank, I did not understand the reasons which made it necessary for one army to slaughter another. Personally, I did not feel a need to kill anybody nor to be killed myself. Be that as it may, recruited into the Seine Militia and duly equipped with uniform and marching boots, I was ordered to present myself at a barber's shop and then report to barracks in the rue de Lourcine at seven the same evening.

I was punctual to the minute. After the roll-call, most of the regiment made a rush for the door and spilled into the road. The street heaved and there was standing room only in the cafés.

Packed tightly together, working men in overalls, working girls in shabby clothes, and soldiers buttoned, gaitered, and unarmed, all bawled the Marseillaise over the clink of glasses, bellowing off key on purpose. Under caps that were astoundingly tall which had peaks as large as a blind man's eye-shade and sported a tricolour badge made of tin, and wearing dark blue jackets with red collar and facings, and blue linen trousers with a red stripe, the men of the Seine Militia roared their defiance at the moon before setting off to overrun Prussia. The uproar in every pothouse was deafening, a solid din of glasses, metal canteens, and raised voices broken now and then by the screech of windows banging in the wind. Suddenly, a drum-roll rose above the pandemonium. A fresh column of men emerged from the barracks and the party spirit which ensued turned into a binge that beggars description. The soldiers who were drinking in the grog-shops ran into the street followed by their relatives and friends who fought for the honour of carrying their knapsacks. Ranks formed and broke into chaotic scrums of soldiers and civilians. Mothers wept, fathers, less demonstrative, staggered under the influence, and children gambolled gleefully, shrieking patriotic songs at the tops of their shrill voices.

Then we all set out across Paris in a mad stampede under gathering storm clouds lashed by forks of white lightning. The heat was unbearable, our knapsacks were heavy, we stopped for a drink at every street corner. Eventually, we reached the station at Aubervilliers. There was a moment of silence broken by the sound of sobbing which was engulfed by another burst of the Marseillaise and then we were herded onto the train like cattle. 'G'night, Jules! See you soon! Be good! Don't forget to write!' Hands were shaken for the very last time, the train whistled and the station retreated behind us.

We were a party of a good fifty men in that box-on-wheels which bore us off. A few blubbed openly. They were jeered at by others who, drunk as lords, stuck lighted candles in their ration bread and kept yelling:

'Bugger Badinguet! Rah-Rah-Rah Rochefort!' Several huddled in a corner by themselves, saying nothing, grim-faced, staring at the wooden floorboards bouncing in the dust. Suddenly the train stopped. I get out. Pitch darkness. Twenty-five minutes past midnight.

Fields stretch away in every direction and, in the distance, lit by flickering flashes of lightning, a small house, a tree are silhouetted against a storm-filled sky. The only sound is the rumble of the engine. Showers of sparks from its chimney scatter along the train like a firework display. Everyone gets out and heads towards the locomotive which looms larger and larger in the night until it is enormous. The stop lasted a good two hours. The signal was showing red and the driver was waiting for it to change. It turned white again. We get back into the trucks but a man comes up at a run waving a lamp, has a word with the driver who immediately reverses us into a siding where we became stationary once more. None of us had any idea where we were. I climb down, find a hillock to sit on, and was just tucking into a piece of bread and a drink when in the distance a noise burst like a hurricane, clattered towards us, shrieking and spitting flames, and an interminable artillery train roared past carrying horses, men, and cannon whose gun-metal collars glinted in a kaleidoscope of lamps. Five minutes later, we were on our way again, our slow progress interrupted by halts which grew longer and longer. Day finally came and, leaning out of the carriage door, wearied by a bone-jarring night, I stare out at the landscape which surrounds us: a succession of chalky downs reaching to the horizon, a belt of pale green, the same green as a watery turquoise, a flat, desolate, lean land—the barren face of Champagne!

Gradually the sun grew brighter. We trundled on and on but in the end we arrived. We had set off at eight in the evening and were delivered at Châlons at three the following afternoon. Two men had been lost on the way, one who had taken a header from the roof of a carriage into a river, and another who had lost his head when it collided with the stanchion of a passing bridge. The rest had helped themselves to the contents of huts and allotments encountered on the way, during our many halts. They yawned, lips swollen with wine and puffy-eyed, or played games, using the length of the carriage to pitch the remains of bushes and chicken cages they had stolen.

Detraining was managed with the same smooth efficiency as entraining had been. Nothing was ready for us: no canteens, no straw, no greatcoats, no weapons, nothing, nothing at all. Just tents deep in filth, alive with fleas, and only just vacated by troops sent up to the frontier. For three days, we scrounged what we could at Mourmelon, guzzling sausage one day, getting a cup of coffee the next, shamelessly fleeced by the villagers, sleeping as best we could, without straw or blankets. None of which was calculated to make us warm to the calling which had been inflicted on us.

As soon as the companies were settled in, they split up. Working men moved into tents occupied by their own kind and their betters likewise. They weren't a bad lot in my tent, for by bribing them with booze we managed to boot out two upstanding specimens whose natural foot-odour had been enhanced by a prolonged, wilful indifference to personal hygiene.

A couple of days passed. We were made to stand guard with sticks, we drank large quantities of brandy, and the bawdy-shops of Mourmelon did a roaring trade. Then suddenly Canrobert decided to review the troops who were lined up behind the colours. I can still see him astride his big horse, bent almost double in the saddle, hair blowing in the wind, waxed moustaches standing out from his whey face. There was mutter-ing in the ranks. Denied supplies and equipment and unconvinced by the Marshal that we wanted for nothing, when he threatened to put an end to our complaints by force, we started bellowing, all together: 'Ta ran ta ra! A hundred thousand dead! Let's go back to Pa-ris, Pa-ris, Pa-ris!'

Canrobert turned even paler with rage and, driving his horse into our midst, he shouted: 'Take your caps off when you're being addressed by a Marshal of France!' There was renewed booing from the men. Then wheeling his mount and followed by his staff officers in a disorderly retreat, he pointed a menacing finger at us and hissed between gritted teeth: 'You'll pay for this, you Parisian troublemakers!'

Two days after this incident, the camp's freezing water supply made me so ill that I needed to be hospitalized: an emergency. After the doctor examined me, I packed up my kit and, escorted by a corporal, set off at a shuffle, hobbling along, sweating under the weight of my knapsack. The hospital was bursting at the seams. I was sent away. So I headed for one of the nearest field dressing-stations. There was an empty bed. I was admitted. At last I could put my knapsack down and, until such time as the MO confined me to bed, I decided to take a turn in the little garden which linked the units of the medical block. Suddenly a man with a bristling beard and bluish-green eyes steps through a door. He thrusts both hands deep in the pockets of a long, snuff-coloured coat and the moment he spots me yells:

'Hey, you! Where the hell do you think you're going?'

I walk up to him and explain how I come to be there. He waves his arms and screams:

'Get back where you came from! You're only allowed to walk in the garden when you've been issued with the regulation dress!'

I go back inside, an orderly appears and brings me a long coat, a pair of trousers, broken-down shoes, and a floppy cap. I took my small hand-mirror and looked at myself in that get-up. What a face, what a rig-out, my God! with brown-ringed eyes and sunken cheeks, short-cropped hair and knobbly nose flaring like a beacon, and with that huge mouse-grey coat, stained red-brown breeches, vast flat-heeled shoes, and gigantic cotton night-cap, I cut an amazingly hideous figure. I couldn't help laughing. I glanced towards the man in the next bed, a well-built Jewish-looking type, who was making a sketch of me in a notepad. We became instant friends. I said my name was Eugène Lejantel, he said he was Francis Emonot. We found that we both knew a number of painters, began discussing art, and forgot our troubles. When it was evening, we were given a bowl of gruel dotted with occasional black lentils and all the liquorice water we could drink, after which I undressed, thrilled to be able to stretch out on a bed without having to keep all my clothes and boots on.

Next morning I was woken up at around six by the sound of banging doors and raised voices. I sat up, rubbed my eyes, and saw the man from the evening before, still wearing his snuff-coloured coat, advancing imperially with a flock of medical orderlies in tow. It was the MO.

The moment he came in, he swivelled his dull-green eyes right and left, stuck his hands in his pockets and bawled:

'Number 1, let's see this leg, this gruesome leg, of yours. Oho! as legs go this one's not going well, that sore's running like a tap. Liniment, lint dressing, half-rations, full-strength liquorice tea.

'Number 2, let's see this throat, this gruesome throat, of yours. This throat is getting worse. We'll snip out those tonsils tomorrow.'

'But doctor . . .'

'I didn't ask for your opinion. You say another word and I'll put you on a bloody diet.'

'But . . .'

'Put this man on a bloody diet. Write down: diet, gargle, full-strength liquorice tea.'

He did the rounds of the rest of the patients in the same manner, prescribing for the VD cases, the wounded, fever, and dysentery the same dose of full-strength liquorice tea.

He got to me, stared me in the face, wrenched back the bed clothes, pummelled my abdomen with his fists, prescribed albumen water, the inescapable tea, and swept out, snorting and shuffling his feet.

Life with our fellow patients was not easy. There were twenty-one of us in the ward. On my left was my friend, the painter, on my right a very large bugler with a face as pock-marked as a thimble and as yellow as a glass of bile. He was a man who had two professions, cobbler by day and pimp by night. Actually he was quite a card and often stood on his head, sometimes his hands, while he told you as candid as could be how he used his boots to persuade his girls to put some vim into their work, or warbled sentimental songs in a tear-jerking voice:

> *Woe is me, I'm full o' sorrow:*
> *Loved only by a l'il sparrer!*

I got into his good books by slipping him 20 sous to buy a litre of wine and it was a good thing we didn't get on the wrong side of him, for the rest of the ward, which had a contingent of pimps from the rue Maubuée, was strongly inclined to make trouble for us.

One particular evening, though there were many such, it was the fifteenth of August, Francis Emonot threatened to punch two men who had taken his towel. The huge uproar that ensued made the rafters ring. Insults rained down on all sides, we were called sissies and fairies. Since there were two of us and nineteen of them, we stood a good chance of being beaten to a jelly when the bugler stepped in, took the most enthusiastic remonstrators to one side, talked them out of it, and persuaded them to return the stolen item. To mark the reconciliation which followed this denouement, Francis and I stumped up 3 francs each and it was decided that the bugler, abetted by his comrades, should attempt to sneak out and bring back meat and wine.

The light had gone out in the MO's window, and in the pharmacy the dispenser finally turned out his. We crawl through the bushes, observe how the land lies, and give the word to the men who move off, hugging the walls, encounter no sentries on their way, give each other a leg-up, and go over the wall into the fields. An hour later they are back, laden with victuals. They pass them over and return to the ward with us. We put out the two night-glims, light candle-ends on the floor, and, sitting in our night-shirts, we form a circle around my bed. We had put away three or four litres and demolished the best part of a leg of mutton, when there was a loud tramping of boots. I snuff the candles by swatting them with my shoes and every man dives into his bed. The door opens, the

MO appears, utters a fearsome 'What the devil!', stumbles in the dark, goes out, and returns with a lamp and the inevitable gaggle of orderlies. I make the most of the respite to remove the remains of the feast from sight. The MO strides through the ward at the double, cursing and blinding and threatening to have us rounded up and put in quod.

Under our blankets we are doubled up with laughter, then a bugle blows at the far end of the ward. The MO puts us all on a starvation diet then leaves, but not before informing us that we will know in pretty short order what sort of stuff he is made of.

When he'd gone, we burst, each of us howling louder than the next man. Guffaws swell to a gale over which the hoots of laughter flow in ripples. The bugler turns cartwheels between the rows of beds, one of his friends advances towards him in similar fashion, a third uses his cot as a trampoline and jumps up and down, arms flung out, night-shirt flapping, his neighbour in the next bed launches into a victorious cancan . . . Then in comes the MO unannounced, orders the four infantrymen he's brought with him to collar the dancing wounded, and informs us that he intends to make a report and pass it on to the appropriate authority.

At last calm is restored. The next day we are forced to ask the orderlies to buy our grub for us. The days pass without further incident. We are starting to feel terminally bored on the ward when one day, at five, the doctor rushes in, orders us to get into uniform and pack our kit.

Ten minutes later we learn that the Prussians are marching on Châlons.

The whole ward is numb with stupefaction. Until that moment we had had no idea what was happening outside. We had heard about our great victory at Sarrebruck and were unprepared for this setback, which left us stunned. The MO examined each man. None has been cured, for we had been given too much liquorice tea and not enough treatment. Even so, he sends the least ill back to their companies and orders the rest to lie on their beds fully dressed, knapsacks at the ready.

Francis and I fell into the latter category. The day wears on, the night passes, nothing happens, but I still have my colic and feel decidedly unwell. Finally, around nine in the morning a long convoy of mule-litters led by men of the Service Corps turns up. We clamber into them in twos. Francis and I are hoisted onto the same mule, but because the painter is very fat and I am so thin, the contraption is instantly unbalanced: I soar while he sinks and ends up under the belly of the beast which, pulled from the front and shoved from behind, kicks and bucks furiously. We proceeded apace in a cloud of dust, blinded, dazed, hanging on to the wicker rail, eyes squeezed shut, laughing and groaning. We got to Châlons more dead than alive. We collapsed onto the ground like exhausted cattle. Then were loaded into railway carriages, left the town, and headed towards . . . where? Nobody knew.

It was now dark. We bowled along the tracks. The hospital cases had been allowed out of the carriages and were roaming about on the walkways. The engine whistled, slowed down, and drew into a station, Rheims, I imagine, though I could not say for sure. We were starving, the Commissariat had overlooked just one thing: to give us a bread ration for the journey. I got off and spotted a buffet that was open. I make a run for it but others were quicker off the mark. When I got there, fighting had broken out. Some were grabbing bottles, others went for the meat, here the bread and there cigars. The owner, beside himself with rage, laid about him with a large jug in defence of his goods. Pushed by their comrades who were now arriving in gangs, the Militia men at the front bore down on the counter, which collapsed and with it brought down the proprietor and his assistants. There followed a general free-for-all. Everything was taken, from matches to toothpicks. Meanwhile a bell clangs and the train starts moving.

Nobody moves a muscle. We sit on the platform and, while the painter's chest heaves and wheezes, I explain the architecture of the sonnet to him. The train reverses along the track to pick us up.

We clamber back into our compartments and take stock of our hard-won booty. To be honest, the provender lacked variety: there was cold cooked meat and more cold cooked meat. We had six strings of garlic sausage, a bright-red tongue, two black puddings, a magnificent slice of Bologna with a silver skin around dark red meat veined with white, four litres of wine, half a bottle of cognac, and an assortment of candle-ends. These we stuck in the necks of our canteens which, suspended by string from the walls of the carriage, swayed as we proceeded. From time to time, when the train rattled over the points where branch-lines joined, we were showered with hot drops of wax which congealed almost instantly in large discs. Still, our uniforms had seen worse.

Wasting not a moment, we set about the repast, which was interrupted by the comings and goings of men who scrambled along the footboard that ran the whole length of the train and knocked at our window, asking for a drink. We sang at the tops of our voices, we drank, we clinked glasses. Never did sick men ever make such a racket or leap around so exuberantly on a moving train! It was like a court of miracles on wheels. The lame did standing jumps, men of unquiet intestines flushed them with generous potations of cognac, the one-eyed saw double, the fever-cases cavorted, painful throats hollered and glugged, it was quite outrageous!

All the excitement died down eventually, however. I took advantage of the lull to poke my nose out of the window. There was not a star to be seen, not even a sliver of moon. Sky and land seemed as one, and in the intense inky blackness lamps fixed on the arms of signals winked like different-coloured eyes. The engine-driver blew his whistle, the engine belched smoke and emitted never-ending volleys of sparks. I shut the window and eyed my companions. Some were snoring, others, unsettled by the jolting of the carriage, grumbled and swore, turning this way and that looking for somewhere to stretch out their legs or wedge their heads which bounced every time the carriage lurched.

I watched them for so long that I was beginning to doze off myself when the train came to a complete stop and woke me up. We were in a station. In the night murk, the stationmaster's office glowed as brightly as a blacksmith's forge. One of my legs was numb, I was shivering with the cold. I get out to try and get warm. I walk up and down the platform, I watch the engine being uncoupled and replaced by another and, as I pass the office, listen to the clack of the telegraph. The operator had his back to me and was leaning a little to his right. From where I stood all I could see was the back of his head and the end of his nose which gleamed pink and glistened with sweat while the rest of his face was hidden in the shadow cast by the shade of a gas light.

I was told to get back on the train where I found my comrades exactly as I had left them. This time, I dropped off and slept soundly—for how long I couldn't say—until I was woken by voices yelling: 'Paris! Paris!' I made a rush for the door. In the distance, against a pale gold strip of sky, rose the black fingers of factory chimneys and works stacks. We were at Saint-Denis. The news spread like wildfire from one carriage to the next. Everybody was on their feet. The train slowed. The Gare du Nord looms up ahead. We are there. We get out, we throw ourselves at the ticket barrier, some of us manage to get through, the rest are halted by porters and troops, we are ordered to board a train which is getting up steam and we're off again, bound God knows where!

Once again we are on the move all day. I grow weary of staring at the never-ending procession of houses and trees which files past me and moreover my colic is no better and is very painful. About four in the afternoon, the train drops its speed and pulls up alongside a platform where waiting for us we find an elderly general around whom bustles a swarm of junior ranks in pink caps, red trousers, and boots with brass spurs. The general inspects us and divides us into two squads. One sets off for the seminary and the other is escorted to the hospital. We are, it seems, at Arras. Francis and I are with the first squad. We are helped onto carts filled with straw and arrive outside a large crouching building which seems about to collapse into the street. We are taken up to the second floor into a ward with perhaps thirty beds in it. We all unpack our knapsacks, comb our hair, and sit down. A doctor arrives.

'What's wrong with you?' he asks the first man.

'Carbuncle, sir.'

'I see. And you?'

'Dysentery, sir.'

'I see. And you?'

'Lump in the groin, sir.'

'You mean none of you have been wounded in action?'

'Never saw action, sir.'

'In that case you can pack up your kit again. The archbishop has only made seminarists' beds available for the wounded.'

I put back the bits and pieces I had taken out of my knapsack and off we hobble, this time to the almshouse in town. There is no room. The nuns do what they can, pushing iron beds together, but it's no good: the rooms are full. Tired of all the delays, I grab a mattress, Francis grabs another, and we go outside and stretch out in the grounds, on a large lawn.

Next morning, I have a word with the warden, a kindly, charming man. I ask permission for the painter and myself to go into town. He agrees, the gates open, and we are free! Now at last we can have lunch, eat real meat and drink real wine! We waste no time but head for the best hotel in town where we are served a succulent meal. There are flowers on the table, magnificent sprays of roses and fuschia blooming in tall glass vases! The waiter brings us steak which bleeds into a lake of butter. The sun joins the party, puts a sparkle into the plates and on the blades of our knives, sifts powdered gold over the water-jugs, and, twinkling through the burgundy lapping in our glasses, pins a blood-red star to the damask table-cloth.

What a slap-up do it turns out to be! My mouth is full and Francis is drunk! The smell of roast meat commingles with the scent of the flowers, the deep red of the wine vies with the crimson of the roses, the waiter who serves us looks like an oaf, we behave like pigs, but we simply don't give a damn. We stuff ourselves on roast meats which keep on coming, we wash down Bordeaux with burgundy and follow cognac with chartreuse. Forget the sour wine and raw spirits we've been drinking ever since we left Paris! Forget the nameless slop and anonymous messes we've been ladling into ourselves so joylessly for almost a month! We are unrecognizable. Our hollow, underfed cheeks glow *bon-viveur* red, and then bawling and shouting, noses in the air, we walk off aimlessly. We walk all round the town in this state.

It starts to get dark, but we've got to get back. The nun in charge of the old men's ward said in a thin, piping voice:

'You must have been very cold last night but now you're going to have a comfortable bed.'

And so saying she herds us into a large room where three smoky night-lights hanging from the ceiling do their worst. I get a freshly made bed and luxuriate between the sheets which still have that delicious newly washed smell on them. The only sounds are the breathing and snores of sleeping men. I am snug and warm, my eyelids droop, I am losing all sense of where I am when a protracted chortle wakes me. I open one eye and see, standing at the foot of my bed, a man staring at me. I sit up. There before me is an aged specimen, tall, cadaverous, with wild eyes and lips that drool spittle into his uncombed beard. I ask him what he wants. No reply. I yell:

'Go away and let me sleep!'

He brandishes his fist. I suspect he is off his head. I roll up a towel and cunningly tie a knot in the end of it. He takes one step forward, I jump out of bed, parry the punch he throws at me, and, in reply, catch him over the left eye with a swing of my towel. He sees stars then lunges at me. I step back and get him with a hefty kick to the stomach. He crumples and as he falls knocks over a chair which skids across the wooden floor. By now the whole dormitory is awake. François runs up in his night-shirt to give me a hand, the nun comes in, the orderlies leap on the lunatic, tan his backside, and, with some difficulty, get him back into bed.

The scene in the dormitory was really quite hilarious. The dull pink glow cast by the dying night-glims was replaced by the glare of three flaring lanterns. The crepuscular ceiling embellished with circles of light which flickered above the smoking wicks now blazed with the bright charms of freshly rendered plaster. The patients, a collection of gruesome, ageless relics—Mr Punch to a man—were all clinging for dear life to the wooden bars which hung on a cord above their beds, hanging on with one hand and making terrified signals with the other. On seeing this spectacle, my anger dissolves, I double up laughing, the painter is quite overcome, and only the nun is not amused. With a mixture of threats and pleading, she manages to restore order in the ward.

Somehow, the night comes to an end. At six in the morning, a drum roll calls us into line. The warden calls the roll. We set off for Rouen.

When we got there, an officer informed the poor unfortunate who was in charge of us that the workhouse was full and could not take us. Meanwhile, we had a wait of one hour. I dump my knapsack in an out-of-the-way corner of the station and, though my stomach is complaining, Francis and I wander off through the town, going into ecstasies over the church of Saint-Ouen and raptures over the quaint old houses. With our admiration on a loose rein, the hour had been up a long time before it occurred to us to make our way back to the station.

'Your mates is long gone,' a porter told us, 'they'll be at Évreux by this time.'

Damn! The next train doesn't leave until nine. Might as well have dinner!

When we got to Évreux, it was well after nightfall. We could hardly go knocking on the hospital doors at that late hour, we would have looked like criminals. It is a superb night, we walk through the town and find ourselves in the country. It was haymaking time and the sheaves had been heaped together. We spy a small haystack in a field, we scoop out two comfortable nests, and I cannot say if it was the evocative smell of our billet or the fragrance of the woods which stirred us, but we both felt the need to talk of old loves. As topics go, it was inexhaustible. Imperceptibly, however, our words falter, our enthusiasm dims, and we fall asleep.

'Blast!' says my comrade as he stretches, 'what time do you reckon it is?'

I open my eyes too. The sun will soon be up, for the wide blue canopy is edged with pink fringes. What a bore! We shall have to go back to the hospital, knock on the door, and bed down in some room impregnated with that fetid reek in which lurks, like a persistent refrain, the acrid fragrance of antiseptic powder.

We trudge disconsolately back to the hospital. They open up but, alas, only one of us is admitted, Francis, and I am packed off to the local school.

Life was becoming impossible and I was toying with the idea of doing a bunk when one day the orderly on duty came down into the schoolyard. I show him my law student's card. He knows Paris and the Latin Quarter. I explain the situation.

'There are no two ways about it,' I said. 'Either Francis comes here or I join him in the hospital.'

He mulls this over and that evening, he comes up to me in bed and whispers in my ear:

'Tomorrow morning, tell them you're feeling worse.'

And lo! next morning at about seven, the doctor walks in, a fine, upstanding man who had only two faults: gruesome breath and the urge to get rid of his patients at any price. Every morning, this scene was repeated:

'Aha! here's a sturdy specimen!' he would cry. 'You look well, there's colour in your cheeks, and your temperature's normal. Out of bed with you, go and get yourself a hot cup of coffee. But no tricks, mind, and no running after women. I'll sign your discharge and you can rejoin your regiment tomorrow.'

Every day, he sent three men packing, whether they were sick or not. That morning, he stops by my bed and says:

'Aha! By my godfathers, you're looking better, my boy!'

I deny it, I say I've never known such agony! He pokes my abdomen.

'But there is an improvement, your abdomen is not as hard.'

I protest. He looks surprised. Then the orderly puts in a quiet word:

'Perhaps he ought to be given an enema, but we don't have either a syringe or an injection pump here. What if we transfer him to hospital?'

'Ah yes, that's an idea,' said the excellent man, delighted to be shot of me, and without further ado he signs a note to admit me. Beaming, I pack my kit and, escorted by a school porter, I walk into the hospital. There I find Francis! By an incredible piece of luck, the Saint-Vincent corridor where he has been put because there is no room in the wards has an empty bed right next to his! At last we are together again! As well as our two beds, five other cots are lined up one after the other against the yellow-washed walls. Their occupants are a linesman, two gunners, a dragoon, and a hussar. The rest of the hospital patients consist of a handful of demented, senile relics, a sprinkling of young men with rickety, twisted legs, and a large cohort of soldiers, the remnant of Mac-Mahon's army who, after being passed from one field hospital to another, had washed up on this shore. Francis and I are the only men wearing the uniform of the Seine Militia. The men in the neighbouring beds were decent enough but, to be honest, not exactly stimulating companions. For the most part, they were the sons of farmers and farm-labourers who had been called up as soon as war was declared.

While I'm taking off my tunic, a nun appears. She is so dainty, so pretty that I can't take my eyes off her. Such big, beautiful eyes! those long blond eyelashes! such pearly teeth! She asks me why I have left the school. I explain in a vague roundabout way that I was turned out due to the non-availability of a . . . er . . . force-pump. She smiles sweetly and says:

'Private, you could have called the thing by its name. We're used to everything here.'

I quite believe the poor girl was used to the very worst, for the soldiers never held back and in her presence were less than modest in their ablutions. In fact, I never saw her blush. She went among them, not speaking, with her eyes on the ground, seemingly oblivious to the crude jokes which flew around her.

God, how she spoiled me! I can still see her of a morning, when the sun snapped the shadow of the barred window on the stone flags, walking slowly towards me down the corridor, with the wide wings of her coif flapping against her face. She would reach the side of my bed bearing a steaming plate on the rim of which one neatly manicured fingernail gleamed.

'The soup's a bit thin this morning,' she would say through her pretty smile, 'so I've brought you some chocolate, drink up while it's still hot.'

Despite the care she lavished on me, I grew terminally bored in that hospital. My friend and I had both sunk to that level of debility which keeps you in bed like some drowsing beast of the field and leaves you struggling to kill the unending hours of insufferable days. The only distractions on offer consisted of lunch and dinner of boiled beef, boiled marrow, boiled prunes, and an inch of wine, but never in sufficient quantities to feed a man.

By simply being polite to the nuns and because I wrote out labels for their pill-boxes, I got the occasional chop or a pear from the hospital orchard. I was therefore rather better off than the rest of the soldiers who were crammed into every cranny of the wards. But for the first few days I was not even able to get my morning commons down. That was the time the doctor did his rounds and chose to perform his operations. The day after I arrived, he slit open a man's thigh from top to bottom. I heard a scream of agony. I shut my eyes but not so tight that I did not see a fountain of blood splash his apron with large red flowers. That morning, I couldn't eat a thing. Little by little, however, I grew hardened until I was able to look the other way and keep my dinner down.

Meanwhile, our situation was becoming intolerable. We had tried, to no avail, to get hold of newspapers and books, and we were reduced to dressing up, such as putting on a hussar's tunic, for a laugh. But such puerile antics quickly wore thin and mostly we just stretched, every twenty minutes or so, exchanging a few words and then burying our heads in our pillows once more.

There wasn't much in the way of conversation to be got out of our comrades. The two gunners and the hussar were too far gone to speak. The dragoon cursed his head off but actually talked. He kept getting out of bed and, wrapped in his great white coat, would make for the latrine whence he returned with evidence of well-trampled excrement on his bare feet. The hospital was short of chamber pots. A few of the illest patients, however, had old saucepans under their beds. These the convalescent cases would toss like cooks and offer the resulting 'hotpot' to the nuns as a joke.

That left only the linesman, a wretched grocer's assistant who had a son and had been called to the colours. He shook with fever all the time and lay there shivering under the bedclothes.

Sitting cross-legged on our beds, we listened while he told us about the battle he had been involved in.

Finding himself somewhere near Frœschweiler, in flat open terrain surrounded by woods, he had seen flashes of red through plumes of white smoke and he had ducked, shaking, dazed by the artillery fire and unnerved by the whine of bullets. Caught up in other regiments, he had marched over mud and mire without seeing a single Prussian, not knowing where he was, hearing all around him groans punctuated by short-lived screams. Then the ranks of soldiers in front of him had suddenly turned tail and in the scrimmage that followed the rout, he had somehow ended up on the ground. He had got up, made a run for it, abandoning his rifle and his knapsack, and finally, exhausted by the forced marches he had endured for a week, drained by fear and weakened by hunger, he had sat down in a ditch. There he had stayed, stupefied, not moving, deafened by the bursting shells, determined he would not try to defend himself or move from where he was. But then he had thought of his wife and started to cry, asking himself what he had done to deserve such treatment. He had picked up a leaf, why he could not say, and still had it. He set great store by it, for he often showed it to us, desiccated and shrivelled, and kept it safe in his pocket.

While he was in this state, an officer holding a pistol passed by, called him a coward, and threatened to beat his brains out if he refused to march. He said: 'I'd sooner that, and get it all over with.' But the officer, just as he was yanking him to his feet, fell, pole-axed, with blood oozing from the back of his neck. He had panicked again, started running, and managed to reach a distant road heaving with fleeing men, black with plodding troopers. Carts drawn by runaway horses careered into them, crushing them and scattering their ranks.

Finally, they had managed to reach shelter. Shouts of treason went up from the huddled knots of men. The regulars seemed to have stomach left for a fight but the recruits refused to go on.

'Let them go and get themselves killed,' they said, meaning the officers, 'it's their job!'

'I got kids. It won't be the government that'll feed them when I'm a goner!'

And they envied the fate of the walking wounded and the sick who could find a safe refuge in the field-hospitals.

'Man, were we scared! I can still hear the voices of men shouting for their mothers and asking for a drink,' he went on, with a shudder. Then he stopped and surveying our corridor with evident delight, continued:

'I don't care, I'm very pleased to be here. Besides, this way my wife can write to me,' and from his trouser pocket he pulled out a bundle of letters and said contentedly:

'Look, my boy wrote to me,' and he showed at the bottom of the page, beneath his wife's laboured handwriting, a series of pen-strokes making a sentence, clearly dictated, which contained 'love to Daddy' and other such sentiments in a bouquet of ink-blots.

We heard this tale at least a score of times and for hours on end were forced to listen to him drone on and on about how delighted he was to have a son. In the end, we stuck our fingers in our ears and tried to sleep to shut out his voice.

This appalling existence seemed set to continue indefinitely when one morning Francis, who, unusually for him, had spent the whole of the previous day prowling round the yard outside, said:

'Listen, Eugène, fancy a sniff of fresh air?'

I prick up my ears.

'There's a recreation yard they keep for the lunatics,' he went on. 'There's no one in it. If we climb onto the roof of the huts, and it's easy because the windows have bars across them, we can get on to the top of the wall, jump and that's it, we're in the country. A short walk from the wall is one of the main gates into Évreux. What do you say?'

I say . . . I say that I'm very ready for an outing. But how will we get back?

'Haven't a clue. Let's go first and think about that later. On your feet, they're coming round with the lunch. We'll go over the wall after.'

I get out of bed. The hospital was short of water so I had been reduced to washing in the Seltzer the nun had managed to get for me. I reach for the siphon, aim it at the painter, who shouts 'fire!', I press the lever, and he gets it full in the face. Then I stand in front of him, I take a squirt to the head, rub my face all over with the froth and dry myself. We're ready, we go down the stairs. There's no one about in the yard. We climb onto the wall. Francis steadies himself and jumps. I straddle the top and cast a quick glance around me: below, a ditch and grass, to my right, one of the town gates; in the distance a forest undulates gently and hoists clumps of red and gold against a strip of pale blue sky. I stand upright, I hear a noise in the yard, I jump. We keep close to the wall and then we are in Évreux!

'Fancy a bite to eat?'

'Motion carried.'

As we proceed in search of a suitable venue, we spot a couple of girls walking along swinging their hips. We follow them and invite them to lunch. They refuse. We insist. They say no, but with less conviction. We insist again and they say yes. We go to their place with a pie, bottles, eggs, and a cold chicken. It seems odd being in a light, airy room decorated with wallpaper flecked with lilac blooms and verdant with large leaves. The casement windows are hung with bright-red damask curtains, there is a mirror on the mantelpiece, an engraving showing Christ answering the Pharisees, six cherry-wood chairs, a circular table with an oilcloth over it showing the kings of France, and a bed with pink cotton eiderdown on it. We set up table and chairs and glance greedily at the girls as they walk round it. It takes some time to lay, however, for we keep stopping them to snatch a kiss, though they are rather ugly and quite stupid. But did that worry us? It was such a long time that we had been anywhere near a woman's lips!

I carve the chicken, corks pop, we drink like fish and guzzle like trolls. Coffee steams in the cups, we gild it with cognac. My gloom lifts, we put a match to the punch, the blue flames from the kirsch flare in the bowl making it hiss and crackle, the girls laugh, hair hanging down in their eyes and bodices plundered. Suddenly, four chimes ring out from the slow church bell. It is four o'clock. Oh my God! the hospital! We have forgotten all about the hospital! I turn pale, Francis looks at me in a panic, we tear ourselves from the arms of our fair colleens, and decamp at top speed.

'How are we going to get in again?' asks the painter.

'We don't have much choice. We'll have our work cut out to get back before dinner time. Let's trust in the Lord and go in through the front door.'

We reach it, we ring the bell. The nun on gate duty opens up and stands there, with her mouth hanging open. We doff our caps and I say, in a voice loud enough for her to hear:

'You know, those people in the Commissariat aren't exactly welcoming, are they? The fat one could hardly bring himself to be polite . . .'

The nun says nothing and we set off at a gallop for the ward. We were only just in time, for I could hear the voice of Sister Angèle who was doling out the rations. I get into bed as quick as a flash and use my hand to hide a love-bite which my girl had left on my neck. The nun looks at me, discovers an unaccustomed sparkle in my eye, and, curious, asks:

'Are you feeling worse?'

I reassure her and reply:

'On the contrary, I'm feeling much better, sister, but having nothing to do and being cooped up is getting me down.'

When I told her how horribly bored I felt, lost in a crowd of soldiers in the middle of nowhere, far from friends and family, she did not answer, but her lips tightened and into her eyes came an indefinable expression of sadness and pity. Yet one day she said to me dryly: 'Being free wouldn't do you any good,' a remark prompted by a conversation she had overheard between Francis and me as we discussed the surpassing charms of Parisian women. But then she had softened her tone and added with that irresistible pouting smile of hers:

'Really, Private, everything is just one big joke to you.'

Next morning the painter and I agreed that straight after lunch we'd go over the wall again. At the appointed hour, we were loitering near the yard but found that the gate was locked!

'Hell's teeth! Still, it can't be helped,' says Francis. 'Best foot forward!'

And he heads straight for the hospital's main entrance. I follow. The nun on the gate asks us where we're going.

'To the Commissariat.'

The door opens and we are outside.

When we got to the town's main square in front of the church and were studying the statues over the west door, I spotted a portly party, with a face like a red moon and a bristling white moustache, who was staring at us in amazement. We stared back brazenly then went on our way. Francis was dying of thirst so we went into a café where, as I sipped my coffee, I glance at the local paper and in it find a name which gave me pause. Actually, I did not know the person who bore it, but the name stirred a memory long forgotten. I recalled that a friend of mine had a relative who was some sort of big noise at Évreux.

'I must go and see him!' I tell the painter.

I ask the proprietor of the café for his address. He does not know it. I leave and call at every baker's and chemist's I pass. Now everybody eats bread and swallows potions. It was not possible that among these upstanding men of industry there was not one who knew the address of Monsieur de Fréchêde. It is vouchsafed to me. I brush the dirt off my greatcoat, buy a black tie and a pair of gloves, and repair to the rue Chartraine where I pull gently on the bell of the iron gate of a large house which rises brick-faced and slate-roofed among the dappled foliage of extensive grounds. A footman shows me in. Monsieur de Fréchêde is out but Madame is at home. I am kept waiting for a matter of moments in a drawing room and then the door opens and an old lady appears. Her manner is so gracious that I am reassured. I explain in a few brief words who I am.

'I have heard', says she with a broad smile, 'a great deal about your family. I do believe that I met your mother at Mme Lezant's during my last visit to Paris. You are most welcome in this house.'

We converse at some length, I, somewhat ill at ease, using my cap to hide the love-bite on my neck, and she, trying to make me accept a gift of money which I refuse.

'Please,' she says at length, 'I am most anxious to be of some help to you. What can I do?'

I reply: 'Well, madame, if you could arrange for me to be sent back to Paris, you would render me a great service. Dispatches might be intercepted any day now, so the papers say. There's talk of another coup d'état or the overthrow of the Empire. I really need to see my mother again. I'm not especially keen on staying here and being taken prisoner if the Prussians come.'

At this point Monsieur de Fréchêde returns. A few words and he is put fully in the picture.

'If you are agreeable,' he said, 'come with me and we'll see what the head physician at the hospital has to say. There's not a minute to waste.'

See the head quack? Oh my God! How would I explain my little outing? I dare not say anything. I follow my protector wondering how it will all turn out. We get to the hospital. The doctor looks at me with astonishment. I do not give him a chance to say a word and trot out, with stupendous glibness, a long litany of lamentations which outline my sorry plight.

Then M. de Fréchêde takes up the theme and, on my behalf, requests a period of two months convalescent leave.

'This man is certainly ill enough', said the doctor, 'to warrant a couple of months leave for recuperation. If my colleagues and the general share my view, your protégé will be able to return to Paris in a matter of days.'

'Splendid,' said M. de Fréchêde. 'I am obliged to you, doctor. I'll have a word with the general this very evening.'

When we are outside in the street, I heave a sigh of relief. I shake the hand of the excellent man who was kind enough to take up my case and hurry off to find Francis. We have just enough time to get back. We reach the hospital entrance. Francis rings the bell. I say good evening to the nun. She stops me:

'Didn't you tell me this morning that you were going to the Commissariat?'

'Absolutely, sister.'

'Well, the general has just left. You're to go and see the doctor in charge and Sister Angèle. They're waiting for you. I expect you'll be able to explain to them what you were doing at the Commissariat.'

Crestfallen, we trudge up the stairs to the ward. Sister Angèle is there, waiting for me. She says:

'I'd never have believed such a thing. You've been out, trailing around the town. You did it yesterday and you've done it again today. Goodness knows what you've been up to.'

'Steady on!' I exclaim.

She gave me such a look that I was silenced.

'The fact remains', she went on, 'that the general happened to see you today in the Square. I denied that you'd gone out and looked everywhere for you in the hospital. The general was right: you weren't here. He asked for your names. I told him who one of you was but refused to tell on the other. But that was wrong of me, very wrong, for you don't deserve it!'

'Oh, I can never thank you enough, sister . . .'

But Sister Angèle wasn't listening. She was extremely cross about the way I'd behaved. There was only one course of action left to me, say nothing, take what was coming, and not try to avoid it. Meanwhile, Francis had been summoned to the doctor's office and because, I can't think why, he was suspected of being a bad influence on me, but also because his constant chaff and banter had made him unpopular with either the doctor or the nuns, he was informed that he would be rejoining his regiment the following day.

'Those damned girls we had lunch with yesterday were registered tarts and they shopped us,' he said furiously. 'The head man told me himself.'

While we were cursing the hussies and lamenting the fact that our uniform made us so easily recognizable, the rumour spread that the Emperor had been taken prisoner and that a Republic had been declared in Paris. I give a franc to an old man who was allowed out to bring me back a copy of the *Gaulois*. The rumour was true. In the hospital, joy was unconfined.

'Badinguet's jiggered! And not before time! The war's over at last!'

Next morning, Francis and I hugged each other and then he left.

'See you soon,' he shouted as he closed the gate, 'meet you in Paris!'

But after that first day, how things changed! How we suffered! How neglected we were! There was no way we could leave the hospital. A sentry marched up and down outside the entrance, posted there in my honour. I was very brave, however, and tried not to take refuge in sleep. I prowled round the yard like a caged animal. I roamed in this manner for twelve solid hours. I got to know my prison like the back of my hand. I knew the places where pellitory and mosses grew, where the walls bulged and cracked. I could no longer stand the thought of my corridor, my mattress now flatter than a pancake, the dirty bedcovers, my filthy underwear which was falling apart. I passed the time by myself, not speaking to anyone, kicking stones round the yard, wandering like a lost soul under the mustard-washed arcades and through the wards, returning to the iron gate from which a flag flew limply, climbing up to the first floor where my bed was, descending to the depths of the sparkling kitchens where copper pans gleamed against bare white walls. I fretted with impatience. At set hours, I watched the comings and goings of civilians and soldiers, toing and froing on every floor, making the cavernous halls resound with their slow footsteps.

I no longer had enough strength to avoid the attentions of the nuns who whisked us off each Sunday to chapel. I became obsessed; I was haunted by one thought: to get away as soon as possible from my horrible gaol. Contributing to my depression was a shortage of cash. My mother had sent me a hundred francs at Dunkirk which was, it seemed, where I was supposed to be. There was no sign of this money. I could see that the time would soon come when I wouldn't have enough to buy tobacco or writing paper.

Meanwhile, one day followed the next. The de Fréchêdes seemed to have forgotten all about me and I put their silence down to my behaviour, of which they had doubtless been informed. Soon, to my mental anguish were added excruciating pains. Badly treated and provoked by all the moving around I had done, my innards flared into revolt. It was so bad that I began to be afraid I would not be able to travel. I hid the pain fearing that the doctor might order me to remain in the hospital. I kept to my bed for a few days. Then, feeling my strength was ebbing, I nevertheless forced myself to my feet and went down to the yard. Sister Angèle had stopped talking to me and when she was doing her evening rounds of the corridors and wards, turning her head away so that she would not see the red glow of tobacco pipes winking in the dark, she would walk straight past me, cool and indifferent, looking the other way.

One morning, however, as I dragged myself around the yard, collapsing onto every bench, she saw me so altered, so pale, that she could not help feeling sorry for me. That evening, after she had looked in on the wards for the last time, I was lying with one elbow on my bolster, staring at the patches of blue light cast by the moon through the corridor windows, when the far door opened and I saw, now wreathed in a silver shimmer, now dark and seemingly clad in funereal black as she passed window or wall, Sister Angèle coming towards me. With a gentle smile she said:

'Tomorrow morning, you will be examined by the doctor. I went to see Mme de Fréchêde today and it's quite likely that you will be sent to Paris in the next few days.'

I sit up in my bed, my face brightens, I wish I could leap about and sing: it was the happiest day of my life! When it is morning, I get up, dress, and, feeling somewhat nervous, make my way to the room where a board of military and doctors is in progress.

One by one, soldiers bared torsos which were pitted with scars or sprouted tufts of hair. The general was picking at a fingernail, the chief constable was fanning himself with a sheet of paper, the medics chatted as they prodded and poked the men. Then finally it is my turn. I am examined from head to foot, hands press my abdomen, which is swollen and tight as a drum, and with one voice the board gives me sixty days convalescent leave. I shall see my mother at last! I shall be reunited with my personal possessions, my books! I cease to feel the red-hot poker that ravages my insides! I skip and prance like a young goat!

I inform my family of the good news. My mother writes me letter after letter, amazed at my non-appearance. Alas, my pass has to be stamped by Divisional HQ at Rouen. It is returned five days later. My papers are now in order, I look for Sister Angèle and ask her if she would request permission for me, before I'm due to leave, to go out so that I can thank the de Fréchêdes who have been so kind to me. She goes straight to the head physician and brings me a note. I hurry off to see the excellent couple. They force me to accept a warm scarf and fifty francs for the journey. I fetch my travel warrant from the Quartermaster and return to the hospital. I've only a matter of minutes left now. I go in search of Sister Angèle, find her in the garden, and, sincerely moved, I say:

'Sister, I'm leaving. However can I repay you for everything you've done for me?'

I reach for her hand which she tries to take back and raise it to my lips. She blushes:

'Goodbye,' she says and then, pointing an admonishing finger, she adds cheerfully: 'Behave yourself, and especially don't fall in with bad company on the way.'

'No need to fear on that score, sister, that's a promise!'

The appointed hour strikes, the gate swings open, I make a dash for the station and leap into a carriage. The train shudders and I have left Évreux behind me.

My compartment is half-full but fortunately I have a window seat. I press my nose to the glass, catch sight of pollarded trees, an outline of hills snaking into the distance, and a bridge spanning a large expanse of water which sparkles in the sun like a shard of broken glass. It is not a particularly cheering sight. I sink back into my corner, looking up from time to time at the telegraph wires which draw black lines across the blue sky. When the train stops, the passengers in my compartment get out, the door closes and then opens again to admit a young woman.

While she sits down and smoothes her dress, I make out her face under the swell of her veil. She is very pretty: eyes of sky-blue, lips flushed with crimson, white teeth, and hair the colour of ripe corn.

I start up a conversation. Her name is Reine and she sits quietly embroidering flowers: we chat like friends. Suddenly she turns pale and is clearly about to faint. I open the top windows and offer her my smelling salts which I had brought with me, just in case, when I left Paris. She thanks me, says it's nothing, then leans against my knapsack and tries to sleep. Fortunately, there were just the two of us in the compartment but the wooden partition which divided the carriage into equal sections was only waist-high so that you could see and, more to the point, hear a crew of country clods and their womenfolk who were shrieking with laughter and making a dickens of a row. I would have gladly handed out a sound thrashing to those morons who dared disturb her slumbers! Instead, I settled for listening to the half-baked political views they exchanged. I soon tire of this. I put my fingers in my ears and I too try to sleep. But the words declaimed by the stationmaster at our last stop—'This train won't reach Paris, the line's cut at Mantes!'—keeps running through my dozing dreams like a persistent refrain. I open my eyes. The girl wakes up too. I don't want to share my misgivings with her. We chat quietly. She tells me she's on the way to join her mother at Sèvres.

'But,' say I, 'this train won't get into Paris before eleven tonight. You'll never have enough time to change stations and make your connection.'

'How will I manage,' says she, 'if my brother isn't there to meet me?'

Hell's teeth! I'm filthy and my belly is on fire! I dare not even think of whisking her off to my bachelor flat, and in any case all I want to do is get to my mother's. What am I to do? I look at Reine in anguish and take her hand. At that moment, the train rattles over the points, the jolt throws her forward, our lips are close, they touch, I press mine to hers, she blushes bright red. Good Lord! her mouth flutters imperceptibly and she returns my kiss, a long drawn-out shiver runs down my spine and as I hang on those two burning brands I feel myself go weak at the knees. Oh Sister Angèle, Sister Angèle, leopards don't change their spots!

Meanwhile the thundering train hurtles on and on, never slowing, rushing us off at full speed towards Mantes. My fears prove groundless: the line is clear. Reine's eyelids droop, her head lolls on my shoulder, her every tremor is transferred to my beard and tickles my lips, I hold her around her supple waist, cradle her in my arms. It's not far to Paris now. We pass docks and warehouses and engine sheds where roaring locomotives are being fired among clouds of red steam. The train stops. The tickets are collected. All things considered, I decide the first thing I shall do is to take Reine to my flat—if, that is, her brother isn't waiting for her at the barrier! All the passengers get out. Her brother is there. 'Five days' she whispers through a kiss and then my pretty bird had flown! Five days later, I was in bed suffering agonies and the Prussians were in Sèvres. I have never seen her since.

My heart is like lead and I heave a deep sigh. But this is no time to be sad! Now I am trundling along in a cab. I recognize my part of town. I draw up outside my mother's house, run up the steps two at a time, tug frantically on the bell, and the maid opens the door. It's the young master! and off she runs to tell my mother who rushes to meet me, turns pale, kisses me, looks at me from head to foot, stands back a step or two, looks again, and kisses me once more. In the meantime, the maid has ransacked the larder.

'I expect you'll be hungry, Monsieur Eugène?'

'Hungry? I should say!'

I devour every last scrap that's put before me and gulp down large glasses of wine. To tell the truth, I have no idea what I'm eating and drinking!

In the end, I go back to my flat to sleep. It is exactly as I had left it. I walk through it, beaming contentedly. Then I sit on the divan and stay there, blissful, in raptures, filling my eyes with the sight of my own things and my books. I undress, nevertheless, get washed all over, knowing that for the first time in two months I shall soon be in a clean bed with lily-white feet and clipped toenails. I jump onto the mattress: it is springy. I snuggle down into my feathery nest, my eyes close, and I float off under full sail to the land of dreams.

I seem to see Francis lighting his immense briar and Sister Angèle gazing down at me with that quizzical look of hers, then Reine is walking towards me and I wake with a start. I tell myself not to be such a fool and bury my head in the pillows, but the pain in my intestines which had faded briefly revives now that the muscles are less tense and I rub my abdomen gently, thinking that at least the worst horrors of dysentery which keeps dragging you to a communal latrine where everyone performs together, without modesty or dignity, were no more! I am in my own apartment and have a bathroom all to myself! And I reflect that you need to have lived cheek by jowl with men in a hospital or camp before you can really appreciate the luxury of a modern lavatory closet and savour the privacy of those little rooms where a man can let his trousers down in comfort.

RENÉE VIVIEN (1877–1909)

The Lady with the She-Wolf

Translated by Elizabeth Fallaize

Told by Monsieur Pierre Lenoir, 69, rue des Dames, Paris.

I cannot tell you why I began to court the lady. She was not beautiful, nor pretty, nor even agreeable. Whereas I myself (ladies, I tell you this without self-conceit) have sometimes been said by others to be not undistinguished. I would not say that Nature has bestowed extraordinary gifts upon me, either in the physical or moral domain but, such as I am, I will admit, I have been very kindly treated by the fair sex. Oh! please be reassured, I am not about to inflict upon you an immodest account of my conquests. I am of a modest nature. Besides, my story does not concern me, as it happens. It concerns the woman, or rather the girl, that is to say the English girl whose curious countenance I found pleasing for a while.

She was a strange creature. When I approached her for the first time, a large beast lay sleeping in the trailing folds of her skirts. The pleasantly banal phrases which facilitate relations between strangers came to my lips. The words themselves are of no account in these circumstances— the art lies in the way in which they are said . . .

But the large beast, lifting up its muzzle, growled in a sinister manner just as I reached the intriguing unknown lady.

I took a step back, despite myself.

'You have a very bad-tempered dog, there, mademoiselle,' I remarked.

'It's a she-wolf,' replied the lady somewhat tartly. 'And, since she sometimes takes against people quite violently and quite inexplicably, I would advise you to keep your distance.'

She silenced the animal with a stern command: 'Helga!'

I beat my retreat, mildly humiliated. A foolish episode, you will agree. I do not know the meaning of fear, but I detest ridicule. The incident displeased me all the more in that I believed I had detected a gleam of sympathy in the eyes of the young lady. She had certainly taken something of a fancy to me. No doubt she must have shared my vexation at our regrettable contretemps. What a pity! A conversation which had begun so well! . . .

Later, I have no idea why, the dreadful animal abandoned its hostility to me. I was able to approach her mistress without fear. I have never seen such a strange face. Beneath the heavy tresses of a dull yet glowing blonde colour, like reddened ashes, flared the grey pallor of her skin. Her emaciated body had the fine and fragile delicacy of a handsome skeleton. (We Parisians all have a touch of the artist about us, you know.) An aura of harsh and solitary pride, of angry recoil and retreat, emanated from this woman. Her yellow eyes resembled those of her she-wolf. They had the same look of sly hostility. Her step was so silent as to be disturbing. No one can ever have walked with so little sound. Her clothing was of a thick material which looked like fur. She was not beautiful, nor pretty, nor charming. But she was, after all, the only woman on board.

I paid court to her, therefore. I followed the rules most soundly based on my already considerable experience. She was adroit enough not to let me see the profound pleasure which my advances caused her. She even succeeded in maintaining her habitual expression of defiance in her yellow eyes. What a marvellous example of feminine wiles! The only result of this ploy was to increase the violence of my attraction to her. Sometimes a long resistance can be an agreeable surprise, rendering victory more triumphant. I am sure you will not contradict me on this point, gentlemen? We all share similar sentiments. There is such a fraternity of feeling between us that conversation is almost impossible. This is the reason I so often shun the monotony of male company, too identical to my own.

I was attracted to the Lady with the she-wolf, admittedly. And, shall I make a confession? The chastity imposed by these floating gaols exacerbated the tumult of my senses. She was a woman . . . And my attentions, which had thus far remained respectful, became more pressing with the passing of each day. I multiplied passionate compliments. I fashioned eloquent and elegant turns of phrase.

You will barely credit the powers of deception this woman displayed! As she listened to me, she affected a faraway look. For all the world she appeared interested only in the froth on the ship's wake, like snow turning into smoke. (Women are not insensible to poetic comparisons.) But, as a long-time student of the psychology of the female face, I knew that those heavy lowered eyelids masked the flickers of passion.

One day I went further, and had begun to accompany a refined expression with a flattering gesture, when she sprang round like a she-wolf to face me.

'Go away,' she commanded with almost savage determination. Her teeth gleamed strangely like those of a wild animal beneath the menacing snarl of her lips.

I smiled, unperturbed. Women, as we know, require a great deal of patience, and one should never believe a word they say. When they order you to leave, that is the moment to stay. I must apologize, gentlemen, for rehearsing such well-worn banalities.

My companion was fixing her large yellow pupils on me.

'You fail to understand me. You continue stupidly to pit yourself against my invincible disdain. I have never known love or hate. I have never met a human being who merited my hatred. Hatred is more tenacious and more patient than love, and it requires a worthy adversary.' She stroked Helga's ungainly head whilst the animal contemplated her with a deep womanly gaze.

'As for love, I am as ignorant of it as you yourself are ignorant of the art, mastered at an early age by my Anglo-Saxon compatriots, of dissimulating the self-conceit inherent in the male sex. Had I been a man, I might have loved a woman. Women have qualities I admire—loyalty in their passions and the capacity for self-sacrifice in affection. They are generally straightforward and sincere. They give without restriction or counting the cost. Their patience is as unfailing as their kindness. They can forgive. They can wait. They possess the highest form of chastity: constancy.'

Fortunately I am sufficiently sharp-witted to be able to grasp what is only hinted at. I smiled deliberately at this outburst of enthusiasm. She glanced absently in my direction and saw what I was thinking.

'Oh you are singularly mistaken. I have come across women with great generosity of spirit and heart. But I have never become attached to one of them. Their sweet nature is in itself a barrier. My soul is not sufficiently elevated to enable me to be patient with their excessive displays of candour and devotion.'

I was beginning to find her pretentious discourses rather tedious. She was turning out to be not only a shrew but a prude and a bluestocking to boot! But she was the only woman on board . . . And her display of superior airs was in any case merely designed to make her forthcoming capitulation all the more precious.

'The sole object of my affections is Helga. And Helga knows that. As for you, you may be a perfectly pleasant young man, but you can have no idea of the depth of my contempt for you.'

She intended to inflame my pride and thus my passion. And she was succeeding, the saucy miss! My blood ran hot with fury and frustrated desire.

'Men who fuss round women, any women they can find, are like dogs sniffing at bitches.'

She cast one of her long yellow glances at me.

'I have spent so long breathing in the snow-filled air of the forest, and have so often felt at one with the vast empty expanses of Whiteness, that my soul has come to resemble that of a she-wolf vanishing into the distance.'

This woman was beginning to frighten me. She noticed my reaction and changed her tone.

'I have a fondness for clarity and freshness,' she continued with a little laugh. 'I recoil from the vulgarity of men as I do from a stale smell of garlic, and I am as disgusted by their sordidity as I am by the reek of sewers. Men (she insisted) only really feel at home in a house of ill-repute. They only like courtesans, recognizing in them their own rapaciousness, their lack of emotional intelligence, their stupid cruelty. They live only for their own self-interest and for debauchery. Morally, I am sickened by men and, physically, I am repulsed by them . . . I have watched men kissing women on the lips whilst indulging in obscene fumblings. The spectacle of a gorilla could not have been more revolting.'

She paused for a moment.

'The most austere of lawmakers only escapes by a miracle the unfortunate consequences of the carnal adventures which endangered his youth. I cannot understand how a woman of any delicacy at all can submit to your filthy embraces without repugnance. As a virgin my disdain for men is equal in its degree of disgust to the nausea felt by the courtesan.'

She is most certainly overplaying her hand, I reflected, even if she is good at it. Most certainly overplaying.

(If we were not in mixed company, gentlemen, I would tell you that I have not always scorned the bordello and that I have even, on many an occasion, picked up pitiful whores off the streets. But for all that the Parisian ladies remain more accommodating than this butter-wouldn't-melt-in-my-mouth performance. I am not in the least self-conceited, but one must know one's own worth, after all.)

And so, judging that the conversation had lasted long enough, I took dignified leave of the Lady with the She-Wolf. Helga, from beneath lowered eyelids, watched me go with a long yellow stare.

Clouds were gathering heavily on the horizon, like towers. Beneath them snaked a strip of murky sky, like a moat. I had the feeling of being crushed by walls of stone.

And the wind was getting up . . .

Seasickness took hold of me. I apologize for this inelegant detail, ladies . . . I was horribly indisposed. I eventually fell asleep towards midnight, in a more lamentable state than I can tell you.

At about two o' clock in the morning, I was awoken by a terrifying crash, followed by an even more terrifying sound of shattering . . . A sense of inexpressible dread loomed in the darkness. I realized that the ship had run aground.

For the first time in my life, I neglected my appearance. I emerged on the bridge improperly dressed.

A chaotic crowd of semi-naked men was already rushing hither and thither . . . They were hauling down the lifeboats in great haste.

At the sight of their hairy limbs and matted chests I could not help recalling, with a smile, something that the Lady with the She-Wolf had said: 'The spectacle of a gorilla could not have been more revolting . . .'

I do not know why this frivolous memory struck me, in the midst of common danger.

The waves looked like monstrous volcanoes enfolded in white smoke. Or rather, perhaps, they looked like nothing on earth. They were themselves, magnificent, terrible, lethal . . . The wind whipped up their towering fury to ever greater heights. The salt stung my eyelids. I shivered in the spray, which filled the air like drizzle. And the pounding of the swell filled my head, destroying all thought.

The Lady with the She-Wolf was there, calmer than ever. And I was faint with fear. I could see Death standing over me, almost close enough to touch. Dazed, I reached up to check my forehead and felt the bones of my skull, horribly prominent. The skeleton within me filled me with dread. I began to cry, stupidly.

My flesh would turn bluish and black, swollen more than a bulging wineskin. The sharks would seize on bits of my severed limbs, floating here and there. And, when my body sank to the bottom of the sea, crabs would crawl sideways over my rotting flesh and feed gluttonously on it.

The wind gusted over the sea . . .

I saw my life pass before my eyes. I reproached myself for the imbecility of my life, a wasted life, a lost life. I tried to remember a single good action I might have committed without intending it, or by mistake. Had I been good for something, useful to someone? My conscience, buried deep within me, replied, as fearsomely as a mute who by some miracle had recovered her voice:

'No!'

The wind gusted over the sea . . .

I dimly recalled the words of our Lord exhorting the sinner to repent and promising salvation to the contrite, even in the very hour of death. I tried to dredge up a few words of prayer from the depths of my memory, as empty as a drained glass . . . And libidinous thoughts came to torment me, like little red devils. The soiled beds of women encountered by chance passed before my eyes. Their stupid obscene invitations filled my ears. The memory of loveless embraces came to me. The horror of Pleasure overwhelmed me.

Faced with the terror of the Mystery of the Void, only the instinct of the animal in rut survived in me, an instinct as powerful in some as the instinct of preservation. It was Life, Life in all its ugliness and crudeness, which howled in wild protest against Annihilation . . .

The wind gusted over the sea . . .

The ideas that come to one at such moments are bizarre, it must be allowed. There was I, a pretty decent man, when all is said and done, held in wide esteem except by a few jealous characters, even loved by a woman or two, reproaching myself so bitterly for a life which has been no better or worse than anyone else's! I must have been the victim of a temporary madness. We were all on the edge of madness, in any case . . .

The Lady with the She-Wolf was staring calmly at the white waves. Oh! they were whiter than snow at dusk! And, seated on her haunches, Helga howled like a bitch. She howled wretchedly, like a bitch baying at the moon . . . She *understood*.

I don't know why that howling froze my veins even more than the sound of the wind and the waves. She was howling at death itself, that damned devilish she-wolf! I wanted to knock her senseless to silence that noise and I searched for a piece of wood, or a spar, an iron bar, anything that would serve to flatten her on the deck. . . . I found nothing.

The lifeboat was ready to leave at last. Men were leaping frantically to safety. Only the Lady with the She-Wolf remained where she was.

'Come aboard!' I shouted to her as I got in.

She approached without haste, followed by Helga.

'Mademoiselle,' said the lieutenant who was more or less in command, 'we cannot take the animal with us. There is only room on board for people.'

'Then I shall stay behind,' she replied, moving away.

Men in a panic were jumping in, with loud and incoherent cries. We had to let her go.

For my own part, I really could not take responsibility for such a flibbertigibbet. And she had been so impertinent to me! You understand, gentlemen, do you not? You would not have behaved otherwise.

So I was saved, or almost. The dawn had come, and lord, what a dawn! A shivering of chilled light, a grey stupor, a mass of creatures and larva-like beings swarming in a twilight limbo . . .

And we saw the blur of land in the distance . . .

Oh! what a joy and comfort to see the safety and welcome of dry land! Ever since that horrible experience, I have taken only one sea voyage and that was the journey back here. I will not be caught out again, that's for certain!

I must be lacking in self-interest, ladies. In the midst of the unutterable uncertainty in which I found myself, saved from Destruction by a mere hair's breadth, I still made the effort to discover what had become of my companions in misfortune. The second lifeboat had been submerged by the frantic assault of too many demented passengers. I watched in horror as it sank. The Lady with the She-Wolf had taken refuge on a broken mast and the quietened beast was with her on this floating wreckage. I was quite certain that the woman would be saved, if her strength and determination did not desert her. I hoped so, with all my heart. But what of the cold, the slow progress and fragility of her improvised vessel, lacking sail and rudder, the dangers of fatigue and feminine weakness!

They were only a short distance from land when the Lady, exhausted, turned towards Helga as if to say: 'I can't go on . . .'

And then something sad and solemn occurred. The she-wolf, *who had understood*, let out her despairing howl so that it reached the land, so near and so inaccessible. Then, raising herself up, she placed her front paws on the shoulders of her mistress, who enfolded her in her arms. Together they disappeared beneath the waves . . .

MARCEL AYMÉ (1902–1967)

The Walking Stick

Translated by Elizabeth Fallaize

Monsieur and Madame Sorbier decided to make the most of Sunday
afternoon and take the children out on a family walk. Mme Sorbier
called through the window to her two boys, Victor and Félicien, who
were playing out in the street throwing filth in each other's faces. They
liked rowdy games of the kind that strike despair in the maternal bosom.

'Come in and put your suits on,' she said. 'We're going out for a walk.
It's a lovely sunny Sunday afternoon.'

Each of the family members dressed up in their Sunday outfits. Victor
and Félicien pulled on their sailor suits with undisguised reluctance. They
were eager to wear men's clothing, but were obliged to wait until the day
of their first communion when they would also get real silver watches.

Their father fastened his detachable stiff collar and arranged a bow tie
over the top of it. As he was about to slip his jacket on he stopped to
scrutinize the left sleeve with a serious expression and said to his wife:

'Mathilde, what would you say if I left my black armband off? In Paris
mourning isn't worn much.'

'You do as you please,' returned Mathilde, frostily. 'It's barely two
months since my Uncle Émile died, but, after all, he was only my
uncle . . . and it obviously doesn't take you long to forget people.'

'Mathilde, you know what your Uncle Émile used to say: "When I'm
gone, my dears . . ." '

'Well of course you're under no obligation to pay respect to my relatives when they pass away, but you will admit that I've always gone into
mourning for all your family. In eight years of marriage I've hardly got
out of black at all . . .'

Sorbier shook his head, looking annoyed, but no reply came to mind.
Giving up the idea, he put his jacket on. But the feeling of virtuous
pleasure that usually accompanies self-denial failed to materialize. He
studied his reflection mournfully in the mirror-fronted wardrobe and
sighed:

'The thing is, it stands out, you know . . . A dark jacket, now, that
wouldn't look so bad . . .'

Sorbier was not over-fussy about his appearance. For going to the office during the week he really didn't mind wearing clothes which were past their best, or had been mended even, but he felt quite rightly that Sundays are for elegant dressing. How indeed could a man be expected to put up with being pushed around all week by his superiors if he didn't have the satisfaction of knowing that he had a Sunday suit in his wardrobe? It's a question of human dignity. And it's perfectly obvious that a black armband lowers the tone of an elegant suit. On the other hand, a bereavement is a bereavement, there is no gainsaying that, especially when you are married and head of the family.

Meanwhile Victor and Félicien were playing hide and seek under the dining-room table. They had been told time and time again that it wasn't a game for indoors. A decorative fruit bowl eventually fell to the floor and smashed. Their mother rushed in when she heard the noise, slapped the one closest at hand and, in order to keep them apart, locked one of them in the WC. Now she could get on with dressing in peace with no fear of a disaster, as the two were separated. When she went back into the bedroom, she saw her husband sitting in the armchair, gazing at the ceiling with a little smile of beatitude, stroking the stiff hairs of his moustache.

'Why are you looking at the ceiling? What are you plotting now, with that little smile of yours?'

'I'd like to . . . You know, Mathilde, an idea came to me, just now. I'd like . . .'

He was murmuring dreamily. His wife pressed him to speak up, already suspecting some new idiocy.

'I'd like,' he said, 'to get Uncle Émile's walking stick out. . . . I hadn't given any thought to Uncle Émile's walking stick before . . . Don't you think that instead of leaving it in the wardrobe drawer, it would be better . . .'

Mathilde compressed her lips and her husband flushed slightly. Obviously, he had been in too much of a hurry wanting the walking stick, with Uncle Émile still warm in his grave, as his wife was making abundantly clear to him, her voice trembling with rage and her eyes moist with indignation:

'Barely two months! A man who worked his whole life! He had never even used his walking stick!'

'Well, exactly . . .'

'Exactly? What do you mean, exactly? There is no sense in saying: exactly. Come on!'

'I am saying: exactly.' And his face took on a closed look, as though he attached some mysterious meaning to his reply.

Mathilde called upon her husband to explain himself. He whistled. She did up her suspenders whilst planning her revenge. At two-thirty everyone was ready on the landing. It appeared that the walk was about to follow the pattern of every Sunday walk: two hours of boredom with a pause in the middle to stand round a bottle of beer in silence. 'Forward march,' said the father. As always. He was about to close the front door when he changed his mind and said, with an innocent air that completely took Mathilde in:

'I've forgotten my watch. You go on down, I'll be with you in a minute, as soon as I've fetched it.'

He ran to the wardrobe, opened the drawer, and took out Uncle Émile's walking stick. The handle was in yellowed bone carved in the shape of a bulldog's head, and it was screwed onto a varnished wooden stick encircled with a gold band. Sorbier had never suspected that the mere act of holding a walking stick in the right hand could confer such an enhanced sense of dignity on a man. When he rejoined his family waiting for him in front of the building, he remained impervious to the furious attack launched by his wife. He announced with all the assurance of a man free to do as he pleases, a man who as head of the family is determined to defend the rights concomitant with the male responsibilities which naturally fell upon him:

'Yes! That's right, I'm using your uncle's walking stick. I see no harm in that. I am thirty-seven years old, I have reached the age where a man with responsibilities may legitimately carry a walking stick. If you want the old man's stick to stay in the wardrobe, I'll buy one of my own, and I promise you that I shan't spare the expense!'

Mathilde remained tight-lipped, fearing what he might take into his head. First they buy a walking stick, then they develop a spending habit, the next thing is a string of mistresses . . . For the first time in years she cast a glance full of fear and admiration at her husband. Even though she resented his lack of reverence for her late uncle, she could not help noticing the easy elegance with which he manipulated the stick. She gave a little sigh, bordering on the affectionate, which Sorbier interpreted as a sign of resentment.

'Go home if your feet are hurting,' he said. 'I shall go on with the children; they'll be more than happy . . .'

'There's nothing wrong with my feet, but what do you mean the children . . .'

'Perhaps you think I can't manage my own children out on a walk? You're suggesting, no doubt, that I'm not much of a father?'

He gave a snort of derision. Victor was walking just ahead of the family, whilst Félicien was holding hands with his mother, who was gripping him tightly. Sorbier registered this and, in need of a bold initiative with which to bolster his authority, he declared high-handedly:

'I find it extraordinary that people try to prevent children from enjoying themselves. Come along, Félicien, let go of your mother's hand.'

'You know perfectly well that when they're together we can't keep them under control,' Mathilde objected. 'They're bound to rip their clothes or end up under the wheels of a car. It's too late once an accident has happened . . .'

Sorbier offered no reply and, giving Félicien's calves a friendly tap with the stick, repeated:

'Come along, Félicien, run off and find your brother. It'll be more fun than walking along at your mother's heel.'

Félicien let go of his mother's hand and ran off to surprise his brother with a sudden kick in the backside. Victor slapped him in return and a beret rolled out into the middle of the road. Mathilde surveyed the results of this paternal initiative with an ironic show of indifference. Sorbier began to laugh and said jovially:

'They're priceless, those two. It would be a real shame not to leave them to enjoy themselves in their own way.'

All the same, he saw the necessity of keeping their amusements within limits.

'Stay just in front of me, within reach of my stick, and play nicely. We've got plenty of time, I'm going to take you on a walk which will be most educational.'

The family made its way along a kilometre of roads and avenues. The father pointed out monuments with his stick and held forth with such cheerfulness and at such length that his wife became exasperated.

'All these streets are full of historical monuments. Over there are the magasins du Louvre, this side is the Ministry of Finance. And there is the statue of Gambetta, who saved our honour in 1870, you remember.'

A bit further on, Victor spotted a naked woman standing on a pedestal, and pointed at her.

'And over there, papa? What's that? Did she save our honour as well?'

His father betrayed a surge of irritation. In a haughty tone he replied:

'It's a woman. Come along now, don't just stand there.'

And he urged Victor forwards with the tip of his stick. He was shocked to hear a boy of Victor's age asking about a naked woman. But his self-control returned almost immediately and, poking his wife with his elbow, he remarked in a roguish tone of barely disguised challenge:

'And a damned shapely woman, actually. You can see an artist's hand there. Look!'

Conscious of the imperfections which she sought with difficulty to disguise beneath her corset, Mathilde took on an air of offended disapproval. Sorbier made things worse by clicking his tongue appreciatively.

'Damned shapely! You surely can't disagree? It's impossible to imagine a woman with a more perfect shape.'

Mathilde replied with an indistinct murmur which was not so much a dissent as a demurral of modesty. Sorbier reacted strongly, as though he had been accused of lying. It seemed to him that the incomparable sense of dignity which Uncle Émile's walking stick had conferred upon him was being hypocritically undermined. Taking Mathilde by the arm, he bundled her forward to stand right in front of the statue.

'Look at the line of the hips, look at the curve of the belly, mm? A slightly rounded belly, just like a belly should be rounded. And the breasts? What about the breasts, then? Have you ever seen anything so beautiful?'

Mathilde was on the verge of tears. Victor and Félicien were following their father's lecture with great interest, and had to hold on to their sides to stop themselves laughing when he invoked the splendours of the curves, which he traced out lovingly with his stick. Mathilde tried several diversions in vain, even expressing her anxiety at seeing the boys taking in the details of this nude study. Sorbier, getting into his stride, spared her nothing and, walking round to the back of the statue, let out a veritable roar of enthusiasm:

'The other side is the same! Just what's needed to sit down, and no more!'

His stick drew two circles in the air, as though to isolate the object of his admiration. Victor and Félicien, already purple from the effort of containing their hilarity, burst into a snort of laughter which exploded through their noses and shook their shoulders. Terrified that this outburst of merriment would be interpreted by their parents as evidence of their depraved instincts, they ran off. This persuaded the father to abandon the statue. Mathilde had heard him out to the end, without even thinking of turning her back on him. She fell mechanically into step behind him, overwhelmed by the image of the naked woman, in all her crushing detail. She caught herself blushing at the size of her own chest, which hid her feet from her view. In a fit of humility, she concluded that she was ridiculous, unworthy of the husband whom she had misjudged. Sorbier appeared to her in a new and prestigious light; he had suddenly acquired a wicked seductiveness, with a halo of perversity. A desire began to stir in her for the pleasures of utter devotion, for the thrill of total obedience and complete submission to the capricious will of her husband. Nevertheless, she was careful to give no outward sign of this revolution in her emotions. Keeping her bearing haughty and her expression supercilious, she maintained a prudent silence, leaving her husband to remonstrate with the children. In an effort which brought the blood to her cheeks, she controlled her breathing so as to minimize her sizeable stomach, without realizing that this made her chest all the more prominent. In any case, Sorbier was not paying any attention to her. Drunk with the fervour of his own invocation to the naked statue, he was repeating to himself some of the turns of phrase which struck him as particularly apt; at the same time, he was enjoying evoking the various body parts of the stone nude. Several times, Mathilde heard him declare in a staccato rhythm: 'thigh, shoulder, belly, shin'. For a moment, she was able to believe that he was planning an unusual recipe for a hotpot, but, after a silence, he added in a burst of nervous laughter: 'And the breasts, oh yes! The breasts!' It was already becoming evident that Sorbier's aesthetic pleasure was no longer strictly pure. The brightness of his eyes and the warmth of his voice provided clues that his wife was familiar with. Unable to maintain her affectation of indifference, she said in a low voice, betraying hurt, but not anger:

'I don't know if you were playing your cards close to your chest, but in the past you never allowed yourself to mention such awful things in my presence. Since you've got hold of Uncle Émile's stick, you've put on a very superior air. If my poor uncle were still alive, he would tell you what your duties are as a husband and father. He would tell you that it isn't fair or reasonable to talk about some trollop's breasts in front of your wife, even stone breasts. You ought to know from what happened to the Corvisons that when a husband starts fooling around it leads to the ruin of his household. And then, I'd like to know, what's the point? What's the point of dreaming about a strange woman's breasts? Dearest, remember the evenings—remember yesterday evening—when my breasts were the only ones in the world. Think about it, you can't possibly have forgotten.'

Mathilde saw her mistake at once. Carried away by a wave of jealousy and affection, she had made the error of drawing attention to her breasts. Not content with having tasted the pleasures of the womanizer, Sorbier now delighted in the opportunity to be cruel and offensive. He looked Mathilde up and down with a pitying, ironic air, and the tip of his stick outlined in space a bulge of insulting proportions. He shook his head in a manner which signified:

' No, no, my poor dear, no, you're quite out of it. Just look at yourself, compare . . .'

His meaning was so clear that Mathilde's cheeks flushed with rage. She tried to get back at him:

'Well, I don't care. I'm only telling you for the children's sake and to try to make you realize how ridiculous you are. When all's said and done you're no spring chicken yourself, you're not exactly a woman's dream. The concierge was saying so only yesterday morning when I came back from fetching the bandages for your varicose veins.'

'That old bag, she's twice tried to kiss me on the stairs! But I told her, the day it takes my fancy to cheat on my wife, there's no shortage of pretty girls in Paris. If a man knows how to go about it—and here Sorbier gave a knowing smile—he can take his pick of the bunch, thank God!'

As he was speaking, a pretty woman went by and her eyes met Sorbier's. Suddenly inspired, he doffed his hat to her and smiled with as much gallantry as he could muster. Slightly surprised, the young woman nodded to him, and even gave a half-smile. Mathilde felt that she was losing her head. Her hand grasped Sorbier's shoulder.

'That woman. Who is she? I've never seen her at our house, or anywhere else. I want to know where you met her.'

Sorbier gave no immediate reply, as though he were contemplating defeat. Mathilde was angrily insistent.

'I don't know,' he murmured in an embarrassed tone. 'I knew her . . . in the past . . . I don't remember exactly.'

Savouring the look of panic which appeared on Mathilde's face, he went off to extract Félicien from a flowerbed. The family continued on out of the Tuileries Gardens and reached the boulevards via the rue Royale.

As they went past a pâtisserie, Félicien complained that he was hungry and Victor claimed to be even hungrier than his brother.

'Mother, I'm hungry. I'm hungrier than him . . .'

Irritated, Mathilde distributed slaps all round. The boys began to cry and whimper more loudly. Mathilde had red swollen eyes herself. The passers-by looked on with sympathetic curiosity at this *mater dolorosa* dragging along two children in tears. Sorbier remained impervious. He walked along ahead of his family, a spring in his step, a roving sparkle in his eye, and roses in his cheeks, turning round only to follow with his eyes a female figure. As he passed in front of the terrace of one of the boulevard cafés, he stopped and allowed them to catch up.

'Let's go in for a drink,' he said. 'The walk has made me quite parched. And we can watch the world go by, women go by . . .'

Mathilde glanced at the café terrace. The luxurious rattan chairs, all identical, the mirrors, the smart uniform of the waiters, and the solemnity of the majordomo filled her with anxiety. The Sunday walk usually finished up in some deserted little café reeking of wood shavings and cheap red wine; a genuine watering hole as Sorbier was fond of saying, where the patron brought the bottles of beer over himself. Mathilde was aghast at the thought of what the prices would be on this smart terrace and felt convinced that her husband was on a slippery slope. Sorbier was already pushing her ahead with what he imagined to be a practised gesture. She resisted.

'It's a very expensive-looking café,' she said. 'We never go into cafés like this. You know we don't.'

'It's just a café. Anyone would think you'd never seen one. I know it like the back of my hand.'

Mathilde smiled humbly and murmured timidly:

'If there were just the two of us, it wouldn't be so bad, it wouldn't be so extravagant. Maybe another day . . .'

Sorbier was growing impatient. It seemed to him that the crowd on the terrace was laughing at his wife's hesitation.

'If you don't feel like going in, you go home with the children. I'm thirsty. You do as you want.'

Without waiting for Mathilde to make her mind up, he began squeezing down between two rows of tables, and the family followed. As he reached the last row of the terrace a couple got up and Sorbier took possession of their abandoned table. He ordered an aperitif for himself, and beer for the children. Mathilde didn't want anything, claiming she had a headache. Husband and wife, each sunk into a rattan armchair, remained in uneasy silence. Sorbier himself appeared ill at ease, worried about how his family might look to this leisured crowd. Several times, he felt that the waiter was looking at him severely. He said to Mathilde:

'Look, order a drink. You look silly! You don't come to a café to refuse a drink, it's ridiculous.'

Eventually she allowed herself to be persuaded and ordered a small glass of draught beer. Sorbier was greatly relieved and felt his good humour returning. He remembered that he had a walking stick and examined the handle with fond attention.

'You can say what you like, a walking stick is the final touch to a man's appearance. I can't imagine how I managed without one.'

He had addressed Mathilde in a friendly tone. In a rush of love and gratitude, she was quick to agree:

'You're right. I would never have thought that a walking stick would suit you so well. I'm glad you thought of getting it out.'

Just at that moment, a woman walked on to the terrace. Her outfit, her make-up, and the glance with which she assessed each of the men were clear signs of her profession. She hesitated between several rows of chairs and, noticing a table free close to the Sorbier family, she came and sat down. Sorbier had been following her progress with interest since she came in. When she was seated, he had no difficulty in catching her eye. Smiles were exchanged, and even winks. The hussy took part in the charade obligingly. No doubt the open way in which Sorbier was looking her over encouraged her to think that Mathilde was not his wife. Leaning forward over his aperitif to get a better look at her, Sorbier was fully occupied in smiling and directing meaningful looks. Mathilde could not pretend not to notice the goings-on but, paralysed by anger and embarrassment, and unwilling to face the shame of a marital dispute in public, she remained silent. However, when Victor and Félicien, curious to know who their father could be smiling at, turned round to face the intruder, Mathilde let out a furious protest.

'It's disgusting. Behaving like that in front of children! A trollop without a penny to her name, no doubt!'

The crowd of drinkers was so dense on the terrace that the waiters were having difficulty keeping up with the orders. The hussy was trying in vain to attract the majordomo's attention and get served. Sorbier conveyed, by means of facial expressions, his indignation at the casual treatment meted out by the staff to an attractive woman. Unable, finally, to contain himself, he remarked in a voice designed to carry, ignoring Mathilde's pressure on his knee recommending silence:

'It's impossible to get served here! My word, this café is going down-hill! When I think what it once was!'

He was delighted to receive in return a long smile of gratitude from the

attractive woman in question. In order to justify to his wife the intervention which he was considering, Sorbier then added, in a show of dandyism
which he himself found overawing and which appalled Mathilde:

'I've been waiting a good quarter of an hour to order a cocktail!'

The word cocktail, which evoked for Mathilde a train of moral
turpitude, naked women, and expensive wax-sealed bottles, was the last
straw. She had a detailed vision of her husband spending the household
savings on taxis, top hats, and extravagant dinners, while she took her
last jewel to the pawnbrokers in order to feed her starving children.

'Waiter, you're wanted over here. It's ridiculous that we can't get a
waiter!'

Sorbier's voice was drowned out by the buzz of conversation. The
young woman shook her head in gratitude and impotence. Carried away
by a wave of gallant impetuosity, Sorbier seized hold of the middle of his
walking stick intending to bang the end on the table. He lifted it up
above his shoulder in a bold and generous gesture . . .

Behind him, a mirrored panel shattered into pieces, pulverized by
Uncle Émile's bulldog. Scarlet, Sorbier sprang up from his armchair. He
was surrounded by a tumult of laughter, comments, and protests. A man
at a neighbouring table complained sharply that there were bits of glass
in his aperitif. People were amused by the consternation of the guilty
party, who stood holding on to his stick with both hands, as if he were
presenting arms.

Mathilde, who had been sunk low in despair, began to recover her
spirits. Sorbier's air of shock and bewilderment revived her; her sagging
bust began to lift majestically. Half standing up she hissed in her husband's ear, with a cruel sneer unaffected by the hilarity which her
response was causing amongst the witnesses to the drama:

'Five hundred francs! That's what your stupidity has cost us! And all
for a slut who was only after your money!'

The manager of the establishment arrived on the scene of the disaster.
A waiter went to fetch the police. Sorbier recited his name and details,
produced his personal documents. Looking suddenly aged, his shoulders
hunched, he stumbled over the same phrases again and again:

'Officer, I didn't do it on purpose . . . it was Uncle Émile's walking
stick . . . I meant to call the waiter with my stick . . .'

Mathilde followed the exchange with a malevolent pleasure, shower-
ing him with sarcastic remarks. In a voice full of resignation, Sorbier
pleaded:

'Please, Mathilde, leave it till later!'

The police officer took pity on his distress and cut short the formalities. The manager also displayed some compassion, affirming that the damage was not that serious and that he could easily sort it out with his insurance company. Distraught with worry, Sorbier sat down again beside Mathilde, who said to him:

'Don't you want a cocktail to buck you up? You must feel in need of something . . .'

His face was so tortured, so humble, that she saw she could do as she pleased and inflict the most painful of humiliations on him. She insisted:

'Whilst you're on a spending spree, you can surely allow yourself a cocktail! You can give me a little sip of it . . .'

Sorbier sighed in distress. He looked round to try to catch the eye of the young woman who had been at the origin of his misfortunes, hoping for the comfort of friendly sympathy. But she, conscious that the mishap had broken the spell, had turned her head away and was smiling at a timorous old gent who couldn't take his eyes off her.

'Just look at your tart,' said Mathilde. 'She's found a man who walks with two sticks!'

Victor and Félicien, with not altogether unconscious cruelty, were keeping themselves amused by reconstructing the accident. Their mother, who was enjoying their game, intervened from time to time to point out some piquant detail in the performance. Sorbier called the waiter over in a weary voice to pay for the drinks. When at last he was able to leave the table Mathilde, who was still lounging in her chair, called him back and said to him in a tone of unbearable sweetness:

'You're forgetting your walking stick, dearest.'

He retraced his steps, took hold of his stick with an awkward gesture and followed his wife, who was propelling the children between two rows of drinkers. His stick was hampering his progress; as he negotiated a table, he knocked off an empty glass which the waiter fortunately managed to catch in mid-air. Mathilde turned her head and jeered:

'My, you're on good form this evening. Have you spotted anything else breakable yet?'

Sorbier reflected that he would take great pleasure in breaking his stick over his wife's back, but it was a passing thought that he did not have the nerve to express out loud. As they left the terrace, he had the further mortification of witnessing the tarty young woman get up and join the elderly gentleman. Mathilde, sharp-eyed as ever, made sure that he knew she had not missed this latest comic twist, but the desire for revenge boiling inside her led her to abandon her ironic stance. Fixing her gaze on her husband's eyes she demanded in the haughty tone familiar to Sorbier's ears:

'Are you going to tell me now why you thought you had the right to take that walking stick? A stick that doesn't even belong to you?'

Sorbier made a vague gesture. He really didn't know . . . Mathilde could have slapped him.

'When a man takes a walking stick, he has a reason. I insist that you tell me why you took Uncle Émile's stick.'

She had come to a halt and taken hold of his jacket. Sorbier saw that she would not let the matter rest until she had an explanation. In a spirit of probity, he scrupulously examined the inner recesses of his soul and, when he found nothing, he fell back on poetic inspiration, in the hope that he might disarm his wife's anger.

'What can I say? Well, it was the sunshine . . . yes, the sunshine . . . you see, when I saw what a lovely day it was, the idea came to me like spring fever. Spring fever can just take you . . .'

Mathilde went through the motions of a fit of laughter, whilst he repeated plaintively:

'Of course, spring fever. If you just tried to understand . . .'

She gave him a shove to start him walking again, as though he were no more than a puppet, and declared between clenched teeth:

'Just wait, my lad, we'll see about spring fever. Don't think I've forgotten your behaviour back there . . .'

Victor and Félicien had taken advantage of the interrogation to slip off ahead on their own. The parents had to hurry to catch them up in the Sunday crowd. Mathilde called to one of the boys:

'Come and take your father's hand and watch out that he doesn't let go.'

Docilely, Sorbier took his son's hand and lengthened his stride. Mathilde ordered him back in the tone of a sergeant major.

' Give him your right hand, he's hurt his wrist . . . Well! What are you waiting for? Don't tell me it's your stick that's the trouble. Just hold it in your left hand. It won't make you look any sillier.'

Sorbier passed his stick over to his left hand and his son over to his right. The stick was becoming more and more of a nuisance; he held it tightly squeezed under his arm and Mathilde was amused by his awkward gait. As he was preparing to take a right turn she called out, in a calm voice which disturbed him:

'No, straight on. Carry on. I've decided to take another route.'

'It's getting late. It's nearly five o'clock you know.'

'You weren't in such a hurry earlier on. I'm still enjoying my walk. We'll go back down the rue Royale in the opposite direction and we'll walk through the Tuileries. It's such a nice walk at this time of year.'

Ever since they left the café she had been meditating her revenge: she would make her humiliated husband retrace in defeat the very same route which he had strode with such arrogance earlier on.

Sorbier walked along with a shuffling gait, his head bowed, his shoulders stooped. It didn't occur to him to look at the women. He was just a poor man looking forward to his paper and his slippers. Mathilde was at his heels, finding every opportunity to underline the gulf between the proud assurance which he had displayed on the first half of their walk, and the subdued air which he wore on the return half.

'Did you see that pretty girl who just passed us? Look round. Earlier on, you were a bit more lively . . .'

In the Tuileries Gardens, Victor and Félicien were allowed to run on ahead, but Sorbier made no attempt to carry his stick in his right hand again. He tried to forget it. Mathilde had retained a very precise memory of each of the places in which her husband had asserted his independence and his lewd taste. She reminded him of each of his comments, before taking them acidly to pieces. When they arrived in front of the statue of the naked woman, she gave a haughty shiver of her chest and declared, looking him up and down:

'Well here's your ironing board! You were very keen on her, earlier on. Haven't you got anything to say, now?'

Sorbier gazed at the statue with an air of melancholy in which Mathilde detected a hint of regret. She took up Uncle Émile's stick and began moving the tip over the stone contours, running down each of the features malevolently as she went.

'Look at that, it's all skin and bones. No shoulders to speak of and no sign of a belly! You'd need strong glasses to see much flesh there.'

Sorbier, eyes in the distance, appeared lost in melancholy thoughts. Mathilde frowned, laid down the stick on the base of the statue and, crossing her arms high up, said to him in a harsh tone:

'Well?'

Sorbier raised his eyes to his wife like a hunted animal. He hesitated for a moment and then, giving a cowardly little gurgle of a laugh, he murmured:

'Of course, she looks too girlish. A beautiful woman should have some flesh on her . . .'

This flattering opinion which she had forced out of her husband brought a flush of pride to Mathilde's cheeks. She took his arm, in a slow and deliberate movement suggesting a definitive repossession, and directed the family on the homeward route. Victor and Félicien had removed the stick from the base of the statue. They ran along in front of their parents, each boy holding on to one end of the stick. Their father looked on with relief, pleased to be spared a burden which now seemed intolerable to him. Sensing his greater degree of ease, Mme Sorbier called to the boys:

'Give the walking stick back to your father. It's not for playing with.'

And, turning to her husband:

'Now you've got it out of the wardrobe, you can bring it every Sunday in future.'

COLETTE (1873–1954)

Gribiche

Translated by Antonia White

I never arrived before quarter past nine. By that time, the temperature
and the smell of the basement of the theatre had already acquired their
full intensity. I shall not give the exact location of the music hall in
which, some time between 1905 and 1910, I was playing a sketch in a
revue. All I need say is that the underground dressing rooms had neither
windows nor ventilators. In our women's quarters, the doors of the rows
of identical cells remained innocently open; the men . . . far less numerous in revues than nowadays . . . dressed on the floor above, almost at
street level. When I arrived, I found myself among women already
acclimatized to the temperature, for they had been in their dressing
rooms since eight o'clock. The steps of the iron staircase clanged
musically under my feet; the last five steps each gave out their particular
note like a xylophone—B, B flat, C, D, and then dropping a fifth to G. I
shall never forget their inevitable refrain. But when fifty pairs of heels
clattered up and down like hail for the big ensembles and dance
numbers, the notes blended into a kind of shrill thunder which made the
plaster walls between each dressing room tremble. Halfway up the staircase a ventilator marked the level of the street. When it was occasionally
opened during the day, it let in the poisonous air of the street, and
fluttering rags of paper, blown there by the wind, clung to its grating,
which was coated with dried mud.

As soon as we reached the floor of our cellar, each of us made some
ritual complaint about the suffocating atmosphere. My neighbour across
the passage, a little green-eyed Basque, always panted for a moment
before opening the door of her dressing room, put her hand on her
heart, sighed: 'Positively filthy!' and then thought no more about it. As
she had short thighs and high insteps, she gummed a kiss-curl on her left
cheek and called herself Carmen Brasero.

Mademoiselle Clara d'Estouteville, known as La Toutou, occupied the
next dressing room. Tall, miraculously fair, slim as women only became
twenty-five years later, she played the silent part of Commère during the
first half of the second act. When she arrived, she would push back the

pale gold swathes of hair on her temples with a transparent hand and murmur: 'Oh, take me out of here or I'll burst!' Then, without bending down, she would kick off her shoes. Sometimes she would hold out her hand. The gesture was hardly one of cordiality; it was merely that she was amused by the involuntary start of surprise which an ordinary hand like my own would give at the touch of her extraordinarily delicate, almost melting fingers. A moment after her arrival, a chilly smell like toothpaste would inform us all that the frail actress was eating her half pound of peppermints. Mademoiselle d'Estouteville's voice was so loud and raucous that it prevented her from playing spoken parts, so that the music hall could only use her exceptional beauty; the beauty of a spun-glass angel. La Toutou had her own method of explaining the situation.

'You see, on the stage I can't say my *a*'s. And however small a part, there's nearly always an *a* in it. And as I can't say my *a*'s . . .'

'But you do say them!' Carmen pointed out.

La Toutou gave her colleague a blue glance, equally sublime in its stupidity, its indignation, and its deceitfulness. The anguish of her indigestion made it even more impressive.

'Look here, dear, you can't have the cheek to pretend you know more about it than Victor de Cottens, who tried me out for his revue at the Folies!'

Her stage costume consisted of strings of imitation diamonds, which occasionally parted to give glimpses of a rose-tinted knee and an adolescent thigh or the tip of a barely formed breast. When this vision, which suggested a dawn glittering with frost, was on her way up to the stage, she passed my other neighbour, Lise Damoiseau, on her way back from impersonating the Queen of Torments. Lise would be invariably holding up her long black velvet robe with both hands, candidly displaying her bow legs. On a long neck built like a tower and slightly widening at the base, Lise carried a head modelled in the richest tones and textures of black and white. The teeth between the sad voluptuous lips were flawless; the enormous dark eyes, whose whites were slightly blue, held and reflected back the light. Her black, oiled hair shone like a river under the moon. She was always given sinister parts to play. In revues, she held sway over the Hall of Poisons and the Paradise of Forbidden Pleasures. Satan, Gilles de Rais, the Nightmare of Opium, the Beheaded Woman, Delilah, and Messalina all took on the features of Lise. She was seldom given a line to speak and the dress designers cleverly disguised her meagre and undistinguished little body. She was far from being vain about her appearance. One night when I was paying her a perfectly sincere compliment she shrugged her shoulders and turned the fixed glitter of her eyes on me.

'M'm, yes,' said Lise. 'My face is all right. And my neck. Down to here, but no further.'

She looked into the great cracked glass that every actress consulted before going up the staircase and judged herself with harsh lucidity.

'I can only get away with it in long skirts.'

After the grand final tableau, Lise Damoiseau went into total eclipse. Shorn of her make-up and huddled into some old black dress, she would carry away her superb head, its long neck muffled in a rabbit-skin scarf, as if it were some object for which she had no further use till tomorrow. Standing under the gas lamp on the pavement outside the stage door, she would give a last smouldering glance before she disappeared down the steps of the métro.

Several other women inhabited the subterranean corridor. There was Liane de Parthenon, a tall big-boned blonde, and Fifi Soada, who boasted of her likeness to Polaire, and Zarzita, who emphasized her resemblance to the beautiful Otero. Zarzita did her hair like Otero, imitated her accent, and pinned up photographs of the famous ballerina on the walls of her dressing room. When she drew one's attention to these, she invariably added, 'The only difference is that *I* can dance!' There was also a dried-up little Englishwoman of unguessable age, with a face like an old nurse's and fantastically agile limbs; there was an Algerian, Miss Ourika, who specialized in the *danse du ventre* and who was all hips; there was . . . there was . . . Their names, which I hardly knew, have long since vanished. All that I heard of them, beyond the dressing rooms near me, was a zoo-like noise composed of Anglo-Saxon grunting, the yawns and sighs of caged creatures, mechanical blasphemies, and a song, always the same song, sung over and over again by a Spanish voice:

> *Tou m'abais fait serment*
> *Dé m'aimer tendrement . . .*

Occasionally, a silence would dominate all the neighbouring noises and give place to the distant hum of the stage; then one of the women would break out of this silence with a scream, a mechanical curse, a yawn, or a tag of song: *Tou m'abais fait serment . . .*

Was I, in those days, too susceptible to the convention of work, glittering display, empty-headedness, punctuality, and rigid probity which reigns in the music hall? Did it inspire me to describe it over and over again with a violent and superficial love and with all its accompaniment of commonplace poetry? Very possibly. The fact remains that during six years of my past life I was still capable of finding relaxation among its monsters and its marvels. In that past there still gleams the head of Lise Damoiseau and the bottomless, radiant imbecility of Mademoiselle d'Estouteville. I still remember with delight a certain Bouboule with beautiful breasts who wept offendedly if she had to play even a tiny part in a high dress and the magnificent, long, shallow-grooved back of some Lola or Pepa or Concha . . . Looking back, I can rediscover some particular acrobat swinging high up from bar to bar of a nickelled trapeze or some particular juggler in the centre of an orbit of balls. It was a world in which fantasy and bureaucracy were oddly interwoven. And I can still plunge at will into that dense, limited element which bore up my inexperience and happily limited my vision and my cares for six whole years.

Everything in it was by no means as gay and as innocent as I have described it elsewhere. Today I want to speak of my debut in that world, of a time when I had neither learned nor forgotten anything of a theatrical milieu in which I had not the faintest chance of succeeding, that of the big spectacular revue. What an astonishing milieu it was! One sex practically eclipsed the other, dominating it, not only by numbers, but by its own particular smell and magnetic atmosphere. This crowd of women reacted like a barometer to any vagary of the weather. It needed only a change of wind or a wet day to send them all into the depths of depression; a depression which expressed itself in tears and curses, in talk of suicide and in irrational terrors and superstitions. I was not a prey to it myself, but having known very few women and been deeply hurt by one single man, I accepted it uncritically. I was even rather impressed by it although it was only latent hysteria; a kind of schoolgirl neurosis which afflicts women who are arbitrarily and pointlessly segregated from the other sex.

My contribution to the programme was entitled 'Maiou-Ouah-Ouah. Sketch'. On the strength of my first '*Dialogues de Bêtes*', the authors of the revue had commissioned me to bark and mew on the stage. The rest of my turn consisted mainly of performing a few dance steps in bronze-coloured tights. On my way to and from the stage I had to pass by the star's dressing room. The leading lady was a remote personage whose door was only open to her personal friends. She never appeared in the corridors except attended by two dressers whose job was to carry her headdresses, powder, comb, and hand mirror and to hold up her trailing flounces. She plays no part in my story but I liked to follow her and smell the trail of amazingly strong scent she left in her wake. It was a sweet, sombre scent; a scent for a beautiful Negress. I was fascinated by it but I was never able to discover its name.

One night, attired in my decorous kimono, I was dressing as usual with my door open. I had finished making up my face and my neck and was heating my curling tongs on a spirit lamp. The quick, hurried little step of Carmen Brasero (I knew it was Carmen by the clatter of her heels) sounded on the stone floor and stopped opposite my dressing room. Without turning around, I wished her good evening and received a hasty warning in reply.

'Hide that! The fire inspectors. I saw those chaps upstairs. I know one of them.'

'But we've all got spirit lamps in our dressing rooms!'

'Of course,' said Carmen. 'But for goodness' sake, hide it. That chap I know's a swine. He makes you open your suitcases.'

I put out the flame, shut the lid, and looked helplessly around my bare cell.

'Where on earth can I hide it?'

'You're pretty green, aren't you? Do you have to be told every single thing? Listen . . . I can hear them coming.'

She turned up her skirt, nipped the little lamp high up between her thighs, and walked off with an assured step.

The fire inspectors, two in number, appeared. They ferreted about and went off, touching their bowler hats. Carmen Brasero returned, fished out my lamp from between her thighs, and laid it down on my make-up shelf.

'Here's the object!'

'Marvellous,' I said. 'I'd never have thought of doing that.'

She laughed like a child who is thoroughly pleased with itself.

'Cigarettes, my handbag, a box of sweets . . . I hide them all like that and nothing ever drops out. Even a loaf that I stole when I was a kid. The baker's wife didn't half shake me! She kept saying, "Have you thrown it in the gutter?" But I held my loaf tight between my thighs and she had to give it up as a bad job. She wasn't half wild! It's these muscles *here* that I've got terrifically strong.'

She was just going off when she changed her mind and said with immense dignity: 'Don't make any mistakes! It's nothing to do with the filthy tricks those Eastern dancers get up to with a bottle! *My* muscles are all on the *outside*!'

I protested that I fully appreciated this and the three feathers, shading from fawn to chestnut, which adorned Carmen's enormous blue straw hat went waving away along the corridor.

The nightly ritual proceeded on its way. 'The Miracle of the Roses' trailed its garlands of dusty flowers. A squadron of eighteenth-century French soldiers galloped up the staircase, banging their arms against the walls with a noise like the clatter of tin cans.

I did my own turn after these female warriors and came down again with whiffs of the smoke of every tobacco in the world in my hair. Tired from sheer force of habit and from the contagion of the tiredness all around me, I sat down in front of the make-up shelf fixed to the wall. Someone came in behind me and sat down on the other cane-topped stool. It was one of the French soldiers. She was young and, to judge by the colour of her eyes, dark. Her breeches were half undone and hanging down; she was breathing heavily through her mouth and not looking in my direction.

'Twenty francs!' she exclaimed suddenly. 'Twenty francs' fine! I'm beyond twenty francs' fine, Monsieur Remondon! They make me laugh!'

But she did not laugh. She made an agonized grimace which showed gums almost as white as her teeth between her made-up lips.

'They fined you twenty francs? Why on earth?'

'Because I undid my breeches on the stairs.'

'And why did you undo . . .'

The French soldier interrupted me: 'Why? Why? You and your whys! Because when you can stick it, you stick it, and when you can't anymore, you can't!'

She leaned back against the wall and closed her eyes. I was afraid she was going to faint, but at the buzz of an electric bell, she leaped to her feet.

'Hell, that's us!'

She rushed away, holding up her breeches with both hands. I watched her down to the end of the passage.

'Whoever's that crazy creature?' asked Mademoiselle d'Estouteville languidly. She was entirely covered in pearls and wearing a breastplate in the form of a heart made of sapphires.

I shrugged my shoulders to show that I had not the least idea. Lise Damoiseau, who was wiping her superb features with a dark rag thick with Vaseline and grease paint, appeared in her doorway.

'It's a girl called Gribiche who's in the chorus. At least that's who I think it is.'

'And what was she doing in your dressing room, Colettevilli?' asked Carmen haughtily.

'She wasn't doing anything. She just came in. She said that Remondon had just let her in for a twenty-franc fine.'

Lise Damoiseau gave a judicious whistle.

'Twenty francs! Lord! Whatever for?'

'Because she took her breeches down on the staircase when she came off the stage.'

'Jolly expensive.'

'We don't know for certain if it's true. Mightn't she just have had a drop too much?'

A woman's scream, shrill and protracted, froze the words on her lips. Lise stood stock-still, holding her make-up rag, with one hand on her hip like the servant in Manet's *Olympe*.

The loudness and the terrible urgency of that scream made all the women who were not up on the stage look out of their dressing rooms. Their sudden appearance gave an odd impression of being part of some stage spectacle. As it was near the end of the show, several of them had already exchanged their stork-printed kimonos for white embroidered camisoles threaded with pale blue ribbon. A great scarf of hair fell over the shoulder of one bent head and all the faces were looking the same way. Lise Damoiseau shut her door, tied a cord around her waist to keep her kimono in place, and went off to find out what had happened, with the key of her dressing room slipped over one finger.

A noise of dragging feet announced the procession which appeared at the end of the passage. Two stagehands were carrying a sagging body: a limp, white, made-up lay figure which kept slipping out of their grasp. They walked slowly, scraping their elbows against the walls.

'Who is it? Who is it?'

'She's dead!'

'She's bleeding from the mouth!'

'No, no, that's her rouge!'

'It's Marcelle Cuvelier! Ah, no, it isn't . . .'

Behind the bearers skipped a little woman wearing a headdress of glittering beads shaped like a crescent moon. She had lost her head a little but not enough to prevent her from enjoying her self-importance as an eyewitness. She kept panting: 'I'm in the same dressing room with her. She fell right down to the bottom of the staircase . . . It came over her just like a stroke . . . Just fancy! Ten steps at least she fell.'

'What's the matter with her, Firmin?' Carmen asked one of the men who was carrying her.

'Couldn't say, I'm sure.' answered Firmin. 'What a smash she went!

But I haven't got time to be doing a nurse's job. There's my transparency for the Pierrots not set up yet!'

'Where are you taking her?'

'Putting her in a cab, I s'pose.'

When they had gone by, Mademoiselle d'Estouteville laid her hand on her sapphire breastplate and half collapsed on her dressing stool. Like Gribiche, the sound of the bell brought her to her feet, her eyes on the mirror.

'My rouge has gone and come off,' she said in her loud schoolboy's voice.

She rubbed some bright pink on her blanched cheeks and went up to make her entrance. Lise Damoiseau, who had returned, had some definite information to give us.

'Her salary was two hundred and ten francs. It came over her like a giddy fit. They don't think she's broken anything. Firmin felt her over to see. So did the dresser. More likely something internal.'

But Carmen pointed to something on the stone floor of the passage: a little star of fresh blood, then another, then still others at regular intervals. Lise tightened her mouth, with its deeply incised corners.

'Well, well!'

They exchanged a knowing look and made no further comment. The little 'Crescent Moon' ran by us again, teetering on her high heels and talking as she went.

'That's all fixed. They've packed her into a taxi. Monsieur Bonnavent's driving it.'

'Where's he driving her to?'

'Her home. I live in her street.'

'Why not the hospital?'

'She didn't want to. At home she's got her mother. She came to when she got outside into the air. She said she didn't need a doctor. Has the bell gone for "Up in the Moon"?'

'It certainly has. La Toutou went up ages ago.'

The Crescent Moon swore violently and rushed away, obliterating the little regularly spaced spots with her glittering heels.

The next day nobody mentioned Gribiche. But at the beginning of the evening show, Crescent Moon appeared breathlessly and confided to Carmen that she had been to see her. Carmen passed the information on to me in a tone of apparent indifference.

'So she's better, then?' I insisted.

'If you like to call it better. She's feverish now.'

She was speaking to the looking glass, concentrated on pencilling a vertical line down the centre of her rather flat upper lip to simulate what she called 'the groove of chastity'.

'Was that all Impéria said?'

'No. She said it's simply unbelievable, the size of their room.'

'Whose room?'

'Gribiche and her mother's. Their Lordships the Management have sent forty-nine francs.'

'What an odd sum.'

In the mirror, Carmen's green eyes met mine harshly.

'It's exactly what's due to Gribiche. Seven days' salary. You heard them say she gets two hundred and ten francs a month.'

My neighbour turned severe and suspicious whenever I gave some proof of inexperience which reminded her that I was an outsider and a novice.

'Won't they give her any more than that?'

'There's nothing to make them. Gribiche doesn't belong to the union.'

'Neither do I.'

'I should have been awfully surprised if you *did*,' observed Carmen with chill formality.

The third evening, when I inquired, 'How's Gribiche?' Lise Damoiseau raised her long eyebrows as if I had made a social gaffe.

'Colettevilli, I notice that when you have an idea in your head, it stays up in the top storey. All other floors vacant and to let.'

'Oh!' sneered Carmen. 'You'll see her again, your precious Gribiche. She'll come back here, playing the interesting invalid.'

'Well, *isn't* she interesting?'

'No more than any other girl who's done the same.'

'You're young,' said Lise Damoiseau. 'Young in the profession I mean, of course.'

'A blind baby could see *that*,' agreed Carmen.

I said nothing. Their cruelty which seemed based on a convention left me with no retort. So did their perspicacity in sensing the bourgeois past that lay behind my inexperience and in guessing that my apparent youth was that of a woman of thirty-two who does not look her age.

It was on the fourth or fifth night that Impéria came rushing in at the end of the show and started whispering volubly to my roommates. Wanting to make a show of indifference in my turn, I stayed on my cane stool, polishing my cheap-looking glass, dusting my make-up shelf, and trying to make it as maniacally tidy as my writing table at home.

Then I mended the hem of my skirt and brushed my short hair. Trying to keep my hair well groomed was a joyless and fruitless task, since I could never succeed in banishing the smell of stale tobacco which returned punctually after each shampoo.

Nevertheless, I was observing my neighbours. Whatever was preoccupying them and making them all so passionately eager to speak brought out all their various characters. Lise stood squarely, her hands on her hips, as if she were in the street market of the rue Lepic, throwing back her magnificent head with the authority of a housewife who will stand no nonsense. Little Impéria kept shifting from one leg to the other, twisting her stubby feet and suffering with the patience of an intelligent pony. Carmen was like all those lively energetic girls in Paris who cut out or finish or sell dresses; girls who instinctively know how to trade on their looks and who are frankly and avidly out for money. Only La Toutou belonged to no definite type, except that she embodied a literary infatuation of the time; the legendary princess, the fairy, the siren, or the perverted angel. Her beauty destined her to be perpetually wringing her hands at the top of a tower or shimmering palely in the depths of a dungeon or swooning on a rock in Liberty draperies dripping with jasper and agate. Suddenly Carmen planted herself in the frame of my open doorway and said all in one breath: 'Well, so what are we going to do? That little Impéria says things are going pretty badly.'

'What's going badly?'

Carmen looked slightly embarrassed.

'Oh! Colettevilli, don't be nasty, dear. Gribiche, of course. Not allowed to get up. Chemist, medicine, dressings, and all that . . .'

'Not to mention food,' added Lise Damoiseau.

'Quite so. Well . . . you get the idea.'

'But where's she been hurt, then?'

'It's her . . . back,' said Lise.

'Stomach,' said Carmen, at the same moment.

Seeing them exchange a conspiratorial look, I began to bristle.

'Trying to make a fool of me, aren't you?'

Lise laid her big, sensible hand on my arm.

'Now, now, don't get your claws out. We'll tell you the whole thing. Gribiche has had a miscarriage. A bad one, four and a half months.'

All four of us fell silent. Mademoiselle d'Estouteville nervously pressed both her hands to her small flat stomach, probably by way of a spell to avert disaster.

'Couldn't we,' I suggested, 'get up a collection between us?'

'A collection, that's the idea,' said Lise. 'That's the word I was looking for and I couldn't get it. I kept saying a "subscription". Come on, La Toutou. How much'll you give for Gribiche?'

'Ten francs,' declared Mademoiselle d'Estouteville without a second's hesitation. She ran to her dressing room with a clinking of sham diamonds and imitation sapphires and returned with two five-franc pieces.

'I'll give five francs,' said Carmen Brasero.

'I'll give five too,' said Lise. 'Not more. I've got my people at home. Will you give something, Colettevilli?'

All I could find in my handbag was my key, my powder, some sous, and a twenty-franc piece. I was awkward enough to hesitate, though only for a fraction of a second.

'Want some change?' asked Lise with prompt tact.

I assured her that I didn't need any and handed the louis to Carmen, who hopped on one foot like a little girl.

'A louis . . . oh, goody, goody! Lise, go and extract some sous out of Madame ——' (she gave the name of the leading lady). 'She's just come down.'

'Not me,' said Lise. 'You or Impéria if you like. I don't go over big in my dressing gown.'

'Impéria, trot around to Madame X. And bring back at least five hundred of the best.'

The little actress straightened her spangled crescent in her mirror and went off to Madame X's dressing room. She did not stay there long.

'Got it?' Lise yelled to her from the distance.

'Got what?'

'The big wad.'

The little actress came into my room and opened her closed fist.

'Ten francs!' said Carmen indignantly.

'Well, what she said was . . .' Impéria began.

Lise put out her big hand, chapped with wet white.

'Save your breath, dear. We know just what she said. That business was slack and her rents weren't coming in on time and things were rotten on the Bourse. That's what our celebrated leading actress said.'

'No,' Impéria corrected. 'She said it was against the rules.'

'What's against the rules?'

'To get up . . . subscriptions.'

Lise whistled with amazement.

'First I've heard of it. Is it true, Toutou?'

Mademoiselle d'Estouteville was languidly undoing her chignon. Every time she pulled out one of the hideous iron hairpins, with their varnish all rubbed off, a twist of gold slid down and unravelled itself on her shoulders.

'I think,' she said, 'you're too clever by half to worry whether it's against the rules. Just don't mention it.'

'You've hit it for once, dear,' said Lise approvingly. She ended rashly: 'Tonight, it's too late. But tomorrow I'll go around with the hat.'

During the night, my imagination was busy with this unknown Gribiche. I had almost forgotten her face when she was conscious but I could remember it very clearly white, with the eyes closed, dangling over a stagehand's arm. The lids were blue and the tip of each separate lash beaded with a little blob of mascara . . . I had never seen a serious accident since I had been on the halls. People who risk their lives daily are extremely careful. The man who rides a bicycle around and around a rimless disc, pitting himself against centrifugal force, the girl whom a knife thrower surrounds with blades, the acrobat who swings from trapeze to trapeze high up in mid-air—I had imagined their possible end just as everyone does. I had imagined it with that vague, secret pleasure we all feel in what inspires us with horror. But I had never dreamed that someone like Gribiche, by falling down a staircase, would kill her secret and lie helpless and penniless.

The idea of the collection was enthusiastically received and everyone swore to secrecy. Nothing else was talked about in the dressing rooms. Our end of the corridor received various dazzling visitors. The 'Sacred Scarab', glittering in purple and green ('*You* know,' Carmen reminded me. 'She's the one who was sick on the stage the night of the dress rehearsal'), and Julia Godard, the queen of male impersonators, who, close to, looked like an old Spanish waiter, came in person to present their ten francs. Their arrival aroused as much curiosity as it would in the street of a little town, for they came from a distant corridor which ran parallel to ours and they featured in tableaux we had never seen. Last of all Poupoute ('wonder quick-change child prodigy') deigned to bring us what she called her 'mite'. She owned to being eight and, dressed as a polo player ('Aristocratic Sports', Tableau 14), she strutted from force of habit, bowed with inveterate grace, and overdid the silvery laugh! When she left our peaceful regions, she made a careful exit backward, waving her little riding whip. Lise Damoiseau heaved an exasperated sigh.

'Has to be seen to be believed! The nerve of Her Majesty! Fourteen if she's a day, my dear! After all that, she coughed up ten francs.'

By dint of one- and two-franc and five-franc pieces and the pretty little gold medals worth ten, the treasurer, Lise Damoiseau, amassed three hundred and eighty-seven francs, which she guarded fiercely in a barley-sugar box.

The troupe of 'Girls' she left out of the affair. ('How on earth can I explain to them when they only talk English that Gribiche got herself in the family way and had a "miss" and all the rest of it?') Nevertheless 'Les Girls' produced twenty-five francs between them. At the last moment, a charming American who danced and sang (he still dances and he is still charming) slipped Carmen a hundred-franc note as he came off the stage, when we thought the 'subscription' was closed.

We received some unexpected help. I won fifty francs for Gribiche playing bezique against a morose and elderly friend. Believe me, fifty francs meant something to him too and made their hole in the pension of a retired official in the Colonial Service. One way and another, we collected over five hundred francs.

'It's crazy,' said Carmen, the night that we counted out five hundred and eighty-seven francs.

'Does Gribiche know?'

Lise shook her splendid head.

'*I'm* not crazy. Impéria's taken her sixty francs for the most pressing things. It's deducted on the account. Look, I've written it all down.'

I leaned for some time over the paper, fascinated by the astonishing contrast between the large childish letters, sloping uncertainly now forward, now backward, and the fluent, assured, majestic figures, all proudly clear and even.

'I bet you're good at sums, Lise!'

She nodded. Her marble chin touched the base of her full, goddess-like neck.

'Quite. I like adding up figures. It's a pity I don't usually have many to add up. I like figures. Look, a 5's pretty, isn't it? So's a 7. Sometimes, at night, I see 5's and 2's swimming on the water like swans . . . See what I mean? There's the swan's head . . . and there's its neck when it's swimming. And there, underneath, it's sitting on the water.'

She brooded dreamily over the pretty 5's and the 2's shaped in the likeness of Leda's lover.

'Queer, isn't it? But that's not the whole story. We're going to take the five hundred and eighty-seven francs to Gribiche.'

'Of course. I suppose Impéria will take care of that.'

Lise proudly brushed aside my supposition with a jerk of her elbow.

'We'll do better than that, I hope. We're not going to fling it at her like a bundle of nonsense. You coming with us? We're going tomorrow at four.'

'But I don't know Gribiche.'

'Nor do we. But there's a right and a wrong way of doing things. Any particular reason for not wanting to come?'

Under such a direct question, reinforced by a severe look, I gave in, while blaming myself for giving in.

'No reason at all. How many of us are going?'

'Three. Impéria's busy. Meet us outside Number 3 —— Street.'

I have always liked new faces, provided I can see them at a certain distance or through a thick pane of glass. During the loneliest years of my life, I lived on ground floors. Beyond the net curtain and the window-pane passed my dear human beings to whom I would not for the world have been the first to speak or hold out my hand. In those days I dedicated to them my passionate unsociability, my inexperience of human creatures, and my fundamental shyness, which had no relation to cowardice. I was not annoyed with myself because the thought of the visit to Gribiche kept me awake part of the night. But I was vexed that a certain peremptory tone could still produce an instinctive reflex of obedience, or at least of acquiescence.

The next day I bought a bunch of Parma violets and took the métro with as much bored resentment as if I were going to pay a ceremonial New Year's Day call. On the pavement of —— Street, Carmen and Lise Damoiseau watched me coming but made no welcoming sign from the distance. They were dressed as if for a funeral except for a lace jabot under Lise's chin and a feather curled like a question mark in Carmen's hat. It was the first time I had seen my comrades by daylight. Four o'clock on a fine May afternoon is ruthless to any defect. I saw with astonishment how young they were and how much their youth had already suffered.

They watched me coming, disappointed themselves perhaps by my everyday appearance. It felt that they were superior to me by a stoicism early and dearly acquired. Remembering what had brought me to this particular street, I felt that solidarity is easier for us than sympathy. And I decided to say 'Good afternoon' to them.

'Isn't that the limit?' said Lise, by way of reply.

'What's the limit? Won't you tell me?'

'Why, that your eyes are blue. I thought they were brown. Greyish-brown or blackish-brown. Some sort of brown, anyway.'

Carmen thrust out a finger gloved in suede and half pulled back the tissue paper which protected my flowers.

'It's Parmas. Looks a bit like a funeral, perhaps. But the moment Gribiche is better . . . Do we go in? It's on the ground floor.'

'Looks out on the yard,' said Lise contemptuously.

Gribiche's house, like many in the region of Batignolles, had been new around 1840. Under its eaves, it still preserved a niche for a statue, and in the courtyard there was a squat drinking fountain with a big brass tap. The whole building was disintegrating from damp and neglect.

'It's not bad,' observed Lise, softening. 'Carmen, did you see the statue holding the globe?'

But she caught the expression on my face and said no more. From a tiny invisible garden, a green branch poked out. I noted for future reference that the Japanese 'Tree of Heaven' is remarkably tenacious of life. Following close behind Lise, we groped about in the darkness under the staircase. In the murk, we could see the faint gleam of a copper door handle.

'Well, aren't you ever going to ring?' whispered Carmen impatiently.

'Go on, ring yourself, then, if you can find the bell! This place is like a shoe cupboard. Here we are, I've found the thing. But it's not electric . . . it's a thing you pull.'

A bell tinkled, crystal clear, and the door opened. By the light of a tiny oil lamp I could make out that a tall, broad woman stood before us.

'Mademoiselle Saure?'

'Yes. In here.'

'Can we see her? We've come on behalf of the Eden Concert Company.'

'Just a minute, ladies.'

She left us alone in the semidarkness, through which gleamed Lise's inflexible face and enormous eyes. Carmen gave her a facetious dig in the ribs without her deigning to smile. She merely said under her breath: 'Smells funny here.'

A faint fragrance did indeed bring to my nostrils the memory of various scents which are at their strongest in autumn. I thought of the garden of the peaceful years of my life; of chrysanthemums and immortelles and the little wild geranium they call Herb Robert. The matron reappeared; her corpulence, outlined against a light background, filling the open frame of the second door.

'Be so good as to come in, ladies. The Couzot girl . . . Mademoiselle Impéria, I should say, told us you were coming.'

'Ah,' repeated Lise. 'Impéria told you we were coming. She shouldn't have . . .'

'Why not?' asked the matron.

'For the surprise. We wanted to make it a surprise.'

The word 'surprise' on which we went through the door permanently linked up for me with the astonishing room inhabited by Gribiche and her mother. 'It's unbelievable, the size of their room . . .' We passed with brutal suddenness from darkness to light. The enormous old room was lit by a single window which opened on the garden of a private house— the garden with the Japanese tree. Thirty years ago Paris possessed—and still possesses—any number of these little houses built to the requirements of unassuming, stay-at-home citizens and tucked away behind the big main buildings which almost stifle them. Three stone steps lead up to them from a yard with anaemic lilacs and geraniums which have all run to leaf and look like vegetables. The one in this particular street was no more imposing than a stage set. Overloaded with blackened stone ornaments and crowned with a plaster pediment, it seemed designed to serve as a backcloth to Gribiche's heavily barred window.

The room seemed all the vaster because there was no furniture in the middle of it. A very narrow bed was squeezed against one wall, the wall furthest away from the light. Gribiche was lying on a divan-bed under the dazzling window. I was soon to know that it was dazzling for only two short hours in the day, the time it took the sun to cross the slice of sky between two five-storey houses.

The three of us ventured across the central void towards Gribiche's bed. It was obvious that she neither recognized us nor knew who we were, so Carmen acted as spokesman.

'Mademoiselle Gribiche, we've all three come on behalf of our comrades at the Eden Concert. This is Madame Lise Damoiseau . . .'

'Of the "Hell of Poisons" and Messalina in "Orgy",' supplemented Lise.

'I'm Mademoiselle Brasero of the "Corrida" and the "Gardens of Murcia". And this is Madame Colettevilli, who plays the sketch "Miaou-Ouah-Ouah". It was Madame Colettevilli who had the idea . . . the idea of the subscription among friends.'

Suddenly embarrassed by her own eloquence, she accomplished her mission by laying a manila envelope, tied up with ribbon, in Gribiche's lap.

'Oh, really . . . I say, really. It's too much. Honestly, you shouldn't . . .' protested Gribiche.

Her voice was high and artificial, like that of a child acting a part. I felt no emotion as I looked at this young girl sitting up in bed. I was, in fact, seeing her for the first time, since she bore no resemblance either to the white, unconscious lay figure or to the French soldier who had incurred a fine of twenty francs. Her fair hair was tied back with a sky-blue ribbon, of that blue which is so unbecoming to most blondes, especially when, like Gribiche, they have thin cheeks, pallid under pink powder, and hollow temples and eye sockets. Her brown eyes ranged from Lise to Carmen, from Carmen to me, and from me to the envelope. I noticed that her breath was so short that I gave the matron a look which asked: 'Isn't she going to die?'

I gave her my flowers, putting on the gay expression which the occasion demanded.

'I hope you like violets?'

'Of course. What an idea! Is there anyone who *doesn't* like violets? Thanks so much. How lovely they smell . . .'

She lifted the scentless bunch to her nostrils.

'It smells lovely here too. It reminds me of the smell of the country where I lived as a child. A bit like the everlastings you hang upside down to dry so as to have flowers in winter . . . What is it that smells so good?'

'All sorts of little odds and ends,' came the matron's voice from behind me. 'Biche, pull your legs up so as Madame Colettevilli can sit down. Do be seated, ladies. I'll bring you up our two chairs.'

Lise accepted her seat with some hesitation, almost as if she had been asked to drink out of a doubtfully clean glass. For a moment that beautiful young woman looked extraordinarily like a prudish chair attendant. Then her slightly knitted eyebrows resumed their natural place on her forehead like two delicate clouds against a pure sky and she sat down, carefully smoothing her skirt over her buttocks.

'Well,' said Carmen. 'Getting better now?'

'Oh, I'll soon be all right,' said Gribiche. 'There's no reason now why I shouldn't get better, is there? Especially with what you've brought me. Everyone's been ever so kind . . .'

Shyly she picked up the envelope but did not open it.

'Will you put it away for me, Mamma?'

She held the envelope out to her mother, and my two companions looked decidedly worried as they saw the money pass from Gribiche's hands into the depths of a capacious apron pocket.

'Aren't you going to count it?' asked Lise.

'Oh!' said Gribiche delicately. 'You wouldn't like me to do that.'

To keep herself in countenance, she kept rolling and unrolling the ribbons of the sky-blue bed jacket, made of cheap thin wool, which hid her nightdress.

She had blushed and even this faint upsurge of blood was enough to start her coughing.

'Stop that coughing now,' her mother urged her sharply. 'You know quite well what I said.'

'I'm not doing it on purpose,' protested Gribiche.

'Why mustn't she cough?' inquired Carmen.

The tall, heavy woman blinked her prominent eyes. Though she was fat, she was neither old nor ugly and still had a ruddy complexion under hair that was turning silver.

'Because of her losses. She's lost a lot, you see. And all that isn't quite settled yet. As soon as she gets coughing, it all starts up again.'

'Naturally,' said Lise. 'Her inside's still weak.'

'It's like . . . It's like a girl I know,' said Carmen eagerly. 'She had an accident last year and things went all wrong.'

'Whatever did she take, then?' asked Lise.

'Why, what does the least harm. A bowl of concentrated soap and after that you run as fast as you can for a quarter of an hour.'

'Really, I can't believe my ears!' exclaimed Madame Gribiche. 'My word, you'd think there was no such thing as progress. A bowl of soapy water and a run! Why, that goes back to the days of Charlemagne! Anyone'd think we lived among the savages!'

After this outburst, which she delivered loudly and impressively, Madame Saure, to give her her right name, relapsed into portentous silence.

Carmen asked with much interest: 'Then she oughtn't to have taken soapy water? According to you, Madame, she'd have done better to have gone to one of those "old wives"?'

'And have herself butchered?' said Madame Saure with biting contempt. 'There's plenty have done that! No doubt they think it funny, being poked about with a curtain ring shoved up a rubber tube! Poor wretches! I don't blame them. I'm just sorry for them. After all, it's nature. A woman, or rather a child, lets a man talk her into it. You can't throw stones at her, can you?'

She flung up her hand pathetically and, in so doing, nearly touched the low ceiling. It was disfigured by concentric brown stains of damp, and cracked here and there in zigzags like streaks of lightning. The middle of it sagged slightly over the tiled floor whose tiles had come unstuck.

'When it rains outside, it rains inside,' said Gribiche, who had seen what I was looking at.

Her mother rebuked her.

'That's not fair, Biche. It only rains in the middle. What d'you expect nowadays for a hundred and forty-five francs a year? It's the floors above that let in the water. The owner doesn't do any repairs. He's been expropriated. Something to do with the house being out of line. But we get over it by not putting any furniture in the middle.'

'A hundred and forty-five francs!' exclaimed Lise enviously. 'Well, that certainly won't ruin you!'

'Oh, no sir, no sir, no sir!' Gribiche said brightly.

I nearly laughed, for anything which disturbed Lise's serenity—envy, avarice, or rage—took away what little feminine softness her statuesque beauty possessed. I tried to catch Carmen's eye and make her smile too, but she was absorbed in some thought of her own and fidgeting with the kiss-curl on her left cheek.

'But, look,' said Carmen, reverting to the other topic, 'if the "old wife" is no better than the soapy water, what's one to do? There isn't all that much choice.'

'No,' said Madame Saure professionally. 'But there is such a thing as education and knowledge.'

'Yes, people keep saying that. And talking about progress and all that . . . But listen, what about Miss Ourika? She went off to Cochin China, you know. Well, we've just heard she's dead.'

'Miss Ourika? What's that you're saying?' said the high, breathless voice of Gribiche.

We turned simultaneously toward the bed as if we had forgotten her.

'She's dead? What did she die of, Miss Ourika?' asked Gribiche urgently.

'But she was . . . she tried to . . .'

To stop her from saying any more, Lise risked a gesture which gave everything away. Gribiche put her hands over her eyes and cried: 'Oh, Mamma! You see, Mamma! You see.'

The tears burst out between her clenched fingers. In three swift steps Madame Saure was at her daughter's side. I thought she was going to take her in her arms. But she pressed her two hands on her chest, just above her breasts, and pushed her down flat on her back. Gribiche made no resistance and slid gently down below the cheap Oriental cushion which supported her. In a broken voice, she kept on saying reproachfully: 'You see, Mamma, you see. I told you so, Mamma . . .'

I could not take my eyes off those maternal hands which could so forcefully push down a small, emaciated body and persuade it to lie prone. Two big hands, red and chapped like a washerwoman's. They disappeared to investigate something under a little blue sateen quilt, under a cretonne sheet which had obviously been changed in our honour. I forced myself to fight down my nervous terror of blood, the terror of seeing it suddenly gush out and spread from its secret channels: blood set free, with its ferruginous smell and its talent for dyeing material bright pink or cheerful red or rusty brown. Lise's head was like a plaster cast; Carmen's rouge showed as two purple patches on her blanched cheeks as they both stared at the bed. I kept repeating to myself: 'I'm not going to faint, I'm not going to faint.' And I bit my tongue to distract from that pressure at the base of the spine so many women feel at the sight of blood or even when they hear a detailed account of an operation.

The two hands reappeared and Madame Saure heaved a sigh of relief: 'Nothing wrong . . . nothing wrong.'

She tossed her silvery hair back from her forehead, which was gleaming with sudden sweat. Her large majestic features which recalled so many portraits of Louis XVI did not succeed in making her face sympathetic. I did not like the way she handled her daughter. It seemed to me that she did so with an expertness and an apprehension which had nothing to do with a mother's anxiety. A great bovine creature, sagacious and agreeable but not in the least reassuring. Wiping her temples, she went off to a table pushed right up against the wall at the far end of the room. The sun had moved on and the room had grown sombre: the imprisoned garden showed black under its 'Tree of Heaven'. In the distance Madame Saure was washing her hands and clattering with some glasses. Because of the distance and the darkness, her forehead seemed as if, any moment, it must touch the ceiling.

'Won't you ladies take a little of my cordial? Biche, you've earned a thimbleful too, ducky. I made it myself.'

She came back to us and filled four little glasses which did not match. The one she offered me spilled over, so that I realized her hand was shaking. Lise took hers without a word, her mouth half open and her eyes fixed on the glass. For the first time, I saw a secret terror in those eyes. Carmen said 'Thank you' mechanically and then seemed to come out of her trance.

'You know,' she said hesitantly. 'You know, I don't think she's awfully strong yet, your daughter . . . If I were you . . . What did the doctor say, Gribiche?'

Gribiche smiled at her with vague, still wet eyes and turned her head on the Oriental cushion. She pursed her lips to reach the greenish-gold oil of a kind of Chartreuse which was in the glass.

'Oh well, the doctor . . .'

She broke off and blushed. I saw how badly she blushed, in uneven patches.

'In the case of women,' said Madame Saure, 'doctors don't always know best.'

Carmen waited for the rest of the answer but it did not come. She swallowed half her liqueur in one gulp and gave an exaggeratedly complimentary 'mmm!'

'It's rather sweet, but very good all the same,' said Lise.

The warmth returned to my stomach with a peppery taste of a kind of homemade Chartreuse that resembled a syrupy cough mixture. My colleagues were sufficiently revived to make conversation.

'Apart from that, is there any news at the theatre?' inquired Gribiche.

She had pulled her plait of fair hair over one shoulder as young girls of those days used to do at bedtime.

'Absolutely not a scrap,' answered Carmen. 'Everything would be as dead as mutton if they weren't rehearsing the new numbers they're putting in for the Grand Prix every day.'

'Are you in the new numbers?'

Lise and Carmen shook their heads serenely.

'We're only in the finale. We're not complaining. We've got quite enough to do as it is. I'm getting sick of this show, anyway. I'll be glad when they put on a new one. In the morning, they're rehearsing a sort of apache sketch.'

'Who?'

Carmen shrugged her shoulders with supreme indifference.

'Some straight actors and actresses. A bitch they call . . . Oh, I can't remember. It'll come back to me. There are quite a lot of them but they're mainly comedians. The management wanted to get Otero but she's going into opera.'

'Never!' said Gribiche excitedly. 'Has she got enough voice?'

'She's got something better than voice, she's got *it*,' said Lise. 'It all goes by intrigue. She's marrying the director of the Opéra, so he can't refuse her anything.'

'What's his name, the director of the Opéra?'

'Search me, dear.'

I half closed my eyes to hear it better, this talk which took me back into a world unhampered by truth or even verisimilitude. A dazzling world, a fairy-like bureaucracy where, in the heart of Paris, 'artistes' did not know the name of Julia Bartet, where it seemed perfectly natural that the great dancer Otero, dying to sing in *Faust* and *Les Huguenots*, should buy the director of the Opéra . . . I forgot the place and the reason which had drawn me back into it.

'Fierval's back from Russia,' said Lise Damoiseau. 'They're giving her the lead in the Winter Revue at the Eden Concert.'

'Did she enjoy her tour in Russia?'

'Like anything. Just fancy, the Tsar rented a box for the whole season just to look in and see her number every night. And every single night, my dear, he sent her round presents by his own pope.'

'His what?' asked Gribiche.

'His pope, dear. It's the same thing as a footman.'

But of course! Naturally! Why not? Ah, go on . . . don't stop! How I loved them like that, swallowing the wildest improbabilities like children the moment they drop their outer shell of tough, hardworking wage earners with a shrewd eye on every sou . . . Let's forget everything except the absurd, the fantastic. Let's even forget this tortured little piece of reality lying flat on her bed beneath a barred window. I hope any moment to hear at the very least that President Loubet is going to elope with Alice de Tender . . . Go on, go on! Don't stop!

'Mamma . . . oh, quick, Mamma.'

The whispered call barely ruffled a silence pregnant with other sensational revelations. But, faint as it was, Madame Saure found it reason enough to rush to the bedside. Gribiche's arm dropped slackly and the little glass which fell from her hand broke on the tiled floor.

'Oh, God!' muttered Madame Saure.

Her two hands dived once more under the sheets. She drew them out quickly, looked at them, and, seeing us on our feet, hid them in the pockets of her apron. Not one of us questioned her.

'You see, Mamma,' moaned Gribiche. 'I told you it was too strong. Why didn't you listen to me? Now, you see . . .'

Carmen made a brave suggestion: 'Shall I call the concierge?'

The tall woman with the hidden hands took a step towards us and we all fell back.

'Quick, quick, get away from here . . . You mustn't call anyone . . . Don't be afraid, I'll look after her. I've got all that's needed. Don't say anything. You'll make bother for me. Get away, quick. Above all, not a word.'

She pushed us back towards the door and I remember that we offered a faint resistance. But Madame Saure drew her hands out of her pockets, perhaps to drive us away. At the sight of them, Carmen started like a frightened horse, while I hustled Lise away, to avoid their contact. I don't know whether it was Lise who opened the door of the room and then the other door. We found ourselves in the mildewed hall under the statue holding the globe, we walked stiffly past the concierge's door, and as soon as we got outside on the pavement, Carmen shot ahead of us, almost at a run.

'Carmen! Wait for us!'

But Carmen did not stop till she was out of breath. Then she stood leaning her back against the wall. The green feather in her hat danced to the measure of her heartbeats. Whether from passionate desire for air, or from sheer gratitude, I turned my face up to the sky which twilight was just beginning to fill with pink clouds and twittering swallows. Carmen laid her hand on her breast, at the place where we believe our heart lies.

'Shall we take something to pull ourselves together?' I suggested. 'Lise, a glass of brandy? Carmen, a pick-me-up?' We were just turning the corner of a street where the narrow terrace of a little wines and spirits bar displayed three iron tables. Carmen shook her head.

'Not there. There's a policeman.'

'What does it matter if there is?'

She did not answer and walked quickly on ahead of us till we came to the Place Clichy, whose bustle seemed to reassure her. We sat down under the awning of a large brasserie.

'A coffee,' said Carmen.

'A coffee,' said Lise. 'As for my dinner tonight . . . my stomach feels as if it were full of lead.'

We stirred our spoons round and round our cups without saying a word. Inside, in the restaurant, the electric lights went on all at once, making us suddenly aware of the blue dusk of approaching evening flooding the square. Carmen let out a great sigh of relief.

'It's a bit stuffy,' said Lise.

'You've got hot walking,' said Carmen. 'Just feel my hand. I know what I'm like. I'll have to put lots of rouge on tonight. I'll put on some 24.'

'Now, I'd look a sight if I put on 24,' retorted Lise. 'I'd look like a beet-root. What *I* need is Creole 2½ and the same ground as a man.'

Carmen leaned politely across the table.

'I think Colettevilli's awfully well made up on the stage, very *natural*. When you're not playing character parts, it's very important to look *natural*.'

I listened to them as if I were only half awake and overhearing a conversation which had begun while I was asleep.

That coffee, though sugared till it was as thick as syrup, how bitter it tasted! Beside us, a flower seller was trying to get rid of her last bunch of lilacs: dark purple lilacs, cut while they were still in the bud, lying on sprays of yew.

' "Les Girls," ' Carmen was saying, 'they've got special stuff they use in England. Colours that make you look pink and white like a baby.'

'But that's no good in character parts, is it, Colettevilli?'

I nodded, my lips on the rim of my cup and my eyes dazzled by an arrow from the setting sun.

Lise turned over the little watch which she pinned to the lapel of her jacket with a silver olive branch whose olives pretended to be jade.

'It's half past five,' she announced.

'I don't give a damn,' said Carmen. 'I'm not going to have any dinner, anyway.'

Half past five! What might have happened in half an hour to that girl on her soaking mattress? All we had done for her was to take her a hand-ful of money. Lise held out her packet of cigarettes to me.

'No, thanks, I don't smoke. Tell me, Lise . . . isn't there anything we can do for Gribiche?'

'Absolutely nothing. Keep out of it. It's a filthy business. I've got my people at home who'd be more upset than me to see me mixed up in anything to do with abortion.'

'Yes. But it was only falling downstairs at the theatre that brought it on.'

She shrugged her shoulders.

'You're an infant. The fall came *after*.'

'After what?'

'After what she'd taken. She fell because she was nearly crazy with whatever it was she took. Colic, giddiness, and what have you. She told Impéria all about it in their dressing room. When she came into yours, she was so far gone, she was at her wits' end. She'd stuffed herself with cotton wool.'

'Her old ma's an abortionist,' said Carmen. 'Gives you a dose to bring it on. She gave her daughter a lot more than a teaspoonful.'

'Anyone can see that Ma Saure's already had some "bothers", as she calls them.'

'How can you tell that?'

'Because she's so frightened. And also because they haven't a bean— no furniture, nothing. I wonder what she can have done to be as hard up as all that.'

'Old murderess,' muttered Carmen. 'Clumsy old beast.'

Neither of them showed any surprise. I saw that they were, both of them, thoroughly aware of and inured to such things. They could contemplate impartially certain risks and certain secret dealings of which I knew nothing. There was a type of criminality which they passively and discreetly acknowledged when confronted with the danger of having a child. They talked of the monstrous in a perfectly matter-of-fact way.

'But what about me?' I suggested rashly. 'Couldn't *I* try? Leaving both of you right out of it, of course. If Gribiche could be got into a hospital! As to what people might say, I don't care a damn. I'm absolutely on my own.'

Lise stared at me with her great eyes.

' 'S true? As absolutely on your own as all that? You haven't anyone at all? No one who's close to you? Not even your family?'

'Oh, yes, there's my family,' I agreed hastily.

'I thought as much,' said Lise.

She stood up as if she considered the subject closed, put on her gloves, and snapped her fingers.

'Excuse me if I leave you now, Colettevilli. As I'm not going to have any dinner, I'm going to take my time getting down to the theatre. I'll go by bus; it'll do me good.'

'Me, too,' said Carmen. 'If we're hungry, we can buy a cheese sandwich off the stage doorkeeper.'

She hesitated a moment before inviting me to join them.

'You coming too?'

'I'd love to, but I've promised to look in at my place first.'

'See you later then. Bye-bye.'

They went off arm in arm across the square, which was now all pink and blue: pink with the lit-up shops and bars, blue with the dusk of the late May afternoon.

My only longing was to get back to my little ground-floor room, to my odd scraps of salvaged furniture, to my books, to the smell of green leaves that sometimes drifted in from the Bois. Most of all I longed for the companion of my good and bad moments, my tabby cat. Once again she welcomed me, sniffing my hands and brooding thoughtfully over the hem of my skirt. Then she sat on the table and opened her golden eyes wide, staring into space at the invisible world which had no secrets for her. Neither of us ate more than a morsel or two and I went off punctually to the theatre.

When I arrived at the Eden Concert, I found Mademoiselle d'Estouteville in a grubby bathrobe, with her feet as bare as an angel's and her cape of golden hair over her shoulders, trying to extract every detail of our visit to Gribiche from Lise and Carmen.

'Did it go off well?'

'Oh, yes, splendidly.'

'Was she pleased?'

'I expect she thought it was better than a slap in the belly with a wet fish.'

'And how is she? Is she coming back soon?'

Lise's face was impenetrable. She was occupied in making herself up for her first appearance as the demon Asmodeus.

'Oh, you know, I think it'll be some time yet. I don't think that girl's awfully strong.'

'Got a decent sort of place?'

'Yes and no, as you might say. There's lots of space. At least, you can breathe there. I'd get the willies, myself, living in such a huge room.'

'Her mother looks after her well?'

'Almost too well!'

'What did she say about the five hundred and eighty-seven francs?'

I took it on myself to answer so as to give Lise a little respite.

'She said we were to thank everyone ever so much . . . everyone who'd taken an interest in her. That she was so awfully touched.'

'How did her face look? Quite normal again?'

'She's got a very babyish face, but you can see she's got much thinner. She'd got her hair tied back in a plait like a kid and a little blue bed jacket. She's very sweet.'

The door of Carmen's dressing room banged, sharply pulled to from inside.

'Who's going to be late?' shouted Lise intelligently. 'Colettevilli, of course. And who'll be to blame. That pain in the neck, Toutou d'Estouteville!'

The harsh voice of Mademoiselle d'Estouteville launched into a volley of insults, calmed down, and resolved into a laugh. Each of us went on to do what we always did: yawn, sing odd snatches of song, curse the stifling airlessness, cough, eat peppermints, and go and fill a tiny water jug at the tap in the passage.

Toward half past eleven, I was dressed again and ready to go home. It was the moment when the heat and lack of oxygen got the better of the dead-beat chorus girls and overworked dressers. As I left my dressing room, I noticed that the door of Carmen's dressing room was still shut and I raised my voice to call out my usual good night. The door opened and Carmen signed to me to come in. She was engaged in weeping as one weeps when one is wearing full stage make-up. Armed with a little tube of blotting paper the size of a pencil, she was pressing it first to her right eyeball, then to her left, between the lids.

'Pay no attention. I've got the . . . I'm unwell.'

'Do you feel ill with it?'

'Oh, no. It's just that I'm so awfully relieved. Fancy, I was six days late. I was terrified of doing what Gribiche did . . . So, I'm so relieved.'

She put her arm on my shoulder, then clasped it around my neck, and, just for the fraction of a second, laid her head on my breast.

I was just turning the corner of the long passage when she called out to me from the distance: 'Good night! Don't have bad dreams!'

I had them all the same. I dreamed of anguished anxieties which had not hitherto fallen to my lot. My dream took place under the plant of ill-fame wormwood. Unfolding its hairy, symbolic leaves one by one, the terrible age-old inducer of abortions grew in my nightmare to monstrous size, like the seed controlled by the fakir's will.

The next evening little Impéria came hobbling hurriedly up to us. I saw her whispering anxiously into Lise's ear. Balanced on one leg, she was clutching the foot that hurt her most with both hands. Lise listened to her, wearing her whitest, most statuesque mask and holding one hand over her mouth. Then she removed her hand and furtively made the sign of the cross.

I am perfectly aware that, in the music-hall world, people make the sign of the cross on the slightest provocation. Nevertheless, I knew at once and unerringly why Lise did so at that moment. Weakly, I made a point of avoiding her till the finale. It was easy and I think she deliberately made it easier still. Afterward, fate played into my hands. In honour of the Grand Prix, the management cut out the sketch 'Miaou-Ouah-Ouah', which did not, I admit, deserve any preferential treatment.

Months and years went by during which I made a public spectacle of myself in various places but reserved the right to say nothing of my private life.

When I felt that I wanted to write the story of Gribiche, I controlled myself and replaced it by a 'blank', a row of dots, an asterisk. Today, when I am allowing myself to describe her end, I naturally suppress her name, that of the music hall, and those of the girls we worked with. By such changes and concealments I can still surround Gribiche's memory with the emblems of silence. Among such emblems are those which, in musical notation, signify the breaking off of the melody. Three hieroglyphs can indicate that break: a mute swallow on the five black wires of the stave; a tiny hatchet cutting across them, and—for the longest pause of all—a fixed pupil under a huge, arched, panic-stricken eyebrow.

The Wall

Translated by Lloyd Alexander

They pushed us into a big white room and I began to blink because the light hurt my eyes. Then I saw a table and four men behind the table, civilians, looking over the papers. They had bunched another group of prisoners in the back and we had to cross the whole room to join them. There were several I knew and some others who must have been foreigners. The two in front of me were blond with round skulls; they looked alike. I suppose they were French. The smaller one kept hitching up his pants; nerves.

It lasted about three hours; I was dizzy and my head was empty; but the room was well heated and I found that pleasant enough: for the past 24 hours we hadn't stopped shivering. The guards brought the prisoners up to the table, one after the other. The four men asked each one his name and occupation. Most of the time they didn't go any further—or they would simply ask a question here and there: 'Did you have anything to do with the sabotage of munitions?' or 'Where were you the morning of the 9th and what were you doing?' They didn't listen to the answers or at least didn't seem to. They were quiet for a moment and then looking straight in front of them began to write. They asked Tom if it were true he was in the International Brigade; Tom couldn't tell them otherwise because of the papers they found in his coat. They didn't ask Juan anything but they wrote for a long time after he told them his name.

'My brother José is the anarchist,' Juan said, 'you know he isn't here any more. I don't belong to any party, I never had anything to do with politics.'

They didn't answer. Juan went on, 'I haven't done anything. I don't want to pay for somebody else.'

His lips trembled. A guard shut him up and took him away. It was my turn.

'Your name is Pablo Ibbieta?'

'Yes.'

The man looked at the papers and asked me, 'Where's Ramon Gris?'

'I don't know.'

'You hid him in your house from the 6th to the 19th.'

'No.'

They wrote for a minute and then the guards took me out. In the corridor Tom and Juan were waiting between two guards. We started walking. Tom asked one of the guards, 'So?'

'So what?' the guard said.

'Was that the cross-examination or the sentence?'

'Sentence.' the guard said.

'What are they going to do with us?'

The guard answered dryly, 'Sentence will be read in your cell.'

As a matter of fact, our cell was one of the hospital cellars. It was terrifically cold there because of the drafts. We shivered all night and it wasn't much better during the day. I had spent the previous five days in a cell in a monastery, a sort of hole in the wall that must have dated from the middle ages: since there were a lot of prisoners and not much room, they locked us up anywhere. I didn't miss my cell; I hadn't suffered too much from the cold but I was alone; after a long time it gets irritating. In the cellar I had company. Juan hardly ever spoke: he was afraid and he was too young to have anything to say. But Tom was a good talker and he knew Spanish well.

There was a bench in the cellar and four mats. When they took us back we sat and waited in silence. After a long moment, Tom said, 'We're screwed.'

'I think so too,' I said, 'but I don't think they'll do anything to the kid.'

'They don't have a thing against him,' said Tom. 'He's the brother of a militiaman and that's all.'

I looked at Juan: he didn't seem to hear. Tom went on, 'You know what they do in Saragossa? They lay the men down on the road and run over them with trucks. A Moroccan deserter told us that. They said it was to save ammunition.'

'It doesn't save gas,' I said.

I was annoyed at Tom: he shouldn't have said that.

'Then there's officers walking along the road,' he went on, 'supervising it all. They stick their hands in their pockets and smoke cigarettes. You think they finish off the guys? Hell no. They let them scream. Sometimes for an hour. The Moroccan said he damned near puked the first time.'

'I don't believe they'll do that here,' I said. 'Unless they're really short on ammunition.'

Day was coming in through four airholes and a round opening they had made in the ceiling on the left, and you could see the sky through it.

Through this hole, usually closed by a trap, they unloaded coal into the cellar. Just below the hole there was a big pile of coal dust; it had been used to heat the hospital but since the beginning of the war the patients were evacuated and the coal stayed there, unused; sometimes it even got rained on because they had forgotten to close the trap.

Tom began to shiver. 'Good Jesus Christ, I'm cold,' he said. 'Here it goes again.'

He got up and began to do exercises. At each movement his shirt opened on his chest, white and hairy. He lay on his back, raised his legs in the air and bicycled. I saw his great rump trembling. Tom was hefty but he had too much fat. I thought how rifle bullets or the sharp points of bayonets would soon be sunk into this mass of tender flesh as in a lump of butter. It wouldn't have made me feel like that if he'd been thin.

I wasn't exactly cold, but I couldn't feel my arms and shoulders any more. Sometimes I had the impression I was missing something and began to look around for my coat and then suddenly remembered they hadn't given me a coat. It was rather uncomfortable. They took our clothes and gave them to their soldiers leaving us only our shirts—and those canvas pants that hospital patients wear in the middle of summer. After a while Tom got up and sat next to me, breathing heavily.

'Warmer?'

'Good Christ, no. But I'm out of wind.'

Around eight o'clock in the evening a major came in with two *falangistas*. He had a sheet of paper in his hand. He asked the guard, 'What are the names of those three?'

'Steinbock, Ibbieta and Mirbal,' the guard said.

The major put on his eyeglasses and scanned the list: 'Steinbock . . . Steinbock . . . oh yes . . . you are sentenced to death. You will be shot tomorrow morning.' He went on looking. 'The other two as well.'

'That's not possible,' Juan said. 'Not me.'

The major looked at him amazed. 'What's your name?'

'Juan Mirbal,' he said.

'Well, your name is there,' said the major. 'You're sentenced.'

'I didn't do anything,' Juan said.

The major shrugged his shoulders and turned to Tom and me.

'You're Basque?'

'Nobody is Basque.'

He looked annoyed. 'They told me there were three Basques. I'm not going to waste my time running after them. Then naturally you don't want a priest?'

We didn't even answer.

He said, 'A Belgian doctor is coming shortly. He is authorized to spend the night with you.' He made a military salute and left.

'What did I tell you,' Tom said. 'We get it.'

'Yes,' I said, 'it's a rotten deal for the kid.'

I said that to be decent but I didn't like the kid. His face was too thin and fear and suffering had disfigured it, twisting all his features. Three days before he was a smart sort of kid, not too bad; but now he looked like an old fairy and I thought how he'd never be young again, even if they were to let him go. It wouldn't have been too hard to have a little pity for him but pity disgusts me, or rather it horrifies me. He hadn't said anything more but he had turned grey; his face and hands were both grey. He sat down again and looked at the ground with round eyes. Tom was good hearted, he wanted to take his arm, but the kid tore himself away violently and made a face.

'Let him alone,' I said in a low voice, 'you can see he's going to blubber.'

Tom obeyed regretfully; he would have liked to comfort the kid, it would have passed his time and he wouldn't have been tempted to think about himself. But it annoyed me: I'd never thought about death because I never had any reason to, but now the reason was here and there was nothing to do but think about it.

Tom began to talk. 'So you think you've knocked guys off, do you?' he asked me. I didn't answer. He began explaining to me that he had knocked off six since the beginning of August; he didn't realize the situation and I could tell he didn't *want* to realize it. I hadn't quite realized it myself, I wondered if it hurt much, I thought of bullets, I imagined their burning hail through my body. All that was beside the real question; but I was calm: we had all night to understand. After a while Tom stopped talking and I watched him out of the corner of my eye; I saw he too had turned grey and he looked rotten; I told myself 'Now it starts.' It was almost dark, a dim glow filtered through the airholes and the pile of coal and made a big stain beneath the spot of sky; I could already see a star through the hole in the ceiling: the night would be pure and icy.

The door opened and two guards came in, followed by a blond man in a tan uniform. He saluted us. 'I am the doctor,' he said. 'I have authorization to help you in these trying hours.'

He had an agreeable and distinguished voice. I said, 'What do you want here?'

'I am at your disposal. I shall do all I can to make your last moments less difficult.'

'What did you come here for? There are others, the hospital's full of them.'

'I was sent here,' he answered with a vague look. 'Ah! Would you like to smoke?' he added hurriedly, 'I have cigarettes and even cigars.'

He offered us English cigarettes and *puros*, but we refused. I looked him in the eyes and he seemed irritated. I said to him, 'You aren't here on an errand of mercy. Besides, I know you. I saw you with the fascists in the barracks yard the day I was arrested.'

I was going to continue, but something surprising suddenly happened to me; the presence of this doctor no longer interested me. Generally when I'm on somebody I don't let go. But the desire to talk left me completely; I shrugged and turned my eyes away. A little later I raised my head; he was watching me curiously. The guards were sitting on a mat. Pedro, the tall thin one, was twiddling his thumbs, the other shook his head from time to time to keep from falling asleep.

'Do you want a light?' Pedro suddenly asked the doctor. The other nodded 'Yes': I think he was about as smart as a log, but he surely wasn't bad. Looking in his cold blue eyes it seemed to me that his only sin was lack of imagination. Pedro went out and came back with an oil lamp which he set on the corner of the bench. It gave a bad light but it was better than nothing: they had left us in the dark the night before. For a long time I watched the circle of light the lamp made on the ceiling. I was fascinated. Then suddenly I woke up, the circle of light disappeared and I felt myself crushed under an enormous weight. It was not the thought of death, or fear; it was nameless. My cheeks burned and my head ached.

I shook myself and looked at my two friends. Tom had hidden his face in his hands. I could only see the fat white nape of his neck. Little Juan was the worst, his mouth was open and his nostrils trembled. The doctor went to him and put his hand on his shoulder to comfort him: but his eyes stayed cold. Then I saw the Belgian's hand drop stealthily along Juan's arm, down to the wrist. Juan paid no attention. The Belgian took his wrist between three fingers, distractedly, the same time drawing back a little and turning his back to me. But I leaned backward and saw him take a watch from his pocket and look at it for a moment, never letting go of the wrist. After a minute he let the hand fall inert and went and leaned his back against the wall, then, as if he suddenly remembered something very important which had to be jotted down on the spot, he took a notebook from his pocket and wrote a few lines. 'Bastard,' I thought angrily, 'let him come and take my pulse. I'll shove my fist in his rotten face.'

He didn't come but I felt him watching me. I raised my head and returned his look. Impersonally, he said to me, 'Doesn't it seem cold to you here?' He looked cold, he was blue.

'I'm not cold,' I told him.

He never took his hard eyes off me. Suddenly I understood and my hands went to my face: I was drenched in sweat. In this cellar, in the midst of winter, in the midst of drafts, I was sweating. I ran my hands through my hair, gummed together with perspiration; at the same time I saw my shirt was damp and sticking to my skin: I had been dripping for an hour and hadn't felt it. But that swine of a Belgian hadn't missed a thing; he had seen the drops rolling down my cheeks and thought: this is the manifestation of an almost pathological state of terror; and he had felt normal and proud of being alive because he was cold. I wanted to stand up and smash his face but no sooner had I made the slightest gesture than my rage and shame were wiped out; I fell back on the bench with indifference.

I satisfied myself by rubbing my neck with my handkerchief because now I felt the sweat dropping from my hair onto my neck and it was unpleasant. I soon gave up rubbing, it was useless; my handkerchief was already soaked and I was still sweating. My buttocks were sweating too and my damp trousers were glued to the bench.

Suddenly Juan spoke. 'You're a doctor?'

'Yes,' the Belgian said.

'Does it hurt . . . very long?'

'Huh? When . . . ? Oh, no,' the Belgian said paternally. 'Not at all. It's over quickly.' He acted as though he were calming a cash customer.

'But I . . . they told me . . . sometimes they have to fire twice.'

'Sometimes,' the Belgian said, nodding. 'It may happen that the first volley reaches no vital organs.'

'Then they have to reload their rifles and aim all over again?' He thought for a moment and then added hoarsely, 'That takes time!'

He had a terrible fear of suffering, it was all he thought about: it was his age. I never thought much about it and it wasn't fear of suffering that made me sweat.

I got up and walked to the pile of coal dust. Tom jumped up and threw me a hateful look: I had annoyed him because my shoes squeaked. I wondered if my face looked as frightened as his: I saw he was sweating too. The sky was superb, no light filtered into the dark corner and I had only to raise my head to see the Big Dipper. But it wasn't like it had been: the night before I could see a great piece of sky from my monastery cell and each hour of the day brought me a different memory. Morning, when the sky was a hard, light blue, I thought of beaches on the Atlantic; at noon I saw the sun and I remembered a bar in Seville where I drank *manzanilla* and ate olives and anchovies; afternoons I was in the shade and I thought of the deep shadow which spreads over half a bull-ring leaving the other half shimmering in sunlight; it was really hard to see the whole world reflected in the sky like that. But now I could watch the sky as much as I pleased, it no longer evoked anything in me. I liked that better. I came back and sat near Tom. A long moment passed.

Tom began speaking in a low voice. He had to talk, without that he wouldn't have been able to recognize himself in his own mind. I thought he was talking to me but he wasn't looking at me. He was undoubtedly afraid to see me as I was, grey and sweating: we were alike and worse than mirrors of each other. He watched the Belgian, the living.

'Do you understand?' he said. 'I don't understand.'

I began to speak in a low voice too. I watched the Belgian. 'Why? What's the matter?'

'Something is going to happen to us that I can't understand.'

There was a strange smell about Tom. It seemed to me I was more sensitive than usual to odours. I grinned. 'You'll understand in a while.'

'It isn't clear,' he said obstinately. 'I want to be brave but first I have to know. . . . Listen, they're going to take us into the courtyard. Good. They're going to stand up in front of us. How many?'

'I don't know. Five or eight. Not more.'

'All right. There'll be eight. Someone'll holler "aim!" and I'll see eight rifles looking at me. I'll think how I'd like to get inside the wall, I'll push against it with my back . . . with every ounce of strength I have, but the wall will stay, like in a nightmare. I can imagine all that. If you only knew how well I can imagine it.'

'All right, all right!' I said, 'I can imagine it too.'

'It must hurt like hell. You know, they aim at the eyes and mouth to disfigure you,' he added mechanically. 'I can feel the wounds already; I've had pains in my head and in my neck for the past hour. Not real pains. Worse. This is what I'm going to feel tomorrow morning. And then what?'

I well understood what he meant but I didn't want to act as if I did. I had pains too, pains in my body like a crowd of tiny scars. I couldn't get used to it. But I was like him, I attached no importance to it. 'After,' I said, 'you'll be pushing up daisies.'

He began to talk to himself: he never stopped watching the Belgian.

The Belgian didn't seem to be listening. I knew what he had come to do; he wasn't interested in what we thought; he came to watch our bodies, bodies dying in agony while yet alive.

'It's like a nightmare,' Tom was saying. 'You want to think something, you always have the impression that it's all right, that you're going to understand and then it slips, it escapes you and fades away. I tell myself there will be nothing afterwards. But I don't understand what it means. Sometimes I almost can . . . and then it fades away and I start thinking about the pains again, bullets, explosions. I'm a materialist, I swear it to you; I'm not going crazy. But something's the matter. I see my corpse; that's not hard but *I'm* the one who sees it, with *my* eyes. I've got to think . . . think that I won't see anything any more and the world will go on for the others. We aren't made to think that, Pablo. Believe me: I've already stayed up a whole night waiting for something. But this isn't the same: this will creep up behind us, Pablo, and we won't be able to prepare for it.'

'Shut up,' I said. 'Do you want me to call a priest?'

He didn't answer. I had already noticed he had the tendency to act like a prophet and call me Pablo, speaking in a toneless voice. I didn't like that: but it seems all the Irish are that way. I had the vague impression he smelled of urine. Fundamentally, I hadn't much sympathy for Tom and I didn't see why, under the pretext of dying together, I should have any more. It would have been different with some others. With Ramon Gris, for example. But I felt alone between Tom and Juan. I liked that better, anyhow: with Ramon I might have been more deeply moved. But I was terribly hard just then and I wanted to stay hard.

He kept on chewing his words, with something like distraction. He certainly talked to keep himself from thinking. He smelled of urine like an old prostate case. Naturally, I agreed with him, I could have said everything he said: it isn't *natural* to die. And since I was going to die, nothing seemed natural to me, not this pile of coal dust, or the bench, or Pedro's ugly face. Only it didn't please me to think the same things as Tom. And I knew that, all through the night, every five minutes, we would keep on thinking things at the same time. I looked at him sideways and for the first time he seemed strange to me: he wore death on his face. My pride was wounded: for the past 24 hours I had lived next to Tom, I had listened to him, I had spoken to him and I knew we had nothing in common. And now we looked as much alike as twin brothers, simply because we were going to die together. Tom took my hand without looking at me.

'Pablo, I wonder . . . I wonder if it's really true that everything ends.'

I took my hand away and said, 'Look between your feet, you pig.'

There was a big puddle between his feet and drops fell from his pants leg.

'What is it?' he asked, frightened.

'You're pissing in your pants,' I told him.

'It isn't true,' he said furiously. 'I'm not pissing. I don't feel anything.'

The Belgian approached us. He asked with false solicitude, 'Do you feel ill?'

Tom did not answer. The Belgian looked at the puddle and said nothing.

'I don't know what it is,' Tom said ferociously. 'But I'm not afraid. I swear I'm not afraid.'

The Belgian did not answer. Tom got up and went to piss in a corner. He came back buttoning his fly, and sat down without a word. The Belgian was taking notes.

All three of us watched him because he was alive. He had the motions of a living human being, the cares of a living human being; he shivered in the cellar the way the living are supposed to shiver; he had an obedient, well-fed body. The rest of us hardly felt ours—not in the same way anyhow. I wanted to feel my pants between my legs but I didn't dare; I watched the Belgian, balancing on his legs, master of his muscles, someone who could think about tomorrow. There we were, three bloodless shadows; we watched him and we sucked his life like vampires.

Finally he went over to little Juan. Did he want to feel his neck for some professional motive or was he obeying an impulse of charity? If he was acting by charity it was the only time during the whole night.

He caressed Juan's head and neck. The kid let himself be handled, his eyes never leaving him, then suddenly, he seized the hand and looked at it strangely. He held the Belgian's hand between his own two hands and there was nothing pleasant about them, two grey pincers gripping this fat and reddish hand. I suspected what was going to happen and Tom must have suspected it too: but the Belgian didn't see a thing, he smiled paternally. After a moment the kid brought the fat red hand to his mouth and tried to bite it. The Belgian pulled away quickly and stumbled back against the wall. For a second he looked at us with horror, he must have suddenly understood that we were not men like him. I began to laugh and one of the guards jumped up. The other was asleep, his wide-open eyes were blank.

I felt relaxed and over-excited at the same time. I didn't want to think any more about what would happen at dawn, at death. It made no sense.

I only found words or emptiness. But as soon as I tried to think of anything else I saw rifle barrels pointing at me. Perhaps I lived through my execution twenty times; once I even thought it was for good: I must have slept a minute. They were dragging me to the wall and I was struggling; I was asking for mercy. I woke up with a start and looked at the Belgian: I was afraid I might have cried out in my sleep. But he was stroking his moustache, he hadn't noticed anything. If I had wanted to, I think I could have slept a while; I had been awake for 48 hours. I was at the end of my rope. But I didn't want to lose two hours of life: they would come to wake me up at dawn, I would follow them, stupefied with sleep and I would have croaked without so much as an 'Oof!'; I didn't want that, I didn't want to die like an animal, I wanted to understand. Then I was afraid of having nightmares. I got up, walked back and forth, and, to change my ideas, I began to think about my past life. A crowd of memories came back to me pell-mell. There were good and bad ones—or at least I called them that *before*. There were faces and incidents. I saw the face of a little *novillero* who was gored in Valencia during the *Feria*, the face of one of my uncles, the face of Ramon Gris. I remembered my whole life: how I was out of work for three months in 1926, how I almost starved to death. I remembered a night I spent on a bench in Granada: I hadn't eaten for three days. I was angry, I didn't want to die. That made me smile. How madly I ran after happiness, after women, after liberty. Why? I wanted to free Spain, I admired Pi y Margall, I joined the anarchist movement, I spoke in public meetings: I took everything as seriously as if I were immortal.

At that moment I felt that I had my whole life in front of me and I thought, 'It's a damned lie.' It was worth nothing because it was finished. I wondered how I'd been able to walk, to laugh with the girls: I wouldn't have moved so much as my little finger if I had only imagined I would die like this. My life was in front of me, shut, closed, like a bag and yet everything inside of it was unfinished. For an instant I tried to judge it. I wanted to tell myself, this is a beautiful life. But I couldn't pass judgement on it; it was only a sketch; I had spent my time counterfeiting eternity, I had understood nothing. I missed nothing: there were so many things I could have missed, the taste of *manzanilla* or the baths I took in summer in a little creek near Cadiz; but death had disenchanted everything.

The Belgian suddenly had a bright idea. 'My friends,' he told us, 'I will undertake—if the military administration will allow it—to send a message for you, a souvenir to those who love you. . . .'

Tom mumbled, 'I don't have anybody.'

I said nothing. Tom waited an instant then looked at me with curiosity. 'You don't have anything to say to Concha?'

'No.'

I hated this tender complicity: it was my own fault, I had talked about Concha the night before, I should have controlled myself. I was with her for a year. Last night I would have given an arm to see her again for five minutes. That was why I talked about her, I couldn't help it. Now I had no more desire to see her, I had nothing more to say to her. I would not even have wanted to hold her in my arms: my body filled me with horror because it was grey and sweating—and I wasn't sure that her body didn't fill me with horror. Concha would cry when she found out I was dead, she would have no taste for life for months afterward. But I was still the one who was going to die. I thought of her soft, beautiful eyes. When she looked at me something passed from her to me. But I knew it was over: if she looked at me *now* the look would stay in her eyes, it wouldn't reach me. I was alone.

Tom was alone too but not in the same way. Sitting cross-legged, he had begun to stare at the bench with a sort of smile, he looked amazed. He put out his hand and touched the wood cautiously as if he were afraid of breaking something, then drew back his hand quickly and shuddered. If I had been Tom I wouldn't have amused myself by touching the bench; this was some more Irish nonsense, but I too found that objects had a funny look: they were more obliterated, less dense than usual. It was enough for me to look at the bench, the lamp, the pile of coal dust, to feel that I was going to die. Naturally I couldn't think clearly about my death but I saw it everywhere, on things, in the way things fell back and kept their distance, discreetly, as people who speak quietly at the bedside of a dying man. It was *his* death which Tom had just touched on the bench.

In the state I was in, if someone had come and told me I could go home quietly, that they would leave me my life whole, it would have left me cold: several hours or several years of waiting is all the same when you have lost the illusion of being eternal. I clung to nothing, in a way I was calm. But it was a horrible calm—beause of my body; my body, I saw with its eyes, I heard with its ears, but it was no longer me, it sweated and trembled by itself and I didn't recognize it any more. I had to touch it and look at it to find out what was happening, as if it were the body of someone else. At times I could still feel it, I felt sinkings, and fallings, as when you're in a plane taking a nose dive, or I felt my heart beating. But that didn't reassure me. Everything that came from my body was all cockeyed. Most of the time it was quiet and I felt no more than a sort of weight, a filthy presence against me; I had the impression of being tied to an enormous vermin. Once I felt my pants and I felt they were damp; I didn't know whether it was sweat or urine, but I went to piss on the coal pile as a precaution.

The Belgian took out his watch, looked at it. He said, 'It is three-thirty.'

Bastard! He must have done it on purpose. Tom jumped; he hadn't noticed time was running out; night surrounded us like a shapeless, sombre mass, I couldn't even remember that it had begun.

Little Juan began to cry. He wrung his hands, pleaded, 'I don't want to die. I don't want to die.'

He ran across the whole cellar waving his arms in the air then fell sobbing on one of the mats. Tom watched him with mournful eyes, without the slightest desire to console him. Because it wasn't worth the trouble: the kid made more noise than we did, but he was less touched: he was like a sick man who defends himself against illness by fever. It's much more serious when there isn't any fever.

He wept: I could clearly see he was pitying himself; he wasn't thinking about death. For one second, one single second, I wanted to weep myself, to weep with pity for myself. But the opposite happened: I glanced at the kid, I saw his thin sobbing shoulders and felt inhuman: I could pity neither the others nor myself. I said to myself, 'I want to die cleanly.'

Tom had gotten up, he placed himself just under the round opening and began to watch for daylight. I was determined to die cleanly and I only thought of that. But ever since the doctor told us the time, I felt time flying, flowing away drop by drop.

It was still dark when I heard Tom's voice: 'Do you hear them?'

Men were marching in the courtyard.

'Yes.'

'What the hell are they doing? They can't shoot in the dark.'

After a while we heard no more. I said to Tom, 'It's day.'

Pedro got up, yawning, and came to blow out the lamp. He said to his buddy, 'Cold as hell.'

The cellar was all grey. We heard shots in the distance.

'It's starting,' I told Tom. 'They must do it in the court in the rear.'

Tom asked the doctor for a cigarette. I didn't want one; I didn't want cigarettes or alcohol. From that moment on they didn't stop firing.

'Do you realize what's happening?' Tom said.

He wanted to add something but kept quiet, watching the door. The door opened and a lieutenant came in with four soldiers. Tom dropped his cigarette.

'Steinbock?'

Tom didn't answer. Pedro pointed him out.

'Juan Mirbal?'

'On the mat.'

'Get up,' the lieutenant said.

Juan did not move. Two soldiers took him under the arms and set him on his feet. But he fell as soon as they released him.

The soldiers hesitated.

'He's not the first sick one,' said the lieutenant. 'You two carry him; they'll fix it up down there.'

He turned to Tom. 'Let's go.'

Tom went out between two soldiers. Two others followed, carrying the kid by the armpits. He hadn't fainted; his eyes were wide open and tears ran down his cheeks. When I wanted to go out the lieutenant stopped me.

'You Ibbieta?'

'Yes.'

'You wait here; they'll come for you later.'

They left. The Belgian and the two gaolers left too, I was alone. I did not understand what was happening to me but I would have liked it better if they had gotten it over with right away. I heard shots at almost regular intervals; I shook with each one of them. I wanted to scream and tear out my hair. But I gritted my teeth and pushed my hands in my pockets because I wanted to stay clean.

After an hour they came to get me and led me to the first floor, to a small room that smelt of cigars and where the heat was stifling. There were two officers sitting smoking in the armchairs, papers on their knees.

'You're Ibbieta?'

'Yes.'

'Where is Ramon Gris?'

'I don't know.'

The one questioning me was short and fat. His eyes were hard behind his glasses. He said to me, 'Come here.'

I went to him. He got up and took my arms, staring at me with a look intended to crush me. At the same time he pinched my biceps with all his might. It wasn't to hurt me, it was only a game: he wanted to dominate me. He also thought he had to blow his stinking breath square in my face. We stayed for a moment like that, and I almost felt like laughing. It takes a lot to intimidate a man who is going to die; it didn't work. He pushed me back violently and sat down again. He said, 'It's his life against yours. You can have yours if you tell us where he is.'

These men dolled up with their riding crops and boots were still going to die. A little later than I, but not too much. They busied themselves looking for names in their crumpled papers, they ran after other men to imprison or suppress them; they had opinions on the future of Spain and on other subjects. Their little activities seemed shocking and burlesque to me; I couldn't put myself in their place, I thought they were insane. The little man was still looking at me, whipping his boots with the riding crop. All his gestures were calculated to give him the look of a live and ferocious beast.

'So? You understand?'

'I don't know where Gris is,' I answered. 'I thought he was in Madrid.'

The other officer raised his pale hand indolently. This indolence was also calculated. I saw through all their little schemes and I was stupefied to find there were men who amused themselves that way.

'You have a quarter of an hour to think it over,' he said slowly. 'Take him to the laundry, bring him back in fifteen minutes. If he still refuses he will be executed on the spot.'

They knew what they were doing: I had passed the night in waiting; then they had made me wait an hour in the cellar while they shot Tom and Juan and now they were locking me up in the laundry; they must have prepared their game the night before. They told themselves that nerves eventually wear out and they hoped to get me that way.

They were badly mistaken. In the laundry I sat on a stool because I felt very weak and I began to think. But not about their proposition. Of course I knew where Gris was; he was hiding with his cousins, four kilometres from the city. I also knew that I would not reveal his hiding place unless they tortured me (but they didn't seem to be thinking about that). All that was perfectly regulated, definite, and in no way interested me. Only I would have liked to understand the reasons for my conduct. I would rather die than give up Gris. Why? I didn't like Ramon Gris any more. My friendship for him had died a little while before dawn at the same time as my love for Concha, at the same time as my desire to live. Undoubtedly I thought highly of him: he was tough. But it was not for this reason that I consented to die in his place; his life had no more value than mine; no life had value. They were going to slap a man up against a wall and shoot at him till he died, whether it was I or Gris or somebody else made no difference. I knew he was more useful than I to the cause of

Spain but I thought to hell with Spain and anarchy; nothing was important. Yet I was there, I could save my skin and give up Gris and I refused to do it. I found that somehow comic; it was obstinacy. I thought, 'I must be stubborn!' And a droll sort of gaiety spread over me.

They came for me and brought me back to the two officers. A rat ran out from under my feet and that amused me. I turned to one of the *falangistas* and said, 'Did you see the rat?'

He didn't answer. He was very sober, he took himself seriously. I wanted to laugh but I held myself back because I was afraid that once I got started I wouldn't be able to stop. The *falangista* had a moustache. I said to him again, 'You ought to shave off your moustache, idiot.' I thought it funny that he would let the hairs of his living being invade his face. He kicked me without great conviction and I kept quiet.

'Well,' said the fat officer, 'have you thought about it?'

I looked at them with curiosity, as insects of a very rare species. I told them, 'I know where he is. He is hidden in the cemetery. In a vault or in the gravediggers' shack.'

It was a farce. I wanted to see them stand up, buckle their belts and give orders busily.

They jumped to their feet. 'Let's go. Molés, go get fifteen men from Lieutenant Lopez. You,' the fat man said, 'I'll let you off if you're telling the truth, but it'll cost you plenty if you're making monkeys out of us.'

They left in a great clatter and I waited peacefully under the guard of *falangistas*. From time to time I smiled, thinking about the spectacle they would make. I felt stunned and malicious. I imagined them lifting up tombstones, opening the doors of the vaults one by one. I represented this situation to myself as if I had been someone else: this prisoner obstinately playing the hero, these grim *falangistas* with their moustaches and their men in uniform running among the graves; it was irresistibly funny. After half an hour the little fat man came back alone. I thought he had come to give the orders to execute me. The others must have stayed in the cemetery.

The officer looked at me. He didn't look at all sheepish. 'Take him into the big courtyard with the others,' he said. 'After the military operations a regular court will decide what happens to him.'

'Then they're not . . . not going to shoot me . . . ?'

'Not now, anyway. What happens afterwards is none of my business.'

I still didn't understand. I asked, 'But why . . .?'

He shrugged his shoulders without answering and the soldiers took me away. In the big courtyard there were about a hundred prisoners, women, children and a few old men. I began walking around the central grass-plot, I was stupefied. At noon they let us eat in the mess hall. Two or three people questioned me. I must have known them, but I didn't answer: I didn't even know where I was.

Around evening they pushed about ten new prisoners into the court. I recognized Garcia, the baker. He said, 'What damned luck you have! I didn't think I'd see you alive.'

'They sentenced me to death,' I said, 'and then they changed their minds. I don't know why.'

'They arrested me at two o'clock,' Garcia said.

'Why?' Garcia had nothing to do with politics.

'I don't know,' he said. 'They arrest everybody who doesn't think the way they do.' He lowered his voice. 'They got Gris.'

I began to tremble. 'When?'

'This morning. He messed it up. He left his cousin's on Tuesday because they had an argument. There were plenty of people to hide him but he didn't want to owe anything to anybody. He said, "I'd go and hide in Ibbieta's place, but they got him, so I'll go hide in the cemetery."'

'In the cemetery?'

'Yes. What a fool. Of course they went by there this morning, that was sure to happen. They found him in the gravediggers' shack. He shot at them and they got him.'

'In the cemetery!'

Everything began to spin and I found myself sitting on the ground: I laughed so hard I cried.

The Man on the Street

Translated by Elizabeth Fallaize

The four men were squashed up together in the taxi. Paris was frozen over. At seven thirty in the morning, the town had a ghastly pallor and the wind was blowing clouds of ice particles along the ground.

The thinnest of the four men occupied the fold-down seat. He had a cigarette hanging on his lower lip and handcuffs on his wrists. The biggest man, wearing a heavy overcoat and a bowler hat, had a thickset chin and smoked his pipe as he watched the railings of the Bois de Boulogne slip past.

'Like me to make a scene?' the man with the handcuffs suggested helpfully. 'Complete with contortions, foaming at the mouth, insults etc.?'

Maigret, removing the cigarette from his mouth and opening the car door, for they had arrived at the Porte de Bagatelle, muttered:

'Don't try to play the wise guy.'

The paths of the Bois de Boulogne were deserted, white as quarried stone, and just as hard. A group of about ten people were stamping their feet on the corner of a bridle path, and a photographer stepped forward to catch the group that was approaching. But P'tit Louis covered his face with his arm, as he had been told to do.

Maigret, looking grumpy, turned his head this way and that like a bear, observing everything, the new blocks on Boulevard Richard-Wallace, with their shutters still closed, the odd workman on his bike coming in from Puteaux, a tram lit up, two concierges who were approaching him, their hands blue with cold.

'All set?' he asked.

The day before he had arranged for the following information to appear in the papers:

THE BAGATELLE MURDER

The police appear for once to have made quick work of a crime which had initially looked impossible to solve. As we reported, on Monday morning a park keeper at the Bois de Boulogne discovered a corpse on a path about a hundred metres from the Porte de Bagatelle.

The body was immediately identified as that of Ernest Borms, a well-known Viennese doctor who had lived in Neuilly for a number of years. Borms was in evening dress. It is thought he was attacked between Sunday night and Monday morning on his way home to his flat on the Boulevard Richard-Wallace.

A bullet fired at point-blank range from a small calibre weapon had entered the heart.

Borms, a handsome man of elegant and youthful appearance, led an active social life.

Barely forty-eight hours after the murder the police have made an arrest. There will be a reconstruction of the crime at the site tomorrow morning, between 7 and 8 a.m.

In years to come the case was to be frequently cited, at the Quai des Orfèvres, as perhaps the most typical example of Maigret's style. But, when it was mentioned in his hearing, Maigret had a strange way of turning his head aside and grunting.

Right! Everything was ready. Almost no onlookers, as predicted. It was no coincidence that he had chosen such an early hour. And even amongst the ten to fifteen people hanging around, some were recognizable as inspectors, trying to look as innocent as possible. One of them, Torrence, adored disguises and had dressed up as a milkman, his boss noted with a shrug.

As long as P'tit Louis didn't overdo it! He was a regular client, arrested the day before for pickpocketing in the metro.

'Give us a hand tomorrow morning and we'll make sure you don't cop it too badly this time.'

They had got him up from the cells.

'Let's get started,' Maigret grunted. 'When you heard someone coming you were hidden over here, weren't you?'

'Yes, that's it, Inspector. I was famished you see? Could have eaten a horse! So, I said to myself, that bloke in the penguin suit must have a fat wallet! "Your money or your life," I whispered in his earhole. And I swear I never intended the gun to go off. It must have been the cold that made my finger slip on the trigger.'

Eleven in the morning. Maigret was pacing up and down his office in the Quai des Orfèvres, smoking pipes and constantly running his hand over the telephone.

'Hello? Is that you Boss? Lucas here. I followed the old bloke who seemed interested in the reconstruction. Nothing gives. Just a crank who goes for a little walk every morning in the Bois.'

'Okay. You can come in.'

Quarter past eleven.

'Hello, Boss? Torrence! I trailed the young man you signalled to me from the corner of your eye. It's his life ambition to be a detective. He's a salesman in a shop on the Champs-Elysées. Shall I come in?'

At five to twelve, at last, a call came through from Janvier.

'I'll be brief, Boss. The bird might fly. I'm watching him through the glass panel in the cabin door. I'm in the bar of the *Nain Jaune* on Boulevard Rochechouart. Yup, he's spotted me. He's got a guilty conscience. He threw something in the river as he crossed over the Seine. He's tried to shake me off at least ten times. Shall I expect you?'

So began a pursuit which was to last five days and five nights, amidst passers-by hurrying on, across a Paris which remained oblivious. They went from bar to bar, from bistro to bistro, with a lone man on one side, and on the other, Maigret and his inspectors relaying each other until they were as harrassed as the man they were trailing.

It was aperitif time when Maigret got out of the taxi opposite the *Nain Jaune*. He found Janvier leaning on the bar. He wasn't trying to keep a low profile, quite the contrary!

'Which one?'

The inspector motioned with his chin at a man sitting at a corner table. The man was looking at them with his light blue-grey eyes, which gave his face a foreign look. Nordic? Slavonic? The latter, probably. He wore a grey overcoat, a well-cut suit, and a soft felt hat.

About thirty-five years old, as far as they could tell. He was pale, closely shaved.

'What'll you have, Boss? Something hot?'

'Okay, a hot toddy . . . What's he having?'

'Brandy. It's his fifth this morning. Don't take any notice if I seem a bit overcome, I've had to follow him from one bistro to another. He's tough, you know. Look at him. He's been like that all day. He wouldn't lower his eyes for all the world.'

It was true. And strange. It wasn't arrogance, nor defiance. He was simply looking at them. If he felt worried, there was no exterior sign of it. His expression was one of sadness, but a calm and studied sadness.

'When he saw you'd noticed him at the Bagatelle, he left at once and I kept close to him. He turned round before he'd gone a hundred metres. Then, instead of leaving the Bois as he'd apparently intended, he set off with huge strides down the first path he came across. He turned round again. He recognized me. He sat down on a bench, despite the cold, and I stopped. Several times, I thought he was about to speak to me, but he went off in the end, shrugging his shoulders.

'At Porte Dauphine I nearly lost him when he jumped into a taxi. It was pure chance that I got one immediately afterwards. He got out at the Place de l'Opéra and rushed down into the metro. I was hard on his heels and we changed line five times before he began to understand that he wasn't going to lose me like that. . . .

'We headed back up above ground, to Place Clichy. Since then we've been going from bar to bar.

'I was waiting for a good place to phone from, where I could keep an eye on him. When he saw me on the phone, he gave a bitter little laugh. I could swear he was waiting for you after that.'

'Report back to the ranch. Tell Lucas and Torrence to be ready to join me at a moment's notice. And we need a photographer from the criminal records office, with a miniature camera.'

'Waiter!' the man shouted. 'How much do I owe you?'

'Three fifty.'

'I bet he's a Pole,' Maigret whispered to Janvier. 'We're off.'

They didn't have far to go . . . They followed their man into a little restaurant and sat down at the next table to his. It was an Italian restaurant, and they ate pasta.

At three o'clock Lucas arrived to take over from Janvier. He and Maigret were in a brasserie opposite the Gare du Nord.

'The photographer?' Maigret asked.

'He's waiting outside to catch him on the way out.'

And indeed, when the Pole left the place, after reading the newspapers, an inspector went straight up to him. At a distance of less than a metre, he pressed a button. The man covered his face with his arm, but it was too late and, in a gesture that showed he had understood, he threw a reproachful look at Maigret.

'Okey-dokey, pal,' mused the inspector, 'I know you don't want to lead us home. But, however patient you might be, I'm just as patient.'

Evening drew in, and a few snowflakes danced in the streets as the man walked on, filling in the time before bed.

'Shall I take over from you for the night, Boss?' Lucas suggested.

'No! I'd prefer you to look into the photograph side. Look through the files, first. Then check the foreign communities. That chap knows Paris. He didn't arrive here yesterday. Someone must know him . . .'

'Shall I get his photo put in the papers?'

Maigret looked with disdain at his subordinate. Hadn't Lucas, who'd worked with him for years, understood the first thing? Did the police have a single piece of proof? Nothing! No witness. A man killed at night in the middle of the Bois de Boulogne. No weapon discovered. No fingerprints. Dr Borms lived alone, and his only employee had no idea where he had been that day.

'Do what I told you! Be off . . .'

It was midnight before the man decided to go into a hotel. Maigret was right behind him. It was a second- or even third-class hotel.

'I'd like a room.'

'Fill in the form please.'

He filled it in, his fingers numb with cold.

He looked Maigret up and down, as if to say:

'You think that's got me bothered! I can write anything down here I want.'

And he did indeed write down the first name that came to him, Nicolas Slaatkovitch, resident of Crakow, arrived in Paris the previous day.

A false name of course. Maigret telephoned CID; the files of rented accommodation were searched, the registers of foreigners checked, and the ports and border posts alerted. No Nicolas Slaatkovitch.

'Do you want a room as well?' asked the hotel owner, with pursed lips. He knew a policeman when he saw one.

'No thanks. I'll spend the night on the stairs.'

Safer that way. He sat down on a step outside room 7. Twice, the door opened. The man peered into the darkness, made out Maigret's shape, and ended up by going to bed. In the morning his chin had a dark shadow and his cheeks bristled. He hadn't been able to change his clothes. He had no comb with him, even, and his hair was tousled.

Lucas made an appearance.

'Shall I take over, Boss?'

Maigret couldn't make up his mind to abandon his man. He watched him pay for the room. He saw him go pale. Maigret guessed the problem.

A little later, as the two men ate their croissants and drank their coffee more or less side by side in a bar, Maigret was proved right as the man openly counted out what he had left. One hundred franc note, two coins of twenty, one of ten, and a few bits of small change. He grimaced bitterly.

Well, he wouldn't get far with that! When he came to the Bois de Boulogne of course, he had just left home. He was freshly shaved, and there wasn't a speck of dust on his newly pressed garments. He must have been expecting to go back home shortly afterwards. He wouldn't even have checked how much he had in his pocket.

It was his identity papers and maybe a few visiting cards that had gone into the Seine, Maigret calculated.

Whatever happened, the man was determined that his home address would not be discovered.

And so the trudge round the streets of those who have no home to go to started up again. Long stops in front of shop windows, at stalls in the street, the occasional entry to a bar, just to be able to sit down, out of the cold, and sessions reading newspapers in brasseries.

One hundred and fifty francs! No more restaurant lunches. The man made do with hard-boiled eggs that he ate standing up at the bar, washed down with a beer, whilst Maigret ate his sandwiches.

The man hesitated for a long while outside a cinema. Hand in his pocket, he jingled his coins. It would be better to last out . . . he walked on, and on.

Hang on a minute! It struck Maigret that this exhausting perambulation was taking him over and over the same ground: from La Trinité church to Place Clichy, Place Clichy to Barbès, via the rue Caulaincourt, Barbès to the Gare du Nord, and down rue La Fayette.

Did the man fear being recognized in other areas? He had surely chosen to keep to the districts furthest away from his home or his hotel, ones he didn't normally visit.

Perhaps, like a lot of foreigners, the Montparnasse area was his usual haunt? Or round the Panthéon?

His clothing—comfortable, sober, well-cut—suggested a man on middle income. A professional man, probably. Ah! He's wearing a wedding ring! Married then!

Maigret was eventually obliged to let Torrence take his place. He dropped in at home. Mme Maigret was displeased: her sister had arrived from Orléans, she had prepared a special dinner and here was her husband, after shaving and changing, announcing that he had to leave again immediately and had no idea when he would be back.

He made a flying visit to the Quai des Orfèvres. 'Did Lucas leave anything for me?'

Yes! There was a note waiting. He had shown the photo around in all the Polish and Russian neighbourhoods. The man was unknown. No luck either with political groups. As a last resort, he had had numerous copies made of the photo. In every area of Paris, police were going from door to door, from concierge to concierge, hawking the picture around the bar owners and the café waiters.

'Hello? Superintendent Maigret? I'm an usherette at the News Theatre on Boulevard de Strasbourg. A Monsieur Torrence told me to let you know he's here, but he daren't come to the phone.'

The man wasn't stupid then. He had worked out that a cinema was the cheapest heated place to spend a few hours. Two francs a ticket, and you were allowed to sit through several showings!

A strange intimacy had developed between follower and followed, between the man whose stubble was more and more pronounced and whose clothes looked increasingly crumpled, and Maigret, who stayed right behind him. There was even a comic detail. They had both caught the same cold. Each had a red nose. They took their handkerchiefs out of their pockets almost in unison and, on one occasion, the man was unable to repress a vague smile as he heard Maigret succumb to a series of sneezes.

After five consecutive sessions of Pathé news, they ended up in a filthy hotel on boulevard de la Chapelle. The same name went down on the register. And Maigret, as before, settled down on the stairway. Only, as it was a hotel used by prostitutes, he had to move every ten minutes for couples who eyed him curiously, and the women were uneasy.

When the man had reached the end of his cash, or the end of his tether, would he head for home? Earlier, he had stayed for quite a while in a brasserie and had taken off his grey overcoat—Maigret had seized the opportunity of looking inside the collar. The garment came from Old England on the boulevard des Italiens. It was off the peg and the shop must have sold dozens of similar coats. There was one clue though. The coat was last year's model, so the man must have been in Paris for at least a year. And he must have hung out somewhere for that time . . .

Maigret began to drink hot toddies, to kill off his cold. His quarry was trying to eke out his cash. He was sticking to coffee, with no brandy, and feeding himself on croissants and hard-boiled eggs.

The news from base was always the same—nothing to report. No one had recognized the Pole's photo. No one had been noticed missing.

No leads on the dead man either. He had a successful practice, made a very comfortable living, had no political activities, led a busy social life, and, as his specialism was nervous illnesses, his clients were mainly women.

Maigret had never previously had the opportunity to pursue this particular question to a conclusion: how long does it take a well-dressed, well-brought-up, well-turned-out man to lose his external veneer when he is forced onto the street?

He knew the answer now: four days. The growing stubble was the most telltale of signs. On the first morning, the man looked like a lawyer, a doctor, an architect, or an industrialist. He could be imagined stepping out of a nice little apartment. A four-day stubble had transformed him to the point where, if his photograph had appeared in the press in connection with the Bois de Boulogne case, he would have been immediately identified as a murderous-looking type.

The cold and the lack of sleep had reddened his eyelids and his cheeks had a feverish glow. His shoes were no longer polished, and had lost their shape. His overcoat was looking tired and his trousers were baggy at the knees.

Even the way he walked the streets had changed. He stuck close to the walls and lowered his gaze when passers-by threw him a glance. And another telltale sign: he turned his head away when he was passing restaurants where diners could be seen seated in front of loaded plates.

'Your last twenty francs, pal,' Maigret calculated. 'And after that?'

Lucas, Torrence, and Janvier stood in for him from time to time, but Maigret handed over to them as little as possible. He would hurtle off to the Quai des Orfèvres to report to the boss.

'You ought to take a break, Maigret.' And Maigret would reply gruffly, touchily, the prey of mixed feelings: 'Is it or is it not my duty to catch the murderer?'

'Of course.'

'Then I'll be off,' he would sigh with a kind of rancour in his voice. 'I wonder where we'll be sleeping tonight . . .'

Only twenty francs left! Less even! When he met up with Torrence, he heard that the man had eaten three hard-boiled eggs and drunk two coffees with brandy in a bar on the corner of the rue Montmartre.

'That's eight francs fifty, eleven francs fifty left.'

Maigret admired him. Far from trying to hide, the man walked along on a level with him, sometimes right beside him, and Maigret had to restrain himself from speaking to him.

'Come on, pal. Isn't it time to spill the beans? There's a nice warm house waiting for you somewhere, your own bed, slippers, a razor. And a good dinner, why not?'

It was not to be. The man was roaming around under the arc lights of Les Halles, like someone with no idea where to go, amongst the piles of cabbages and carrots, stepping out of the way when a train whistle blew, or a lorry loaded with fresh produce passed by.

'No cash for a room tonight!'

It was eight degrees below freezing that evening. The man bought himself some hot sausages that a woman stallholder was cooking in the open air. He would stink of garlic and grease all night long!

At one point he tried to sneak into one of the warehouses and lie down in a corner. A policeman, whom Maigret had no time to tip off, sent him on his way. Now, he was hobbling along. The banks of the Seine. The Pont des Arts. He'd better not take it into his head to throw himself in the river! Maigret didn't feel up to jumping after him into the dark waters towing along lumps of ice.

He was following the towpath. Tramps were muttering complaints. Under the bridges, all the good places were taken.

In a little street near the Place Maubert, through the windows of a strange bistro, old men could be seen asleep, their heads on the table. Twenty sous, with a glass of red wine thrown in! The man looked at him through the darkness, gave a fatalistic gesture of the hands, and pushed open the door. As it opened and closed, a nauseating smell hit Maigret in the face. He decided to stay outside. He called to an officer, put him on watch outside on the pavement, and went off to phone Lucas, on duty that night.

'We've been looking for you for an hour, boss. We've found him! Through a concierge. His name is Stéphan Strevski, an architect, age 34, born in Warsaw, came to France three years ago. Works for an interior designer on the Faubourg Saint-Honoré. Married to a Hungarian woman, a beauty who goes by the name of Dora. They rent a flat for twelve thousand francs a month in the Passy area, rue de la Pompe. No political connections. The concierge has never seen the victim. Stéphan went out on Monday morning earlier than usual. She was surprised not to see him come home, but she wasn't worried, given that . . .'

'What time is it?'

'Half past three. I'm on my own in the office. I've had some beer sent up, but it's too cold.'

'Listen, Lucas. Here's what . . . Yes! I know. It's too late for the morning ones. But this evening's? Okay?'

That morning a silent reek of misery seemed to seep from the man's clothing. His eyes were sunken. The look he darted at Maigret, in the pale dawn, expressed eloquent reproach.

Hadn't he been pushed, step by step but still at vertiginous speed, on to the bottom rung of the ladder? He turned up the collar of his coat. He didn't leave the district but, with an embittered scowl, dived into a bistro which had just opened its doors. He downed four glasses of spirits, as if to wash away the rank taste that the previous night had left in his mouth and in his breast.

Well, that was that. His pockets were empty now. Nothing for it but to walk the streets, slippery with black ice. He must be aching all over. He was limping with his left leg. Every now and again, he stopped and looked around him despairingly.

Now that he wasn't going into cafés, where there were telephones, Maigret was unable to get anyone to take over. The banks of the Seine again! And the man fingered the second-hand books in a mechanical gesture, turning over the pages, sometimes checking the authenticity of an engraving or a print! An icy wind swept over the river. In front of the moving barges, the water was making clinking noises as lumps of ice came into contact with each other, like spangles.

In the distance, Maigret could make out HQ and his office window. He just hoped Lucas . . .

He did not yet know that this dreadful inquiry was set to become a classic, with every detail recounted by generations of inspectors to the ones below. The silliest thing was that it was a ridiculous detail which affected him the most: the man had a pimple on his forehead, a pimple which, when you looked closely, was more likely a boil and which seemed to be turning from red to violet.

He just hoped Lucas . . .

At midday the man, who certainly seemed at home in Paris, made his way to the soup kitchen right at the end of the boulevard Saint-Germain. He took his place in the queue of down-and-outs. An old man spoke to him, but he pretended not to understand. Then another, his face pitted with pox marks, tried him in Russian.

Maigret crossed over to the opposite pavement, hesitated, had no choice but to eat a sandwich in a bistro. He kept his shoulder turned away, so that the man could not see him eating.

The vagrants were moving forward slowly, being allowed in groups of four or six into the room where they were served with a bowl of hot soup. The queue was lengthening. Every now and again the people at the back started pushing, and there were protests.

One o'clock. The boy arrived at the end of the street and began running, his head bent forward.

'Read the *Intran* . . . The *Intran* . . .'

The boy was also trying to get there ahead of anyone else. He could recognize his likely customers from a distance. He took no notice of the queue of beggars.

'Read . . .'

Humbly, the man raised his hand, drew the boy's attention.

The others looked on. So he had enough money to buy a paper?

Maigret hailed the boy himself, unfolded the paper, and, to his relief, found what he was looking for on the first page—a photograph of a young woman, pretty and smiling.

A DISTURBING DISAPPEARANCE

We have been informed of the disappearance, four days ago, of a young Polish woman, Mme Dora Strevski, who has not returned to her home in Passy, 17 rue de la Pompe.

A troubling feature is the fact that her husband, M. Stéphan Strevski himself disappeared the previous day, Monday, and the concierge, who alerted the police, declares . . .

The man had only five or six metres to go, in the queue which was carrying him forward, before being allotted his bowl of steaming soup. He broke rank at that moment, crossed over the street, almost got run over by a bus, reached the pavement just as Maigret arrived at the same spot.

'I am at your disposal,' he declared. 'Take me away, I'll answer all your questions.'

Everyone was waiting in the corridor back at CID—Lucas, Janvier, Torrence, and others who had not been working on the case but who were in the know. As Maigret passed him, Lucas made a gesture which meant 'Success'.

A door opened and closed. Beer and sandwiches on the table.

'Have something to eat first.'

Awkwardness. The mouthfuls refused to go down. The man finally spoke.

'As long as she's gone, and is safe . . .'

Maigret had a sudden urge to poke the stove.

'When I read the account of the murder in the papers . . . I had suspected Dora of having an affair with that man for some time. I realized she wasn't his only mistress and I knew Dora and her impetuous character. You know? If he had wanted to drop her, I was sure she was capable of . . . And she always carried a mother-of-pearl revolver in her bag. When the papers announced the reconstitution of the crime, I wanted to see.'

Maigret would have liked to warn him, as the English police do, that 'anything you say may be taken down and used against you.'

The man still hadn't taken his overcoat off. He was still wearing a hat.

'Now that she's in safety. Or I suppose she is . . .'

He looked round him in anguish. A suspicion had crossed his mind.

'She must have understood, when I didn't come home. I knew it would end badly, that Borms wasn't the man for her, she wouldn't accept being a plaything and she would come back to me. She went out alone on Sunday evening, as she had started to do, recently. She must have killed him when . . .'

Maigret blew his nose. He blew it at length. A ray of sunshine, that piercing winter sunshine which accompanies freezing weather, was coming through the window. The pimple, the boil, shone on the forehead of the person he still thought of as the man.

'Yes, your wife killed him. When she understood that he didn't take her seriously. And you, you understood that she had killed. And you didn't want . . .'

Suddenly, he walked up to the Pole.

'I'm sorry, old man' he muttered, as if he were speaking to an old friend. 'It was my job to find out the truth, wasn't it? My duty to . . .'

He opened the door.

'Bring in Mme Dora Strevski. Lucas, you carry on, I . . .'

And he didn't set foot again in CID for two days. The Boss telephoned him at home.

'Well now Maigret, she admitted everything, you know. And by the way, how's your cold? I've been told . . .'

'It's nothing, Boss. I'm fine. All be over in 24 hours. And how is he?'

'What? Who?'

'The man!'

'Oh! I see. He went to the best lawyer in Paris. He's hoping . . . Well, you know, *crime passionnel* cases . . .'

Maigret went back to bed and knocked himself out with liberal doses of hot toddy and aspirin. Whenever, after that, people tried to talk to him about the case, he would grunt:

'Case? What case?' in a way that discouraged further questions.

And the man came to see him, once or twice a week, kept him abreast of the lawyer's hopes.

It was not quite an acquittal: a year's suspended sentence.

And it was the man who taught Maigret to play chess.

An Errand

Translated by Dorothy S. Blair

When she is the only one at the foot of the mortar-stones, the hen only scratches with one paw. For she has, so she thinks, plenty of time to choose her grains of corn.

Penda certainly was not the only girl in M'Badane, but she had only to appear for the most beautiful to seem almost ugly. Of all the girls in the village Penda was the most beautiful, and, far from being fastidious and difficult to please as might have been expected, she was only too anxious to find a husband, as she was afraid of growing into an old maid, for she had already turned sixteen. On their side suitors were not lacking: every single day her girl-friends' brothers and fathers, young men and old men from other villages, sent *griots* and *dialis* bearing gifts and fine words to ask her hand in marriage.

If it had only depended on herself, Penda would certainly by now have had a baby tied on her back, either good, or bad-tempered and crying. But in the matter of marriage, as in all things, a girl must submit to her father's will. It is her father who must decide whom she is to belong to: a prince, a rich *dioula* or a common *badolo* who sweats in the fields in the sun; it is for her father to say if he wishes to bestow her on a powerful *marabout* or an insignificant *talibé*.

Now Mor, the father of Penda, had demanded neither the immense bride-price of a rich man, nor the meagre possessions of a *badolo*; still less had he thought of offering his daughter to a *marabout* or to a *marabout's* disciple in order to enlarge his place in paradise.

Mor simply told all those who came to ask for his daughter, whether for themselves, for their masters, for their sons, or for their brothers:

'I will give Penda without demanding bride-price or gifts, to the man who will kill an ox and send me the meat by the agency of a hyena; but when it arrives not a single morsel of the animal must be missing.'

But how can you entrust meat, even dried meat, to a hyena, and prevent her from touching it?

That was more difficult than making the round-eared Narr-the-Moor keep a secret. It was more difficult than entrusting a calabash full of honey to a child and expect him not even to dip his little finger in. You might as well try to prevent the sun from leaving his home in the morning or retiring to bed at the end of the day. You might as well forbid the thirsty sand to drink the first drops of the first rains. Entrust meat to Bouki-the-Hyena? You might as well entrust a pat of butter to a burning fire. Entrust meat to Bouki and prevent her from touching it?

It was an impossible task, so said the *griots* as they wended their way home to their masters; so said the mothers who had come on their sons' behalf; so said the old men who had come to ask for the beautiful Penda for themselves.

A day's walk from M'Badane lay the village of N'Diour. The inhabitants of N'Diour were by no means ordinary folk; they were, or so they believed, the only men and the only women, since earliest times, to have tamed the double-dealing hyenas, with whom in fact they lived in perfect peace and good understanding. It is true that the people of N'Diour did their share to maintain these good relations. Every Friday they killed a bull which they offered to Bouki-the-Hyena and her tribe.

Of all the young men of N'Diour, Birane was the best at wrestling as well as at working in the fields; he was also the most handsome. When his *griot* brought back the presents that Mor had refused, and told him the conditions which Penda's father had laid down, Birane said to himself,

'I shall be the one to win Penda for my bed.'

He killed an ox, dried the meat, and put it in a goatskin; the skin was enclosed in a coarse cotton bag and the whole thing placed in the middle of a truss of straw.

On Friday, when Bouki came with her family to partake of the offering given by the people of N'Diour, Birane went to her and said,

'My *griot*, who has no more sense than a babe at the breast, and who is as stupid as an ox, has brought back the fine gifts that I sent to Penda, the daughter of Mor of M'Badane. I am certain that if you, whose wisdom is great and whose tongue is as honey, took this simple truss of straw to M'Badane to the house of Mor, you would only need to say, "Birane asks for your daughter", for him to grant her to you.'

'I have grown old, Birane, and my back is no longer very strong, but M'Bar, the eldest of my children, is full of vigour and he has inherited a little of my wisdom. He will go to M'Badane for you, and I am sure that he will acquit himself well of your mission.'

M'Bar set off very early in the morning, the truss of straw on his back. When the dew moistened the truss of straw the pleasant odour of the meat began to float in the air. M'Bar-the-Hyena stopped, lifted his nose, sniffed to the right, sniffed to the left, then resumed his way, a little less hurriedly it seemed. The smell grew stronger, the hyena stopped again, bared his teeth, thrust his nose to the right, to the left, into the air, then turned round and sniffed to the four winds.

He resumed his journey, but now hesitating all the time, as if held back by this penetrating, insistent smell which seemed to come from all directions.

Not being able to resist it any longer, M'Bar left the track that led from N'Diour to M'Badane, made huge circling detours in the veld, ferreting to the right, ferreting to the left, continually retracing his steps, and took three whole days instead of one to reach M'Badane.

M'Bar was certainly not in the best of tempers when he entered Mor's home. He did not wear the pleasant expression of a messenger who comes to ask a great favour. This smell of meat that had impregnated all the grass and all the bushes of the veld, and still impregnated the huts of M'Badane and the courtyard of Mor's home, had made him forget on the way from N'Diour all the wisdom that old Bouki had instilled into him, and stifled the gracious words that one always expects from a petitioner. M'Bar scarcely even unclenched his teeth to say: '*Assalamou aleykoum!*' and nobody could even hear his greeting; but as he threw down the truss of straw from his back that had bent under its weight, he muttered in a voice that was more than disagreeable,

'Birane of N'Diour sends you this truss of straw and asks you for your daughter.'

Under the very eyes of M'Bar-the-Hyena, first astonished, then indignant, then covetous, Mor cut the liana ropes that bound the truss of straw, opened it up, and took out the bag of coarse cotton; from the coarse cotton bag he took out the goatskin, and from the goatskin the pieces of dried meat.

'Go,' Mor said to M'Bar-the-Hyena, who nearly burst with rage at the sight of all that meat that he had unsuspectingly carried for three days, and which was spread out there without his being able to touch a single bit (for the folk of M'Badane were not like the inhabitants of N'Diour, and in M'Badane hunting spears were lying all round). 'Go,' said Mor, 'go and tell Birane that I give him my daughter. Tell him that he is not only the most spirited and the strongest of all the young men of N'Diour, but he is also the shrewdest. He has managed to entrust meat to you, hyena; he will be able to keep a sharp watch on his wife and outwit all tricks.'

But M'Bar had certainly not heard the last words of Mor, which were so flattering to the man who had sent him on this errand; he was already out of the house and leaving the village, for he recalled having seen on his long and tortuous path innumerable trusses of straw.

Indeed as soon as he reached the first fields of M'Badane he found some trusses of straw. He cut the bonds, rummaged inside them, scattered them all around without finding anything that resembled flesh or even bones. He ran to the right, he ran to the left, ferreting, rummaging, scattering all the trusses of straw that he found in the fields, so that it eventually took him another three days to get back to the village of N'Diour.

'What!' asked Birane, when he saw him arrive sweating and panting. 'Haven't you done my errand yet, M'Bar? What have you been doing for six days when you barely needed two days to get to M'Badane and back?'

'What I did on the way is none of your business,' said M'Bar-the-Hyena in a curt voice. 'Suffice to say, if it gives you pleasure, that Mor gives you his daughter.'

And without waiting for the thanks that Birane would no doubt have lavished on him, M'Bar went off to rummage in other trusses of straw.

And since that day, hyenas have never run errands for anyone at all.

The Guest

Translated by Justin O'Brien

The schoolmaster was watching the two men climb towards him. One was on horseback, the other on foot. They had not yet tackled the abrupt rise leading to the schoolhouse built on the hillside. They were toiling onwards, making slow progress in the snow, among the stones, on the vast expanse of the high, deserted plateau. From time to time the horse stumbled. Without hearing anything yet, he could see the breath issuing from the horse's nostrils. One of the men, at least, knew the region. They were following the trail although it had disappeared days ago under a layer of dirty white snow. The schoolmaster calculated that it would take them half an hour to get on to the hill. It was cold; he went back into the school to get a sweater.

He crossed the empty, frigid classroom. On the blackboard the four rivers of France, drawn with four different coloured chalks, had been flowing towards their estuaries for the past three days. Snow had suddenly fallen in mid-October after eight months of drought without the transition of rain, and the twenty pupils, more or less, who lived in the villages scattered over the plateau had stopped coming. With fair weather they would return. Daru now heated only the single room that was his lodging, adjoining the classroom and giving also on to the plateau to the east. Like the class windows, his window looked to the south too. On that side the school was a few kilometres from the point where the plateau began to slope towards the south. In clear weather could be seen the purple mass of the mountain range where the gap opened on to the desert.

Somewhat warmed, Daru returned to the window from which he had first seen the two men. They were no longer visible. Hence they must have tackled the rise. The sky was not so dark, for the snow had stopped falling during the night. The morning had opened with a dirty light which had scarcely become brighter as the ceiling of clouds lifted. At two in the afternoon it seemed as if the day were merely beginning. But still this was better than those three days when the thick snow was falling amidst unbroken darkness with little gusts of wind that rattled the double door of the classroom. Then Daru had spent long hours in his room, leaving it only to go to the shed and feed the chickens or get some coal. Fortunately the delivery truck from Tadjid, the nearest village to the north, had brought his supplies two days before the blizzard. It would return in forty-eight hours.

Besides, he had enough to resist a siege, for the little room was cluttered with bags of wheat that the administration left as a stock to distribute to those of his pupils whose families had suffered from the drought. Actually they had all been victims because they were all poor. Every day Daru would distribute a ration to the children. They had missed it, he knew, during these bad days. Possibly one of the fathers or big brothers would come this afternoon and he could supply them with grain. It was just a matter of carrying them over to the next harvest. Now shiploads of wheat were arriving from France and the worst was over. But it would be hard to forget that poverty, that army of ragged ghosts wandering in the sunlight, the plateaux burned to a cinder month after month, the earth shrivelled up little by little, literally scorched, every stone bursting into dust under one's foot. The sheep had died then by thousands and even a few men, here and there, sometimes without anyone's knowing.

In contrast with such poverty, he who lived almost like a monk in his remote schoolhouse, none the less satisfied with the little he had and with the rough life, had felt like a lord with his whitewashed walls, his narrow couch, his unpainted shelves, his well, and his weekly provision of water and food. And suddenly this snow, without warning, without the foretaste of rain. This is the way the region was, cruel to live in, even without men—who didn't help matters either. But Daru had been born here. Everywhere else, he felt exiled.

He stepped out on to the terrace in front of the schoolhouse. The two men were now half-way up the slope. He recognized the horseman as Balducci, the old gendarme he had known for a long time. Balducci was holding on the end of a rope an Arab who was walking behind him with hands bound and head lowered. The gendarme waved a greeting to which Daru did not reply, lost as he was in contemplation of the Arab dressed in a faded blue jellaba, his feet in sandals but covered with socks of heavy raw wool, his head surmounted by a narrow, short *chèche*. They were approaching. Balducci was holding back his horse in order not to hurt the Arab, and the group was advancing slowly.

Within earshot, Balducci shouted: 'One hour to do the three kilo-metres from El Ameur!' Daru did not answer. Short and square in his thick sweater, he watched them climb. Not once had the Arab raised his head. 'Hello,' said Daru when they got up on to the terrace. 'Come in and warm up.' Balducci painfully got down from his horse without letting go the rope. From under his bristling moustache he smiled at the school-master. His little dark eyes, deep-set under a tanned forehead, and his mouth surrounded with wrinkles made him look attentive and studious. Daru took the bridle, led the horse to the shed, and came back to the two men, who were now waiting for him in the school. He led them into his room. 'I am going to heat up the classroom,' he said. 'We'll be more comfortable there.' When he entered the room again, Balducci was on the couch. He had undone the rope tying him to the Arab, who had squatted near the stove. His hands still bound, the *chèche* pushed back on his head, he was looking towards the window. At first Daru noticed only his huge lips, fat, smooth, almost negroid; yet his nose was straight, his eyes were dark and full of fever. The *chèche* revealed an obstinate fore-head and, under the weathered skin now rather discoloured by the cold, the whole face had a restless and rebellious look that struck Daru when the Arab, turning his face towards him, looked him straight in the eyes. 'Go into the other room,' said the schoolmaster, 'and I'll make you some mint tea.' 'Thanks,' Balducci said. 'What a nuisance! How I long for retirement.' And addressing his prisoner in Arabic: 'Come on, you.' The Arab got up and, slowly, holding his bound wrists in front of him, went into the classroom.

With the tea, Daru brought a chair. But Balducci was already enthroned on the nearest pupil's desk and the Arab had squatted against the teacher's platform facing the stove, which stood between the desk and the window. When he held out the glass of tea to the prisoner, Daru hesitated at the sight of his bound hands. 'He might perhaps be untied.' 'Certainly,' said Balducci. 'That was for the journey.' He started to get to his feet. But Daru, setting the glass on the floor, had knelt beside the Arab. Without saying anything, the Arab watched him with his feverish eyes. Once his hands were free, he rubbed his swollen wrists against each other, took the glass of tea, and sucked up the burning liquid in swift little sips.

'Good,' said Daru. 'And where are you headed for?'

Balducci withdrew his moustache from the tea. 'Here, my boy.'

'Odd pupils! And you're spending the night?'

'No. I'm going back to El Ameur. And you will deliver this fellow to Tinguit. He is expected at police headquarters.'

Balducci was looking at Daru with a friendly little smile.

'What's this story?' asked the schoolmaster. 'Are you pulling my leg?'

'No, my boy. Those are the orders.'

'The orders? I'm not . . .' Daru hesitated, not wanting to hurt the old Corsican. 'I mean, that's not my job.'

'What! What's the meaning of that? In wartime people do all kinds of jobs.'

'Then I'll wait for the declaration of war!'

Balducci nodded.

'O.K. But the orders exist and they concern you too. Things are brewing, it appears. There is talk of a forthcoming revolt. We are mobilized, in a way.'

Daru still had his obstinate look.

'Listen, my boy,' Balducci said. 'I like you and you must understand. There's only a dozen of us at El Ameur to patrol throughout the whole territory of a small department and I must get back in a hurry. I was told to hand this man over to you and return without delay. He couldn't be kept there. His village was beginning to stir; they wanted to take him back. You must take him to Tinguit tomorrow before the day is over. Twenty kilometres shouldn't worry a husky fellow like you. After that, all will be over. You'll come back to the pupils and your comfortable life.'

Behind the wall the horse could be heard snorting and pawing the earth. Daru was looking out of the window. Decidedly, the weather was clearing and the light was increasing over the snowy plateau. When all the snow was melted, the sun would take over again and once more would burn the fields of stone. For days, still, the unchanging sky would shed its dry light on the solitary expanse where nothing had any connexion with man.

'After all,' he said, turning around towards Balducci, 'what did he do?' And, before the gendarme had opened his mouth, he asked: 'Does he speak French?'

'No, not a word. We had been looking for him for a month, but they were hiding him. He killed his cousin.'

'Is he against us?'

'I don't think so. But you can never be sure.'

'Why did he kill?'

'A family squabble, I think. One owed the other grain, it seems. It's not at all clear. In short, he killed his cousin with a billhook. You know, like a sheep, *kreezk!*'

Balducci made the gesture of drawing a blade across his throat and the Arab, his attention attracted, watched him with a sort of anxiety. Daru felt a sudden wrath against the man, against all men with their rotten spite, their tireless hates, their blood lust.

But the kettle was singing on the stove. He served Balducci more tea, hesitated, then served the Arab again, who, a second time, drank avidly. His raised arms made the jellaba fall open and the schoolmaster saw his thin, muscular chest.

'Thanks, my boy,' Balducci said. 'And now, I'm off.'

He got up and went towards the Arab, taking a small rope from his pocket.

'What are you doing?' Daru asked dryly.

Balducci, disconcerted, showed him the rope.

'Don't bother.'

The old gendarme hesitated. 'It's up to you. Of course, you are armed?'

'I have my shot gun.'

'Where?'

'In the trunk.'

'You ought to have it near your bed.'

'Why? I have nothing to fear.'

'You're mad. If there's an uprising, no one is safe, we're all in the same boat.'

'I'll defend myself. I'll have time to see them coming.'

Balducci began to laugh, then suddenly the moustache covered the white teeth.

'You'll have time? O.K. That's just what I was saying. You have always been a little cracked. That's why I like you, my son was like that.'

At the same time he took out his revolver and put it on the desk.

'Keep it; I don't need two weapons from here to El Ameur.'

The revolver shone against the black paint of the gable. When the gendarme turned towards him, the schoolmaster caught the smell of leather and horseflesh.

'Listen, Balducci,' Daru said suddenly, 'every bit of this disgusts me, and most of all your fellow here. But I won't hand him over. Fight, yes, if I have to. But not that.'

The old gendarme stood in front of him and looked at him severely.

'You're being a fool,' he said slowly. 'I don't like it either. You don't get used to putting a rope on a man even after years of it, and you're even ashamed—yes, ashamed. But you can't let them have their way.'

'I won't hand him over,' Daru said again.

'It's an order, my boy, and I repeat it.'

'That's right. Repeat to them what I've said to you: I won't hand him over.'

Balducci made a visible effort to reflect. He looked at the Arab and at Daru. At last he decided.

'No, I won't tell them anything. If you want to drop us, go ahead; I'll not denounce you. I have an order to deliver the prisoner and I'm doing so. And now you'll just sign this paper for me.'

'There's no need. I'll not deny that you left him with me.'

'Don't be mean with me. I know you'll tell the truth. You're from hereabouts and you are a man. But you must sign, that's the rule.'

Daru opened his drawer, took out a little square bottle of purple ink, the red wooden penholder with the 'sergeant-major' pen he used for making models of penmanship, and signed. The gendarme carefully folded the paper and put it into his wallet. Then he moved towards the door.

'I'll see you off,' Daru said.

'No,' said Balducci. 'There's no use being polite. You insulted me.'

He looked at the Arab, motionless in the same spot, sniffed peevishly, and turned away towards the door. 'Goodbye, son,' he said. The door shut behind him. Balducci appeared suddenly outside the window and then disappeared. His footsteps were muffled by the snow. The horse stirred on the other side of the wall and several chickens fluttered in fright. A moment later Balducci reappeared outside the window leading the horse by the bridle. He walked towards the little rise without turning round and disappeared from sight with the horse following him. A big stone could be heard bouncing down. Daru walked back towards the prisoner, who, without stirring, never took his eyes off him. 'Wait,' the schoolmaster said in Arabic and went towards the bedroom. As he was going through the door, he had a second thought, went to the desk, took the revolver, and stuck it in his pocket. Then, without looking back, he went into his room.

For some time he lay on his couch watching the sky gradually close over, listening to the silence. It was this silence that had seemed painful to him during the first days here, after the war. He had requested a post in the little town at the base of the foothills separating the upper plateaux from the desert. There, rocky walls, green and black to the north, pink and lavender to the south, marked the frontier of eternal summer. He had been named to a post farther north, on the plateau itself. In the beginning, the solitude and the silence had been hard for him on these wastelands peopled only by stones. Occasionally, furrows suggested cultivation, but they had been dug to uncover a certain kind of stone good for building. The only ploughing here was to harvest rocks. Elsewhere a thin layer of soil accumulated in the hollows would be scraped out to enrich paltry village gardens. This is the way it was: bare rock covered three-quarters of the region. Towns sprang up, flourished, then disappeared; men came by, loved one another or fought bitterly, then died. No one in this desert, neither he nor his guest, mattered. And yet, outside this desert neither of them, Daru knew, could have really lived.

When he got up, no noise came from the classroom. He was amazed at the unmixed joy he derived from the mere thought that the Arab might have fled and that he would be alone with no decision to make. But the prisoner was there. He had merely stretched out between the stove and the desk. With eyes open, he was staring at the ceiling. In that position, his thick lips were particularly noticeable, giving him a pouting look. 'Come,' said Daru. The Arab got up and followed him. In the bedroom, the schoolmaster pointed to a chair near the table under the window. The Arab sat down without taking his eyes off Daru.

'Are you hungry?'

'Yes,' the prisoner said.

Daru set the table for two. He took flour and oil, shaped a cake in a frying-pan, and lighted the little stove that functioned on bottled gas. While the cake was cooking, he went out to the shed to get cheese, eggs, dates, and condensed milk. When the cake was done he set it on the window sill to cool, heated some condensed milk diluted with water, and beat up the eggs into an omelette. In one of his motions he knocked against the revolver stuck in his right pocket. He set the bowl down, went into the classroom, and put the revolver in his desk drawer. When he came back to the room, night was falling. He put on the light and served the Arab. 'Eat,' he said. The Arab took a piece of the cake, lifted it eagerly to his mouth, and stopped short.

'And you?' he asked.

'After you. I'll eat too.'

The thick lips opened slightly. The Arab hesitated, then bit into the cake determinedly.

The meal over, the Arab looked at the schoolmaster. 'Are you the judge?'

'No, I'm simply keeping you until tomorrow.'

'Why do you eat with me?'

'I'm hungry.'

The Arab fell silent. Daru got up and went out. He brought back a folding bed from the shed, set it up between the table and the stove, at right-angles to his own bed. From a large suitcase which, upright in a corner, served as a shelf for papers, he took two blankets and arranged them on the camp bed. Then he stopped, felt useless, and sat down on his bed. There was nothing more to do or to get ready. He had to look at this man. He looked at him, therefore, trying to imagine his face bursting with rage. He couldn't do so. He could see nothing but the dark yet shining eyes and the animal mouth.

'Why did you kill him?' he asked in a voice whose hostile tone surprised him.

The Arab looked away.

'He ran away. I ran after him.'

He raised his eyes to Daru again and they were full of a sort of woeful interrogation. 'Now what will they do to me?'

'Are you afraid?'

He stiffened, turning his eyes away.

'Are you sorry?'

The Arab stared at him open-mouthed. Obviously he did not understand. Daru's annoyance was growing. At the same time he felt awkward and self-conscious with his big body wedged between the two beds.

'Lie down there,' he said impatiently. 'That's your bed.'

The Arab didn't move. He called to Daru:

'Tell me!'

The schoolmaster looked at him.

'Is the gendarme coming back tomorrow?'

'I don't know.'

'Are you coming with us?'

'I don't know. Why?'

The prisoner got up and stretched out on top of the blankets, his feet towards the window. The light from the electric bulb shone straight into his eyes and he closed them at once.

'Why?' Daru repeated, standing beside the bed.

The Arab opened his eyes under the blinding light and looked at him, trying not to blink.

'Come with us,' he said.

In the middle of the night, Daru was still not asleep. He had gone to bed after undressing completely; he generally slept naked. But, when he suddenly realized that he had nothing on, hesitated. He felt vulnerable and the temptation came to him to put on his clothes again. Then he shrugged his shoulders; after all, he wasn't a child and, if need be, he could break his adversary in two. From his bed he could observe him, lying on his back, still motionless with his eyes closed under the harsh light. When Daru turned out the light, the darkness seemed to coagulate all of a sudden. Little by little, the night came back to life in the window where the starless sky was stirring gently. The schoolmaster soon made out the body lying at his feet. The Arab still did not move, but his eyes seemed open. A faint wind was prowling around the schoolhouse. Perhaps it would drive away the clouds and the sun would reappear.

During the night the wind increased. The hens fluttered a little and then were silent. The Arab turned over on his side with his back to Daru, who thought he heard him moan. Then he listened for his guest's breathing, become heavier and more regular. He listened to that breath so close to him and mused without being able to go to sleep. In this room where he had been sleeping alone for a year, this presence bothered him. But it bothered him also by imposing on him a sort of brotherhood he knew well but refused to accept in the present circumstances. Men who share the same rooms, soldiers or prisoners, develop a strange alliance as if, having cast off their armour with their clothing, they fraternized every evening, over and above their differences, in the ancient community of dream and fatigue. But Daru shook himself; he didn't like such musings, and it was essential to sleep.

A little later, however, when the Arab stirred slightly, the schoolmaster was still not asleep. When the prisoner made a second move, he stiffened, on the alert. The Arab was lifting himself slowly on his arms with almost the motion of a sleepwalker. Seated upright in bed, he waited motionless without turning his head towards Daru, as if he were listening attentively. Daru did not stir; it had just occurred to him that the revolver was still in the drawer of his desk. It was better to act at once. Yet he continued to observe the prisoner, who, with the same slithery motion, put his feet on the ground, waited again, then began to stand up slowly. Daru was about to call out to him when the Arab began to walk, in a quite natural but extraordinarily silent way. He was heading towards the door at the end of the room that opened into the shed. He lifted the latch with caution and went out, pushing the door behind him but without shutting it. Daru had not stirred. 'He is running away,' he merely thought. 'Good riddance!' Yet he listened attentively. The hens were not fluttering; the guest must be on the plateau. A faint sound of water reached him, and he didn't know what it was until the Arab again stood framed in the doorway, closed the door carefully, and came back to bed without a sound. Then Daru turned his back on him and fell asleep. Still later he seemed, from the depths of his sleep, to hear furtive steps around the schoolhouse. 'I'm dreaming! I'm dreaming!' he repeated to himself. And he went on sleeping.

When he awoke, the sky was clear; the loose window let in a cold, pure air. The Arab was asleep, hunched up under the blankets now, his mouth open, utterly relaxed. But when Daru shook him, he started dreadfully, staring at Daru with wild eyes as if he had never seen him and such a frightened expression that the schoolmaster stepped back. 'Don't be afraid. It's me. You must eat.' The Arab nodded his head and said yes. Calm had returned to his face, but his expression was vacant and listless.

The coffee was ready. They drank it seated together on the folding bed as they munched their pieces of the cake. Then Daru led the Arab to the shed and showed him the tap where he washed. He went back into the room, folded the blankets and the bed, made his own bed and put the room in order. Then he went through the classroom and out on to the terrace. The sun was already rising in the blue sky; a soft, bright light was bathing the deserted plateau. On the ridge the snow was melting in spots. The stones were about to reappear. Crouched on the edge of the plateau, the schoolmaster looked at the deserted expanse. He thought of Balducci. He had hurt him, for he had sent him off in a way as if he didn't want to be associated with him. He could still hear the gendarme's farewell and, without knowing why, he felt strangely empty and vulnerable. At that moment, from the other side of the schoolhouse, the prisoner coughed. Daru listened to him almost despite himself and then, furious, threw a pebble that whistled through the air before sinking into the snow. That man's stupid crime revolted him, but to hand him over was contrary to honour. Merely thinking of it made him smart with humiliation. And he cursed at one and the same time his own people who had sent him this Arab and the Arab too who had dared to kill and not managed to get away. Daru got up, walked in a circle on the terrace, waited motionless, and then went back into the schoolhouse.

The Arab, leaning over the cement floor of the shed, was washing his teeth with two fingers. Daru looked at him and said: 'Come.' He went back into the room ahead of the prisoner. He slipped a hunting-jacket on over his sweater and put on walking shoes. Standing, he waited until the Arab had put on his *clèche* and sandals. They went into the classroom and the schoolmaster pointed to the exit, saying: 'Go ahead.' The fellow didn't budge. 'I'm coming,' said Daru. The Arab went out. Daru went back into the room and made a package of pieces of rusk, dates, and sugar. In the classroom, before going out, he hesitated a second in front of his desk, then crossed the threshold and locked the door. 'That's the way,' he said. He started towards the east, followed by the prisoner. But, a short distance from the schoolhouse, he thought he heard a slight sound behind them. He retraced his steps and examined the surroundings of the house; there was no one there. The Arab watched him without seeming to understand. 'Come on,' said Daru.

They walked for an hour and rested beside a sharp peak of limestone. The snow was melting faster and faster and the sun was drinking up the puddles at once, rapidly cleaning the plateau, which gradually dried and vibrated like the air itself. When they resumed walking, the ground rang under their feet. From time to time a bird rent the space in front of them with a joyful cry. Daru breathed in deeply the fresh morning light. He felt a sort of rapture before the vast familiar expanse, now almost entirely yellow under its dome of blue sky. They walked an hour more, descending towards the south. They reached a level height made up of crumbly rocks. From there on, the plateau sloped down, eastward, towards a low plain where there were a few spindly trees and, to the south, towards outcroppings of rock that gave the landscape a chaotic look.

Daru surveyed the two directions. There was nothing but the sky on the horizon. Not a man could be seen. He turned towards the Arab, who was looking at him blankly. Daru held out the package to him. 'Take it,' he said. 'There are dates, bread, and sugar. You can hold out for two days. Here are a thousand francs too.' The Arab took the package and the money but kept his full hands at chest level as if he didn't know what to do with what was being given him. 'Now look,' the schoolmaster said as he pointed in the direction of the east, 'there's the way to Tinguit. You have a two-hour walk. At Tinguit you'll find the administration and the police. They are expecting you.' The Arab looked towards the east, still holding the package and the money against his chest. Daru took his elbow and turned him rather roughly towards the south. At the foot of the height on which they stood could be seen a faint path. 'That's the trail across the plateau. In a day's walk from here you'll find pasture lands and the first nomads. They'll take you in and shelter you according to their law.' The Arab had now turned towards Daru and a sort of panic was visible in his expression. 'Listen,' he said. Daru shook his head: 'No, be quiet. Now I'm leaving you.' He turned his back on him, took two long steps in the direction of the school, looked hesitantly at the motionless Arab, and started off again. For a few minutes he heard nothing but his own step resounding on the cold ground and did not turn his head. A moment later, however, he turned around. The Arab was still there on the edge of the hill, his arms hanging now, and he was looking at the schoolmaster. Daru felt something rise in his throat. But he swore with impatience, waved vaguely, and started off again. He had already gone some distance when he again stopped and looked. There was no longer anyone on the hill.

Daru hesitated. The sun was now rather high in the sky and was beginning to beat down on his head. The schoolmaster retraced his steps, at first somewhat uncertainly, then with decision. When he reached the little hill, he was bathed in sweat. He climbed it as fast as he could and stopped, out of breath, at the top. The rock-fields to the south stood out sharply against the blue sky, but on the plain to the east a steamy heat was already rising. And in that slight haze, Daru, with heavy heart, made out the Arab walking slowly on the road to prison.

A little later, standing before the window of the classroom, the schoolmaster was watching the clear light bathing the whole surface of the plateau, but he hardly saw it. Behind him on the blackboard, among the winding French rivers, sprawled the clumsily chalked-up words he had just read: 'You handed over our brother. You will pay for this.' Daru looked at the sky, the plateau, and, beyond, the invisible lands stretching all the way to the sea. In this vast landscape he had loved so much, he was alone.

Monologue

Translated by Patrick O'Brien

The monologue is her form of revenge.
Flaubert

The silly bastards! I drew the curtains they keep the stupid coloured lanterns and the fairy lights on the Christmas trees out of the apartment but the noises come in through the walls. Engines revving brakes and now here they are starting their horns big shots is what they take themselves for behind the wheel of their dreary middle-class family cars their lousy semisports jobs their miserable little Dauphines their white convertibles. A white convertible with black seats that's terrific and the fellows whistled when I went by with slanting sunglasses on my nose and a Hermès scarf on my head and now they think they're going to impress me with their filthy old wrecks and their bawling klaxons! If they all smashed into one another right under my windows how happy I should be happy. The swine they are shattering my eardrums I've no more plugs the last two are jamming the telephone bell they are utterly repulsive yet still I'd rather have my ears shattered than hear the telephone not ringing. Stop the uproar the silence: sleep. And I shan't get a wink yesterday I couldn't either I was so sick with horror because it was the day before today. I've taken so many sleeping pills they don't work anymore and that doctor is a sadist he gives them to me in the form of suppositories and I can't stuff myself like a gun. I've got to get some rest I have to I must be able to cope with Tristan tomorrow: no tears no shouting. 'This is an absurd position. A ghastly mess, even from the point of view of dough! A child needs its mother.' I'm going to have another sleepless night my nerves will be completely frazzled I'll make a cock of it. Bastards! They thump thump in my head I can see them I can hear them. They are stuffing themselves with cheap foie gras and burned turkey they drool over it Albert and Madame Nanard Etiennette their snooty offspring my mother: it's flying in the face of nature that my own brother my own mother should prefer my ex-husband to me. I've nothing whatever to say to them only just let them stop preventing me sleeping; you get so you are fit to be shut up you confess everything, true or false, they needn't count on that though I'm tough they won't get me down.

Celebrations with them, how they stank: it was ghastly enough quite ghastly enough on ordinary days! I always loathed Christmas Easter July 14. Papa lifted Nanard onto his shoulder so that he could see the fireworks and I stayed there on the ground squashed between them just at prick level and that randy crowd's smell of sex and Mama said 'there she is snivelling again' they stuffed an ice into my hand there was nothing I wanted to do with it I threw it away they sighed I couldn't be slapped on a July 14 evening. As for him he never touched me I was the one he liked best: 'proper little God-damn woman.' But when he kicked the bucket she didn't bother to hold in anymore and she used to swipe me across the face with her rings. I never slapped Sylvie once. Nanard was the king. She used to take him into her bed in the morning and I heard them tickling one another he says it's untrue I'm disgusting of course he's not going to confess they never do confess indeed maybe he's forgotten they are very good at forgetting anything inconvenient and I say they are shits on account of I do remember: she used to wander about her brothel of a room half naked in her white silk dressing gown with its stains and cigarette holes and he clung around her legs it makes you really sick mothers with their little male jobs and I was supposed to be like them no thank you very much indeed. I wanted decent children clean children I didn't want Francis to become a fairy like Nanard. Nanard with his five kids he's a bugger for all that you can't deceive me you really must hate women to have married that cow.

It's not stopping. How many of them are there? In the streets of Paris hundreds of thousands. And it's the same in every town all over the world: three thousand million and it'll get worse and worse: famines there are not nearly enough more and more and more people: even the sky's infested with them presently they will be as thick in space as they are on the motorways and the moon you can't look at it anymore without thinking that there are cunts up there spouting away. I used to like the moon it was like me; and they've mucked it up like they muck everything up they were revolting those photos—a dreary greyish dusty thing anyone at all can trample about on.

I was clean straight uncompromising. No cheating: I've had that in my bones since I was a child. I can see myself now a quaint little brat in a ragged dress Mama looked after me so badly and the kind lady simpering 'And so we love our little brother do we?' And I answered calmly 'I hate him.' The icy chill: Mama's look. It was perfectly natural that I should have been jealous all the books say so: the astonishing thing the thing I like is that I should have admitted it. No compromise no act: that proper little woman was me all right. I'm clean I'm straight I don't join in any act: that makes them mad they hate being seen through they want you to believe the stuff they hand out or at least to pretend to.

Here's some of their bloody nonsense now—rushing up the stairs laughter voices all in a tizzy. What the hell sense does that make, all working themselves up at a set date a set time just because you start using a new calendar? All my life it's made me sick, this sort of hysterical crap. I ought to tell the story of my life. Lots of women do it people print them people talk about them they strut about very pleased with themselves my book would be more interesting than all their balls: it's made me sweat but I've lived and I've lived without lies without sham how furious it would make them to see my name and picture in the shop windows and everyone would learn the real genuine truth. I'd have a whole raft of men at my feet again they're such grovelling creatures that the most dreadful slob once she's famous they make a wild rush for her. Maybe I should meet one who would know how to love me.

My father loved me. No one else. Everything comes from that. All Albert thought of was slipping off I loved him quite madly poor fool that I was. How I suffered in those days, young and as straight as they come! So of course you do silly things: maybe it was a put-up job what is there to show he didn't know Olivier? A filthy plot it knocked me completely to pieces.

Now of course that just had to happen they are dancing right over my head. My night is wrecked finished tomorrow I shall be a rag I shall have to dope myself to manage Tristan and the whole thing will end in the shit. You mustn't do it! Swine! It's all that matters to me in life sleep. Swine. They are allowed to shatter my ears and trample on me and they're making the most of it. 'The dreary bitch downstairs can't make a fuss it's New Year's Day.' Laugh away I'll find some way of getting even she'll bitch you the dreary bitch I've never let anyone walk over me ever. Albert was livid. 'No need to make a scene!' oh yes indeed there was! He was dancing with Nina belly to belly she was sticking out her big tits she stank of scent but underneath it you got a whiff of bidet and he was jigging about with a prick on him like a bull. Scenes I've made scenes all right in my life. I've always been that proper little woman who answered 'I hate him' fearless open as a book dead straight.

They're going to break through the ceiling and come down on my head. I can see them from here it's too revolting they're rubbing together sex to sex the women the respectable women it makes them wet they're charmed with themselves because the fellow's tail is standing up. And each one of them is getting ready to give his best friend a pair of horns his dearly beloved girlfriend they'll do it that very night in the bathroom not even lying down dress hitched up on their sweating asses when you go and pee you'll tread in the mess like at Rose's the night of my scene. Maybe it's on the edge of a blue party that couple upstairs they're in their fifties at that age they need whorehouse tricks to be able to thread the needle. I'm sure Albert and his good lady have whore parties you can see from Christine's face she's ready for anything at all he wouldn't have to hold himself back with her. Poor bleeder that I was at twenty too simple-minded too shamefaced. Touching, that awkwardness: I did really deserve to be loved. Oh I've been done dirt life's given me no sort of a break.

Hell I'm dying of thirst I'm hungry but it would slay me to get up out of my armchair and go to the kitchen. You freeze to death in this hole only if I turn up the central heating the air will dry out completely there's no spit left in my mouth my nose is burning. What a bleeding mess their civilization. They can muck up the moon but can't heat a house. If they had any sense they'd invent robots that would go and fetch me fruit juice when I want some and see to the house without my having to be sweet to them and listen to all their crap.

Mariette's not coming tomorrow fine I'm sick of her old father's cancer. At least I've disciplined *her* she keeps more or less in her place. There are some that put on rubber gloves to do the washing up and play the lady that I cannot bear. I don't want them to be sluts either so you find hairs in the salad and finger marks on the doors. Tristan is a cunt. I treat my dailies very well. But I want them to do their jobs properly without making a fuss or telling me the story of their lives. For that you have to train them just as you have to train children to make worthwhile grown-ups out of them.

Tristan has not trained Francis: that bitch of a Mariette is leaving me in the lurch. The drawing room will be a pigsty after they've been here. They'll come with a plushy present everyone will kiss everyone else I will hand around little cakes Francis will make the answers his father has gone over with him he lies like a grown-up man. I should have made a decent child of him. I shall tell Tristan a kid deprived of his mother always ends up by going to the bad he'll turn into a hooligan or a fairy you don't want that. My serious thoughtful voice makes me feel sick: what I should really like to do is scream it's unnatural to take a child away from its mother! But I'm dependent on him. 'Threaten him with divorce,' said Dédé. That made him laugh. Men hold together so the law is so unfair and he has so much pull that it's him that would get the decree. He would keep Francis and not another penny and you can whistle for the rent. Nothing to be done against this filthy blackmail—an allowance and the flat in exchange for Francis. I am at his mercy. No money you can't stand up for yourself you're less than nothing a zero twice over. What a numskull I didn't give a damn about money unselfish half-wit. I didn't twist their arms a quarter enough. If I had stayed with Florent I should have made myself a pretty little nest egg. Tristan fell for me fell right on his face I had pity on him. And there you are! This puffed-up little pseudo-Napoleon leaves me flat because I don't swoon go down on my knees in admiration before him. I'll fix him. I'll tell him I'm going to tell Francis the truth: I'm not ill I live alone because your swine of a father ditched me he buttered me up then he tortured me he even knocked me about. Go into hysterics in front of the boy bleed to death on their doormat that or something else. I have weapons I'll use them he'll come back to me I shan't go on rotting all alone in this dump with those people on the next floor who trample me underfoot and the ones next door who wake me every morning with their radio and no one to bring me so much as a crust when I'm hungry. All those fat cows have a man to protect them and kids to wait on them and me nothing: this can't go on. For a fortnight now the plumber hasn't come a woman on her own they think they can do anything how despicable people are when you're down they stamp on you. I kick back I keep my end up but a woman alone is spat on. The concierge gives a dirty laugh. At ten in the morning it is *in concordance with the law* to have the radio on: if he thinks I'm impressed by his long words. I had them on the telephone four nights running they knew it was me but impossible to pin it I laughed and laughed: they've coped by having calls stopped I'll find something else. What? Drips like that sleep at night work all day go for a walk on Sunday there's nothing you can get a hold on. A man under my roof. The plumber would have come the concierge would say good day politely the neighbours would turn the volume down. Bloody hell, I want to be treated with respect I want my husband my son my home like everybody else.

A little boy of eleven it would be fun to take him to the circus to the zoo. I'd train him right away. He was easier to handle than Sylvie. She was a tough one to cope with soft and cunning like that slug Albert. Oh, I don't hold it against her poor little creep they all put her against me and she was at the age when girls loathe their mothers they call that ambivalence but it's hatred. There's another of those truths that make them mad. Etiennette dripped with fury when I told her to look at Claudie's diary. She didn't want to look, like those women who don't go to the doctor because they're afraid of having cancer so you're still the dear little mama of a dear little daughter. Sylvie was not a dear little anything I had a dose of that when I read her diary: but as for me I look things straight in the face. I didn't let it worry me all that much I knew all I had to do was wait and one day she would understand and she would say I was the one who was in the right and not them and cram it down their throats. I was patient never did I raise a hand against her. I took care of myself of course. I told her, 'You won't get me down.' Obstinate as a mule whining for hours on end days on end over a whim there wasn't the slightest reason for her to see Tristan again. A girl needs a father I ought to know if anybody does: but nobody's ever said she needs two. Albert was quite enough of a nuisance already he was taking everything the law allowed him and more I had to struggle every inch of the way he'd have corrupted her if I hadn't fought. The frocks he gave her it was immoral. I didn't want my daughter to turn into a whore like my mother. Skirts up to her knees at seventy paint all over her face! When I passed her in the street the other day I crossed over to the other sidewalk. With her strutting along like that what a fool I should have looked if she had put on the great reconciliation act. I'm sure her place is as squalid as ever with the cash she flings away at the hairdresser's she could afford herself a cleaning woman.

No more horns blowing I preferred that row to hearing them roaring and bellowing in the street: car doors slamming they shout they laugh some of them are singing they are drunk already and upstairs that racket goes on. They're making me ill there's a foul taste in my mouth and these two little pimples on my thigh they horrify me. I take care I only eat health foods but even so there are people who muck about with them hands more or less clean there's no hygiene anywhere in the world the air is polluted not only because of the cars and the factories but also these millions of filthy mouths swallowing it in and belching it out from morning till night: when I think I'm swimming in their breath I feel like rushing off into the very middle of the desert: how can you keep your body clean in such a lousy disgusting world you're contaminated through all the pores of your skin and yet I was healthy clean I can't bear them infecting me. If I had to go to bed there's not one of them that would move a finger to look after me. I could croak any minute with my poor overloaded heart no one would know anything about it that terrifies the guts out of me. They'll find a rotting corpse behind the door I'll stink I'll have shat the rats will have eaten my nose. Die alone live alone no I can't bear it. I need to have a man I want Tristan to come back lousy dunghill of a world they are shouting they are laughing and here I am withering on the shelf: forty-three it's too soon it's unfair I want to live. Big-time life that's me: the convertible the apartment the dresses everything. Florent shelled out and no horsing around—except a little in bed right's right—all he wanted to do was to go to bed with me and show me off in smart joints I was lovely my loveliest time all my girlfriends were dying with envy. It makes me sick to think of those days nobody takes me out anymore I just stay here stewing in my own shit. I'm sick of it I'm sick of it sick sick sick sick sick sick sick sick sick sick sick sick sick sick sick sick sick sick sick sick sick sick sick sick sick sick sick sick sick sick sick sick sick sick sick sick sick sick sick sick sick sick sick sick sick sick sick sick sick sick sick sick sick sick sick sick sick sick sick sick sick sick sick sick sick sick sick sick sick sick sick sick sick sick sick sick sick sick sick sick sick sick sick.

That bastard Tristan I want him to have me out to a restaurant to a theatre I'll insist upon it I don't insist nearly enough all he does is come drooling along here either by himself or with the kid sits there with a mealy-mouthed smirk on his face and at the end of an hour he drools off again. Not so much as a sign of life even on New Year's Eve! Swine! I'm bored black I'm bored through the ground it's inhuman. If I slept that would kill the time. But there is this noise outside. And inside my head they are giving that dirty laugh and saying, 'She's all alone.' They'll laugh the other side of their faces when Tristan comes back to me. He'll come back I'll make him I certainly will. I'll go to the couturiers again I'll give cocktail parties evening parties my picture will be in *Vogue* with a neck-line plunging to there I have better breasts than anyone. 'Have you seen the picture of Murielle?' They will be utterly fucked and Francis will tell them about how we go to the zoo the circus the skating rink I'll spoil him that'll make them choke on their lies their slanders. Such hatred! Clear-sighted too clear-sighted. They don't like being seen through: as for me I'm straight I don't join their act I tear masks off. They don't forgive me for that. A mother jealous of her daughter so now I've seen everything. She flung me at Albert's head to get rid of me for other reasons too no I don't want to believe it. What a dirty trick to have urged me into that marriage me so vital alive a burning flame and him stuffy middle-class coldhearted prick like limp macaroni. I would have known the kind of man to suit Sylvie. I had her under control yes I was firm but

I was always affectionate always ready to talk I wanted to be a friend to her and I would have kissed my mother's hands if she had behaved like that to me. But what a thankless heart. She's dead and so all right what of it? The dead are not saints. She wouldn't cooperate she never confided in me at all. There was someone in her life a boy or maybe a girl who can tell this generation is so twisted. But there wasn't a precaution she didn't take. Not a single letter in her drawers and the last two years not a single page of diary: if she went on keeping one she hid it terribly well even after her death I didn't find anything. Blind with fury just because I was doing my duty as a mother. Me the selfish one when she ran away like that it would have been in my interest to have left her with her father. Without her I still had a chance of making a new life for myself. It was for her own good that I was having none of it. Christine with her three great lumps of children it would have suited her down to the ground to have had a big fifteen-year-old girl she could have given all the chores to poor lamb she had no notion the hysterics she put on for the benefit of the police. . . . Yes the police. Was I supposed to put on kid gloves? What are the police there for? Stray cats? Albert offering me money to give up Sylvie! Always this money how grovelling men are they think everything can be bought anyhow I didn't give a damn about his money it was peanuts compared with what Tristan allows me. And even if I had been broke I'd never have sold my daughter. 'Why don't you let her go, that chick only brings you headaches' Dédé said to me. She doesn't understand a mother's feelings she never thinks of anything but her own pleasure. But one must not always be at the receiving end one must also know how to give. I had a great deal to give Sylvie I should have made her into a fine girl: and I asked nothing from her for myself. I was completely devoted. Such ingratitude! It was perfectly natural I should ask that teacher's help. According to her diary Sylvie worshiped her and I thought she'd hold her bloody tongue the lousy half-baked intellectual. No doubt there was much more between them than I imagined I've always been so clean-minded I never see any harm these alleged brain workers are all bull dykes. Sylvie's snivelling and fuss after it and my mother who told me on the phone I had no right to intermeddle with my daughter's friendships. That was the very word she used *intermeddle*. 'Oh as far as that was concerned you never intermeddled. And don't you begin now if you please.' Straight just like that. And I hung up. My own mother it's utterly unnatural. In the end Sylvie would have realized. That was one of the things that really shattered me at the cemetery. I said to myself 'A little later she would have said I was in the right.' The ghastliness of remembering the blue sky all those flowers Albert crying in front of everyone Christ you exercise some self-control. I controlled myself yet I knew very well I'd never recover from the blow. It was me they were burying. I have been buried. They've all got together to cover me over deep. Even on this night not a sign of life. They know very well that nights when there are celebrations everybody laughing gorging stuffing one another the lonely ones the bereaved kill themselves just like that. It would suit them beautifully if I were to vanish they hide me in a hole but it doesn't work I'm a burr in their pants. I don't intend to oblige them, thank you very much indeed. I want to live I want to come to life again. Tristan will come back to me I'll be done right by I'll get out of this filthy hole. If I talked to him now I should feel better maybe I'd be able to sleep. He must be at home he's an early bedder, he saves himself up. Be calm friendly don't get his back up otherwise my night is shot to hell.

He doesn't answer. Either he's not there or he doesn't want to answer. He's jammed the bell he doesn't want to listen to what I have to say. They sit in judgement upon me find me guilty not one of them ever listens to me. I never punished Sylvie without listening to what she had to say first it was she who clammed up who wouldn't talk. Only yesterday he wouldn't let me say a quarter of what I had to say and I could hear him dozing at the other end of the line. It's disheartening. I reason I explain I prove: patiently step by step I force them to the truth I think they're following me and then I ask 'What have I just said?' They don't know they stuff themselves with mental earplugs and if a remark happens to get through their answer is just so much balls. I start over again I pile up fresh arguments: same result. Albert is a champion at that game but Tristan is not so bad either. 'You ought to take me away with Francis for the holidays.' He doesn't answer he talks of something else. Children have to listen but they manage they forget. 'What have I said, Sylvie?' 'You said when one is messy in small things one is messy in big ones and I must tidy my room before I go out.' And then the next day she did not tidy it. When I force Tristan to listen to me and he can't find anything to reply—a boy needs his mother a mother can't do without her child it's so obvious that even the crookedest mind can't deny it—he goes to the door flies down the stairs four at a time while I shout down the well and cut myself off short in case the neighbours think I'm cracked: how cowardly it is he knows I loathe scenes particularly as I've an odd sort of a reputation in this house of course I have they behave so weirdly— unnaturally—that sometimes I do the same. Oh what the hell I used to behave so well it gave me a pain in the ass Tristan's casualness his big laugh his loud voice I should have liked to see him drop down dead when he used to horse around in public with Sylvie.

Wind! It's suddenly started to blow like fury how I should like an enormous disaster that would sweep everything away and me with it a typhoon a cyclone it would be restful to die if there were no one left to think about me: give up my body my poor little life to them no! But for everybody to plunge into nothingness that would be fine: I'm tired of fighting them even when I'm alone they harry me it's exhausting I wish it would all come to an end! Alas! I shan't have my typhoon I never have anything I want. It's only a little very ordinary wind it'll have torn off a few tiles a few chimney pots everything is mean and piddling in this world nature's as bad as men. I'm the only one that has splendid dreams and it would have been better to choke them right away everything disappoints me always.

Perhaps I ought to stuff up these sleeping things and go to bed. But I'm still too wide awake I'd only writhe about. If I had got him on the phone if we'd talked pleasantly I should have calmed down. He doesn't give a fuck. Here I am torn to pieces by heartbreaking memories I call him and he doesn't answer. Don't bawl him out don't begin by bawling him out that would muck up everything. I dread tomorrow. I shall have to be ready before four o'clock I shan't have had a wink of sleep I'll go out and buy petits fours that Francis will tread into the carpet he'll break one of my little ornaments he's not been properly brought up that child as clumsy as his father who'll drop ash all over the place and if I say anything at all Tristan will blow right up he never let me keep my house as it ought to be yet after all it's enormously important. Just now it's perfect the drawing room polished shining like the moon used to be. By seven tomorrow evening it'll be utterly filthy I'll have to spring-clean it even though I'll be all washed out. Explaining everything to him from *a* to *z* will wash me right out. He's tough. What a clot I was to drop Florent for him! Florent and I we understood one another he coughed up I lay on my back it was cleaner than those capers where you hand out tender words to one another. I'm too softhearted I thought it was a terrific proof of love when he offered to marry me and there was Sylvie the ungrateful little thing I wanted her to have a real home and a mother no one could say a thing against a married woman a banker's wife. For my part it gave me a pain in the ass to play the lady to be friends with crashing bores. Not so surprising that I burst out now and then. 'You're setting about it the wrong way with Tristan' Dédé used to tell me. Then later on 'I told you so!' It's true I'm headstrong I take the bit between my teeth I don't calculate. Maybe I should have learned to compromise if it hadn't been for all those disappointments. Tristan made me utterly sick I let him know it. People can't bear being told what you really think of them. They want you to believe their fine words or at least to pretend to. As for me I'm clear-sighted I'm frank I tear masks off. The dear kind lady simpering 'So we love our little brother do we?' and my collected little voice: 'I hate him.' I'm still that proper little woman who says what she thinks and doesn't cheat. It made my guts grind to hear him holding forth and all those bloody fools on their knees before him. I came clumping along in my big boots I cut their fine words down to size for them—progress prosperity the future of mankind happiness peace aid for the under-developed countries peace upon earth. I'm not a racist but don't give a fuck for Algerians Jews Negroes in just the same way I don't give a fuck for Chinks Russians Yanks Frenchmen. I don't give a fuck for humanity what has it ever done for me I ask you. If they are such bleeding fools as to murder one another bomb one another plaster one another with napalm wipe one another out I'm not going to weep my eyes out. A million children have been massacred so what? Children are never anything but the seed of bastards it unclutters the planet a little they all admit it's overpopulated don't they? If I were the earth it would disgust me, all this vermin on my back, I'd shake it off. I'm quite willing to die if they all die too. I'm not going to go all soft-centred about kids that mean nothing to me. My own daughter's dead and they've stolen my son from me.

I should have won her back. I'd have made her into a worthwhile person. But it would have taken me time. Tristan did not help me the selfish bastard our quarrels bored him he used to say to me 'Leave her in peace.' You ought not to have children in a way Dédé is right they only give you one bloody headache after another. But if you do have them you ought to bring them up properly. Tristan always took Sylvie's side: now even if I had been wrong—let's say I might have been sometimes for the sake of argument—from an educational point of view it's disastrous for one parent to run out on the other. He was on her side even when I was right. Over that little Jeanne for example. It quite touches my heart to think of her again her moist adoring gaze: they can be very sweet little girls she reminded me of my own childhood badly dressed neglected slapped scolded by that concierge of a mother of hers always on the edge of tears: she thought I was lovely she stroked my furs she did little things for me and I slipped her pennies when no one was looking I gave her sweeties poor pet. She was the same age as Sylvie I should have liked them to be friends Sylvie disappointed me bitterly. She whined 'Being with Jeanne bores me.' I told her she was a heartless thing I scolded her I punished her. Tristan stood up for her on the grounds that you can't force liking that battle lasted for ages I wanted Sylvie to learn generosity in the end it was little Jeanne who backed out.

It's quietened down a bit up there. Footsteps voices in the staircase car doors slamming there's still their bloody fool dance music but they aren't dancing anymore. I know what they're at. This is the moment they make love on beds on sofas on the ground in cars the time for being sick sick sick when they bring up the turkey and the caviar it's filthy I have a feeling there's a smell of vomit I'm going to burn a joss stick. If only I could sleep I'm wide awake dawn is far away still this is a ghastly hour of the night and Sylvie died without understanding me I'll never get over it. This smell of incense is the same as at the funeral service: the candles the flowers the catafalque. My despair. Dead: It was impossible! For hours and hours I sat there by her body thinking no of course not she'll wake up I'll wake up. All that effort all those struggles scenes sacrifices—all in vain. My life's work gone up in smoke. I left nothing to chance; and chance at its cruellest reached out and hit me. Sylvie is dead. Five years already. She is dead. Forever. I can't bear it. Help it hurts it hurts too much get me out of here I can't bear the breakdown to start again no help me I can't bear it any longer don't leave me alone. . . .

Who to call? Albert Bernard would hang up like a flash: he blubbered in front of everybody but tonight he's gorged and had fun and I'm the one that remembers and weeps. My mother: after all a mother is a mother I never did her any harm she was the one who mucked up my childhood she insulted me she presumed to tell me. . . . I want her to take back what she said I won't go on living with those words in my ears a daughter can't bear being cursed by her mother even if she's the ultimate word in tarts.

'Was it you who called me? . . . It surprised me too but after all on a night like this it could happen you might think of my grief and say to yourself that a mother and daughter can't be on bad terms all their lives long; above all since I really can't see what you can possibly blame me for. . . . Don't shout like that. . . .'

She has hung up. She wants peace. She poisons my life the bitch I'll have to settle her hash. What hatred! She's always hated me: she killed two birds with one stone in marrying me to Albert. She made sure of her fun and my unhappiness. I didn't want to admit it I'm too clean too pure but it's staringly obvious. It was she who hooked him at the physical

culture class and she treated herself to him slut that she was it can't have
been very inviting to stuff her but what with all the men who'd been
there before she must have known a whole bagful of tricks like getting
astride over the guy I can just imagine it it's perfectly revolting the way
respectable women make love. She was too long in the tooth to keep him
she made use of me they cackled behind my back and went to work
again: one day when I came back unexpectedly she was all red. How old
was she when she stopped? Maybe she treats herself to gigolos she's not
so poor as she says she's no doubt kept jewels that she sells off on the sly.
I think that after you're fifty you ought to have the decency to give it up:
I gave it up well before ever since I went into mourning. It doesn't interest me anymore I'm blocked I never think of those things anymore even
in dreams. That old bag it makes you shudder to think of between her
legs she drips with scent but underneath she smells she used to make up
she titivated she didn't wash not what I call wash when she pretended
to use a douche it was only to show Nanard her backside. Her son her
son-in-law: it makes you feel like throwing up. They would say, 'You've
got a filthy mind.' They know how to cope. If you point out that they're
walking in shit they scream it's you that have dirty feet. My dear little
girlfriends would have liked to have a go with my husband women
they're all filthy bitches and there he was shouting at me, 'You are
contemptible.' Jealousy is not contemptible real love has a beak and
claws. I was not one of those women who will put up with sharing or
whorehouse parties like Christine I wanted us to be a clean proper couple a decent couple. I can control myself but I'm not a complete drip I've
never been afraid of making a scene. I did not allow anyone to make fun
of me I can look back over my past—nothing unwholesome nothing
dubious. I'm the white blackbird.

Poor white blackbird: it's the only one in the world. That's what
maddens them: I'm something too far above them. They'd like to do
away with me they've shut me up in a cage. Shut in locked in I'll end by
dying of boredom really dying. It seems that that happens to babies even,
when no one looks after them. The perfect crime that leaves no trace.
Five years of this torture already. That ass Tristan who says travel you've
plenty of money. Plenty to travel on the cheap like with Albert in the old
days: you don't catch me doing that again. Being poor is revolting at any
time but when you travel! . . . I'm not a snob I showed Tristan I wasn't
impressed by deluxe palace hotels and women dripping with pearls the
fancy doormen. But second-rate boardinghouses and cheap restaurants,
no *sir*. Dubious sheets filthy tablecloths sleep in other people's sweat in

other people's filth eat with badly washed knives and forks you might catch lice or the pox and the smells make me sick: quite apart from the fact that I get deadly constipated because those johns where everybody goes turn me off like a tap: the brotherhood of shit only a very little for me please. Then what earthly point is there in travelling alone? We had fun Dédé and I it's terrific two pretty girls in a convertible their hair streaming in the wind: we made a terrific impression in Rome at night on the Piazza del Popolo. I've had fun with other friends too. But alone? What sort of impression do you make on beaches in casinos if you haven't got a man with you? Ruins museums I had my bellyful of them with Tristan. I'm not a hysterical enthusiast I don't swoon at the sight of broken columns or tumbledown old shacks. The people of former times my foot they're dead that's the only thing they have over the living but in their own day they were just as sickening. Picturesqueness: I don't fall for that not for one minute. Stinking filth dirty washing cabbage stalks what a pretentious fool you have to be to go into ecstasies over that! And it's the same thing everywhere all the time whether they're stuffing themselves with chips paella or pizza it's the same crew a filthy crew the rich who trample over you the poor who hate you for your money the old who dodder the young who sneer the men who show off the women who open their legs. I'd rather stay at home reading a thriller although they've become so dreary nowadays. The TV too what a clapped-out set of fools! I was made for another planet altogether I mistook the way.

Why do they have to make all that din right under my windows? They're standing there by their cars they can't make up their minds to put their stinking feet into them. What can they be going on and on about? Snotty little beasts snotty little beastesses grotesque in their miniskirts and their tights I hope they catch their deaths haven't they any mothers then? And the boys with their hair down their necks. From a distance those ones seem more or less clean. But all those louse-breeding beatniks if the chief of police had any sort of drive he'd toss them all into the brig. The youth of today! They drug they stuff one another they respect nothing. I'm going to pour a bucket of water on their heads. They might break open the door and beat me up I'm defenceless I'd better shut the window again. Rose's daughter is one of that sort it seems and Rose plays the elder sister they're always together in one another's pockets. Yet she used to hold her in so she even boxed her ears she didn't bother to bring her to reason she was impulsive arbitrary: I loathe capriciousness. Oh, Rose will pay for it all right as Dédé says she'll have Danielle on her hands pregnant. . . . I should have made a lovely person of Sylvie. I'd have given her dresses jewels I'd have been proud of her we should have gone out together. There's no justice in the world. That's what makes me so mad—the injustice. When I think of the sort of mother I was! Tristan acknowledges it: I've forced him to acknowledge it. And then after that he tells me he's ready for anything rather than let me have Francis: they don't give a damn for logic they say absolutely anything at all and then escape at the run. He races down the stairs four at a time while I shout down the well after him. I won't be had like that. I'll force him to do me justice: cross my heart. He'll give me back my place in the home my place on earth. I'll make a splendid child of Francis they'll see what kind of a mother I am.

They are killing me the bastards. The idea of the party tomorrow destroys me. I must win. I must I must I must I must I must. I'll tell my fortune with the cards. No. If it went wrong I'd throw myself out of the window no I mustn't it would suit them too well. Think of something else. Cheerful things. The boy from Bordeaux. We expected nothing from one another we asked one another no questions we made one another no promises we bedded down and made love. It lasted three weeks and he left for Africa I wept wept. It's a memory that does me good. Things like that only happen once in a lifetime. What a pity! When I think back over it it seems to me that if anyone had loved me properly I should have been affection itself. Turds they bored me to death they trample everyone down right left and centre everyone can die in his hole for all they care husbands deceive their wives mothers toss off their sons not a word about it sealed lips that carefulness disgusts me and the way they don't have the courage of their convictions. 'But come really your brother is too closefisted' it was Albert who pointed it out to me I'm too noble-minded to bother with trifles like that but it's true they had stuffed down three times as much as us and the bill was divided fifty-fifty thousands of little things like that. And afterward he blamed me—'You shouldn't have repeated it to him.' On the beach we went at it hammer and tongs. Etiennette cried you would have said the tears on her cheeks were melting suet. 'Now that he knows he'll turn over a new leaf' I told her. I was simpleminded—I thought they were capable of turning over new leaves I thought you could bring them up by making them see reason. 'Come Sylvie let's think it over. You know how much that frock costs? And how many times will you ever put it on? We'll send it back.' It always had to be begun again at the beginning I wore myself out. Nanard will go on being closefisted to the end of his days. Albert more deceitful lying secretive than ever. Tristan always just as self-satisfied just as pompous. I was knocking myself out for nothing. When I tried to teach Etiennette how to dress Nanard bawled me out—she was twenty-two and I was dressing her up as an elderly schoolteacher! She went on cramming herself into little gaudy dresses. And Rose who shouted out 'Oh you are cruel!' I had spoken to her out of loyalty women have to stand by one another. Who has ever shown me any gratitude? I've lent them money without asking for interest not one has been grateful to me for it indeed some have whined when I asked to be paid back. Girlfriends I overwhelmed with presents accused me of showing off. And you ought to see how briskly they slipped away all those people I had done good turns to yet God knows I asked for nothing much in return. I'm not one of those people who thinks they have a right to everything. Aunt Marguerite: 'Would you lend us your apartment while you're on your cruise this summer?' Lend it hell hotels aren't built just for dogs and if they can't afford to put up in Paris they can stay in their own rotten hole. An apartment's holy I should have felt raped. . . . It's like Dédé. 'You mustn't let yourself be eaten up' she tells me. But she'd be delighted to swallow me whole. 'Have you an evening coat you can lend me? You never go out.' No I never go out but I did go out: they're my dresses my coats they remind me of masses of things I don't want a strumpet to take my place in them. And afterward they'd smell. If I were to die Mama and Nanard would share my leavings. No no I want to live until the moths have eaten the lot or else if I have cancer I'll destroy them all. I've had enough of people making a good thing out of me—Dédé worst of all. She drank my whiskey she showed off in my convertible. Now she's playing the great-hearted friend. But she never bothered to ring me from Courchevel tonight of all nights. When her cuckold of a husband is travelling and she's bored why yes then she brings her fat backside here even when I don't want to see her at all. But it's New Year's Day I'm alone I'm eating my heart out. She's dancing she's having fun she doesn't think of me for a single minute. Nobody ever thinks of me. As if I were wiped off the face of the earth. As if I had never existed. Do I exist? Oh! I pinched myself so hard I shall have a bruise.

What silence! Not a car left not a footstep in the street not a sound in the house the silence of death. The silence of a death chamber and their eyes on me their eyes that condemn me unheard and without appeal. Oh how strong they are! Everything they felt remorse for they clapped it onto my back the perfect scapegoat and at last they could invent an excuse for their hatred. My grief has not lessened it. Yet I should have thought the devil himself would have been sorry for me.

All my life it will be two o'clock in the afternoon one Tuesday in June. 'Mademoiselle is too fast asleep I can't get her to wake up.' My heart missed a beat I rushed in calling 'Sylvie are you ill?' She looked as though she were asleep she was still warm. It had been all over some hours before the doctor told me. I screamed I went up and down the room like a madwoman. Sylvie Sylvie why have you done this to me? I can see her now calm relaxed and me out of my mind and the note for her father that didn't mean a thing I tore it up it was all part of the act it was only an act I was sure I am sure—a mother knows her own daughter—she had not meant to die but she had overdone the dose she was dead how appalling! It's too easy with these drugs anyone can get just like that: these teenage girls will play at suicide for a mere nothing: Sylvie went along with the fashion—she never woke up. And they all came they kissed Sylvie not one of them kissed me and my mother shouted at me 'You've killed her!' My mother my own mother. They made her be quiet but their faces their silence the weight of their silence. Yes, if I were one of those mothers who get up at seven in the morning she would have been saved I live according to another rhythm there's nothing criminal about that how could I have guessed? I was always there when she came back from school many mothers can't say as much always ready to talk to question her it was she who shut herself up in her room pretending she wanted to work. I never failed her. And my mother she who neglected me left me by myself how she dared! I couldn't manage any reply my head was spinning I no longer knew where I was. 'If I'd gone to give her a kiss that night when I came in. . . .' But I didn't want to wake her and during the afternoon she had seemed to me almost cheerful. . . . Those days, what a torment! A score of times I thought I was going to crack up. School friends teachers put flowers on the coffin without addressing a word to me: if a girl kills herself the mother is guilty: that's the way their minds worked out of hatred for their own mothers. All in at the kill. I almost let myself be got down. After the funeral I fell ill. Over and over again I said to myself, 'If I had got up at seven. . . . If I had gone to give her a kiss when I came in. . . .' It seemed to me that everybody had heard my mother's shout I didn't dare go out anymore I crept along by the wall the sun clamped me in the pillory I thought people were looking at me whispering pointing enough of that enough I'd rather die this minute than live through that time again. I lost more than twenty pounds, a skeleton, my sense of balance went I staggered. 'Psychosomatic,' said the doctor. Tristan gave me money for the nursing home. You'd never believe the questions I asked myself it might have driven me crazy. A phony suicide she had meant to hurt someone—who? I hadn't watched her closely enough I ought never to have left her for a moment I ought to have had her followed held an inquiry unmasked the guilty person a boy or a girl maybe that whore of a teacher. 'No Madame there was no one in her life.' They wouldn't yield an inch the two bitches and their eyes were murdering me: they all of them keep up the conspiracy of lies even beyond death itself. But they didn't deceive me. I know. At her age and with things as they are today it's impossible that there was no one. Perhaps she was pregnant or she'd fallen into the clutches of a lezzy or she'd got in with an immoral lot someone was blackmailing her and having her threatening to tell me everything. Oh, I must stop picturing things. You could have told me everything my Sylvie I would have got you out of that filthy mess. It must certainly have been a filthy mess for her to have written to Albert, *Papa please forgive me but I can't bear it any-more.* She couldn't talk to him or to the others: they tried to get to her, but they were strangers. I was the only one she could have confided in.

Without them. Without their hatred. Bastards! You nearly got me down but you didn't quite succeed. I'm not your scapegoat: your remorse—I've thrown it off. I've told you what I think of you each one has had his dose and I'm not afraid of your hatred I walk clean through it. Bastards! They are the ones who killed her. They flung mud at me they put her against me they treated her as a martyr that flattered her all girls adore playing the martyr: she took her part seriously she distrusted me she told me nothing. Poor pet. She needed my support my advice they deprived her of them they condemned her to silence she couldn't get herself out of her mess all by herself she set up this act and it killed her. Murderers! They killed Sylvie my little Sylvie my darling. I loved you. No mother on earth could have been more devoted: I never thought of anything but your own good. I open the photograph album I look at all the Sylvies. The rather drawn child's face the closed face of the adolescent. Looking deep into the eyes of my seventeen-year-old girl they murdered I say 'I was the best of mothers. You would have thanked me later on.'

Crying has comforted me and I'm beginning to feel sleepy. I mustn't go to sleep in this armchair I should wake everything would be mucked up all over again. Take my suppositories go to bed. Set the alarm clock for noon to have time to get myself ready. I must win. A man in the house my little boy I'll kiss at bedtime all this unused affection. And then it would mean rehabilitation. What? I'm going to sleep I'm relaxing. It'll be a swipe in the eye for them. Tristan is somebody they respect him. I want him to bear witness for me: they'll be forced to do me justice. I'll call him. Convince him this very night.

'Was it you who phoned me? Oh, I thought it was you. You were asleep forgive me but I'm glad to hear your voice it's so revolting tonight nobody's given the slightest sign of life yet they know that when you've had a great sorrow you can't bear celebrations all this noise these lights did you notice Paris has never been so lit up as this year they've money to waste it would be better if they were to reduce the rates I shut myself up at home so as not to see it. I can't get off to sleep I'm too sad too lonely I brood about things I must talk it over with you without any quarrelling a good friendly talk listen now what I have to say to you is really very important I shan't be able to get a wink until it's settled. You're listening to me, right? I've been thinking it over all night I had nothing else to do and I assure you this is an absurd position it can't go on like this after all we are still married what a waste these two apartments you could sell yours for at least twenty million and I'd not get in your way never fear no question of taking up married life again we're no longer in love I'd shut myself up in the room at the back don't interrupt you could have all the Fanny Hills you like I don't give a hoot but since we're still friends there's no reason why we shouldn't live under the same roof. And it's essential for Francis. Just think of him for a moment I've been doing nothing else all night and I'm tearing myself to pieces. It's bad for a child to have parents who are separated they grow sly vicious untruthful they get complexes they don't develop properly. I want Francis to develop properly. You have no right to deprive him of a real home. . . . Yes yes we do have to go over all this again you always get out of it but this time I insist on your listening to me. It's too selfish indeed it's even unnatural to deprive a son of his mother a mother of her son. For no reason. I've no vices I don't drink I don't drug and you've admitted I was the most devoted of mothers. Well then? Don't interrupt. If you're thinking about your fun I tell you again I shan't prevent you from having girls. Don't tell me I'm impossible to live with that I ate you up that I wore you out. Yes I was rather difficult it's natural for me to take the bit between my teeth: but if you'd had a little patience and if you'd tried to understand me and had known how to talk to me instead of growing pig-headed things would have gone along better between us you're not a saint either so don't you think it; anyhow that's all water under the bridge: I've changed: as you know very well I've suffered I've matured I can stand things I used not to be able to stand let me speak you don't have to be afraid of scenes it'll be an easygoing coexistence and the child will be happy as he has a right to be I can't see what possible objection you can have. . . . Why isn't this a time for talking it over? It's a time that suits me beautifully. You can give up five minutes of sleep for me after all for my part I shan't get a wink until the matter's settled don't always be so selfish it's too dreadful to prevent people sleeping it sends them out of their minds I can't bear it. Seven years now I've been rotting here all alone like an outcast and that filthy gang laughing at me you certainly owe me my revenge let me speak you owe me a great deal you know because you gave me the madly-in-love stuff I ditched Florent and broke with my friends and now you leave me flat all your friends turn their backs on me: why did you pretend to love me? Sometimes I wonder whether it wasn't a put-up job. . . . Yes a put-up job—it's so unbelievable that terrific passion and now this dropping me. . . . You hadn't realized? Hadn't realized what? Don't you tell me again that I married you out of interest I had Florent I could have had barrowloads and get this straight the idea of being your wife didn't dazzle me at all you're not Napoleon whatever you may think don't tell me that again or I shall scream you didn't say anything but I can hear you turning the words over in your mouth don't say them it's untrue it's so untrue it makes you scream you gave me the madly-in-love jazz and I fell for it. . . . No don't say listen Murielle to me I know your answers by heart you've gone over and over them a hundred times no more guff it doesn't wash with me and don't you put on that exasperated look yes I said that exasperated look I can see you in the receiver. You've been even more of a cad than Albert he was young when we married you were forty-five you ought to understand the nature of your responsibilities. But still all right the past's past. I promise you I shan't reproach you. We wipe everything out we set off again on a fresh footing I can be sweet and charming you know if people aren't too beastly to me. So come on now tell me it's agreed tomorrow we'll settle the details.

'Swine! You're taking your revenge you're torturing me because I haven't drooled in admiration before you but as for me money doesn't impress me nor fine airs nor fine words. "Never not for anything on earth" we'll see all right we'll see. I shall stand up for myself. I'll talk to Francis I'll tell him what you are. And if I killed myself in front of him do you think that would be a pretty thing for him to remember? . . . No it's not blackmail you silly bastard with the life I lead it wouldn't mean a thing to me to do myself in. You mustn't push people too far they reach a point when they're capable of anything indeed there are mothers who kill themselves with their children. . . .'

Swine! Turd! He's hung up. . . . He doesn't answer he won't answer. Swine. Oh! My heart's failing I'm going to die. It hurts it hurts too much they're slowly torturing me to death I can't bear it any longer I'll kill myself in his drawing room I'll slash my veins when they come back there'll be blood everywhere and I shall be dead. . . . Oh! I hit it too hard I've cracked my skull it's them I ought to bash. Head against the wall no no I shan't go mad they shan't let me down I'll stand up for myself I'll find weapons. What weapons swine swine I can't breathe my heart's going to give I must calm down. . . .

Oh God. Let it be true that you exist. Let there be a heaven and a hell I'll stroll along the walks of Paradise with my little boy and my beloved daughter and they will all be writhing in the flames of envy I'll watch them roasting and howling I'll laugh I'll laugh and the children will laugh with me. You owe me this revenge, God. I insist that you grant it me.

The Lily of the Valley Lay-by

Translated by Barbara Wright

'Time to get up, Pierre!'

Pierre was sleeping with the obstinate calm of the twenty-year-old who has blind confidence in his mother's vigilance. No danger of his old woman letting him oversleep, she who was so nervous and slept so badly herself. He turned over heavily to face the wall, taking refuge behind his powerful back and the nape of his shaven neck. She watched him, remembering the so recent dawns when she had had to wake him to send him to the village school. He looked as if he had fallen fast asleep again, but she didn't insist. She knew that for him the night was over, his day had started, and that from now on his routine would follow its inexorable pattern.

A quarter of an hour later he joined her in the kitchen and she poured out his chocolate into a big flowered bowl. He gazed at the black rectangle of the window in front of him.

'It's still dark,' he said, 'but even so the days are getting longer. I'll be able to switch off the headlights in less than an hour.'

She seemed to be dreaming—she who had not left Boullay-les-Troux for the last fifteen years.

'Yes, spring's almost here. Down there on the Riviera, you may even find the apricot trees in blossom.'

'Well—the Riviera! We don't go any farther south than Lyons on this trip. And in any case, even if there were any we'd hardly have time to look at them.'

He stood up and, out of pure respect for his mother—for according to peasant tradition no man ever washes the dishes—he rinsed out his bowl under the tap in the sink.

'When will I see you?'

'The day after tomorrow, as usual. In the evening. A straightforward round trip to Lyons, sleeping in the cab with my pal Gaston.'

'As usual,' she murmured to herself. 'I still can't get used to it. Well, since you seem to like it . . .'

He shrugged his shoulders:

'No choice!'

The monumental shadow of the articulated lorry could be made out against the horizon as it whitened with the dawn. Slowly, Pierre walked round it. It was the same every morning, his reunion, after the night, with this enormous toy that warmed the cockles of his heart. He would never have admitted it to his old woman, but he would really have preferred to make his bed in it and sleep there. It was all very well to lock everything up, but as the lorry was so gigantic it had no real defence against attacks of all kinds—someone might run into it, it could be dismantled and some of its removable parts stolen. It wasn't even unthinkable that the vehicle itself might be stolen, with all its load; such a thing had been known, however unlikely it might seem.

But this time too, everything seemed to be in order, though there was a washing job to be done straightaway. Pierre rested a little ladder against the radiator grille and began to clean the huge windscreen. The windscreen is the conscience of the vehicle. All the rest of it can remain muddy and dusty, if need be, but the windscreen must be absolutely impeccable.

Next he went down on his knees, almost religiously, in front of the headlights, and wiped them. He blew on their glass and polished them with a white rag as carefully and tenderly as a mother cleaning her baby's face. Then he returned the little ladder to its place against the slatted sides of the lorry and climbed up into the cab, threw himself on to the seat and pressed the starter.

On the Quai du Point-du-Jour, the Boulogne-Billancourt, at the corner of the rue de Seine, there is an old, lopsided block of flats whose decrepitude is in startling contrast to the café on the ground floor with its flamboyant neon lighting, its nickel-plating and its multicoloured pinball machines. Gaston lived by himself in a tiny room on the sixth floor. But he was ready and waiting outside the bistro, and the lorry barely had to stop to pick him up.

'Okay, Pop?'

'Okay.'

It was always as regular as clockwork. Gaston would observe a ritual silence for three minutes. Then he'd start to unpack the travelling bag he'd hauled up on to the seat between Pierre and himself, and spread out his thermos flasks, knapsacks, mess tins, and parcels with a speed that revealed a long-established routine. Gaston was a wiry little man, not so young any more, with a calm watchful face. He gave the impression of being dominated by the pessimistic wisdom of the weak man accustomed since childhood to warding off the blows of a world which he knows from long experience to be fundamentally hostile. After he had sorted everything out, he would follow on with an undressing session. He swapped his shoes for felt slippers, his jacket for a thick, polo-neck sweater, his beret for a balaclava helmet, and even tried to take his trousers off, a delicate operation because there was very little room and he was on shifting ground.

Pierre didn't need to watch him to see his manoeuvres. While keeping his eyes fixed on the labyrinth of congested streets leading to the outer boulevards, he missed nothing of the familiar commotion taking place on his right.

'Look, you've only just got dressed to come down, but you have to undress again the moment you're on board,' he commented.

Gaston didn't condescend to reply.

'I wonder why you don't come down from your room in your nightshirt. That way you'd kill two birds with one stone, don't you think?'

Gaston was perched on the back of his seat. When the lorry started off again at a green light, he let himself gently topple over on to the bunk fixed up behind the seats. His voice was heard one last time:

'When you have any intelligent questions to ask me, you can wake me up.'

Five minutes later the lorry was hurtling down the slip-road leading into the outer boulevards, where there was already a good deal of traffic even at this early hour. For Pierre, this was merely an uninspiring preliminary. The real motorway travellers were indistinguishable in this stream of delivery vans, private cars, and workers' buses. You had to wait until they were filtered out at the exits to Rungis, Orly, Longjumeau and Corbeil-Essonnes, and at the turn-off to Fontainebleau, before, with the Fleury-Mérogis tollgate, you finally reached the threshold of the great concrete ribbon.

When he later stopped behind four other big lorries waiting to go through the barrier, he had two reasons to be pleased. Not only was he driving, but as Gaston was asleep he wouldn't make him miss the entry to the A6 motorway. He solemnly held out his card to the attendant, took it back, got into gear, and started rolling along the smooth, white road leading to the heart of France.

Having filled up at the Joigny service station—this too was a ritual— he drove off again at cruising speed until the Pouilly-en-Auxois exit, then slowed down and pulled into the Lily of the valley lay-by for their eight o'clock snack. Hardly had the vehicle come to a halt under the beeches in the little wood than Gaston shot up from behind the seats and began to collect the components of his breakfast. This too was immutable routine.

Pierre jumped out. Wearing a tight-fitting blue nylon track-suit and moccasins, he looked like an athlete in training. Moreover, he tried out a few exercises, hopped about boxing with an imaginary opponent, then ran off in impeccable style. When he came back, hot and panting, Gaston had just got into his 'day clothes'. Then, no hurry, he laid out a real French breakfast on one of the tables in the lay-by—coffee, hot milk, croissants, butter, jam, and honey.

'What I like about you,' Pierre observed, 'is the way you go in for comfort. It's as if you always travel with either your mother's kitchen or a bit of a three-star hotel.'

'There's an age for everything,' replied Gaston, pouring a trickle of honey into the half-opened side of a croissant. 'For thirty years, every morning before work, I kept to a diet of dry white wine. White Charentes, and nothing else. Until the day I realized that I had a stomach and kidneys. Then that was that. No more alcohol, no more tobacco. Coffee with milk for yours truly! Plus toast and marmalade. Like an old granny at Claridges. And I'll tell you something worth hearing . . .'

He interrupted himself to bite into a croissant. Pierre sat down next to him.

'What about it, then, that something worth hearing?'

'Well, I'm wondering whether I'm not going to give up coffee with milk, which isn't so easy to digest, and switch to tea with lemon. Because, well, tea with lemon, you can't beat it.'

'In that case, while you're about it, why not eggs and bacon, like the English?'

'Oh no! Anything but that! Nothing salty for breakfast! No—breakfast, you understand, needs to be . . . how can I put it? It needs to be pleasant, no, affectionate, no, maternal. That's it, maternal! Breakfast should somehow take you back to your childhood. Because the start of the day isn't all that amusing. So we need something soft and reassuring to wake us up properly. Something hot and sweet, then, that's what we need.'

'And what about your flannel belt?'

'That's just it! That's maternal, too! Do you see the connection, or did you just say that without thinking?'

'I don't see it; no.'

'Babies' nappies! My flannel belt is a return to nappies.'

'Are you having me on? And what about the feeding bottle, then, when do you have that?'

'My dear fellow, look at me and take a leaf out of my book. Because I have at least one advantage over you. I have been your age, and nobody, not even the good Lord, can take that away from me. Whereas you, you can't be absolutely sure of getting to be my age one day.'

'Well, what *I* have to say is that all this guff about age, it leaves me cold. I believe people are either dim or bright, once and for all, and for life.'

'Yes and no. Because, you see, there are degrees of dimness, and I believe there's a special age for it. After that, things tend to get better.'

'And in your opinion, what is that special age, as you call it?'

'It all depends on the person.'

'For me, for example, it wouldn't be twenty-one, would it?'

'Why precisely twenty-one?'

'Because I *am* precisely twenty-one.'

Gaston gave him an ironic look as he sipped his coffee.

'Ever since we've been on the road together, yes, I've been observing you and looking for your dim side.'

'And you can't find it, because I don't smoke and I don't like everlasting little glasses of white wine.'

'Yes, but don't you see, there's a difference between being dim in little ways and in big ways. Tobacco and white wine, that's just little ways. They can kill you, but only in the long run.'

'Whereas when you're dim in a big way, that can kill you at one fell swoop?'

'Yes, that's right. Me, when I was your age, no, I was younger than that, I must have been eighteen, I joined the Resistance.'

'And that was being dim in a big way?'

'In an enormous way! I didn't give a single thought to the danger. Obviously, luck was on my side. But my best pal, who was with me, he didn't come out of it. Arrested, deported, missing. Why? What was the good of it? I've been asking myself that for the last thirty years.'

'Well, I'm not in any danger in that direction,' Pierre observed.

'No, not in that direction.'

'Which means that you're still looking for my way of being enormously dim, and you haven't found it yet?'

'I haven't found it yet, no. I haven't found it yet, but I'm beginning to get a whiff of it . . .'

Two days later, Pierre and Gaston and their lorry were once again at the same matutinal hour at the Fleury-Mérogis tollgate. This time it was Gaston who was holding the joystick and Pierre, sitting on his right, felt as always slightly frustrated at starting the day in the role of second in command. He wouldn't have allowed such an unreasonable feeling to show for anything in the world; in any case, he barely even admitted it to himself, but that was why he was in a slightly sour mood.

'Hi, Bébert! You on duty again today?'

It was so strange, Gaston's need to fraternize with that race apart, the somewhat mysterious, somewhat despicable race of tollgate attendants. In Pierre's eyes, the official entry to the motorway was invested with a ceremonial value that should not be disturbed by useless chat.

'Well yes,' the employee explained. 'I switched with Tiénot, he's gone to his sister's wedding.'

'Ah,' Gaston concluded, 'then we won't see you on Friday?'

'Well no, it'll be Tiénot.'

'See you next week then.'

'Okay, have a good trip!'

Gaston passed the toll card to Pierre. The vehicle started rolling along the motorway. Gaston changed each gear placidly, without any frantic acceleration. They settled down into the euphoria produced by the cruising speed of the enormous vehicle and the dawn of a day that promised to be superb. Pierre, firmly ensconced in his seat, was fiddling with the toll card.

'You know, those chaps who work at the tollgates—I don't understand them. They belong, and yet they don't belong.'

Gaston could see he was going to launch out into one of those lucubrations in which he refused to follow him.

'They belong, they belong—they belong to what?'

'To the motorway, of course! They stand on the threshold! Then, in the evenings, when they're off duty, they get on their motorbikes and go back to their farms. But then—what about the motorway?'

'The motorway—what of it?' Gaston asked irritably.

'Oh hell, make an effort, can't you! Don't you feel, when you come through the gate, when you have your toll card in your hand, don't you feel that something's happened? After that you belt along the concrete line, it's straight, it's clean, it's quick, it doesn't do you any favours. You're in another world. You're in something new. That's the motorway, hell! You belong to it!'

Gaston persisted in his incomprehension.

'No, for me the motorway's just a job, that's all there is to it. I might even say I find it a bit monotonous. Especially with a crate like ours. Of course, when I was young, I wouldn't have minded racing down here at two hundred kilometres an hour in a Maserati. But chugging along with forty tonnes behind you, I find the ordinary main roads much more amusing, with all their level crossings and little bistros.'

'Okay,' Pierre conceded, 'I agree about doing two hundred in a Maserati. As a matter of fact, I've already done that.'

'*You*'ve done that? You've done two hundred on a motorway in a Maserati?'

'Well, it wasn't exactly a Maserati. It was an old Chrysler, Bernard's you know, the one he souped up. We got up to a hundred and eighty on the motorway.'

'That's not the same thing at all.'

'Oh come on, you aren't going to quibble over twenty kilometres!'

'I'm not quibbling, I'm just saying: it's not the same.'

'Okay, but I'm telling you: I still prefer our crate.'

'Explain.'

'Because in the Maserati . . .'

'In the souped-up Chrysler . . .'

'It's the same thing, you're stuck down on the ground. You're not in control. Whereas our contraption, it's high up, you're in control.'

'And you need to be in control?'

'I like the motorway. So I want to see. Here, look at that line running straight off into the horizon! That's really nice, isn't it? You don't see that when you're flat on your stomach on the ground.'

Gaston shook his head indulgently.

'What you ought to do, you know, you ought to fly a plane. Then you really would be in control!'

Pierre was indignant.

'You haven't understood a thing, or else you're getting at me. A plane's no good. It's too high. With the motorway, you have to be on it. You have to belong to it. You mustn't leave it.'

That morning the Lily of the valley lay-by was bathed in such smiling colours under the young sun that the motorway in comparison might have seemed a hell of noise and concrete. Gaston had started cleaning up the cab and had brought out a whole panoply of cloths, feather dusters, brushes and polishes, watched ironically by Pierre, who had got out to stretch his legs.

'I reckon this cab is where I spend most of the hours of my life. So it might just as well be clean,' he explained, as if talking to himself.

Pierre wandered off, attracted by the atmosphere of living freshness in the little wood. The farther he went under the budding trees, the fainter the roar of the traffic became. He felt in the grip of a strange, unknown emotion, his whole being moved to a tenderness he had never yet experienced, unless perhaps when, many years before, he had approached his baby sister's cot for the first time. The delicate foliage was humming with bird song and insect flight. He took a deep breath, as if he had finally emerged into the open air from a long, asphyxiating tunnel.

Suddenly, he stopped. Not far away he perceived a charming tableau. A blonde girl in a pink dress, sitting in the grass. She didn't see him. She had eyes only for three or four cows peacefully grazing in the meadow. Pierre felt he had to see her better, to speak to her. He walked on. Suddenly, he was stopped. A fence loomed up in front of him. A menacing wire fence, almost like that round a prison or concentration camp, its top bristling with rolls of barbed wire. Pierre belonged to the motorway. A lay-by is no place for escapism. The distant hum of the traffic woke him from his dream. Nevertheless, he stayed there mesmerized, his fingers gripping the wire, staring at the blonde patch over by the foot of the old mulberry tree. Finally a well-known signal reached his ears—the lorry's horn. Gaston was becoming impatient. He must go back. Pierre dragged himself out of his contemplation and returned to reality, to the articulated lorry, to the motorway.

Gaston was driving. He was still absorbed in his spring cleaning, was Gaston.

'At least it's cleaner, now,' he observed with satisfaction.

Pierre said nothing. Pierre wasn't there. He was still gripping the wire fence on the perimeter of the lay-by. He was happy. He smiled at the angels floating invisibly in the pure sky.

'You're very quiet all of a sudden. Haven't you got anything to say?' Gaston finally marvelled.

'Me? No. What do you want me to say?'

'No idea.'

Pierre shook himself, and tried to come back to the real world.

'Well, you know,' he finally sighed, 'it's spring!'

The trailer had been detached and was resting on its prop. The lorry was free to leave the Lyons depot while the warehousemen unloaded the cargo.

'The good thing about an articulated lorry,' Gaston, who was driving, said appreciatively, 'is that we can clear off with the tractor while they're loading or unloading. Then it's almost like a private jalopy.'

'Yes, but there are times when we ought each to have our own tractor,' Pierre objected.

'Why do you say that? You want to go off on your own?'

'No, I say that for you. Because we're heading for the cafeteria, now, and I know you don't like that much. If you had your own jalopy you could go on to old mother Maraude's hash house; you always say there's nothing like her special little dishes.'

'It's true that with you, we always have to eat like greased lightning in a place like a dentist's surgery.'

'The cafeteria's quick, and it's clean. And there's a choice.'

They joined the queue, pushing their trays along the shelf below the display of waiting food. Gaston's scowl expressed his total disapproval. Pierre chose raw vegetables and a grill, Gaston a pâté de campagne and tripe. Next they had to find a table where there was a bit of room.

'Did you see the variety?' said Pierre triumphantly. 'And we didn't have to wait a second.'

Then, noticing Gaston's plate, he said, astonished:

'What's that?'

'In theory, it's supposed to be tripe,' said Gaston prudently.

'Only natural, in Lyons.'

'Yes, but what isn't natural is that it's going to be cold.'

'Shouldn't have had that,' said Pierre, and he pointed to his raw vegetables. 'These don't get cold.'

Gaston shrugged his shoulders.

'Your famous rapidity, then, is going to make me start my lunch with the plat de résistance. Otherwise my tripe's going to turn into solid fat. And cold tripe is impossible. Im-pos-sible. Never forget that. If that's the only thing you learn from me, you won't have wasted your time. That's why I prefer to wait a while, having a drink with my pals in a little bistro. The patronne herself brings you her special dish of the day, hot and perfectly cooked. That's what I think about speed. As for the cooking, the least said the better. Because in these cafeterias, I've no idea why, they don't dare season the grub. For instance, tripe, it's supposed to be cooked with onions, garlic, thyme, bay leaves, cloves, and a lot of pepper. Very hot and highly seasoned. Whereas this!—just taste it—you'd think it was boiled noodles for someone on a saltless diet!'

'Should have had something else. You had a choice.'

'A choice! Don't talk to me about choice! I'll tell you something worth knowing: in a restaurant, the less choice you have, the better it is. If you're offered seventy-five dishes, you'd do better to leave, it'll all be bad. The good cook only knows one thing: her dish of the day.'

'Have a coke then, that'll make you feel better!'

'Coke with tripe!'

'Make up your mind! You've been telling me for the last ten minutes that it isn't tripe.'

They ate in silence, each following his own train of thought. It was Pierre who finally expressed his conclusion:

'Basically, you know, we don't exactly see the job in the same way. I obviously belong to the motorway, I'm the A6. Whereas you're still living on the main roads—you're the N7.'

The fine weather seemed indestructible. More than ever, the Lily of the valley lay-by deserved its name. Gaston was lying not far from the vehicle, sucking a bit of grass and looking at the sky through the delicate branches of an aspen tree. Pierre had headed swiftly for the far end of the lay-by. His fingers gripping the wire fence, he scrutinized the meadow. Disappointment. The cows were there sure enough, but there was no cowgirl to be seen. He waited, hesitated, and then decided to pee through the fence.

'Make yourself at home!'

The young voice with the Burgundy accent came from behind a bush to his left. Pierre hastily covered up.

'If there's a fence, it's for a good reason. It's to keep out the motorway filth. All that pollution!'

Pierre was trying to reconcile the somewhat distant and idealized image he had been carrying round in his head for the last ten days with the very concrete image of the girl in front of his eyes. He had imagined her taller, slimmer, and above all, not so young. She was a real adolescent, a bit rustic at that, and without a trace of make-up on her freckled little mug. He immediately decided that he liked her even better that way.

'Do you come here often?'

That was all he could find to say, in his embarrassment.

'Sometimes. So do you, I think. I recognize your lorry.'

There was a silence full of the rustle of spring.

'It's peaceful here, so close to the motorway. The Lily of the valley lay-by. Why's it called that? Are there any lilies of the valley round here?'

'There used to be,' the girl said. 'It used to be a wood. Yes, it was full of lilies of the valley in the spring. When they built the motorway, the wood disappeared. Swallowed up, buried under the motorway, as if by an earthquake. So the lilies of the valley—they've had it!'

There was a further silence. She sat down on the ground, leaning her shoulder against the fence.

'We pass this way twice a week,' Pierre explained. 'Only, of course, every other time we're going back to Paris. So we're on the other side of the motorway. To come here we'd have to walk across both carriageways. It's dangerous, and anyway you aren't allowed to. What about you, have you got a farm round here?'

'My parents have, yes. At Lusigny. Lusigny-lès-Beaune. It's five hundred metres away, maybe less. But my brother's gone to live in town. He's an electrician in Beaune. He doesn't want to cultivate the soil, as he puts it. So we don't know what'll happen to the farm when our old man's too old.'

'Obviously; that's progress,' said Pierre with approval.

The wind floated gently through the trees. The lorry's horn sounded.

'I must go,' said Pierre. 'See you soon, maybe.'

The girl stood up.

'Goodbye!'

Pierre started off, but came back immediately.

'What's your name?'

'Marinette. What's yours?'

'Pierre.'

Shortly afterwards, Gaston thought that something had changed in his companion's way of thinking. He was suddenly worrying about married people!

'There are times,' Pierre said, 'when I wonder how our married pals get on. All week on the road. So, when you're at home, obviously all you want to do is sleep. And naturally, no question of going for a run in the car. So the little woman is bound to feel neglected.'

Then, after a silence:

'But you were married in the old days, weren't you?'

'Yes, in the old days,' Gaston admitted without enthusiasm.

'And?'

'And—she did the same as me.'

'What the same as you?'

'Well yes of course, I was always away. She went away too.'

'But *you* came back.'

'And she didn't come back. She went to live with a chap who owns a grocery. A chap who's always there!'

And after a meditative pause he concluded with these words, heavy with menace:

'Basically, the motorway and women, you know, they don't go together.'

According to custom, Gaston should have washed the vehicle every other time. This is standard practice with every team of lorry drivers. But it was almost always Pierre who took the initiative, and Gaston took the theft of his turn philosophically. Clearly, they took a different view of aesthetics and hygiene, in regard to both themselves and the tool of their trade.

That day Gaston was lounging on the seat while Pierre aimed such a solid, deafening sheet of water on to the bodywork that it interrupted the few remarks they exchanged through the open window.

'Think you've given it enough?' asked Gaston.

'Enough what?'

'Enough elbow grease. Do you think you're in a beauty parlour?'

Without answering, Pierre turned off the hose and brought a dripping sponge out of a bucket.

'When we teamed up, I quite understood that you didn't like dolls, lucky charms, transfers, and all the stuff other men stick on the lorries,' Gaston went on.

'No, you're right,' Pierre agreed. 'I don't think it suits the lorry's type of beauty.'

'And in your opinion, what is that type of beauty?'

'It's a useful, suitable, functional beauty, you might say. A beauty that's like the motorway. Nothing extraneous, you see, nothing that dangles, or that doesn't have a use. Nothing to make it look pretty.'

'You must admit that I took it all off straightaway, including the gorgeous Veedol girl with the naked thighs who used to skate on the radiator.'

'You could have left that one,' Pierre acknowledged, picking up his hose again.

'Well well,' Gaston marvelled. 'Would Monsieur be becoming more human? It must be the spring. You ought to paint some little flowers on the bodywork.'

In the din made by the water lashing the metal, Pierre could barely hear.

'What on the bodywork?'

'I said: you ought to paint some little flowers on the bodywork. Some lilies of the valley, for instance.'

The jet was aimed at Gaston's face, and he hastily cranked up the window.

This same day, during the customary stop at the Lily of the valley lay-by, there was an incident that worried Gaston more than it amused him. Pierre, who thought he was asleep in the bunk, opened the back of the trailer and took out the little metal ladder they used when they wanted to climb up on to the roof. Then he went over to the far end of the lay-by. An evil genie sometimes seems to take charge of events. The scene that followed must have been visible from some point in the road, which describes a wide curve at that spot. What happened was that two motor-way cops on motor bikes appeared just at the moment when Pierre had leaned the ladder against the fence and was beginning to climb up it. Confronted, questioned, he had to come down. Gaston intervened. They had it out, with exaggerated gestures. One of the cops spread out the whole paraphernalia of the perfect bureaucrat on one of the wings of the vehicle and buried himself in paperwork, while Gaston put the ladder away. Then the cops went off on their mounts like two horsemen of the Apocalypse, and the lorry continued on its way to Lyons.

After a very long silence, Pierre, who was driving, spoke first.

'You see that village over there? Every time I pass it I think of my own village. That dwarfish church, and the houses huddled all around, it's like Parlines, near Puy-de-la-Chaux. Now that really is the sticks, even for the Auvergne, which is a place full of cows and coal merchants who keep little cafés. Not more than twenty years ago, the people and the animals used to sleep in the same room. At the far end, the cows; on the left, the pigsty; on the right, the hen house, even though it did have a sort of cat-flap to let the birds out. By the window, the dining table, and on either side of it two big beds which had to accommodate the whole family. So that not a scrap of heat was wasted in the winter. But the atmosphere when you suddenly came in from outside! You could cut it with a knife!'

'But you don't know anything about that, you're too young,' Gaston objected.

'No, but that's where I was born. It's what you might call hereditary, and I sometimes wonder whether I ever really got free of it. It's like the floor. Just mud. No question of tiles or wood. But then—no need to wipe your feet when you came in! The mud from the fields what was sticking on to your soles, and the mud inside the house, it was all the same, no harm in mixing it. That's the thing I particularly appreciate in our job: to be able to work in moccasins with flexible soles. And yet it wasn't all bad in our village. For example, they used wood for heating and cooking. Say what you like, that's not the same thing as the gas and electricity we had later, when my old girl got widowed and we moved to Boullay. It's a living heat. And the decorated Christmas tree . . .'

Gaston was becoming impatient.

'But why are you telling me all this?'

'Why? No idea. Because I was thinking about it.'

'You want me to tell you? That ladder business. You think it was to go and chat up Marinette? Not only that. It was more to get away from the motorway, and back to your Parlines-by-Puy or whatever!'

'Ah, hell! You wouldn't understand.'

'Just because I was born in Pantin, I wouldn't understand that you're suffering from the typical nostalgia of the hayseed?'

'How should I know? You think I understand it myself? No, really, there are times when life becomes too complicated!'

'And Saturday nights, do you sometimes go dancing?'

Pierre would have preferred to sit down with Marinette and just be there with her in silence, but that barrier, that wire fence his fingers were gripping, created a distance between them which forced them to talk to each other.

'Sometimes, yes,' Marinette replied evasively. 'But it's a long way. There's never any dances at Lusigny. So we go to Beaune. My parents don't like me to go alone. The neighbours' daughter has to come with me. Jeannette, she's a serious-minded girl. They trust me with her.'

Pierre was dreaming.

'One Saturday I'll come and fetch you at Lusigny. We'll go to Beaune. We'll take Jeannette with us, since that's the way it is.'

'Are you going to come and fetch me with your forty-tonne lorry?' the realistic Marinette asked, amazed.

'Oh no! I've got a motorbike, a 350cc.'

'Three on a motorbike won't be very comfortable.'

There was a despondent silence. She didn't seem too keen, Pierre thought. On the other hand, though, could it have been the fact that she wanted it to happen right away that made her immediately see all the material obstacles?

'But we can dance here,' she said suddenly, as if she had just made a discovery.

Pierre didn't understand.

'Here?'

'Yes, I've got my little transistor,' she said, bending down and picking up the radio from the tall grass.

'With this fence between us?'

'Some dances, you don't touch each other. The jerk, for instance.'

She switched on the radio. Some sweet, rather slow music began to fill the air.

'Is *that* the jerk?' asked Pierre.

'No, that'd be more like a waltz. Shall we try, even so?'

And without waiting for his answer, holding the transistor, she began to gyrate, under Pierre's mesmerized gaze.

'Aren't you going to dance, then?'

Awkwardly at first, and then with more abandon, he followed suit. Thirty metres away, Gaston, coming to fetch the companion who seemed to have grown deaf to all his signals, stopped in amazement at the sight of that strange, sad scene, the boy and the girl, both radiating youth, dancing a Viennese waltz *together*, separated by a barbed wire fence.

When they set off again, Gaston took the wheel. Pierre stretched out his hand to the dashboard radio. Immediately, Marinette's waltz came on the air. Pierre leaned back, as if lost in a happy dream. It suddenly seemed to him that the landscape he saw going by all round him was in marvellous accord with this music, as if there were a profound affinity between this flowering Burgundy and the imperial Vienna of the Strauss family. Attractive, noble old residences, harmonious undulations, soft green meadows, succeeded each other before his eyes.

'It's funny how beautiful the countryside is round here,' he finally said. 'I've been through it dozens of times but I never noticed it before.'

'It's the music that does that,' Gaston explained. 'It's like in the movies. When they play the right sort of music with a scene, it has much more effect on you.'

'There's the windscreen too,' Pierre added.

'The windscreen? What d'you mean?'

'The windscreen, you know, the glass that protects the landscape.'

'Ah, because you think that's what the windscreen is for—to protect the landscape?'

'In a way, yes. And by that very fact it makes the landscape more beautiful. But I couldn't tell you why.'

Then, after a moment's thought, he corrected himself.

'I could, though; I do know why.'

'Come on, then. Why would the windscreen make the landscape more beautiful?'

'When I was little, I used to like going to town and looking in the shop windows. Especially on Christmas Eve. Everything in the windows was nicely arranged on velvet, with tinsel and little branches of Christmas trees. But the window, it's forbidding, it won't let you touch. When you went into the shop and got them to show you something they took out of the window, it was never so nice. It had lost its charm, if you see what I mean. So here, with the windscreen, well, the landscape's like a shop window. Nicely arranged, but impossible to touch. Maybe that's why it's more beautiful.'

'In short,' Gaston concluded, 'if I understand right, the motorway is full of beautiful things, but only to look at. No point in stopping and holding out your hand. Don't touch, forbidden, hands off!'

Gaston fell silent. He wanted to add something, to follow his idea through to its conclusion, but he hesitated. He didn't want to be too unkind to this Pierrot, who was so young and so awkward. Even so, he finally made up his mind:

'The thing is,' he said in a low voice, 'it isn't only the landscape that the motorway makes it impossible to touch. It's the girls, too. The landscape behind a windscreen, the girls behind a fence—everything in a shop window. Don't touch, forbidden, hands off! That's what the motorway is.'

Pierre hadn't moved. His passivity irritated Gaston. He exploded:

'Isn't that right, Pierrot?' he yelled.

Pierre jumped, and gave him a distracted look.

The enormous, immobile shadow of the vehicle rose up against the star-spangled sky. There was a faint light inside the cab. Gaston, in his night clothes but with a pair of steel-rimmed spectacles on his nose, was immersed in a novel. Pierre, lying on the bunk, was worried by this prolonged vigil.

'What're you doing?' he asked in a sleepy voice.

'You can see perfectly well: I'm reading.'

'What're you reading?'

'When you're talking to me and when I'm talking to you, I'm not reading any more. I stop reading. You can't do everything at the same time. So, before we started talking, I was reading a novel. *The Venus of the Sands*, it's called.'

'*The Venus of the Sands*?' 'Yes, *The Venus of the Sands*.'

'What's it about?'

'It takes place in the desert. In the Tassili, to be precise. That must be somewhere in the south of the Sahara. It's caravaneers. Men who cross the desert with camels carrying goods.'

'Is it interesting?'

'Contrary to what anyone might think, it has a certain connection with us.'

'Meaning?'

'My caravaneers, they walk all day long across the sand with their camels. They transport goods from one place to another. In a way, they're the lorry drivers of that time. Or else, we're the caravaneers of today. You simply substitute the camels for the lorry and the desert for the motorway, and it becomes the same thing.'

'Mmm,' murmured Pierre, half asleep.

But Gaston, engrossed in his subject, continued:

'And then, there's the oases. The caravaneers' lay-bys are the oases. There, there's springs, palm trees, and girls waiting for them. That's why the book's called *The Venus of the Sands*. She's a fantastic girl who lives by an oasis. So, obviously, the caravaneers dream of her. Here, listen to this:

'*The young tribesman had got down from his white mehari*—that's what we'd call a camel—*from his white mehari and was looking for Ayesha*—that's the girl's name—*in the shade of the palm grove. He couldn't find her because she was hiding near the well, watching the young man's efforts through the slit in her veil, which she had pulled down over her face. At last he caught sight of her and recognized her indistinct silhouette through the branches of a pink tamarisk tree. She stood up when she saw him approach, for it is not correct for a seated woman to speak to a man.* You see, in these countries they still have a sense of hierarchy.

' "*Ayesha,*" *he said,* "*I have travelled for a week across the sandstone of the Tassili, but every time my eyes closed under the burning furnace of the sun, your tender face appeared to me. Ayesha, flower of the Sahel, have you once thought of me in all that time?*"

'*The girl revealed the mauve gaze of her dark eyes and the white radiance of her smile.*

' "*Ahmed, son of Dahmani,*" *she said,* "*that is what you say tonight. But with the first glimmering of the dawn, you will bid your white mehari to arise, and you will depart towards the north without a backward glance. In truth, I believe you love your camel and your desert more than you love me!*"

'What do you say to that, eh?'

Pierre turned over in his bunk. Gaston heard a sort of groan in which he thought he could make out a name: 'Marinette!'

They were approaching the Lily of the valley lay-by; Pierre was at the wheel. Gaston was dozing behind him on the bunk.

The vehicle entered the turn-off and stopped.

'I'm going to get out for a moment,' Pierre explained.

'I'm not budging,' came the answer from the bunk.

Pierre walked ahead under the trees. Grey skies had obliterated the colours and the bird song. There was a kind of disenchanted, morose, almost menacing expectancy in the air. Pierre reached the fence. He could see neither cows nor cowgirl. He stayed there for a moment, disappointed, his fingers gripping the fence. Should he call out? There was no point. Clearly, no one was there, and that was why the charm had been broken. Suddenly, as if he had come to an abrupt decision, Pierre turned round and strode back to the lorry. He took his place and drove off.

'You didn't waste any time,' the bunk commented.

The lorry went hurtling along the turn-off and rejoined the motorway, regardless. A Porsche coming up like a meteor swerved violently to the left, flashing indignant headlights. Stepping savagely on the accelerator, changing gear like a virtuoso, Pierre brought the lorry up to its maximum speed, though unfortunately it was fully loaded. Then came the Beaune exit. The vehicle charged into it. Gaston's flabbergasted head, wearing its balaclava, shot up from behind the seats.

'What the fuck are you doing? Have you gone raving mad?'

'Lusigny, Lusigny-lès-Beaune,' Pierre muttered through clenched teeth. 'I have to go there.'

'But you realize what that's going to cost us? You don't care. What time shall we get to Lyons this evening? After that business with the ladder, do you really think you can go on playing the fool?'

'A little detour, that's all! Let me have just half an hour.'

'Half an hour my foot!'

The lorry stopped at the tollman's window. Pierre handed him his card.

'Lusigny, Lusigny-lès-Beaune? You know where that is?'

The man made a vague gesture and replied with a few unintelligible words.

'What?'

Another, even vaguer, gesture, accompanied by obscure sounds.

'Okay, okay!' Pierre concluded, driving off.

'Look,' said Gaston, 'you don't even know where you're going?'

'Lusigny. Lusigny-lès-Beaune. That's clear, isn't it? Five hundred metres away, Marinette said.'

The vehicle went on for a while, and then stopped by a little old woman holding an umbrella in one hand and a basket in the other. Scared, she jumped aside.

'Excuse me, Madame—which way to Lusigny-lès-Beaune?'

'To the industrial zone? Which one do you mean?'

'No, Lusigny. Lusigny-lès-Beaune.'

'Which way to the Rhône? But that's nowhere near here!'

Gaston thought it was time for him to intervene, so, leaning over Pierre's shoulder, he pronounced distinctly:

'No, Madame. We are looking for Lusigny. Lusigny-lès-Beaune.'

The old woman waxed indignant. 'Well! I'm a silly old crone, am I! Huh! The modern generation!' And she marched off.

'Shit!' muttered Pierre, letting in the clutch.

The lorry crawled on for almost another kilometre, then slowed down even more when a man pushing a cow in front of him came into view through Gaston's window. Gaston immediately questioned him. Without stopping, without a word, the man waved his arm to the right.

'Have to turn right,' said Gaston.

With some difficulty, the heavy lorry started down a minor road. Up came a boy riding a big cart horse with a potato sack in place of a saddle.

'Hey, young feller, Lusigny, Lusigny-lès-Beaune? Do you know it?'

The boy looked at him stupidly.

'Oh come on! Do you or don't you know it? Lusigny?'

There was a silence. Then the horse stretched out its neck, revealed an enormous expanse of yellow teeth, and let out a comic neigh. Immediately the boy, as if by contagion, burst into demented laughter.

'Forget it,' Gaston advised. 'You can see he's an imbecile.'

'But what sort of a lousy hole is this!' Pierre exploded. 'They're doing it on purpose, aren't they?'

They came to a junction with a little cart track. There was a signpost, but its arm had disappeared. Pierre jumped down on to the bank and inspected the grass round the post. He finally found an iron arm covered in green mould bearing the names of several villages, including that of Lusigny.

'Here! You see? Lusigny, three kilometres,' he said triumphantly.

'Yes, but she told you five hundred metres,' Gaston reminded him.

'Which goes to show that we goofed!'

The lorry began to move, and turned into the track.

'You aren't going to take us down there!' exclaimed Gaston.

'Yes I am, why not? Look, there's no problem.'

The lorry advanced, rocking like a ship. Branches scraped its sides, others brushed against the windscreen.

'We aren't out of the wood yet,' Gaston groaned.

'Defeatism brings bad luck.'

'Sometimes, it's simply foresight. Huh! Look what's coming towards us!'

Advancing round a bend, there was a farm tractor towing a cart that blocked the whole width of the road. Both stopped. Pierre got out and exchanged a few words with the man on the tractor. Then he went back to his place beside Gaston.

'He says we can pass a bit farther on. He's going to reverse.'

A delicate manoeuvre began. The lorry crawled on at a walking pace, pursuing the tractor, impeded by its cart. Eventually they arrived at a point where the track was slightly wider. The lorry kept as far to the right as it could without imprudence. The tractor began to pass it. The cart couldn't make it. The lorry reversed a few metres, then went forward again, steering to the right. The way was clear for the cart, but the bulk of the lorry was leaning dangerously over to the right. Pierre stepped on the accelerator. The engine roared to no avail. The right-hand wheels were embedded in grass and soft earth.

'That's it! We're stuck!' Gaston observed with gloomy satisfaction.

'Don't worry, I have it all worked out.'

'You have it all worked out?'

'Yes, look, we've got a tractor, haven't we? It'll tow us out!'

Pierre got out, and Gaston saw him parleying with the tractor driver. The man made a gesture of refusal. Pierre pulled out his wallet. Another refusal. Finally the tractor began to move, and the cart passed the lorry. Gaston jumped down and ran to catch up the tractor.

'Hey, we're going to Lusigny. Lusigny-lès-Beaune. Do you know where it is?'

The driver gestured in the direction he was going himself. Shattered, Gaston went back to Pierre, who was searching the back of the cab, looking for a cable.

'Great news,' he told him. 'We have to turn round.'

But they hadn't reached that point yet. Pierre had unwound the cable and got under the radiator to fix it to the winch. Then he went off more or less at random with the other end of the cable, looking for something to anchor it to. He hesitated in front of one tree, then another, and finally decided on an ancient wayside cross standing at the intersection with a mud path. He wound the cable round the bottom of the plinth and returned to the cab. The engine of the winch began to hum, and they could see the cable slowly moving towards them, twisting and turning on the stones in the path, then becoming taut and vibrating. Pierre switched off, as if he wanted to meditate before the final effort. Then he started to winch up again, bending over the steering wheel as if to participate in the effort that would get the forty-tonne lorry out of the rut. Gaston watched the operation from a short distance behind the cab. He knew that if a man is standing in the wrong place when a steel cable breaks, he can have both his legs severed by one fell whiplash. The vehicle shuddered, then very slowly began to extricate itself from the soft earth. His eyes fixed on the ground, Pierre followed the progress of the lorry, metre by metre. Gaston was the first to see the cross begin to list in an alarming fashion, and then suddenly crash down on to the grass, just when the four wheels of the trailer were finally beginning to get a grip on the road.

'The cross! Look what you've done!'

Relieved at having got out of that particular difficulty, Pierre shrugged his shoulders.

'We'll end up in prison, you'll see,' Gaston insisted.

'If that bastard had only helped us with his tractor, it wouldn't have happened.'

'You can tell that to the gendarmes!'

The lorry resumed its bumpy progress along the uneven road.

'The scenery is certainly very pretty, but don't forget that we have to turn round.'

'We're bound to get somewhere soon.'

And indeed, a kilometre farther on they arrived at a little village square, with a grocery-cum-bar, chemist's shop, and rows of rusty tubes supporting the folded tarpaulins of an absent market. On the far side was a war memorial, with its statue of a private soldier going over the top with fixed bayonet, his boot treading underfoot a German spiked helmet. It wasn't exactly ideal for manoeuvring the lorry, but there was no choice. Gaston got out to direct operations. They had to take advantage of a sloping alleyway and introduce the fore part of the tractor into it, then reverse, turning the wheel hard to the left. The trouble was that the next time they couldn't use the alleyway to give the lorry more room. It had to back up as far as possible, right up to the war memorial.

Gaston ran from behind the trailer to the cab window, giving Pierre directions.

'Straight ahead as far as you can go! . . . A bit more . . . Stop . . . Right hand down now . . . Back . . . Stop . . . Left hand down . . . Straight ahead . . .'

It was really like moving around on a pocket handkerchief. The absence of passers-by or inhabitants further accentuated the malaise the two men had felt since the start of their escapade. What sort of country had they ventured into? Would they ever get out of it?

The most difficult operation was still to come, for while the tractor's bumper was practically brushing against the chemist's window, the back of the trailer was now directly threatening the war memorial. But Gaston had a quick eye. He shouted, ran up and down, exerted himself. Good old Gaston, who detested wasted effort and the unforeseen, he'd really come into his own today!

If the lorry advanced just one more centimetre it would smash into the shop window, with its display of cough drops, tisanes, and rheumatism belts. Pierre turned the wheel as far as it would go and began to reverse. He had a vague feeling that Gaston was being too careful, and making him waste precious centimetres with each manoeuvre. You always had to force him a bit! He reversed. Gaston's voice reached him, from a distance but quite clearly.

'Come on! Gently. More. More. Gently. Stop, that's it.'

But Pierre was convinced that he still had a good metre to play with. That little bit extra would mean avoiding one more turn. So he went on reversing. Gaston's voice rose in panic.

'Stop! Hold it! Stop, for Christ's sake!'

There was a scraping sound, then a muffled impact. Pierre finally stopped, and jumped out.

The private soldier, who had been holding his bayonet in both hands, no longer possessed his bayonet, or his hands, or his arms. He had defended himself valiantly, however, for there was a huge scratch along the metal side of the trailer. Gaston bent down and picked up some fragments of bronze.

'Well, so now he's lost his arms,' Pierre observed. 'But after all, that isn't so bad for a disabled ex-serviceman, is it?'

Gaston shrugged his shoulders.

'This time we really will have to go to the gendarmerie. No getting out of it. You and your lousy Sticks-lès-Beaune, that's it for today!'

The formalities kept them nearly two hours, and night had fallen when they left the gendarmerie. Gaston had noticed that Pierre— sombre, resolute, and as if beside himself with suppressed rage—hadn't even asked the gendarmes the way to Lusigny. What had they been doing in this village with their forty-tonner? Their answer to this question was that they had been in urgent need of a spare part, someone had told them about a garage, a whole series of misunderstandings.

All they had to do now was get back to the motorway. Gaston took the wheel. Pierre was still locked in a stormy silence. They had travelled about two kilometres when they heard a succession of crackling sounds so loud that they drowned the noise of the engine.

'*Now* what is it?' said Gaston anxiously.

'Nothing,' Pierre grunted. 'It isn't coming from the engine.'

They drove on until they came to a pale but blinding light blocking the way. Gaston stopped.

'Hold it,' said Pierre. 'I'll go and see.'

He jumped down from the cab. It was only a Bengal light burning itself out on the road. Pierre was just about to climb in again when a wild, grotesque fanfare rang out, and he was surrounded by a group of masked dancers brandishing torches. Some had toy whistles, others had trumpets. Pierre struggled, trying to escape from this absurd round dance. He was deluged with confetti, a Pierrot enveloped him in streamers, the mask of a pink pig stuck a paper tongue into his face.

'Stop it, you bastards!'

A firework exploded under his feet. Pierre grabbed the pink pig by the lapels, shook him furiously, and crashed his fist into his snout, which crumpled under the blow. The others came to the rescue. Pierre was tripped up, and fell. Then Gaston leaped down from the cab with a torch. He yelled:

'That's enough, you lot of morons! *We* aren't here for laughs. We've met your gendarmes, you know. We'll go and fetch them!'

The tumult abated. The lads took off their masks and revealed the hilarious faces of young peasants in festive mood. They were all wearing in their lapels the beribboned tricolour of young conscripts.

'Hell! We've just got called up, so we're celebrating! That's all!'

'And anyway, what the fuck're you doing here at this hour with that crate? You moving house?'

They put their fingers to their temples, with howls of laughter.

'Yeah, that's it, they're moving house!'

Pierre rubbed his back. Gaston hurriedly pushed him over to the lorry and shoved him up into the cab before things turned nasty again.

Driving along the motorway, he kept a watch out of the corner of his eye on the embittered face, the obstinate profile of his companion, which was intermittently visible in the harsh streaks of light coming from the sparse traffic.

'You know, your Lusigny,' he finally declared. 'I'm beginning to wonder whether it even exists. Or whether your Marinette wasn't making a monkey of you.'

'It's quite possible that Lusigny doesn't exist,' Pierre replied after a silence. 'But that Marinette was making a monkey of me—no.'

'Then if she wasn't making a monkey of you, tell me why she gave you the name of a village that doesn't exist?'

There was another silence, then Gaston heard this answer, which mesmerized him:

'It could be that Marinette doesn't exist, either. A girl who doesn't exist, it's only natural she should live in a village that doesn't exist, isn't it?'

It was broad daylight the next day when the lorry, on its way back to Paris, approached the Lily of the valley lay-by. Pierre was at the wheel. He was in the same sombre mood as the day before, and only broke his silence by muttered abuse. Hunched up in his corner, Gaston watched him anxiously. A car passed them and swerved back to the right a little too quickly. Pierre exploded:

'Huh! Tourists! They just clutter up the roads! Then there's accidents, and they always blame it on the lorry drivers! Why don't they go by train if they want to have fun on their holidays!'

Gaston looked round. A two-horsepower Citroën was also, with much effort, trying to pass them.

'Even the two legged beasties are trying to get in on the act! And driven by a woman, what's more. But if she can't go as fast as us, why is she so keen on passing us?'

To Gaston's great surprise Pierre nevertheless slowed down, and the Citroën passed them with no more difficulty. As she went by, the woman thanked them with a little wave.

'You're being very decent,' Gaston observed, 'but after yesterday's goings-on we can't waste any more time.'

Then he noticed that Pierre was continuing to slow down, had switched on his right-hand directional signal, and was pulling over on to the verge of the motorway. He realized why when he saw the Lily of the valley lay-by on the other side of the road.

'Oh no, shit! You aren't going to start all over again!'

Without a word, Pierre jumped down from the cab. It would be very difficult to cross both sides of the motorway, where the traffic was heavy and rapid in both directions. But obviously, this didn't worry Pierre. He seemed to have become blind.

'Pierre—you've gone mad! Watch out, for Christ's sake!'

Pierre just barely missed a Mercedes, which protested with a prolonged screech of its horn. He started off again and reached the central reservation. He jumped over it and started to rush across the Paris–Provence carriageway. A lorry brushed against him and forced him to stop. He started off again with a desperate leap to try to avoid a Citroën DS. One more leap. An impact sent him spinning, another knocked him over towards the ground, but before he reached it he was projected into the air by a staggering blow. 'It was as if the cars were playing football with him,' Gaston was to describe it later. Tyres screeched, horns sounded. There was a general hold-up.

Gaston was the first to reach Pierre. Helped by three motorists, he got him back to their lorry. Pierre's blood-soaked head rolled inertly from side to side. Gaston immobilized it between his hands. He looked him in the eyes with tenderness and grief. Then Pierre's lips began to move. He was trying to say something. He stammered. And slowly, the words began to form.

'The motorway . . .' he murmured. 'The motorway . . . You see, Gaston, when you belong to the motorway . . . you mustn't try to leave it.'

Later, the articulated lorry, driven by Gaston, was back on the road. It was preceded by an ambulance surmounted by its revolving light. Soon the ambulance turned right into the Beaune exit. The lorry passed it, and carried on in the direction of Paris. The ambulance slowed down in the access road and passed a signpost on which Pierre, being unconscious, was unable to read: *Lusigny-lès-Beaune 0.5 km.*

CHRISTIANE BAROCHE (b. 1935)

Do You Remember the Rue d'Orchampt?

Translated by Elizabeth Fallaize

I had no sense of premonition. Anyway, it wasn't fate that I encountered that evening but memory. The twists and turns of our destiny most often follow the biddings of memory.

Patrice Miodan had asked me round, with the Dorianos. I am not certain that he realized, when he issued his . . . no really, it was not an invitation. He had murmured one day, at very short notice and in that curiously syncopated voice of his, which never manages to catch up with what he's thinking, 'perhaps if we had dinner together on Friday, we could . . .'. With him, all conditionals remain just that and we, well we never learned how to give them a foothold. I think I would like to whisper the end of the sentence to him, make him a present of it. He so plainly suffers from his verbal tangles, from the way in which his impulse towards others fails to get through, to cross the barrier of his lips, gets no further than his eyes. But, when it comes down to it, I don't listen to him; there would be no point, anyway, I catch his eye. And he sighs with relief.

Doriano, in contrast, has no difficulty with words. Sometimes I wish that he did, or that someone would make difficulties for him. I wish that his silences could be as populated as his speech, but he is rarely quiet and when words fail him, everything suddenly reverberates around him as if in the heart of a void. So in the end I prefer him to speak.

And we found ourselves, on that Friday, in the rue de l'Orient, outside a firmly closed door. Jean-Paul and Clotilde laughed. It was what they were expecting, they said, but for me, that red door had something malevolent about it which I reacted violently against. I am quite incapable of waiting, it's the only thing I really can't bear. Waiting is a kind of rusting away. To a certain extent, I wasn't surprised either, and I didn't feel cross with Patrice, I simply refused to wait patiently, I refused absolutely.

Clotilde sat down on the steps, eyes instantly closing. She's lucky that way, she doesn't have to wait, she goes to sleep.

It was warm, for a February night. The moon was rising over Montmartre, fat, yellow, and lacklustre. A gaslight from the beginning of the century. It wasn't late, it was eight o'clock. Yet the rue Lepic was deserted. What a bizarre district the Butte is, a kind of island, calm, almost totally asleep, but encircled by hustle and bustle. The boulevard below exports noise, light, passers-by who wander off up the hill but hasten back down, as though halted halfway up by a barrier of bird-lime. Really, it's not a place where you might dawdle, where you might seek out some ill-defined pleasure, it's no den of multiple lures. Despite what everyone believes, people live there, just like anywhere else, but in an even quieter way.

Bursts of rock and roll came from a one-storey house. On the other side of the windows, shadows moved about, in rhythmic yet anarchic patterns, following a logic which escaped us because we were party only to whiffs of sound. A singer currently in vogue lived there and what was coming to us intermittently was the embryonic shape of his performance, an early draft.

Clotilde was dozing, her head slightly drooping, propped up against the bannister. I have always seen her be severe and concentrated when she sleeps, stubbornly determined, I would even say, in a way which makes her look almost spiteful.

Jean-Paul was talking, talking away . . . I didn't want to hear what he was saying. My own evasions take an ambulatory form, I walk, taking whatever turning I come to, blindly, mechanically, seeking only a state of hypnotic torpor, putting each foot forward one after the next, with no idea of where I'm going. Or, in fact, I do find out, but later; some ill-defined, terribly effective force, jogs my memory of a route I have taken before without noticing. Very often it stops at that, a sudden resurgence, harmless, with no consequence. At other times the upsurge of memory overwhelms everything. The lives I've led before must be present, surely, in that recognition of the unknown.

The rue de l'Orient is short, turns a fairly sharp corner, tumbles over steps, over ivy, over a wall, passes between antiquated houses with closed shutters. None of that mattered to me, I was walking on, walking away from that door behind which no one was waiting for me with the sole purpose of forcing me to wait. And the flavour of long gone days suddenly rose deliciously in my throat.

Jean-Paul had followed me automatically. He was still talking. About himself, probably, or about the creative process, which brings him back to himself. That's the fastest route to a man, the path he constantly works on marking out, littering it with signs. I no longer felt like reading them, making sense of them. There are people whose habit it is to make concentric dives down into themselves, driven by competing forces. At first they're centripetal and some listeners are caught up spellbound in the eddy. But, in my experience, maelstroms eventually end up ejecting their harvests. I have been floating on the edges of danger for a long while. I like Doriano though; I don't find him fascinating, I don't listen to him properly any more, I watch him spinning round and the circles have gradually got smaller. Or perhaps I've jumped ship. It's sad, in any case, I'm well aware.

By some miracle, luck was suddenly on my side, and all the streetlights around us went out. We were just coming to the top of a flight of steps and, in the road below, the trees whipped up a swell of darkness outside the windows of the houses. I didn't feel worried, it was just a local power failure. Beyond the avenues plunged into darkness by my fault, the neon lights of Paris-by-night vibrated like the rides in a theme park, the world continued to go round.

And anyway I like the night-time. The daytime hands me over to passions, to constraints that I can't escape, to males. Night-time is when men come to me. The fact that Doriano stopped talking is proof of that. Even if it's just fear that sends them to me—but fear of what?—I couldn't care less, they come to me naked, calm and loving, nursery rhymes hovering on their lips, and they nest in me like trusting birds. I'm weary of falcons and eagles.

Silence had descended with the darkness. The silence of towns. In the countryside, night makes a dreadful din. There, in that street that I had still not identified, life had not stopped because of the power failure, it was hibernating, settling into the dark eiderdown with meticulous little satisfactions. Since there was no sign of the power coming back on, since the TV screen remained dark, couples, I felt sure, were feeling their way to bed, plumping the pillows and slipping between the sheets, sighing with pleasure. It was a night to keep an eye on, to watch out for contours taking shape as the eye slowly becomes accustomed to the depths of the darkness, to the whiteness enclosed in it, pearly ink. And I realized where I was. Oh, it was ages ago. Fifteen years, it was fifteen years ago . . .

Doriano was hauling me away from the walls, urging me, 'they're bound to be back by now, come on Marianne, we must have made a mistake about the time.' He set off ahead of me. His jerky step betrayed a monstrous desire to run, barely controlled. I know why he didn't dare, he was afraid I'd call him back, that I'd make him listen to me. But the lights came on again, and I followed him.

Patrice and Dana had indeed returned. In their house, all up and down stairs, Baudelairean sofas elongated by the dim light made you want to let something die in you, divest yourself of a habit, the most prosaic one preferably, and dream of horizons forever out of reach, of sleeping pasts, against a background of tango music; the world of clocks had no place here, time did not divide itself up into pointlessly exact measurements.

What did we talk about? I retain a memory of luxuriant smiles, ringing out, I can bring precisely to mind the vague gestures which Patrice suspends at the end of each of his sentences as if they were excuses. Words were evading him, as usual, and his hands flew recreating them from nothing, from the halo of the lamps, from the fluid movement of the curtains hanging at the half-open windows, from our shadows on the walls, larger and fleshier than our real selves. When it comes down to it, he is perfectly able to make himself understood.

Dana let her head slide into the hollow of the cushions; she looks like an Egyptian cat with her black eyes—in fact they're almost yellow but her thick eyelashes cast a deep shadow—and her eyes were shining, gleaming, signalling soft caresses like satiny skin. We never managed to say so but we were fond of each other. And we still are, in fact, we see each other, we get madly excited at the idea of playing with the fire of ideas without resorting to words and we embrace, our hands suddenly clasped, 'Marianne, we should meet more often.' Yes I remember it all. And yet I was absent.

In those moments which stand out bizarrely framed in the everyday, like open casements, I am both present and wandering elsewhere; that's when a line from Robbie Burns comes into my head, obsessive, pressing in its invitation, 'My heart's in the Highlands, a-chasing the deer'. The line takes me over, hounds me, buzzes in my ear and I take off towards the high moors to chase my own prey.

I expect I carried on as usual, contemplating my friends engaged in their spirited existences, joining in with them only through a touch on their wrist, a kiss on their cheek, a laugh. Gestures suffice. They represent my entire presence to others, the mask of attendance behind which I escape far away. I am there, in the flesh, profuse like my caresses. Others are taken in and that's good. Why upset them, what for? They tell me things, they relax, they show their emotions. They unburden themselves and I am there for them, a calm warm presence, looking deep into their eyes and smiling at their smiling mouths, it's important . . . isn't it? I'm fond of them and they know it. That's enough. I don't expect much more than that myself, and they are not so different.

Knowledge does not change my memories, does not feed them. Colours them slightly perhaps.

When the time came, the red door closed behind me, that's all. If I could have—but one can't—I would have stayed there with them, they would soon have forgotten me, would have given up their night to me. I am not a voyeur and all bodily encounters come to much the same, no, it was something both more straightforward and more complicated than that. Whether they desired each other or not was of no interest to me, it was only the house that I was after. The ceilings were hiding very high up, on a level with Patrice who is tall.

I have no idea if she possesses or if he parades that brittle fragility that one attributes instinctively to an interminable body. But what I can guess about him suggests something muted. In the room under the eaves where he usually works the sofas are low, the lamps are at floor level. When he's standing up he must feel lost, must take refuge in the walnut colouring of the beams, and take wing, certainly, towards some opacity that the dim light is insufficient to dissolve and that can only be captured through the imaginary. Women are reassured by proximity, men need the illusions of space.

I took the Dorianos home as quickly as possible. I was worn out—driving has never tired me—I was worn out from the desire to be alone. Jean-Paul was reviewing the evening. He and Patrice are both musicians. For one of them music is a ship, for the other an abyss. Contrary to what one might think from what I've said about him, it's not Doriano who submerges himself, plunging down into melodic chasms. But it's difficult to be more specific, or to be sure . . .

I dropped my friends off in front of their door, I couldn't find the patience to listen to any more about composition and counterpoint. The Doriano 'I, me' had suddenly reached saturation point.

And I had an appointment. An appointment with a street.

An almost fanatical willpower made me park the car in the same space that I had only just vacated. Everything had . . . gone quiet is not the word. Died down. Everything had died down. The singer was standing in front of his house, smoking a cigarette, his dog was mooching around the doorways, taking its time, lifting its leg, giving little whimpers as it followed up old trails. The man and the dog watched me go by, with no particular surprise. They looked alike, both with the tranquil air, vacant, on the heavy side, of those who have no anxieties and who are ready for bed, their day finished. I sometimes envy those kinds of people, and at other times, I feel sorry for them. On that particular evening I felt sorry for them.

The Miodans' window was dark. On the top floor the curtain still flapped against the half-open window. I had turned my head and slowed down and the man behind me remarked casually 'sometimes he goes off around this time, into the waters of the night, but today they had visitors. He's a strange bloke, does the same kind of work as me, more or less, so the concierge at no. 5 said, but I never hear anything, not a sound coming from his house.'

I recognized the voice now. It had always seemed to me to be rather artificial, when I heard it on his records, on the radio, well, it was his own. Banal, of course. It's easy to get the wrong idea about people who get caught up by fame.

'Why did you tell me that?'

'No bloody idea! But don't worry your head about it, it's just I like talking to people, that's all.'

He whistled at the dog, made a gesture in my direction, his hands sketched a proposal, he waited a moment then went in, shrugging his shoulders. I should have followed him in. Only, it would have been so disarmingly easy; I need a bit more of a battle to arouse my interest, no longer in the first flush of youth, either.

What time was it ? In the waters of the night . . . Thinking of that phrase, I felt as though as I was going up a river with lazy bends, passing alongside banks unchanged for centuries.

Beneath the ivy the flight of steps in rue Tholozé was black as soot. The plant had thrown out branches in all directions and some of them were creeping out beyond the pavements. Others had slipped in between two stones, progressively pulling them loose and blistering the rendering with their growth. Above the rue d'Orchampt, the stems had nothing but empty space to cling on to and they had gradually been forced into bends, criss-crossing each other in a noisy jumble, full of the rustle of birds taking frantic flight. In the past, rats used to climb up to the nests to swallow the eggs, and I was already on the lookout for the double red glow of their watchful eyes as they ran past. Nothing had changed.

It was dark. Sudden gusts of wind made the lights sway. The wind in Paris . . . It arrives from nowhere, starts up between two rows of buildings and then stops dead when it reaches the end. It couldn't be said to blow, or even breathe. In the rue Lepic, in any case, it dances backwards, from the Place J.-B. Clément to the Place Blanche. How I had loved that wind, that ivy, those narrow steps.

14 rue d'Orchampt. I lived there. On the seventh floor. Only one window. I lived there to lean on the little balcony, to put my cheek, my forehead, my lips against the glass. Over a long period, I have tried and failed to work out the nature of that bizarre fascination. In the beginning, like all girls of twenty, I didn't live somewhere, no, I lived with someone. I was young. Well, at that age, usually, one is young. But perhaps I was born old, or else youthfulness took hold of me straightaway, for ever, until death. I don't feel as though I have changed my status, or that I could do. I am. Lots of people would find that a reassuring conviction.

HE was an actor. Jean something, Jean Béranger, there! It's funny, his face, his body escape me completely; I remember his hands, which I hated because they destroyed my nocturnal world simply by reaching out to the lamps. I suppose he never understood, or even guessed, he called me his prude. In fact I was far from having false modesty, far from having true modesty, of no interest to me. But nothing weighed on me, nothing mattered when I stood touching the glass, looking right down over the town. From the window I could sweep down over the town, into the town, it was as if I were pulled in different directions by it, but suspended somewhere else, in a tranquil space that nothing could disturb.

Jean would leave home early, bound in amorous haste for the theatre; for him acting on stage was like life, only better. When it comes down to it, we spent eight months passing each other in corridors and meeting up in beds without getting to know each other well. He was happy that I would wait for him and I was happy to wait. That encapsulates the difference. Waiting for time to immobilize or to accelerate? I don't know, I waited. That convinced him that I was in love. Apart from my strange mania for plunging straight back into darkness what he had just illuminated, with the casual flick of a finger, nothing separated us; the path we travelled together was strewn with kisses and embraces. Nothing but. Love and fresh air. Because we almost never ate together, almost never. We made love. We hardly spoke. He secretly gloried in this exclusively physical passion I know, he told people, who naturally told me. Men often have vanities of this kind which deprive them of a superior kind of pride—but just a minute! Aphorisms like this come with indifference or priggishness. At the time, he amused me, though I didn't make the effort to discover why and that was just as well.

I sat down on the doorstep, back against the wall. I had sat there dozens of times, in the early days, because Jean only had one key. In the end he found the spare one and gave it to me, without a second thought but with the feeling he was offering me the moon.

I had never really moved in. He thought I was staying and I thought so too. I was just passing. As far as men are concerned I've carried on just passing. I am loath to settle down, it's not their fault, to settle down in THEIR life. Yet I grow attached to surroundings and, like everyone else, I encumber myself with objects. But they only stay with me for a while. As soon as they grow familiar, I become bored and get rid of them. When all's said and done, my lovers slip through my fingers in the same way.

The street's cats came to walk round me. They hadn't changed either.

Why I stayed sitting there, I don't know. I must have dozed a bit. Then a rapid step, the clinking of a metal object being run along a railing, bar after bar, the honeyed smell of pipe tobacco . . . fifteen years were wiped out.

We looked each other over. He had aged and knew it. 'I drink too much.' He sat down beside me. 'I won't ask you if you've come back. After all, you never left.'

He picked up my handbag, opened it, took a cigarette out of a crushed packet, lit it, and held it out to me. I wanted to tell him that I hardly smoked now because I no longer waited, but he wouldn't have wanted to believe me. His gestures attached to long-gone moments had the same effect on me as those childhood photos which people bring out of the album with an unnatural pleasure, because they are nearly dead and no longer sure they ever lived.

'Come up, go on, I won't eat you. And you can see your bloody window. That's what you've come for, isn't it?'

On the stairs the light went out between the third and fourth floor.

'No point trying, Marianne, it won't come back on again any more than it did fifteen years ago.'

And I went on up to the seventh, without having to put a hand out. It stank of sour heat, of wax polish, of rehashed smells. The smells had certainly grown in substance anyway.

He opened his door and put his hand out to the light switch but, instead of the flood of light which he used to inflict on me in the past, the modest beams of a little hanging lamp flickered over the curtains.

'As you see, I finally . . . got the message.'

His tone betrayed volumes of painfully acquired certainties. I was slightly suspicious, he had always liked play-acting.

'I didn't think you'd have stayed on here, Jean.'

'Why not?'

'I don't know, not very much room, perhaps.'

'And not very expensive. My acting is no better than before and I'm not paid much better than before.'

His mouth had lost all trace of softness. I made no attempt to reply or to offer any comfort, he had gone well beyond that kind of thing. All the same, I was surprised. The theatre meant so much to him. And he had never been no good, in my view. He was passionate about acting, and that was all I saw. Passion can make up for a lot.

'I know what's become of you. First an easy lay, then a name. Okay, calm down . . .'

I was surprised, that was all.

'If I'd run into you I would have told you to your face you were a whore, only I didn't run into you. And then I began to feel sorry for *them*. You were all right, you always came out of it unscathed, just the same as you went in. It put years on them, or else they turned to drink. From a distance you could have been taken for a bit of a bitch, that's what it looked like. But it wasn't that. After all, I should know, shouldn't I?'

'I'm not sure what you're talking about.'

'There have been many men in your life, Marianne. I never understood why, you don't need them. At first, you wanted them, that was the obvious thing to think, or else it was ambition. Why not? They were all doing well, often rich, nearly always handsome. They all had reputations, good or bad, but they had them. Only they never seemed to be of much use to you. Not in bed or anywhere else. Later I noticed they were all alike and I couldn't be arsed to work out if they were all like ME or else if I was simply the same type. That was hard to take, that. So I told myself that you just picked them up, like people might adopt a dog in the winter, a dog that they'll abandon on a motorway the following summer, and replace with another one of the same breed in November time. I could see you still had that look of an old sow embarrassed by your own company and I started to add things up, to remember certain things, and bring myself down a peg or two all by myself. It was then that the theatre gave up on me. In all the roles I was given to play, there was an answer to everything, even to obscure things, even to the questions that had no answers. I'm an actor because I need someone to pull the strings. And in that respect, life trumps the most successful of plays every time. Only in life you haven't got the script written down for you to help you cope.'

He gave a rather nasty laugh.

'You see Marianne, I didn't love you and in a way, that's a pity, because you trampled all over my little illusions. While I was about it, if I'd been able to indulge in a proper bout of misery, real bleeding heart stuff, no holds barred, if I'd been able to wallow in wanting desperately to kill you or to take you by force, then, that would have achieved something, that would have helped me get you out of my system. Grief can be very salutary. It's incredible how being madly in love predisposes you to forgetting someone. Yes, if I'd been crazy about you, hooked on you, I would have been in a state for at least a fortnight. After that, it would have been easy to build on the capital. I would have bawled my eyes out, I would have found someone else, that's the way the game goes. I would have had my moments of melancholy. Instead of all that, I asked myself, I'm still asking myself, why you left, what I'd done, etc. There was no other man, that's always the first thought. You had nothing particular to go to. At the time, you remember, you were following up a number of possibilities, all going equally well and all of no interest to you. You were gifted. Gifted with gifts. The only thing that sparked off anything in you was painting. But you didn't paint. What a joke. I'm pretty certain you still found me attractive . . . I really didn't understand. And worst of all, I didn't know if there was anything to understand.'

He sighed.

'I thought that people usually left a note, even if writing to someone seems pathetic, you leave a note to say you're leaving when you go . . . I turned the room upside down. I didn't find anything of course. So, there we are. I've lived my life telling myself I was bound to see you again, otherwise it would be simply impossible, and I didn't believe it for a minute. But here you are.'

He was standing behind me. I was aware of the smell of his breath on my neck and of the closeness of his body. I wasn't worried by it. He was right. It was true that I had still found him attractive, fifteen years earlier.

He was waiting. He was waiting for me to speak and I didn't know how to go about it.

'Am I being a pain? Is it such a pain to explain to me?'

'In the past, it was too difficult, first because things were not clear in my own mind, and second because you would have said I had no real reasons.'

'I wasn't that stupid!'

'It's not a question of intelligence, Jean. You would have shrugged your shoulders, you were totally unprepared. I can tell you, it wasn't your fault. Not really. You were acting in *The Exchange*, do you remember? You were in a little company that performed in university theatres. And you left even earlier than usual to go to the theatres at the Cité Universitaire, in Antony, at Nanterre. Sometimes you acted with rage, sometimes with passion, depending on whether you'd slept or not. The woman leading the company, that director, she really annoyed me. She recreated the world every night, she invented the theatre for you, made it into a kind of complicated stagecraft in which Artaud, Stanislavski, Planchon were mixed in with Wilson and Andy Warhol. You were all transfixed by it, half-asleep but transfixed. She had a brash charm, a certain know-how, and her eyes looked drugged up. The actors were her drug, because you all stayed on, it could have just as well have been a barman, a lorry driver, a queer looking for a drink. It could have been anyone at all with two ears who could keep their mouth shut. And with a cock, sometimes. So as not to finish the night alone. She would have got herself infected with the pox rather than be on her own. On top of that, at 3 a.m., when you were all yawning wide like empty wineskins, she would start switching from the realist to the fantastic, she would get a second wind that was positively mythomaniac. With a certain genius, I have to say. While that was going on, I was waiting at this window, perfectly patiently. Are you beginning to understand? Every evening, Jean, every evening, I had a hunk of bread and an apple for dinner, leaning on the balustrade.

Jean moved. The bedsprings murmured gently, as if in protest. He was lying down and would go to sleep. When it comes down to it, that's why I didn't leave a message, fifteen years ago. Jean needed to ask himself things, contrary to what he had been saying, he only needed questions. Answers can be awkward sometimes, destroying the only end there is to love affairs, the one you've built yourself around the unbearable.

At this window, standing up for hours, sometimes kneeling on a stool. Silence would suddenly fall, like an angel. How else could it be put, the household angel of a peace beyond our time. At the bottom end of the rue d'Orchampt, where it hooks on to the rue de la Mire, with its constant to-and-fro of cars, its hullabaloo as the swarm of children are called in from windows, and they don't want to come in, don't want to go to bed, the smithy was taking its time over closing up. The blacksmith was a woman, in fact, not a man. She was stocky like an iron pot with her hands settled on her hips.

I see her now. That woman wrought the absolute. Her workmen left the place about seven o'clock in the evening and the rusty pile of salvaged metals seemed to subside for the night. The woman stayed on. I never found out where she lived exactly. Nothing in her existence appeared to fit her for everyday life. And when I say that she stayed on in that lair, that means that she continued to buzz about. She would come to the doorway, take deep breaths, go back inside and clanging noises would start up, in a bunch or alone, patterned or at random. More than sounds, voices. Soul in the iron. A red spot with brief gleams glowed until morning. I know, I'm sure, that she lay on a straw mattress or a chair, in her passing torpors, keeping an eye out only for the fire. A vestal virgin aged sixty. Not particularly chaste, so they said. The blacksmith had died in the war, she hadn't remarried. One of the workmen, always the same one, didn't leave with the others some nights. And on those nights the workshop reverberated with high notes, gasping for hours on end in shifting red flushes. Those fragile peals were his. An old man with wrists like tree trunks.

I never attempted to conceal myself when I watched the two of them. Often, in the middle of the night, the woman would lift her head and return my look, shaking her head. Perhaps she made comments about me. I was certain that I had come across Venus and Vulcan. Sometimes mythology gets it right.

As I've got older, I've learned hundreds of ways of extracting happiness from nothing at all; at the time, I was only half-aware of them. So I never got up the nerve to go and talk to my blacksmiths. Now I would. But the smithy is dead, it seems. In any case, night is turning its fire into ashes.

Anyway, they were not the only ones I spied on, with affection. I didn't know that she was envious, I only recently understood that she was. A couple is only ever the achievement of an equilibrium. Some people manage it. It doesn't matter how! In my case, I'm circling round it, I've flushed out the deer and I'm following the track. It's . . . a delicate set of scales. I used them to weigh my Samarcands and my Golconda treasures. I got it right, I expect, but without knowing it. And that's not the essential thing, the essential thing is to be demanding . . .

In the studio more or less opposite the window where I would stay on watch all night, another couple was visible. Less picturesque, or rather, picturesque in a different way. Both of them over fifty, and no pretence. I always had the impression that they were approaching old age with relief. Thank goodness, life won't have to be lived much longer. What a pleasure to anticipate the rest shortly to come. Knowing it's round the corner, we're not quite there yet and the last few yards are divine.

Especially when they go on and on. The ideal would be to get a good glimpse of death ahead, in a backward glancing profile, and to be able to constantly measure the distance to it. Those two, almost old people, were contemplating it from quite a distance still, but glad to have spotted it ahead. I suppose that that's what they were admiring every evening for twenty minutes, that distance, that margin of security. They would open up the French windows—neither of them was a painter, their room was the only exhibition behind the glass—and then they could see IT coming, from anywhere on the horizon. They would open the windows and lean on the rail.

I could look right into the depths of the room and they had known for ages that I did look. Very soon, in fact, they started giving me a wave of the hand, with a smile on her part, a word or two even, one of those phrases that you call out into the empty air and which are meant for someone.

For twenty minutes. You could feel that they were settled into the comfort of a tried and tested routine. It must have been at least thirty years ago that they had found the exact place where the elbow or the wrist should be wedged to feel just right, to be in the best position to wait. There was an element of provocation, of course, but well mannered, calm. Careful.

Their story was a straightforward one. It was made up of details, of the appropriation of their own details. An ancient livery of furniture and curtains, acquired after long deliberation and kept in use until the end. Theirs. Because the furniture stays behind, becomes covered with the hoary frost of the dust of the years, sinks beneath a tangle of spiders' webs, but stays behind. It does die, later. Much later. Yes, it was straightforward. A big double bed, in dark wood, with a white cotton bedspread and a red eiderdown. On the floor, stained almost black, a red carpet and, on the carpet, a chamber pot. White, in the kind of china that is no longer made, the kind which stays cool to the skin. And the two of them in that room, clutching at their coarse red linen curtains? They were white, in the long and roomy old-fashioned nightgowns which warm the air round bare legs. People knew how to live, in the past.

So. They scanned the darkness or the evening sky, with nightfall barely begun, and closed the windows on themselves, reassured to have issued an invitation which death had not accepted. It's very straightforward. They went off to bed and, as it was very high like a white cliff, they used a little oak stool highly polished by their naked feet, up we go! Lying side by side. I could see their hands close enough together to touch. I don't know where the light came from. Then it was dark. Beneath their eiderdown they must have lain enjoying the outline of the sky through the windows, but eventually, one of them got up and I saw only their fingers slowly pulling the curtains to. That was all. The show was over.

It was generally just about then that Jean came home, still animated by the theatre or by the tidal wave of words which sprang from their conversations after the performance.

He flooded everything with garish light. In that period of his life, he needed the 'footlights', the 'spotlight', he needed the illusion that he was being looked at. An actor is often a peremptory identity solely in the eyes of others. And those eyes can look away . . .

'The day before, Jean, the day before I left, you got home later than usual. They had been in bed for ages, my Philemon and Baucis and the smithy was only running on dogged exhaustion. You came home drunk with words, in love once again with your leader though exasperated by the stupid woman who could not let you return to your solitude since you furnished hers. So you wanted light, wine, a bit of flesh you could call your own and a travesty of love, you wanted me to be Helen or Ariel, available to satisfy your desire still clothed in the garb of an Ancient Greek or in Prospero's doublet.'

And Jean slept on. He was snoring behind me, as I had expected.

I opened the shutter very quietly; the studio opposite had dark green curtains, new ones, carelessly pulled to. Down below in the smithy, in the creaking silence, bits of scrap iron were rusting away, piled up in a random order and creating their own through the sheer force of their weight. As for the garden, which my gaze had so often lingered in, felt at home in, a tangle of a garden, a mildly crazy garden, it had been disciplined by the Paris authorities, twelve floors of concrete had sprung up there, with the statutory green space in front, if you please, a lawn and a maple tree. What a lack of respect, for goodness sake! That was where I had my night of revelation, in Pascalian style, that was where I caught myself by the collar.

Jean, then, aroused and in irritatingly excitable mode, had pushed me down against my will onto the bed. For the first time since I had known him I had one of those morose, resigned reflexes, 'it'll all be over much more quickly if I let him get on with it.'

Naturally he had gone to sleep straight away afterwards; it was indeed over.

Everything was. Or rather, the little that had existed between us. Not really because of that fiasco of a union, which had united him with what? My genitals, that was all. It was all so stupid, in a way, because I'd finally understood after spending so much time thinking it over. Lost time . . . I was made for solitude, for choice, for never having to submit and never having to impose. For not belonging to anyone and not owning anything. Above all a human being.

I would never—I told myself that night and I've been repeating it ever since, not pig-headedly, just with that kind of unreasonable certitude that comes from the guts—I would never be able to put up with what is implied by the word couple. I have no need to be dependent. Banal, perhaps, but I'm not so sure. The word freedom, so degraded nowadays, means above all choice. And who really chooses?

I had not been able to bring myself to explain this to Jean, in the past. What would he have understood by it? 'I don't love you' instead of the only phrase I could have managed, 'I'm leaving'? So, I had got up, noiselessly, I'd taken a last look at the street as if to seek confirmation there, and then I'd left.

Afterwards, oh afterwards, the pattern often repeated itself. Humanity proceeds in twos, no doubt that's what keeps it going. Myself, I have walked alone in my life. Sometimes accompanied for a few months, for a few weeks. But permanency tends to slip in between men and women, they settle down under the cover of love and they stop. It's the persistence after the first stab of heartbreak that I don't like, I have a surgeon's instinct. And then, I get bored easily. The moment always comes when I feel like getting the hell out. Other people stay, that's up to them. When it comes down to it, it's true, I'm an old sow fed up with the company she keeps. People come up with phrases that go deep, only they don't realize.

Jean was sleeping with the same insistence as Clotilde, the same conviction. I closed the door without him stirring, I went down the stairs for the second time, there would be no other. Dawn was already breaking.

The little electric whine of the dustbin carts in the early morning streets of an empty Paris, half-asleep, mumbling, not quite with it, made me feel quite jaunty. I fetched the car under the eyes of an intrigued concierge just taking her bins in. Heaven knows what she took me for!

Yes, I had chosen, I had elected for solitude. On this subject I am, oh, not indulgent towards the mania people have for pairing up, and badly, nine times out of ten—that would mean I find excuses for them; I have become less intransigent. Now, I can watch them get together, struggle in the little labyrinths of disagreements, fail to call off the hounds; I can see them try again, on the same footing, under the same flag with the same pointless agitation or see them discover with great difficulty that moment in the couple equal to zero in which the forces on the two sides neutralize each other. What an expression! I can witness with indifference that meltdown of two personalities into a rather mongrel duo. And then, each us places our pride where we can—mine is borrowed from Cyrano and doesn't fly very high but it flies alone! Why shouldn't other people pay a heavy price for the illusion that they can conquer the universe in a little band? Because, alas, there are also those false promises, the children!

I didn't go back to that district, mainly because the Miodans moved house. There were works in the area, the road was being lengthened, the studios pulled down. The smithy. . . . I don't know about the smithy, does that make any difference? Everything changed, moved on, progressed . . . it's well known what that means.

Jean Béranger . . . no point in mentioning his name, I know nothing more about him. However, he did have a surprise for me up his sleeve. When I found myself back in the street, at dawn, relieved of the burden of a memory and confirmed, let's be frank, in a decision I had made rather than in my choices, I looked up, I looked *behind me.*

Jean was at the window. He was smoking. There was nothing to look out at, but nevertheless, he was looking out.

I might as well admit, that gave me a turn.

The Check-up

Translated by Elizabeth Fallaize

Then, I want you to blindfold your eyes, said the child to the doctor. His
mother had stayed behind in the waiting room. Dr Mettetal had taken
over the practice from his father, who had himself taken it over from his
father, and nothing had changed in this middle-class flat in the rue
Fontaine, since the grandfather had set himself up there at the turn of the
century. Objects brought back from a series of journeys to the East were
piled up in locked glass cases, barely identifiable in their dusty clutter.
Carpets deadened the sound of footfalls. A Buddha's head still sat on the
solid desk, but the succession of pictures of women which had taken
their turn there had lost their pride of place, removed by the hands
which had cherished them—Dr Mettetal was a bachelor. He was a tall
young man whose appearance fitted his name, thin, stiff, with long bony
hands, a complexion which sometimes veered towards an opaque blue,
sometimes towards a grey veined transparency, with a beauty in his face
which was more of a recollection of beauty or a nostalgia for it than an
immediately striking impression—it was impossible to contemplate him
without a sickly-sweet sensation rising in the throat, a deathly impression, as if a succubus had etched a filigree patterning on his skin, withering and retracting the flesh with successive cuts of a scalpel, insinuating
itself into the bone of his high Slav cheeks, shading in a mauve circle
round his eyes, making them float in a vague and aimless melancholy.
Shortly after the death of his father, as if suddenly liberated, he had
brought to an end the tradition of general medicine skilfully practised
from father to son, and chosen paediatrics as his specialism. Dr Mettetal
had a single glory of which he was justly proud: he had a splendid head of
hair, long and fine, but vigorous in growth, which he tossed backwards,
either side of a parting, after he had given it an energetic brushing; even
the child, who was not inclined to observe such things, was dazzled
by the hair's electric blondness and managed to forget his fear—the
consulting room did smell strongly of ether—as he thought that he
would like to touch it. Dr Mettetal calmly repeated his injunction: I want

you to get undressed. And the child just as calmly repeated his reply, but he looked directly into the doctor's eyes and his voice betrayed a commanding lack of certainty: then, I want you to blindfold your eyes. Dr Mettetal told himself that he must retain his self-control: I'm not going to blindfold my eyes because I have to examine you, young sir, and how do you expect me to examine you with my eyes blindfolded? That's simply ridiculous, the child responded, in the United States they examine people through sheets of paper. You're certainly well informed, said the doctor taking on an amused look. And you should be better informed, said the child. Right, get undressed or I'll call your mother in. My mother's always on my side, said the child. But why the devil don't you want to get undressed? I don't mind getting undressed, said the child, but not until you've blindfolded your eyes. Perhaps you feel cold? It is a bit chilly. Shall I turn up the heating? If you insist. Will you get undressed? Yes, when you've blindfolded your eyes. Look here this isn't a game of blind man's buff, exploded the doctor, where do you think you are? I'm going straight off to fetch your mother. Don't you think we should try to solve this little problem ourselves? asked the child gravely. Yes, you're right, said the doctor, so will you explain to me why you want me to blindfold my eyes? So you can't see me, said the child. And why's that? I don't know you well enough, why should I do you the favour of letting you look at my body? My word, you must think you're Isabelle Adjani, said the doctor. In a sense, said the child who now seemed quite sure of himself, already convinced that he would get his way. Well I swear to you that I won't look at you, I'll keep my eyes closed, but let me listen to your heart, and unbutton your shirt at least! To speed up the negotiations, Dr Mettetal had unwound his stethoscope and was preparing to put it to his ears. I refuse, said the child, you're cheating, I want you to blindfold your eyes. But how can I examine you? I'll guide your hand, said the child. But I'll be forced to touch you, and that's a kind of seeing, I'll see you in my imagination. You can imagine as much as you like, but you won't see me. Are you sure you wouldn't like me to wear gloves as well? No, no, the blindfold will do. You're as stubborn as a mule. And you like wasting time, if we hadn't spent so long arguing this whole business would be settled by now. What do you want me to use as a blindfold? asked the doctor, defeated. My scarf, replied the child, who half a second earlier had no answer, here you are, and he held out the inky-coloured bit of wool knitted by his mother. And do you want to check it? asked the doctor. Yes, said the child. Dr Mettetal tied the scarf round his head, taking care not to catch his hair in it, the child went behind him and added another knot, then positioned himself in front of the doctor and waved his hands before his eyes. Can you see anything? asked the child. Yes, said the doctor. You're lying, said the child—I tried it before I came out, that scarf is perfect. Then the child tiptoed off, like someone about to play a trick, and bent down to undo his shoelaces. His movements seemed to perform a secret dance, joyful and intimately triumphant. What are you doing? said the doctor, automatically advancing the cup of his stethoscope. What you asked me to do, dear doctor, I'm getting undressed. Before starting on his shirt, the child looked all round him to make sure that no one could see him—that the door of the consulting room was firmly shut, that the glass in the window was properly frosted; he bent down to look through the narrow channel which ran along the wooden sill, but it looked out over a park, he even went up to the large archaic X-ray machine and touched it as though to check that it wasn't a living being. Then, one by one, he undid the buttons on his shirt, enacting his sacred pantomime. Beneath his shirt he wore a white vest. He took it off at last, in such a rapid movement that his hair, made electric by the friction of the vest, stood out from his head like a crown. He was naked: the painting of a woman sitting alone in a field hung over his head, he threw a glance of pity at her, and folded his arm across his chest. You can come over, said the child, trembling. You come over, said the doctor. The child approached his outstretched hands, turned round to present the doctor with his back; he hung his head like a defeated animal. The doctor did not dare palpate him, scarcely to touch him, asked the child to breathe through his mouth, then to cough; the child did as he was asked. Then he put an ear to the boy's skinny shoulder blade, and knocked his fist against several places on his back. Come in, said the child. That's an old joke, said the doctor, all children say that. You see, said the child, it's best to try and normalize the situation. You think that's possible, said the doctor, we must make a pretty picture! Yes, said the child. And as the doctor gently took hold of each side of his body to turn him round, the child slipped out of his grasp in fright—let me do it, he said. He raised his head again towards the woman in the painting as if to ask for encouragement. And now, said the child, are you going to listen to . . . my heart? That's right, said the doctor, haven't you had it done before? Yes, said the child. Well, said the doctor, it doesn't hurt, does it? Yes, said the child, it does hurt. You mean it feels cold? Not just that, said the child, and he took a step forward, and pulled the doctor's hand towards him, groping for the heart. So now you see, said the child, with difficulty. No, I promise you I don't see anything at all. But now you see, repeated the child, you've seen . . . No, I can only hear your heart-beat, it's very slightly irregular. You've seen, said the child, tell me the truth. But what do you want me to see? You're saying that to be nice to me, said the child, you've seen but you don't want to say so—if you've seen, you might as well take off your blindfold . . . The child's voice was close to tears. No, said the doctor, I shan't take it off until you tell me to, you can take it off for me and I hope you're not a kleptomaniac, my pockets are always full. Oh, said the child, as if this idea might make him laugh, you're a kind man. A kind of man? A kind man, said the child. You can get dressed, said the doctor. The child took a step backwards and seized his vest, which he had laid out ready on the chair, facing the right way round—his skin was impatient to be clothed again. May I take the blindfold off? asked the doctor in a voice that was too loud, under-estimating the proximity of his patient who was silently executing his rapid movements a few paces from the doctor. You may, said the child. He threw a last furtive look at the woman in the painting—he hadn't even noticed that she had a finger lifted to her lips, as if she were saying 'ssh'. The woman was protecting the sleep of someone lying at the edge of the frame. The title of the painting, engraved on the surrounding, had become illegible; perhaps it was called *The Secret*. The doctor's eyelids were fluttering, you've brought me back from miles away, he said, laugh-ing, that was a real kidnapping. May I touch your hair? said the child. Why? said the doctor. No special reason, just to thank you, because it's nice hair. The child was at last touching the doctor's hair. When the doctor lay dying, and his veins were overwhelmed by a terrible cold and dessication, he recalled that scene and it brought a glow more potent than any morphine.

There Is No Exile

Translated by Marjolijn de Jager

The particular morning, I'd finished the housework a little earlier, by nine o'clock. Mother had put on her veil, taken her basket; in the opening of the door, she repeated as she had been repeating every day for three years: 'Not until we had been chased out of our own country did I find myself forced to go out to market like a man.'

'Our men have other things to do,' I answered, as I'd been answering every day for three years.

'May God protect us!'

I saw Mother to the staircase, then watched her go down heavily because of her legs: 'May God protect us,' I said again to myself as I went back in.

The cries began around ten o'clock, more or less. They were coming from the apartment next door and soon changed into shrieks. All three of us, my two sisters—Aïcha, Anissa, and I—recognized it by the way in which the women received it: it was death.

Aïcha, the eldest, ran to the door, opened it in order to hear more clearly: 'May misfortune stay away from us,' she mumbled. 'Death has paid the Smaïn family a visit.'

At that moment, Mother came in. She put the basket on the floor, stopped where she stood, her face distraught, and began to beat her chest spasmodically with her hands. She was uttering little stifled cries, as when she was about to get sick.

Anissa, although she was the youngest of us, never lost her calm. She ran to close the door, lifted Mother's veil, took her by the shoulders and made her sit down on a mattress.

'Now don't get yourself in that state on account of someone else's misfortune,' she said. 'Don't forget you have a bad heart. May God shelter and keep us always.'

While she repeated the phrase several more times, she went to get some water and sprinkled it on Mother, who now, stretched out full length on the mattress, was moaning. Then Anissa washed her entire face, took a bottle of cologne from the wardrobe, opened it, and put it under her nostrils.

'No!' Mother said. 'Bring me some lemon.'

And she started to moan again.

Anissa continued to bustle about. I was just watching her. I've always been slow to react. I'd begun to listen to the sobs outside that hadn't ceased, would surely not cease before nightfall. There were five or six women in the Smaïn family, and they were all lamenting in chorus, each one settling, forever it seemed, into the muddled outbreak of their grief. Later, of course, they'd have to prepare the meal, busy themselves with the poor, wash the body. . . . There are so many things to do, the day of a burial.

For now, the voices of the hired mourners, all alike without any one of them distinguishable from the other if only by a more anguished tone, were making one long, gasping chant, and I knew that it would hang over the entire day like a fog in winter.

'Who actually died over there?' I asked Mother, who had almost quieted down.

'Their young son,' she said, inhaling the lemon deeply. 'A car drove over him in front of the door. I was coming home when my eyes saw him twisting one last time, like a worm. The ambulance took him to the hospital, but he was already dead.'

Then she began to sigh again.

'Those poor people,' she was saying, 'they saw him go out jumping with life and now they're going to bring him back in a bloodstained sheet.'

She raised herself halfway, repeated: 'jumping with life.' Then she fell back down on the mattress and said nothing other than the ritual formulas to keep misfortune away. But the low voice she always used to address God had a touch of hardness, vehemence.

'This day has an evil smell,' I said, still standing in front of Mother, motionlessly. 'I've sensed it since this morning, but I didn't know then that it was the smell of death.'

'You have to add: May God protect us!' Mother said sharply. Then she raised her eyes to me. We were alone in the room, Anissa and Aïcha had gone back to the kitchen.

'What's the matter with you?' she said. 'You look pale. Are you feeling sick, too?'

'May God protect us!' I said and left the room.

At noon, Omar was the first one home. The weeping continued. I'd attended to the meal while listening to the threnody and its modulations. I was growing used to them. I thought Omar would start asking questions. But no. He must have heard about it in the street.

He pulled Aïcha into a room. Then I heard them whispering. When some important event occurred, Omar spoke first to Aïcha in this way, because she was the eldest and the most serious one. Previously, Father used to do the same thing, but outside, with Omar, for he was the only son.

So there was something new; and it had nothing to do with death visiting the Smaïn family. I wasn't curious at all. Today is the day of death, all the rest becomes immaterial.

'Isn't that so?' I said to Anissa, who jumped.

'What's the matter now?'

'Nothing,' I said without belabouring the point, for I was familiar with her always disconcerted answers whenever I'd start thinking out loud. Even this morning . . .

But why this sudden, blatant desire to stare at myself in a mirror, to confront my own image at some length, and to say, while letting my hair fall down my back so that Anissa would gaze upon it: 'Look. At twenty-five, after having been married, after having lost my two children one after the other, having been divorced, after this exile and after this war, here I am busy admiring myself, smiling at myself like a young girl, like you . . .'

'Like me!' Anissa said, and she shrugged her shoulders.

Father came home a little late because it was Friday and he'd gone to say the prayer of *dhor* at the mosque. He immediately asked why they were in mourning.

'Death has visited the Smaïns,' I said, running toward him to kiss his hand. 'It has taken their young son away.'

'Those poor people,' he said after a silence.

I helped him get settled in his usual place, on the same mattress. Then, as I put his meal in front of him and made sure he didn't have to wait for anything, I forgot about the neighbours for a while. I liked to serve Father; it was, I think, the only household task I enjoyed. Especially now. Since our departure, Father had aged a great deal. He gave too much thought to those who weren't with us, even though he never spoke of them, unless a letter arrived from Algeria and he asked Omar to read it.

In the middle of the meal I heard Mother murmur: 'They can't possibly feel like eating today.'

'The body is still at the hospital,' someone said.

317

Father said nothing. He rarely spoke during meals.

'I'm not really hungry,' I said, getting up, to excuse myself.

The sobs outside seemed more muffled, but I could still distinguish their singsong. Their gentle singsong. This is the moment, I said to myself, when grief becomes familiar, and pleasurable, and nostalgic. This is the moment when you weep almost voluptuously, for this gift of tears is a gift without end. This was the moment when the bodies of my children would turn cold fast, so fast, and when I knew it. . . .

At the end of the meal, Aïcha came into the kitchen, where I was by myself. First she went to close the windows that looked out over the neighbouring terraces, through which the weeping reached me. But I could still hear it. And, oddly, it was that which made me so tranquil today, a little gloomy.

'There are some women coming this afternoon to see you and to propose marriage,' she began. 'Father says the candidate is suitable in every way.'

Without answering, I turned my back to her and went to the window.

'Now what's your problem?' she said a little sharply.

'I need some air,' I said and opened the window all the way, so that the song could come in. It had already been a while since the breathing of death had become, for me, 'the song'.

Aïcha remained a moment without answering. 'When Father goes out, you'll attend to yourself a little,' she said at last. 'These women know very well that we're refugees like so many others, and that they're not going to find you dressed like a queen. But you should look your best, nevertheless.'

'They've stopped weeping,' I remarked, 'or perhaps they're already tired,' I said, thinking of that strange fatigue that grasps us at the depth of our sorrow.

'Why don't you keep your mind on the women who're coming?' Aïcha replied in a slightly louder voice.

Father had left. Omar too, when Hafsa arrived. Like us, she was Algerian and we'd known her there, a young girl of twenty with an education. She was a teacher but had been working only since her mother and she had been exiled, as had so many others. 'An honourable woman doesn't work outside her home,' her mother used to say. She still said it, but with a sigh of helplessness. One had to live, and there was no man in their household now.

Hafsa found Mother and Anissa in the process of preparing pastries, as if these were a must for refugees like us. But her sense of protocol was instinctive in Mother; an inheritance from her past life that she could not readily abandon.

'These women you're waiting for,' I asked, 'who are they?'

'Refugees like us,' Aïcha exclaimed. 'You don't really think we'd give you away in marriage to strangers?' Then with heart and soul: 'Remember,' she said, 'the day we return to our own country, we shall all go back home, all of us, without exception.'

'The day that we return,' Hafsa, standing in the middle of the room, suddenly cried out, her eyes wide with dreams. 'The day that we return to our country!' she repeated. 'How I'd like to go back there on foot, the better to feel the Algerian soil under my feet, the better to see all our women, one after the other, all the widows, and all the orphans, and finally all the men, exhausted, sad perhaps, but free—free! And then I'll take a bit of soil in my hands, oh, just a tiny handful of soil, and I'll say to them: "See, my brothers, see these drops of blood in these grains of soil in this hand, that's how much Algeria has bled throughout her body, all over her vast body, that's how much Algeria has paid for our freedom and for this, our return, with her own soil. But her martyrdom now speaks in terms of grace. So you see, my brothers . . ."'

'The day that we return,' Mother repeated softly in the silence that followed . . . 'If God wills it.'

It was then that the cries began again through the open window. Like an orchestra that brusquely starts a piece of music. Then, in a different tone, Hafsa reminded us: 'I'm here for the lesson.'

Aïcha pulled her into the next room.

During their meeting, I didn't know what to do. The windows of the kitchen and of the other two rooms looked out over the terraces. I went from one to the other, opening them, closing them, opening them again. All of this without hurrying, as if I weren't listening to the song.

Anissa caught me in my rounds.

'You can tell they're not Algerian,' she said. 'They're not even accustomed to being in mourning.'

'At home, in the mountains,' Mother answered, 'the dead have nobody to weep over them before they grow cold.'

'Weeping serves no purpose,' Anissa was stoic, 'whether you die in your bed or on the bare ground for your country.'

'What do you know about it?' I suddenly said to her. 'You're too young to know.'

'Soon they're going to bury him,' Mother whispered.

Then she raised her head and looked at me. I had once again closed the window behind me. I couldn't hear anything anymore.

'They're going to bury him this very day,' Mother said again a little louder, 'that's our custom.'

'They shouldn't,' I said. 'It's a hateful custom to deliver a body to the earth when beauty still shines on it. Really quite hateful. . . . It seems to me they're burying him while he's still shivering, still . . .' (but I couldn't control my voice any longer).

'Stop thinking about your children!' Mother said. 'The earth that was thrown on them is a blanket of gold. My poor daughter, stop thinking about your children!' Mother said again.

'I'm not thinking about anything,' I said. 'No, really. I don't want to think about anything. About anything at all.'

It was already four o'clock in the afternoon when they came in. From the kitchen where I was hiding, I heard them exclaim, once the normal phrases of courtesy had been uttered: 'What is that weeping?'

'May misfortune stay far away from us! May God protect us!'

'It gives me goose bumps,' the third one was saying. 'I've almost forgotten death and tears, these days. I've forgotten them, even though our hearts are always heavy.'

'That is the will of God,' the second one would respond.

In a placid voice, Mother explained the reason for the mourning next door as she invited them into the only room we had been able to furnish decently. Anissa, close by me, was already making the first comments on the way the women looked. She was questioning Aïcha, who had been with Mother to welcome them. I had opened the window again and watched them exchange their first impressions.

'What are you thinking?' Anissa said, her eye still on me.

'Nothing,' I said feebly; then, after a pause: 'I was thinking of the different faces of fate. I was thinking of God's will. Behind that wall, there is a dead person and women going mad with grief. Here, in our house, other women are talking of marriage . . . I was thinking of that difference.'

'Just stop "thinking," ' Aïcha cut in sharply. Then to Hafsa, who was coming in: 'You ought to be teaching *her*, not me. She spends all her time thinking. You'd almost believe she's read as many books as you have.'

'And why not?' Hafsa asked.

'I don't need to learn French,' I answered. 'What purpose would it serve? Father has taught us all our language. "That's all you need," he always says.'

'It's useful to know languages other than your own,' Hafsa said slowly. 'It's like knowing other people, other countries.'

I didn't answer. Perhaps she was right. Perhaps you ought to learn and not waste your time letting your mind wander, like mine, through the deserted corridors of the past. Perhaps I should take lessons and study French, or anything else. But I, I never felt the need to jostle my body or my mind. . . . Aïcha was different. Like a man: hard and hardworking. She was thirty. She hadn't seen her husband in three years, who was still incarcerated in Barberousse prison, where he had been since the first days of the war. Yet, she was getting an education and didn't settle for household work. Now, after just a few months of Hafsa's lessons, Omar no longer read her husband's infrequent letters, the few that might reach her. She managed to decipher them by herself. Sometimes I caught myself being envious of her.

'Hafsa,' she said, 'it's time for my sister to go in and greet these ladies. Please go with her.'

But Hafsa didn't want to. Aïcha insisted, and I was watching them play their little game of politeness.

'Does anyone know if they've come for the body yet?' I asked.

'What! Didn't you hear the chanters just now?' Anissa said.

'So that's why the weeping stopped for a moment,' I said. 'It's strange, as soon as some parts of the Koranic verses are chanted, the women immediately stop weeping. And yet, that's the most painful moment, I know it all too well myself. As long as the body is there in front of you, it seems the child isn't quite dead yet, can't be dead, you see? . . . Then comes the moment when the men get up, and that is to take him, wrapped in a sheet, on their shoulders. That's how he leaves, quickly, as on the day that he came. . . . For me, may God forgive me, they can chant Koranic verses all they want, the house is still empty after they've gone, completely empty. . . .'

Hafsa was listening, her head leaning toward the window. With a shiver, she turned toward me. She seemed younger even than Anissa, then.

'My God,' she said, emotion in her voice, 'I've just turned twenty and yet I've never encountered death. Never in my whole life!'

'Haven't you lost anyone in your family in this war?' Anissa asked.

'Oh yes,' she said, 'but the news always comes by mail. And death by mail, you see, I can't believe it. A first cousin of mine died under the guillotine as one of the first in Barberousse. Well, I've never shed a tear over him because I cannot believe that he's dead. And yet he was like a

brother to me, I swear. But I just can't believe he's dead, you understand?' she said in a voice already wrapped in tears.

'Those who've died for the Cause aren't really dead,' Anissa answered
with a touch of pride.

'So, let's think of the present. Let's think about today,' Aïcha said in a
dry voice. 'The rest is in God's hand.'

There were three of them: an old woman who had to be the suitor's
mother and who hastily put on her glasses as soon as I arrived; two other
women, seated side by side, resembled each other. Hafsa, who'd come in
behind me, sat down next to me. I lowered my eyes.

I knew my part, it was one I'd played before; stay mute like this, eyes
lowered, and patiently let myself be examined until the very end: it was
simple. Everything is simple, beforehand, for a girl who's being married
off.

Mother was talking. I was barely listening. I knew the themes to
be developed all too well: Mother was talking about our sad state as
refugees; then they'd be exchanging opinions on when the end might be
announced: '. . . another Ramadan to be spent away from home . . .
perhaps this was the last one . . . perhaps, if God wills it! Of course, we
were saying the same thing last year, and the year before that. . . . Let's
not complain too much. . . . In any event, victory is certain, all our men
say the same thing. And we, we know the day of our return will come. . . .
We should be thinking of those who stayed behind. . . . We should be
thinking of those who are suffering. . . . The Algerian people are a people
whom God loves. . . . And our fighters are made of steel. . . .' Then they'd
come back to the tale of the flight, to the different means by which each
one had left her soil where the fires were burning. . . . Then they'd evoke
the sadness of exile, the heart yearning for its country. . . . And the fear of
dying far from the land of one's birth. . . . Then. . . . 'But may God be
praised and may he grant our prayers!'

This time it lasted a bit longer; an hour perhaps, or more. Until the
time came to serve coffee. By then, I was hardly listening at all. I too was
thinking in my own way of this exile, of these sombre days.

I was thinking how everything had changed, how on the day of my
first engagement we had been in the long, bright living room of our
house in the hills of Algiers; how we'd been prosperous then, we had
prosperity and peace; how Father used to laugh, how he used to give
thanks to God for the abundance of his home . . . And I, I wasn't as I was
today, my soul grey, gloomy and with this idea of death beating faintly

inside me since the morning. . . . Yes, I was thinking how everything had changed and that, still, in some way everything remained the same. They were still concerned with marrying me off. And why exactly? I suddenly wondered. And why exactly? I repeated to myself, feeling something like fury inside me, or its echo. Just so I could have worries that never change whether it's peace or wartime, so I could wake up in the middle of the night and question myself on what it is that sleeps in the depths of the heart of the man sharing my bed. . . . Just so I could give birth and weep, for life never comes unaccompanied to a woman, death is always right behind, furtive, quick, and smiling at the mothers. . . . Yes, why indeed? I said to myself.

Coffee had now been served. Mother was inviting them to drink.

'We won't take even one sip,' the old woman began, 'before you've given us your word about your daughter.'

'Yes,' the other one said, 'my brother impressed upon us that we weren't to come back without your promising to give her to him as his wife.'

I was listening to Mother avoid answering, have herself be begged hypocritically, and then again invite them to drink. Aïcha joined in with her. The women were repeating their request. . . . It was all as it should be.

The game went on a few minutes longer. Mother invoked the father's authority: 'I, of course, would give her to you. . . . I know you are people of means. . . . But there is her father.'

'Her father has already said yes to my brother,' one of the two women who resembled each other replied. 'The question remains only to be discussed between us.'

'Yes,' said the second one, 'it's up to us now. Let's settle the question.'

I raised my head; it was then, I think, that I met Hafsa's gaze. There was, deep in her eyes, a strange light, surely of interest or of irony, I don't know, but you could feel Hafsa as an outsider, attentive and curious at the same time, but an outsider. I met that look.

'I don't want to marry,' I said. 'I don't want to marry,' I repeated, barely shouting.

There was much commotion in the room: Mother got up with a deep sigh; Aïcha was blushing, I saw. And the two women who turned to me, with the same slow movement of shock: 'And why not?' one of them asked.

'My son,' the old woman exclaimed with some arrogance, 'my son is a man of science. In a few days he is leaving for the Orient.'

'Of course,' Mother said with touching haste. 'We know he's a scholar. We know him to have a righteous heart.... Of course....'

'It's not because of your son,' I said. 'But I don't want to get married. I see the future before my eyes, it's totally black. I don't know how to explain it, surely it must come from God.... But I see the future totally black before my eyes!' I said again, sobbing, as Aïcha led me out of the room in silence.

Later, but why even tell the rest, except that I was consumed with shame and I didn't understand. Only Hafsa stayed close to me after the women had left.

'You're engaged,' she said sadly. 'Your mother said she'd give you away. Will you accept?' and she stared at me with imploring eyes.

'What difference does it make?' I said and really thought inside myself: What difference does it make? 'I don't know what came over me before. But they were all talking about the present and its changes and its misfortunes. And I was saying to myself: of what possible use is it to be suffering like this, far away from home, if I have to continue here as before in Algiers, to stay home and sit and pretend.... Perhaps when life changes, everything should change with it, absolutely everything. I was thinking of all that,' I said, 'but I don't even know if that's bad or good.... You, you're smart, and you know these things, perhaps you'll understand....'

'I do understand,' she said, hesitating as if she were going to start talking and then preferred to remain silent.

'Open the window,' I said. 'It's almost dark.'

She went to open it and then came back to my bed where I'd been lying down to cry, without reason, crying for shame and fatigue all at the same time. In the silence that followed, I was feeling distant, pondering the night that little by little engulfed the room. The sounds from the kitchen, where my sisters were, seemed to be coming from somewhere else.

Then Hafsa began to speak: 'Your father,' she said, 'once spoke of exile, of our present exile, and he said—oh, I remember it well, for nobody speaks like your father—he said: "There is no exile for any man loved by God. There is no exile for the one who is on God's path. There are only trials." '

She went on a while, but I've forgotten the rest, except that she repeated *we* very often with a note of passion. She said that word with a peculiar vehemence, so much so that I began to wonder toward the end whether that word really meant the two of us alone, or rather other women, all the women of our country.

To tell the truth, even if I'd known, what could I have answered? Hafsa was too knowledgeable for me. And that's what I would have liked to have told her when she stopped talking, perhaps in the expectation that I would speak.

But it was another voice that answered, a woman's voice that rose, through the open window, rose straight as an arrow toward the sky, that rounded itself out, spread out in its flight, a flight ample as a bird's after the storm, then came falling back down in sudden torrents.

'The other women have grown silent,' I said. 'The only one left to weep now is the mother. . . . Such is life,' I added a moment later. 'There are those who forget or who simply sleep. And then there are those who keep bumping into the walls of the past. May God take pity on them!'

'Those are the true exiles,' said Hafsa.

Tunis, March 1959

RENÉ DEPESTRE (b. 1926)

The Negro with the White Shadow

Translated by Elizabeth Fallaize

That October, the imminent demise of Dieuveille Alcindor was the only topic of conversation amongst the inhabitants of the place known as Cap-Rouge. Alcindor was a mere will o' the wisp suspended beneath the machete of destiny. His life might fall victim to the fatal blade at any moment. The corner of his brain which was still lit up didn't know whether his legs were on daytime or night-time, whether it was cold or whether the sun was shining in his balls. The latter no longer took pride of place in his life. Evil forces were preventing him from having any control over his toes or over the sunlit heights of his soul. When a negro goes to the dogs like that, it's time to order his coffin and call in père Savane.

Jérôme Cançon-Fer, the most important healer in Cap-Rouge, confirmed the diagnosis of the other *houngans* of the hamlet in the direst of terms. When a negro has lost contact with his feet and his balls, the Cap-Rouge or the distant island of Guinea of life are all the same to him!

'Poor dearly departed Ti-Dor. There was a negro who lived his life at high octane. He had a water-melon in place of a heart. He worked hard and showed courage in the face of tribulations, both his own and other people's. And as to casting a spell over women, and especially to getting them pregnant, it would take a corncob to even begin to match this vigorous fighting cock's equipment!'

Originally from Tortuga Island, Dieuveille Alcindor had settled in Cap-Rouge, in the south-west of Haiti, a few months after the Yankees had 'pacified' the country. According to the tales of the time, Alcindor had joined the ranks of the rebel Cacos who had fought against the marine fuseliers in the mountains of the North. Narrowly escaping execution, he had suffered all sorts of vicissitudes in his subsequent flight and had landed up by chance on the plateau of Cap-Rouge. On arrival, he had acquired for virtually nothing a patch of land which was really just a few squares of thorny brush overrun by snakes, large black lizards, and the loathsome crows. No one had wanted it. After dark people went out of their way to avoid this accursed ground: it was said to be a meeting-place for all the zombies, werewolves, wild boar-men, and other evil spirits of the area.

It was a heroic act on Dieuveille Alcindor's part to take on such a place. He told himself that Atibon-Legba, the King of Haiti's evil places, would help him get these diabolical intruders off his land. Several times, Alcindor thought he was beaten: the tender shoots he planted in the morning rarely survived to greet the moon and the stars, despite the care he took of them. But an iron will drove him on to put his heart and soul into toil and struggle. After several years, the 'accursed savannah' was no longer recognizable, transformed at last by his efforts into a land resplendent with good health; fruit trees, maize, sweet potatoes, African peas, manioc, and even heavy water-consumers like malanga, yams, and sugar cane saw off the nightmare of thorn bushes and cacti. And this triumph of greenery was quickly inhabited by the song of ortolans, thrushes, turtle-doves, hummingbirds, village weavers, carpenter birds, guinea-fowl, and other wandering musicians, all contributing to the score. From that time on, Dieuveille Alcindor ceased to be the 'evil foreign spirit' of Cap-Rouge. He was no longer left out of the *coumbites*,[1] the voodoo ceremonies, the *bandes-raras*,[2] and the other community activities of the hamlet.

Now, in every field, people crossed themselves or spat their grief into the dust when they turned their eyes towards the straw roof beneath which Alcindor's identity was gradually coming to pieces. An atmosphere of funereal vigil already surrounded his house. The crows were back, perched amongst the leaves of the calabash trees. The odour of an impending death gave a new vigour to their eternal mourning cries. Buffalo, Alcindor's hunting dog, let off a lugubrious howl at the sky from time to time. The living Christian souls kept quiet: Cécilia, Alcindor's legal wife; Marianna, his young garden-wife; Dorée, his female companion in the seasons-under-the-sea; Andréus, his brother-in-law; Lerminier and Emulsion-Scott, his neighbours; and of course the children, each one the fruit of a different storm—all these *Alcindorian* people, by the grace of God and of Atibon-Legba, all crept around on tiptoe, afraid that a clumsy gesture, a chair knocked over, an object dropped, a sneeze insufficiently bottled up, might create a stir in the hut which could be fatal to Alcindor, struggling for his life on the cosmic tightrope. He was visibly nothing more than a bag of bones, topped by a

---

[1] Form of cooperative work in the countryside.

[2] Carnival processions in the countryside.

face which had become so sharply delineated that, if the dying man were to venture a last wish, it was likely to be cut off before it left his lips.

But, as Dieuveille Alcindor was later to say himself, even in this desperate state, he was far from believing in his heart of hearts that the cause of his life was lost. Despite the verdict of the *houngans,* despite his loved ones' grief, his dog's *libera* for the dead, and the timely return of the crows, somewhere deep within his will to live was irrepressible, like a dolphin on heat leaping up out of the water. A negro of his draught does not cross over to the other side like a colt stepping over a cactus hedge. The lid on Dieuveille Alcindor's mahogany coffin was not about to be nailed down just yet, may his balls be struck by lightning first! His father, dearly departed Aristhène Alcindor, had died at the ripe old age of ninety-two and at the funeral, dearly departed General Mabial Limabial, his maternal grandfather, was still able to help bear the coffin to the cemetery at the age of over a hundred. A heart like his with the potential of a palm-tree doesn't give up when it's reached the height of a poppy. It was still aiming a sure and certain greeting at the blue sky.

O Jesus-Mary-Joseph, O papa Guédé Nibo, if Dieuveille Alcindor even once in his life ever let the love arrow that lives in his shorts drag in the mud, then let his soul be carried off like a thornlamp, let it be made into a heap of blasted coal! But if, on the other hand, you recognize that his head is always filled with the rosebay and nightingales beloved by living Christian souls, o *loas* of Guinea, angels of the stars, then permit the royal palm tree of the Alcindors to keep the promise of his roots in the world beyond; let him spend a few more seasons of rain and flowers in Cap-Rouge buried in the flesh of the young negro girls who turn sixteen this year!

Yes, when a good dozen more of them have ripened in the sun of his fabulous member, then he will be ready to embrace death, his duty to fill with wonder carried out to the full. Let him continue to plough and impregnate a few more of the fertile fields which are clamouring for the attentions of Alcindor's ploughshare! Let him dabble his bare feet of the Tropics in the eager fountains of the young negresses of Cap-Rouge for the greater good of the plants, the torrents, the rainfall, and the future hopes of the region!

It was Andréus Limabial who caught the name of Okil Okilon on the lips of the dying man. He understood immediately that his brother-in-law wanted to throw a final dice. Why had no one thought of Okilon and his skills? Probably because of his reputation of taking the side of evil spirits against the well-being of living Christian souls. Okilon was known to be a downright assassin. Not only did he hasten the departure of his patients, but after the burial he would go and wake them up again and force them to work as zombies on his land. He was an enemy of life. Alcindor knew that as well as anyone. But, nevertheless, he was asking for him. The wish of a dying man is sacred. Perhaps for the first time in his life, Okil Okilon was about to find himself coming across a negro better hung than himself!

Okil Okilon arrived at the Alcindor household at dusk. He was amazed by his summons to the deathbed of someone like Dieuveille Alcindor, who had never acknowledged him. It had often occurred to him that this negro with the reputation of a stallion would make a prize piece in his collection of zombies. He had never imagined that his wish would be granted so soon. Okilon's left eye gleamed with unbounded joy, whilst his right eye endeavoured to track down with the help of an enormous magnifying glass the symptoms of the illness which was carrying Alcindor off. With the help of the magnifying glass he explored the sick man's body at length, pore by pore, taking each ball in turn, as if he were dealing with the delicate mechanism of a clock. When he had finished his examination, the famous *bocor*[3] took a little red flag out of his pocket and began to wave it over Alcindor's body as a signal of victory.

'General Dieuveille Alcindor,' declared Okilon, 'your cure is called *houari*.[4] That's the seed that I saw shining in the magnifying glass over most of your organs. In the same magnifying glass I saw a rainbow arch between your heart and your privates. Yes, all the colours of life are still lit in that fine negro flesh of yours. The *houari* is the red and black shield of nature which is going to ward off the attacks of that damned malaria which has sworn to get you. General Houari is the benefactor of the blood of living Christian souls! He will go on guard in you henceforth! Everyone here present, raise your voices in gratitude to the red and black epaulettes of General Houari!

'Long live Papa-Houari, and thanks be to him, now and ever shall be, so be it, amen!' cried out the family in unison.

Now, nobody could take their eyes off the miraculous kernel which master Okilon held delicately between his thumb and index finger. It was a sort of red and black nut, slightly oval in shape, of the same size as an ortolan's egg.

'Mammy Cécilia,' said Okilon, 'for three days you must give an infusion of *houari* to that lucky husband of yours. In order to get this

[3] A *houngan* practising black magic.
[4] A type of wild nut.

royal medicine to have its full effect, the nut must be passed over the fire. Not just any wood fire. In the case of Dieuveille Alcindor, the youngest woman of the household must pass naked over the hearth three times so that her young blood can mix with the protective power of the fire. My name is not Okil Okilon if, on the fourth day following the treatment, our patient is not ready to rise from his bed and climb a coconut tree!'

Okilon handed over the sachet of *houaris* to Cécilia Alcindor. He put the magnifying glass back in its leather pouch and, before taking his leave, thought it necessary to insist on an important detail of the prescription:

'Above all, don't forget that if the *houari* is to produce the miraculous effect we want, it must first of all pass through the fire of the most intrepid vagina of the household. And I mean the most lyrically vaginal fire of the household! Goodbye!'

'Goodbye, master Okilon,' called the family, dumbfounded.

Cécilia Alcindor straightaway set about preparing the health-giving prescription. She lit a virile fire of pinewood beneath the arbour. Marianna, the young garden-wife known for her charms, stripped off completely. Three times over, she performed a dance of life worthy of her seventeen years above the flames which leapt up joyfully between her open legs. No one had realized up to then that the swell of her breasts and her buttocks beneath her dress hid such marvels of sparkling good form. When she had blessed the fire, instead of getting dressed she went into the room where Dieuveille lay and repeated over his body, without touching him, the ritual dance which she had just performed over the fire.

Cécilia, meanwhile, had had what seemed to her an inspired idea. Why not infuse three kernels of *houari* at once for poor Dieuveille? Three would surely have more effect overnight than just one. Three generals, that would make a whole army headquarters to outsmart the manoeuvres of the enemy sickness in papa Ti-Dor's body!

A moment later, Alcindor had the impression he was rediscovering in the spoonfuls being administered to him the flavour of Marianna's fresh hormones, drunk at the fountain of her seventeen years . . .

The next morning, when Cécilia went in to say good morning to her husband, she remained rooted to the spot in the doorway for several minutes. Then the whole of Cap-Rouge jumped as she began screaming in horror. Instead of the painfully familiar face of papa Ti-Dor, she saw a white man's mask on the pillow. Andréus, Dorée, Marianna, and Emulsion-Scott were forced to the same indisputable conclusion: a white man lay sleeping in Dieuveille Alcindor's place. There was a headlong rush outside to the edge of the property. Buffalo followed them out of the room, howling lugubriously. The hamlet was mobilized in an instant. A group of brave volunteers eventually formed, with Okil Okilon at their head. Okilon was the first to venture into Alcindor's bedroom: he took three steps before passing out. The other *houngans*, sticking closely together, waited for a considerable time before advancing towards the bed of the white ghost. The stranger woke up and stared at them blankly. Tonton Dérance, the most senior of the 'leaf-doctors', had a sudden inspiration:

'Monsieur,' he said respectfully, 'could you tell us what has happened to Dieuveille Alcindor, beloved son of Cap-Rouge?'

When he heard this name, the stranger suddenly sat up. He looked down at his hands and his legs. He rubbed his eyes as though to convince himself that he was not the victim of a hallucination. He asked for a mirror. As soon as he was placed in the presence of his own image, he let out such a harrowing scream that the scalp of everyone who heard it for miles around turned into a hedgehog. Dieuveille Alcindor had just been faced with the image of a white man bursting with health who was none other than Dieuveille Alcindor himself! Once again he found himself alone in the room, his terrified visitors having taken to their heels.

'When will my Calvary end?' Dieuveille Alcindor asked himself. Since he had been taken away from Cap-Rouge, his despair had proceeded through countless stations. He wasn't carrying his cross on his shoulders, like Papa-Jésus, it was dispersed throughout his body, diffuse, flesh of his most intimate flesh, incorporated in each of his pigments. Even his shadow had not remained loyal to him. He carried his longing to be a native-born negro with him wherever he went, and neither the sun nor women could help him.

For the doctors of Port-au-Prince, Dieuveille Alcindor was the strange case that had been sent to them from Jacmel. They were carrying out all sorts of research and observations on the peasant from Cap-Rouge who had become as white as a Dane after drinking a decoction of *houari*. They had before their very eyes a human phenomenon whose genetic adventure could be of interest to international scientific milieux. The correspondent of the United Press International alerted world opinion to the dangerous precedent that Alcindor represented for the future of white hegemony of the planet. Dieuveille Alcindor's photo appeared on the front of *Time Magazine*. In all the great capitals of the world, people asked what would happen to white supremacy if all the negroes of the earth suddenly decided to launch an offensive with this extraordinary *houari* from the Haitian brush. Unscrupulous traffickers could start smuggling this biological narcotic across the Carribbean, Brazil, and Africa. No white man would ever again feel safe in the skin he has by divine right. The press in South Africa were already predicting the crossing of the lowest of the Bantus into Afrikaner identity. The tides of 'negro barbarism' were becoming uncontrollable . . .

Dieuveille Alcindor was kept under observation for several months in Port-au-Prince. His return to Jacmel brought no change to his condition of double existence. Hundreds of people were waiting for him at the entry to the small town and he was carried in triumph. He was asked for his impressions of his stay in the capital. He contented himself with murmuring in reply that he had lived his time there harrowed by his desire to recover the negro from Tortuga Island. The prettiest girls in Jacmel were begging for his autograph. What would he sign with? He bore his cross on his soul. His princely sex organ had fallen asleep. The white shroud that Okil Okilon had cut exactly to his size caused him discomfort in every fold and twist of his zombie's body.

He arrived in Cap-Rouge the same January afternoon. He had spent months encountering the loneliness and the mockery of fame. At the sight of his hamlet perched in the intimate blue of the dusk, he picked up a handful of soil and sprinkled it gently over his head. He felt a strange mixture of hatred and love, despair and desperate hope. His tears could have taught the whole world something. The inhabitants of Cap-Rouge took flight at his approach. He walked the full distance to his house along a path even more deserted than the pavements of his life. The rosebay and the begonias of yesteryear shrank back from his approach with the same reaction of terror as the humans and the animals. He found his key on the doorstep already rusting away. He threw himself down on a chair covered in dust and cobwebs. He sank into sleep anchored by the ghost ship which he had become. The following day, he tried in vain to scrape up a friend. He soon learned that zombies have no friends.

The next morning, at the edge of a field of corn, he heard a rustling of leaves behind him: it was Marianna. He looked in her eyes and discovered straightaway that his white man's face was as lovingly received as the negro one he had lost. He entered Marianna superbly. For years and years afterwards their lovemaking had a fantastic influence on the pattern of rainfall and on the quantity of the crops of Cap-Rouge.

FRÉDÉRIC FAJARDIE (b. 1947)

The Underwear of the Woman Up Above

Translated by Elizabeth Fallaize

He was standing waiting, hands in his pockets, under the close surveillance of two of his colleagues.

His gaze was lost somewhere in the distance, over towards the grey-green river and its deserted banks.

The man in his forties with the vacant air was David Koppelmann and he felt weary, wretched, and sunk in gloom.

Superintendent Koppelmann lent a fevered brow against the cold glass of the window.

The contrast between the overheated interior of the building and the outside temperature was turning the condensation into a thin layer of frost, vaguely reminiscent of lace.

He leant back slightly, searched through one of his pockets and brought out a crumpled packet of Chesterfields.

With an unsteady hand, he lit a cigarette and, half turning round, examined a door bearing a plate with the words: 'Police Complaints Authority'.

The two inspectors who were 'escorting' him exchanged an amused look and then the younger one drew closer and challenged:

'Hey you, Koppelmann, how much did you get paid for pulling that dirty trick of yours?'

Without turning round, the Superintendent replied in a hard-edged voice:

'Lay off, you little shit. I'm still your superior officer.'

The other man gave a tremulous laugh, and turned towards the older inspector, who gave a warning signal.

The wait got longer and longer.

The two inspectors had sat down on a bench and were talking women, cars, horses . . . As time went by their surveillance had slackened, as if Koppelmann, still standing slightly hunched over in front of the window, was unlikely to attempt an escape or indulge in heroics.

So they were taken by surprise when the Superintendent opened the window.

The older of the two inspectors rushed at him, then pulled up short and stood stock still, open-mouthed.

With a melancholy smile, Koppelmann said to him:

'Well, what? It's a paper aeroplane, that's all.'

The inspector shook his head with a disapproving air, recognizing the summons from the Complaints Authority.

Then, in a pained tone of voice, he advised:

'Koppelmann, in your position, I wouldn't make things worse for yourself with displays of idiotic behaviour.'

Koppelmann scrutinized his colleague carefully then threw the paper aeroplane out into the courtyard of the Police Headquarters. There was something childish in his attitude, like a kid deliberately defying the rules.

'It's taken off!' he observed in a neutral tone.

'So have you!' retorted the inspector who was unable, nevertheless, to take his eyes off the scrap of paper carried off by a wind from the west.

'I haven't taken off,' said Koppelmann, after a long silence. Then, with a touch of sharpness, he added: 'On the contrary, I've just come down to earth.'

'Yeah, and landed in the nick!' said the young inspector who had come up to join them.

His older colleague saw Koppelmann withdraw. He was particularly sorry because he would have liked to have engaged the Superintendent in conversation, tried to understand what had led him to this form of professional suicide.

So it was in a brusque tone that he instructed his colleague:

'Go and have a game of pinball. No, go and have a hundred games. At the double!'

'Pardon?'

'Go on, scarper!'

The man turned crimson, bit back the torrent of insults on his lips, then left, taking such enormous strides that he almost slipped right over on the polished floor.

'What a shit!' said the inspector.

'We're all shits!' replied Koppelmann.

'What do you mean, all?'

'You, me, the big shots behind that door, Gagarin, Cousteau, out there in space or at the bottom of the sea. Man is in his essence a little shit.'

'You're not much of a laugh!'

Koppelmann smiled:

'That is also man's grandeur. The guy who knows fundamentally, coldly, definitively, and I would even say courageously, that he's nothing but a poor little shit, that guy has the advantage, morally and intellectually, over the big shits.'

'The big shits?' questioned the inspector, frowning.

'Yes. The big shits that run the world. You know, the presidents, the generals, the capitalists, or the bureaucrats. Those guys, the big megalomaniac shits, their only role in life is to reinforce the State, and to mould it in their own image.'

'How do you see it all working? I mean: in practice.'

Koppelmann paused for thought and automatically reached for his packet of Chesterfields. Realizing that it was empty, he screwed it up into a ball and threw it out of the window. Then, noticing the packet of Gauloises held out by the inspector, he helped himself and lit his cigarette with a hand trembling with nervous tension.

Finally, he slowly exhaled the smoke and, gazing fixedly at a barge on the river, replied:

'When I see barges on the Seine in winter, only in winter, it makes me think of *L'Atalante*. I was mad about Juliette Dita Parlo when I was twenty.'

'You didn't answer my question.'

'What question?' Koppelmann asked, turning towards him.

'Well . . . You said something or other about the State, the big shits.'

'Yes. I'll put it in simple terms: the State is moulded by the big shits. The big shits are essentially shitty. Conclusion: the State is essentially shitty.'

The inspector gave a short bark of laughter.

'You're awe-inspiring, you are.'

Koppelmann jumped.

'Shit—I can't believe you said that.'

'Why?'

Koppelmann returned his attention to the river and then, in an almost husky voice, replied:

'That's what she used to say to me. She used to laugh as well, when she said it.'

'Who did?'

'Miss Lizzy.'

'Who?'

Koppelmann waved his hands in a gesture of helplessness.

'You wouldn't understand.'

'Try me. By the way, do you mind me calling you "tu"?'

Koppelmann shook his head.

'I'm up for dismissal. It could happen.'

The inspector waved his hands in a gesture of helplessness, one of those gestures which accompanies phrases of the kind: 'You went looking for it, didn't you?'

Then he decided to wait a bit longer before tackling the central question.

'Miss who?'

'Miss Lizzy. I should say "Dizzy Miss Lizzy", because that's what I called her . . . Yeah, a modern story, hang on, what do they call it? Ah yes, in tune with its times.'

'Come on Koppelmann, don't make me beg for it: spill the beans!'

'There was a girl who lived in the flat up above me. I used to hear her high heels on the floorboards . . . At first, it left me cold. And then bit by bit, I got to like the sound, I'd wait for it, listen out for it . . . And then I started thinking that there, thirty centimetres above my head, were her high heels, her feet, her ankles, her thighs. I started thinking about the underwear of the woman up above. I started thinking that without that blasted ceiling, I could reach out my arm and touch her warm thighs. I needed them, those warm thighs. Maybe because I was alone. I even wanted to die, strangled by her warm thighs. In the end, I couldn't stand it any longer.'

'You were really hooked,' noted the inspector.

'Totally hooked, that's right! I recorded the sound of the heels and then I would play it back at night through my earphones. I used to listen to it like some people count sheep, but you've got to be twisted to count sheep—why not count pink elephants in swimming trunks while you're about it. Anyway, I had an hour of recorded female footsteps . . .'

'That wasn't enough?' questioned the inspector, puzzled.

'Hang on, I went on to a more acute phase! One day I moved my wardrobe and I put it under the girl's route, her route to the bathroom. I stuck some pillows and blankets up there, and I lay down with my nose right up against the ceiling.'

'What?'

'You heard. I spent two hours up there every day.'

'But why?'

'I had no idea. And then in the end, I realized. Give or take a few centimetres of flooring and plaster, a few miserable centimetres, she was trampling over me. She was walking on my face, piercing my cheeks with her pointed heels. She was wading through my flesh, between the ribs. She was crushing my cock and my balls . . .'

'Christ you're a pervert, a real pervert, you are!'

Koppelmann burst out laughing then put a friendly hand on the inspector's shoulder.

'No, no mate! I love looking at a woman from underneath. Try it, lie down on the floor, and ask your girlfriend to stand over you, just above your head, her ankles against your ears. It's like being back at school! Like when you used to bend over to look up the teacher's skirt when she was going up the stairs a few steps ahead of you.'

The inspector thought about it, with a puzzled air, searching through his childhood memories. Then, convinced, he nodded his head and asked: 'And then?'

'Then? You know up to then I'd been discreet, silent, self-effacing. One day she was walking about in new shoes with stiletto heels . . . It was long after the wardrobe episode, you know? Well I put on a Stones record, *Satisfaction*, and let it rip. The footsteps stopped, straightaway. I played it again, ten times. Each time the footsteps stopped. So I had got myself identified. Next I had to let her know who I was. I put on *She's not there*, by the Zombies, then *Go now* by the Moody Blues, *Gloria* by Them. I was playing *Dizzie Miss Lizzie* at top volume when the doorbell rang.

'Was it her?'

'It was her. She looked at me, I took her hand, pulled her inside, kissed her . . .'

'Fantastic! Nice work! And you married her and spent your honeymoon on top of the wardrobe for old times' sake.'

Koppelmann looked gloomy.

'No. I slept with her. But she took exception to my fantasies and, suddenly, her footsteps, up above, started to annoy me. More and more. In fact I couldn't bear them.'

'But . . . But why?'

'I told you, I'm a little shit of the manic depressive variety. So I moved.'

The inspector waved his hands in a gesture of helplessness.

'I don't understand you.'

'There's nothing to understand. Look around you, open your eyes! On the roads, bandits are robbing travellers. Others are robbing corpses dug up from Paris cemeteries. In Italy blokes are pillaging trains as if they were in the American West in the nineteenth century. Add to that that there are pirate ships off the coast of Thailand and you see what a marvellous epoch we're living in, in 1985. And, since you're not completely brainless, you can make the connection between this giant step backwards and what the powers-that-be are always telling us about information technology and everyday life. Get it?'

'Ok, you've got a point. But why did you let out all the guys locked up in your police cells?'

Koppelmann made an evasive gesture, as if to say that that was a matter of very little consequence.

'What was it? Four whores? A transvestite? Two thugs? Guys arrested for thefts from parked vehicles, drunkenness on the public highway, non-payment of restaurant bills, insults to police officers, and rebellion?'

'You'd also got a bloke locked up who'd eaten his wife in daily portions of a hundred grams. Very nice!'

'Trifles, mate. Nothing but little shits. I said to them: "Go in peace and sin no more."'

'But why? Why?'

Koppelmann walked nervously up and down and, taking the heavens as witness, declared:

'He wants to know why! To see them run, of course! See them run like rats out of all the exits of the Police Station while their guards looked on in amazement!'

'It's not right to do just as you please like that, because otherwise . . . Well, where would it end! . . . Hey, what's up with you?'

Koppelmann lurched his way over to the bench, then said, with the air of a man at the end of his tether:

'I feel tired! And depressed! I've been tired and depressed for months!'

The inspector bent down and stared into Koppelmann's eyes at length before asking, with a faint shadow of a smile:

'Is that what you're going to tell them?'

The Superintendent gave him a crafty look and—with the air of a man in perfect health—replied:

'That's what I'm going to tell them. This time.'

And, very slowly, Koppelmann closed his eye in a wink addressed to the inspector.

The latter smiled. Timidly at first and then broadly.

And he winked back, repeating:

'You're awe-inspiring, you are! Yes, truly awe-inspiring!'

ANNIE SAUMONT (b. 1927)

The Finest Story in the World

Translated by Elizabeth Fallaize

Okay. Let's get things properly organized. Yes. The list. As usual.

She tears a page out from her notebook. Someone's gone off with my pencil again.

dry-cleaner's
Medical bumph
parent's evening—Charlène
appointment paediatrician
water hydrangeas
paint velux
adaptor
cleaning stuff
frozen food order

She gets back from the dry-cleaner's. Crosses that off. She fills in the medical expenses claim form. Jean had flu then asthma. Jean's the one who docsn't want to go and live with his mother. She sticks the stamps on the form. Must get Pascal to sign it and send it off to his firm's insurance.

Parent's evening. Five o'clock sharp. She can drop the baby off at the playgroup.

Velux. That can wait.

There's another thing—not on the list, in her head—always being shelved, always back on the table that will have to get done one day, her wild dream of writing the finest story in the world.

Yes, everyone knows. *The Finest Story in the World* goes back nearly a century. For Kipling it was the story of the writer who tries to tell the finest story in the world but who abandons his project when the bank clerk holding the key to the story falls in love with the young salesgirl taken on by the tobacconist. And loses all interest in the story.

Woman, then, is an obstacle to writing.

But there are women who write.

She writes.

When she gets a spare minute. When everything is sparkling. When the final of the Cupwinner's Cup is live on television and she can forget that she lives with a man who needs a sympathetic listener in the evenings. After a good dinner.

She starts cooking. She starts writing. The osso bucco bubbles gently then turns to cinders. She opens all the windows, puts the charred pan in to soak. Gets out a tin of sausages with lentils, meal-in-a-minute. No way is a burnt dinner going to mean the end of the finest story in the world. She's going to get this story written. Just as soon as she's scrawled an affectionate invitation to Aunt Josiane to come for the weekend—poor Aunt Josiane, lonely and depressed.

vacuum bag
tax payment
repot geraniums
clear chest of drawers
shorten curtains

She's writing.

She's writing in her notebooks. She enters it into the Mac. She writes while the baby's asleep. She writes between bouts of anxiety—has he vomited his bottle? That little spot on his cheek that she noticed just now, could it be the first symptom of some infectious illness? Why is he so quiet? She runs to check if he's still breathing.

She's writing. She's not writing. Charlène is whining, nobody likes me. Charlène is complaining that she's fat and ugly. Don't be so silly. Look at yourself in the mirror. I got D in my end of term test. Ooh! that's rather different. Charlène resolves to give up chocolate eclairs and to go through her homework in future with her mother.

go through homework
sort out winter clothes
ironing
mothball cupboards
senior citizens' club visit
press-studs, 50 cm velcro tape
fruit vegetables
subscription TV magazine

Jean wants to have his friends round one Saturday evening. For a mega rock and rap session. She shudders. Had no idea what she was taking on when she agreed to be a stepmum. Chin up, others have been in the same boat. Listen Jean, we'll see. Just now I have to write. And it's time for your basketball training.

Write? says Jean. Write to who? Nobody writes any more. What for, with mobiles. . . .

She's not writing. She is writing. In between she decides that the kids can use the garage and make sandwiches in the kitchen on condition that . . . But what's the point in having conditions when the promises are bound to be broken, recriminations inevitable . . . Don't let Jean get on at you advises Pascal, retreating to the safety of his study. This from a man who has never been able to say no to his son.

From a man who has a study.

A room of one's own. How can she sort out a refuge for herself in a house of modest proportions in which the children all have their own room and Dad has a study?

There is no bar on writing the finest story in the world on the kitchen table. Nor on thinking about questions of syntax whilst stirring the tomato coulis with a wooden spoon.

Charlène's long hair is infested with vermin. The school nurse said to take emergency measures. Don't want my hair shaved off. The shampoo guarantees the nits will die a perfumed death. To be repeated twice more this week. Nits in the baby's hair. Bugs in the word processing system. Women and computers, Jean sniggers. You just pressed *shift* when you should've pressed *alt*. Shall I put it right for you, he suggests, good Samaritan. Okay, for the rock and rap session she will supply an enormous pizza and a whole crate of cans of coke. She will send Charlène off to her best friend's house for the night. And suggest to Pascal that it's about time they visited the grandmothers. She and Pascal and the baby will stay with one or other of them until Sunday afternoon. Heaving out through the hatchback a mountain of stuff, folding cot, high chair, pack of nappies, jars of baby food, inflatable bath, cleansing milk. Hello stranger. Thought you'd forgotten you had parents. Armelle—(Jean again)—Armelle, is my Beachmania T-shirt ready? Still in the dirty washing basket! I've got nothing left to wear.

Baby's gums are sore. Can she imagine writing the finest story in the world with her right hand, whilst rocking a baby with teeth coming through in the crook of her left arm?

I hate to disturb you, says Pascal, I don't suppose by any chance you've seen . . .

Have I seen, haven't I seen, what can I say (the missing folder, the watch that Pascal takes off and puts down in a different place every night, the credit card that he is quite sure he put away in its case, Jean's gameboy, Charlène's fluorescent pogs). See nothing, say nothing, hear nothing, keeping her head down, she writes. Ever since she was a kid she's dreamed of being a writer. Without ever telling her parents, they would have shrugged their shoulders, where does she get these funny ideas. Her mother would have added that girls need only

Yes: spin wool and keep house.

Peace at last. Then the telephone.

Elsa, her best friend from way back. Hello Armelle, Gérard is having an affair.

Look Elsa, you've thought this too many times before.

Armelle, this time I swear he is.

The tenth time at least (the twentieth even?) that Elsa has rung her in desperation, Help he's having an affair. That could be the subject of the saddest story in the world. And the most farcical.

The computer is purring. Charlène, watch the plug. Have I saved it. Pascal opens the door a crack, Armelle, would you have a second to read over my article, you're so good at spelling.

Charlène is complaining, the baby is just ridiculous, throws everything he's given on the floor. Next time, young man, I am not picking your car up. The Ferrari crashes noisily to the floor. Too bad, I warned you. The baby starts howling.

Just at that moment the health visitor rings at the door. Sorry, just a routine visit, don't take it the wrong way.

She doesn't take it the wrong way. Sighs.

While I'm here I wanted to let you know that the old lady next door is having problems remembering things. Perhaps you could, discreetly . . . Mum, you said you'd help me make some paper flowers, the teacher wants them for the school fête. You haven't got time ? Don't be surprised then when I don't get to move up to secondary school next year.

Wednesday. The kids out of school in the neighbourhood are making a racket. The play area down the street is showered in bits of glass. It takes her for ever to pick them up. What is the best way to give meaning to life? Write the finest story in the world or rid the planet of broken glass?

Or take a lover. She'll pick a good one. Rich and loving and generous. She'll talk to him. When they've made love. Pascal goes to sleep after lovemaking. The lover will listen to her. She'll tell him about writing, about how demanding it is. He'll understand.

He'll take her away from this place. Somewhere where no one needs her any more. Pascal will have to cope with Jean's behaviour, Charlène's moods, his aspirations in senior management, his choice of tie, the baby's vaccinations. And the plumbing. Far away beneath a panoramic blue sky she'll open her notebooks and fill them up in future without wasting any pages on lists of domestic tasks, blissfully untroubled by thoughts of shopping baskets.

No. There would be regrets and remorse. The pain of having hurt and betrayed. There would be anguish. The sky has turned grey.

And the finest story in the world will never be written.

MONIQUE PROULX (b. 1952)

Public Transit

Translated by Matt Cohen

Her raincoat rustled stiffly as she jumped between the tracks. She didn't fall, which was surprising for a body so tall and uncoordinated. And now she stands peacefully, her purse hanging securely from her shoulder. She is doing as the others are doing, she is waiting for the subway—but not in order to get in, obviously.

The news spreads like stomach flu through the rush-hour crowd, everyone in the Berri station gathers at the platform to watch; people realize that they are witnessing, right before their eyes, the unfolding of a drama, and it makes them happy and excited, most of them have never seen a real suicide—in flesh and raincoat, as I was telling you.

A certain Conrad is among the crowd; he sells shoes at Pegabo and he's a little shorter than average, which means he is unable to see the show. But he instantly understands that something unusual is happening and he moves closer, like the others, trying to be part of the adventure. People are murmuring to each other like old friends; 'She's in desperate straits,' calls out a tall man who can see everything and has probably read a lot. Conrad manages to elbow his way to the front row and then he sees her. She is wearing glasses, is in her thirties, not too attractive, eclipsed by her ordinariness, and by the big black raincoat which fits her awkwardly. She turns her back on everyone, as though to state that this whole scene has nothing to do with her, then she slowly makes her way towards the black mouth of the tunnel, where the rumble of a moving train can already be heard. To see her like that, so peaceful, it's impossible to understand—she's not the type to have been disappointed in love, she's not the type to have been through anything, and maybe that's reason enough for her to stand resignedly in front of a homicidal subway train.

Someone near Conrad screams, 'Somebody *do* something!' and Conrad, after a slightly confused delay, realizes that this hare-brained call has come from himself. Around him the others signal their agreement by nodding their heads fatalistically, yes, of course, something must be done, but what, what can you do about death and isn't it already too late, the train is coming, poor poor girl, poor children poor parents of this poor girl. The train is coming, Conrad doesn't want to be the one, he never did, the train is coming, its mechanical howl is rising like a fever, it's too late for the controllers, too late to discuss things with the girl and convince her—of what, in fact? Miss, life *is* worth the trouble, stay alive, miss, if no one loves you I will love you . . . How could she believe him, he who loves only men? Suddenly Conrad leaps into the trench and, without thinking, jumps on the girl, half knocking her out; his strength unleashed, he throws her onto the platform like a bale of hay and hurls himself after her.

Just then, out of the blue, a television crew appears in front of Conrad. Dazed by the spotlights, he is raised to the crowd's shoulders and applauded. The girl in the raincoat takes off her glasses and her raincoat. Underneath she is as beautiful as the girls in the before-and-after beauty parlour ads. She explains to Conrad that it was all a live televised test of everyday heroism, he is the winner, is he happy? Conrad is interviewed on 'The Journal' and 'Pam Wallin Live', he's on the front pages of all the next day's newspapers, Jean Chrétien gives him a tie, the Pope faxes him forgiveness for his sins, he gets the Legion of Honour and the St. Jean Baptiste Cross.

The whole thing makes Conrad sick. He has to change jobs because women are harassing him—are you the one who's the hero, can I touch you? . . . Now he doesn't use the subway any more. He walks. And when he finds himself stopped at a red light, beside a blind man, for example, he doesn't help him cross the street the way he would have before, no sir; he gives him a discreet little shove so he'll fall on his face.

Biographical Notes

MARCEL AYMÉ (1902–67). A somewhat controversial figure, Aymé was a non-conformist who attacked hypocrisy in a number of quarters, including the intellectual left and the legal establishment. Brought up on a farm in the Jura, his novels, plays, and short stories often use rural settings to great effect. His immensely popular novel *The Green Mare* (1933) upset some critics with its bawdy rural humour, but it was subsequently made into a highly successful film. His best-known short story collection is *The Walker-through-Walls* (1943), marked by a strong vein of fantasy and comedy.

HONORÉ DE BALZAC (1799–1850). One of France's best-known nineteenth-century novelists and author of *The Human Comedy*, which groups together over eighty separate short stories and novels, depicting a huge range of social and geographical spheres of French contemporary life. His family intended him to be a lawyer, but, after a slow start, Balzac became an immensely popular writer, famously working furiously late into the night clad in a monk's robe in order to fulfil his ambition to be 'society's secretary', and to meet his many deadlines. A great deal of his work has been translated into English, including, amongst the short stories, *Selected Short Stories* (Penguin Classics) and *The Unknown Master-piece*. Novels include *Père Goriot* (1834), *Eugénie Grandet* (1833), *Lost Illusions* (1837), and *Cousin Bette* (1846).

CHRISTIANE BAROCHE (b. 1935). By training a scientist at the Curie Institute in Paris, Baroche is the author of a number of novels, poetry, and some noted collections of short stories, including *Chambres, avec vue sur le passé* (1978) which won the Goncourt prize for the best short story collection. In 1995 she published a novel entitled *La Rage au bois dormant* which takes up the story of Madame de Merteuil, the heroine of Laclos's *Dangerous Liaisons*, after her disfigurement from smallpox and flight from Paris. None of her work is currently translated into English, with the exception of the story in this volume.

SIMONE DE BEAUVOIR (1908–86). Novelist, philosopher, autobiographer, and author of *The Second Sex* (1949), a founding text of twentieth-century feminism. Her two short story collections are both translated into English: *The Woman Destroyed* (1968) and *When Things of the Spirit Come First*, published in 1979 but written in the 1930s. Much of Beauvoir's work is available in translation, including *Memoirs of a Dutiful Daughter* (1958), her first volume of autobiography describing her Catholic bourgeois upbringing, and her means of escape from it; *A Very Easy Death* (1964), an account of her mother's death; and the novels *She Came to Stay* (1943) and *The Mandarins* (1954), winner of the Goncourt prize.

Biographical Notes

ALBERT CAMUS (1913–60). Born and brought up in Algeria, Camus went to France for treatment for tuberculosis in 1942 and became a well-known resistance figure. His novels *The Outsider* (1942), a fictional vision of the absurd, and *The Plague* (1947), an allegorical representation of the German Occupation and of totalitarian regimes in general, made him one of the most widely read authors of twentieth-century France. His short story collection *Exile and the Kingdom* (1957) won him the Nobel prize for literature; he died in a car accident three years later before completing *The First Man*, released in 1994 and also translated into English.

COLETTE (full name Sidonie-Gabrielle Colette, 1873–1954). Born in Burgundy, Colette went to Paris at the age of 20 when she married Willy (Henri Gauthers-Villars), under whose tutelage she produced her four hugely successful Claudine novels, which include *Claudine at School* (1900) and *Claudine in Paris* (1901). Later she left Willy, became a music-hall artiste, and embarked on a series of independent works almost all of which are translated into English—see, for example, *Cheri* (1920) and *Break of Day* (1928). She became a major figure of the literary establishment in later life. A hundred of her stories are available in English in *The Collected Stories of Colette*.

ALPHONSE DAUDET (1840–97). Usually associated with the Naturalist tradition of French writing, Daudet published stories and novels relating principally to scenes of life in Provence, where he was brought up, or to the Franco-Prussian War (1870–1), which ended in humiliating defeat for France and the loss of two captured provinces, Alsace and Lorraine. Collections available in English include *Letters from My Windmill* (1869), *La Belle Nivernaise and Other Stories*, and *Monday Tales* (1873).

RENÉ DEPESTRE (b. 1926). Born in Haiti, Depestre's early work was an exuberant defence of revolution. Since 1946, he has mainly lived in exile, including fifteen years in Cuba, which he left in 1979 to work with Unesco in Paris. An opponent of 'negritude', the literary and cultural movement of black solidarity which arose in the 1930s, Depestre went on to write lyrical poetry and prose celebrating love and eroticism, such as *A Rainbow for the Christian West* (1967), *The Festival of the Greasy Pole* (1979), and *Vegetations of Splendour* (1973).

BIRAGO DIOP (1906–89). Senegalese writer born in Dakar. After qualifying as a vet he was appointed to work in Western Sudan, where he began to collect the folk-tales and legends of French West Africa. *Tales of Amadou Koumba* (1966) collects together stories taken from a trilogy of volumes of tales published between 1947 and 1963. Diop also published other short fiction, poems, and autobiographical volumes. He became an ambassador for the newly independent republic of Senegal in the early 1960s.

ASSIA DJEBAR (pseudonym of Fatima-Zohra Imalayène, b. 1936). Born in Algeria, Djebar studied in Algiers, Tunis, and Paris before taking up a university teaching post in history. Currently living mainly in France, Djebar has also worked in the theatre and cinema, directing a number of films. Her work foregrounds Algerian women's experience of the family, of social constraints, and of the effects of the Algerian War, the struggle for independence from France lasting from 1954 to 1962. *Women of Algiers in their Apartments,* her first collection of short stories, was published in 1980; also available in translation is the novel *So Vast the Prison* and *Fantasia: An Algerian Cavalcade* (1985), interspersing autobiographical anecdote with accounts of the French conquest of Algeria.

FRÉDÉRIC FAJARDIE (b. 1947). Popular contemporary writer who has published more than forty novels and collections of short stories, as well as writing scripts for cinema and TV films. Many of his titles include the word 'noir', flagging his connection to the tradition of the 'roman noir' or thriller, and to detective fiction. His work has a strong political, anarchist tendency. None of it is yet available in English, with the exception of the story included here.

GUSTAVE FLAUBERT (1821–80). Flaubert's only collection of short stories, *Three Tales* (1887), was published very near the end of his life. By that time a celebrated writer, today he is considered one of the great figures of world literature. His first major work, *Madame Bovary* (1857), a tale of provincial adultery and frustration, displays the ideals of perfection of style and composition to which he remained committed throughout his writing. *A Sentimental Education* (1869) follows the unremarkable adventures of a hero of Flaubert's own generation, set against the events of the Second Empire. *Salammbô* (1862), set in Carthage, and the unfinished *Bouvard and Pécuchet,* on which he was working at the time of his death, are also available in English.

THÉOPHILE GAUTIER (1811–72). Poet, critic, and novelist, associated with the formalist Art for Art's Sake movement that emerged in France during the 1830s. Gautier's preface to his novel *Mademoiselle de Maupin* (1835–6, available in English), designed to scandalize a bourgeois audience with its sexual confusions, became the manifesto of the movement. Baudelaire dedicated his *Flowers of Evil* to Gautier. His short story collections often emphasize the fantastic; story collections available in English include *Tales before Supper* and *Great Ghost Stories: Mummy's Foot and Tree Ghosts.*

HERVÉ GUIBERT (1955–91). Journalist, photographer, and author of more than twenty books, Guibert became a household name with a work entitled *To the Friend Who Did Not Save My Life* (1990), dealing with his fight against AIDS. Far from being merely a grim journal, the work raised issues that touched a wide audience; three other books appeared in his lifetime, including a follow-up, *The Compassion Protocol* (1991). He died in 1991, aged 36. Posthumously published works available in English include *The Man in the Red Hat* (1992), a novel, and *Cytomegalovirus* (1992), a hospital diary.

JORIS-KARL HUYSMANS (1848–1907). A writer initially associated with Émile Zola and the literary project of Naturalism, Huysmans published *Against Nature* in

1884, a novel which was to attain cult status as a bible of decadence and dandyism, the dominant mode of the *fin de siècle*. The short story 'Knapsack at the Ready' was part of a collection of stories all by representatives of the Naturalist movement, entitled *Les Soirées de Médan* (1880). Also available in English are: *Là-bas (Down There)* (1891), his second major novel, and *The Cathedral* (1898), a work marking his return to Catholicism.

GUY DE MAUPASSANT (1850–93). Born and brought up by his mother in Normandy, where many of his short stories are set, Maupassant achieved great success with the form during his lifetime and is today considered one of its finest practitioners. The meanness of the Normandy peasant, the horrors of the Franco-Prussian War, in which he took part, and the hypocrisy of bourgeois society were constant themes in a body of work marked by a deep pessimism. He died insane in an asylum, aged 42. There are many translated collections of his stories, including *A Day in the Country*, *Mademoiselle Fifi*, and *The Horla*. His best-known novel *Pierre and Jean* (1888) is also available in English.

PROSPER MÉRIMÉE (1803–70). An inspector of historical monuments who worked tirelessly to conserve France's architectural heritage, Mérimée was also the author of *Carmen* (1847), the tale which provided the basis for Bizet's popular opera, and of a relatively small number of other short stories whose reputation has made him one of the best-known French practitioners of the genre. Most of the stories create tragic outcomes, undercut by irony and ambiguity. *Carmen and Other Stories* contains five of his most famous stories.

MONIQUE PROULX (b. 1952). A young French-Canadian writer, Monique Proulx has published two novels, *Le Sexe des étoiles* (1987) and *L'Homme invisible à la fenêtre* (1993), and two collections of short stories, which have been highly praised for their incisive, jewel-like qualities. She also writes film scripts. Her collection *Montreal Dawns* (1996), offering a vivid portrait of contemporary Montreal, is currently being translated into English.

MARQUIS DE SADE (1740–1814). A scandalous figure who spent twelve years in prison for assaults and attempted murders of prostitutes, and the last years of his life confined to a mental asylum, Sade's erotic writing exploring the pleasure and power of evil is today considered a classic. He wrote in many genres, including novels such as *Justine, Philosophy in the Bedroom* (1791), and *The 120 Days of Sodom* (1904). A collection of his short stories is available as *The Misfortunes of Virtue and Other Early Tales*.

JEAN-PAUL SARTRE (1905–80). Philosopher, dramatist, novelist, and biographer, exponent of a brand of existentialism which deeply marked post-Second World War intellectual life in France. His best-known philosophical work *Being and Nothingness* appeared in 1943, four years after his novel *Nausea*, which explores its protagonist's gradual realization of the contingency and absurdity of life. The short story collection *The Wall and Other Stories* was published in 1939; the trilogy *The Roads to Freedom* began to appear from 1945 onwards. Most of Sartre's plays, his biographies of Genet and Flaubert, and his slim volume of autobiography, *The Words* (1963) are available in English translation.

ANNIE SAUMONT (b. 1927). The translator into French of John Fowles, and author of three novels, Saumont published her first collection of short stories in 1969. With twenty collections now to her name, she has become one of France's leading contemporary French short story writers. Combining humour with sympathy, and an eye for the everyday, her stories are peopled with modest characters, often leading a marginal existence. She won the Goncourt prize for the short story in 1981 for *Quelquefois dans les cérémonies. I'm No Truck: Sixteen Stories* (1991), winner of the Prix Nova, is available in English.

GEORGES SIMENON (1903–89). Belgian author of thousands of short stories and hundreds of popular novels, Simenon is known worldwide for his creation of the detective figure Maigret. The character was created in 1931 and went on to appear in eighty or so novels and stories, many of which were adapted for television. A large number are currently available in English—see, for example, *Maigret's Pipe: Sixteen Stories, Maigret's Christmas: Nine Stories*, and *Maigret in Montmartre*. The detailed locations and the way in which the detective comes to understand the criminal with whom he is dealing make the stories endlessly fascinating.

STENDHAL (pseudonym of Henri Beyle, 1783–1842). Best known for his two great novels, *The Red and The Black* (1830), recounting the fortunes of a carpenter's son inspired by Napoleon's example to rise up through society's ranks, and *The Charterhouse of Parma* (1839), set in Stendhal's beloved Italy, in which the hero again dies young, after finding love. Italy was a place of great happiness and beauty for Stendhal and the eight stories of the *Italian Chronicles* are all set there. His study of amorous passion, entitled *Love* (1822), is available in English, as is his autobiographical work published posthumously, *The Life of Henry Brulard* (1890).

MICHEL TOURNIER (b. 1924). Born in Paris, Tournier studied philosophy before gaining success with his first novel *Friday* (1967), an imaginative reworking of Defoe's *Robinson Crusoe*. Tournier belongs to a long tradition of philosopher novelists in France but has also written short stories, autobiographical essays, and fiction for children. Much of his work is available in English, including: *The Erl-King* (1970), which won the Goncourt prize and recounts a garage mechanic's search for truth; and *Golden Droplet* (1985), the story of a North African boy who comes to France as an immigrant worker. His two collections of short stories are *Fetishist and Other Stories* (1978) and *Midnight Love Feast* (1989).

VILLIERS DE L'ISLE-ADAM (1838–89). An impoverished aristocrat, Villiers pursued a visionary idealism in the face of his material difficulties. His short stories, at first published individually in literary reviews, were collected together as *Cruel Tales* (1883), followed by a second volume five years later. In the tradition of the supernatural and the fantastic, they nevertheless occasionally display savage irony. His stage play *Axel* (1886), available in translation, is also full of occult allusion. In contrast, the novel *Eve of the Future Eden* (1886) breaks new ground as an experiment in science fiction.

RENÉE VIVIEN (1877–1909). Born Pauline Tarn in London, she was educated partly in Paris and set up home there in 1899. Passionately involved with Nathalie Barney, Vivien became an alcoholic and depressive, dying at the age of 31. She published ten poetry collections, a short novel, and a collection of stories under the name Vivien as well as poems and prose under the name Paule Riversdale. Available in English are her poetry collections *A Woman Appeared to Me* (1904) and *At the Sweet Hour of Hand in Hand* (1906); and the short stories *Woman of the Wolf and Other Stories* (1904).

EMILE ZOLA (1840–1902). Author of the novel cycle *The Rougon-Macquart*, charting in twenty novels the history of a family under the Second Empire, Zola promoted a scientific view of literature termed 'Naturalism', in which the influence of heredity and milieu played a prominent part. Most of the novels in the cycle have been translated e.g. *Nana* (1880), the adventures of a courtesan; *Germinal* (1885) recounting a strike in a mining community; *Earth* (1887), representing peasant life. He also wrote eleven other novels, poetry, newspaper articles (including his famous intervention in the Dreyfus affair), and five collections of short stories, some of which are available as *Attack on the Mill and Other Stories*.